The Solstice Court

THRICE KINGDOM SERIES
BOOK TWO

JADE JUNIPER

Contact Info: https://jadejuniper.carrd.co/

Cover Art: little_lis_art

Cover Formatting: Whimberry Books

Editor: Yumi Yamamoto

Map Cartography: Shyanne Garland

Author Photo: Han Jutting

Imprint logo: Lindsay Lamp

ISBN: 9798336926132 (paperback)

979-8-9904198-0-3 (hardcover)

ASIN: B0CRR4TZ7T

First Edition: September 20, 2024

JADE JUNIPER

This one was always for my dad:
The man who believed I was capable of writing a book,
long before I could read.
Anything I accomplish is due to you teaching me I can.

Excerpts from...

BETHYNG COMPENDIUM

Silver salmon Era eleven ed.

Proven theories

Everything has magick.

Everyone has magick. (though some may not wield it).

A person can only wield, or hold one form of magick in one lifetime.

Magick is the manifestation of willpower.

Working theories

Magick's strength can be inherited.

Magick can build up in a person over time, with use.

Magick manifests in a person between the ages of 12-19

If a child has one magick-wielding parent and one non-wielding, they are half likely
to wirld magick themselves.

Drawbacks of wielding magick: An over inundation of magick can lead to: indigestion,
fatigue, dizziness, migraines, auras and death.

Manifestations of magick

Holding Sway: The body's manifestation of magick.*
Mind Melding: The mind's manifestation of magick.
Bond Wielding: The soul's manifestation of magick.

*Not to be confused with Sway, a gesture-led, non-verbal language
predating the magickal manifestation.

Proven Theories on Souls

Everything has a soul.

Everyone has a soul.

Souls can be split.

Souls can be paired.

Souls can be tethered and Bonded.

A Soul without both a vessel and wielder returns to the Summerlands.

Otherworldly Soul Splitting

Soulmates (Elastor), Twinsouls (Xenkesh) Soulbursts (Alora)

A soul, upon creation, may split into two.

If split in the Summerlands, these souls do not reforge into one.

While acting as two separate entities, they are drawn to fuse.

This bond is "otherworldly" and have little to no study beyond the principles of
a "worldly" Bond.

Worldly Soul Splitting

A worldly being may create a tether between a soul and themselves (the wielder).
To do this, their soul is split, via intention and attachment, and placed into the Bonded soul.

Through this method, a Bond is created.

A Bond is lifelong.

A Bonded soul will follow its wielder to the Summerlands, with or without a vessel.

Worldly split souls reforge and untether themselves once returned to the Summerlands.

Further thoughts on Souls

Pairing

Any two, or more*, souls can pair.

Pairing is a worldly magick, done with intent. By means of body, mind and soul.

Pairing souls gives two, or more, souls a similar essence.

Pairing allows a shared willpower and magick cache (between wielder).

Paired souls are not tethered nor soulmates*.
"They are not one, but close. Kindred." - Monk Konnri, soul specialist.

Unpairing: Souls cannot unpair until returned to the Summerlands.
"An individual claiming the ability to assist in an 'unpairing' is selling komodai bane."
- Monk Konnri, soul specialist.

Paramours: Becoming Paramours is a pairing done during a ritual known as
Handfasting.

Pairing should not be confused with Tethering, which gives Bondwielders access to
Bonded soul's soul-language in order to directly affect Bond (&therefore it's counterparts)

Soulmates have this bond inherently, rendering ritualistic pairings moot.

---

 * Basha's pairings to all three of his paramours lended proof to this theory
 * Also known as Twin souls (Xenkesh), or Soulbursts (Alora)

The Wheel of the Year

Thrice's Seasons

Winter
Winter Solstice
First Thaw

IRON WOLF
WHIRLWIND
SILVER SALMON

Spring
Spring Equinox
Hearttide

THE WARRIOR
IRON BEAR
THUNDERSTORM

Summer
Summer Solstice
First Harvest

KING CRAB
THE MONARCH
GLOAM SABLE

Autumn
Autumn Equnox
Nighttide

ZEPHYR BREEZE
ELECTRIC EEL
THE ARCHER

The Wheel of the Year was agreed upon in the first Year of King Ellas' rule and the establishment of the Thrice Kingdoms: Year One of the Warrior Star, during the Iron Bear's moon alignment, known as Warrior Era One, Iron Bear Moon.

The Thrice Kingdoms

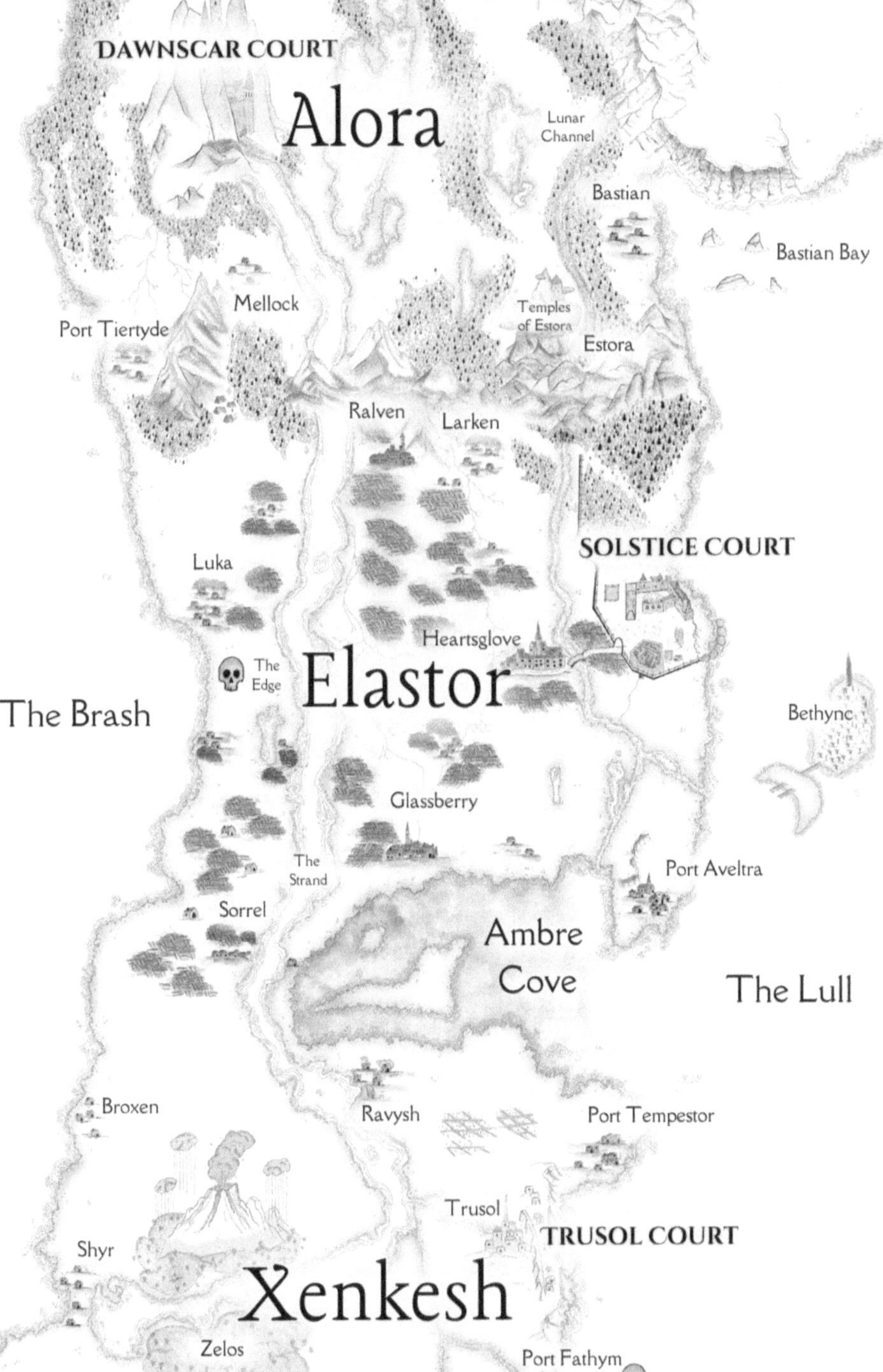

Elowren

It had been two weeks of laborious travel on elkback. Beyond the bone-cracking ache in his back and the chafing of his thighs, the deep lurch of exhaustion nearly dragged Elowren from his saddle numerous times; a rather unking-like spectacle even by his standards. His elk, Cinnamon, trudged forward, powdered with snow, leading a small army. Elowren slouched forward and counted Cinnamon's hoof-prints stamped into the recent flurry that clung to the frozen ground.

A northern wind whipped through the passage and he and his soldiers plodded on, heads low to fight the shards of ice. He tightened the fastenings of his overcoat, relieved Elize had convinced him to bring it. He had called her fussy for it, but regretted his teasing now that he shivered. He missed his daughter, nimble-limbed and everywhere at once; excited for his arms one moment, then scampering away the next. The thought of her warmed him and he chuckled to himself, the fog of breath blowing up in a puff.

The pristine smell of snow welcomed an end to the journey. Elowren sighed. Once, he would have made this journey gladly. The newest destruction, left in the village of Luka, however, had put an end to that. The air had shifted from a home seasoned with fresh baked bread and laughter to a smoldering village and the cries of a child over the fortnight.

Elowren pried his thoughts away from Luka. Dwelling on the atrocity wouldn't help that child. It wouldn't bring families back. What he aimed for now was preventing such heedless violence from happening on his lands again. A foreboding tension writhed in his stomach. He had let these attacks, these 'accidents,' go on far too long. Not anymore. Tonight he would walk into Dawnscar Court not as a friend, but as a King: his least favorite mask to wear.

He pulled at the leather tie holding back his heavy bundle of thick black braids peppered with silver. He hoped he wouldn't be the only one at this meeting showing signs of age. Elowren didn't believe himself a vain man, but the firm wrinkles on his brown brow had bothered him more than he willingly admitted.

He tapped his elk's reins again, the stomp of soldiers picking up pace on his cue. Upon reaching a small summit, Elowren caressed Cinnamon's ashen, auburn fur in praise. Dusk shimmered at the edges of the mountains. Dawnscar beheld between the elk's branch of antlers. The Kingdom of Alora held the same allure as a snowflake —beautiful, but filled with jagged edges and sharp lines. Dawnscar Keep, Alora's capital, spiked like a stalagmite from the mountains. Its spires and sapphire flags lifted to the clouds more in a warning than a declaration.

They descended. Then, a bend in the cold valley relieved into signs of life. Pale smoke billowed behind thick, high walls of blizzard stone. Gates set in the wall groaned open and the last rays of sun shone off polished bits of blue beneath the black surface.

Two Alorans leveraged their bodies to drag down pulleys and open the double door gates. Elowren had the urge to assist them with his magick as they hauled the ropes down with effort.

An inner courtyard parted into view. Over a dozen Aloran soldiers on large wolves greeted his entourage. Indigo padding accentuated otherwise dull plated armor on both wolves and riders. The soldiers held impassive stares, but the wolves had hackles raised and amber eyes alert on their party of elk. Elowren patted Cinnamon's haunches as he dismounted, knowing his elk must be nearly as anxious as he.

"If you think the iron wolves are terrifying," he told Cinnamon, "you should meet the Iron Queen."

Cinnamon appeared unamused.

"Elowren, you've gone gray!" A large wolf moved to the front of the pack and atop it Elowren recognized Castiel, Regent and friend to Alora's throne. Castiel slid off his mount like a dancer, his fur-lined tunic plummeted low in the front, his cleavage a mockery to the cold.

"Only to flatter you." Elowren gestured to Castiel's hair, silver spilled like fine silk down his shoulders. "But as expected, I've fallen short of your glory."

Castiel's laugh rang a deep, metallic singsong. "You can continue your sweet-talk while we get your soldiers settled."

"My entourage will accompany me in the throne room this evening."

Castiel quirked a brow and gave a mocking smile. "Alright then. Let's get your elk to the dens and I'll personally take you to our dear friend-Queen."

They walked the frosted exterior of the keep until the wolves' den fed into stables with stairs that beckoned them in from the cold. Castiel chattered away about his time at sea. He either cared little about or overlooked Elowren's somber mood.

Despite the chill outside, the air in the keep grew muggy. A familiar and pungent aroma wafted through Elowren's nose from the hot springs dwelling below the stone floors. His boots thawed as heat rose beneath them. Dawnscar's walls had been carved from the mountain itself. Enkindled sconces lined the hall and steam seeped through the cracks, giving his walk a hazy, dimly lit appearance. He had forgotten how cavernous the keep was. Elowren tilted his head to view the spiral of obsidian stairs that made up the spires. A tunnel of open-air halls and locked doors. He hoped his rooms wouldn't be too high up.

Castiel swung the throne room doors open without pause or decorum and Elowren snapped away from his distractions. Illija sensed weaknesses like wolves smelled fear, and he needed this to go well.

The noble continued his swagger up the steps and past a line of courtiers to stand by his queen. He then waved an arm in gesture. "Look my dear, Elowren has decided to pay us a visit before First Thaw." The room tittered, but no amount of flamboyance could draw Elowren's attention away from the woman who sat at its center.

He felt simultaneously over dressed and humbled by Illija. She sat on her throne, legs crossed, arms languid at her sides. She had not bothered with court attire but dressed in well-worn riding leathers that caressed her body in depthless azure. Her black hair spun into a partial bun, while the rest pooled around her. The supple delicacy of her features combatted her demeanor. Illija's posture harmonized with her personality. On the surface was an airy confidence, a natural regality Elowren himself could only emulate. Below it, he knew, was his childhood friend; sweet smiles with wild zinnias in her hair.

He tried to rescind the thought. Too late; her brown eyes and heavy lashes narrowed with irritation. Elowren chastised himself for the slip, remembering his mind no longer purely belonged to him.

He returned her stare with one more forgiving. Though, he was not the guilty party here.

"I'm sure you're aware of why I've come," Elowren began. It was important he spoke first. He needed her to understand the severity, that he hadn't come simply as himself. "But I would like to speak candidly and openly, for both our nobility's benefit."

Small chuckles came from the Alorans, silenced by a wave of Illija's hand.

"Then please, speak freely on whatever brought you here." She regarded his soldiers. "And with half of your kingdom in tow."

"I assure you, Illija," Elowren said, "this is not even an eighth of Elastor's forces, but I'm hoping my words will be enough."

Illija raised her brows. "Threats, Elowren? From you?"

"Understanding is what I seek here today," Elowren said with firm correction. "You may do what you want with the information, but I wish you to realize our current situation cannot remain the same."

Illija shifted her attention to her nails, while her lovely, curved lips slanted in a frown. "I wasn't aware we had a situation. You made it clear you intended to stay out of mine."

"I made it clear Elastor would stay out of it," Elowren said, "but Elastor can't do so when the edge of our lands is scourged by war."

"Alora has never attacked your people," she said, tone bored.

"And yet my people are dying."

"As are mine."

"My people," Elowren said, "are dying for your war."

"This," Illija hissed, "is not my war."

"Then withdraw your armies from Xenkesh. Stop using my lands as your personal training grounds."

"I intend to. I just intend to kill Amarus before I do it."

"Illija," Elowren pleaded. "He is the father to your children. Is there no other way?"

The brown of her eyes hardened like sap. "He is father to none as far as I'm concerned, and no, there is not."

Elowren rubbed at the tension in his jaw. He'd expected the adversity, he still hated it. "Then I have no choice but to close my borders to you."

Illija grew still, her expression devoid of emotion. To many, she might have been unreadable, but he recognized the fear there. He withheld the urge to roll his shoulders in discomfort.

"That's as good as waging war on us, and you know it," she said. "We both rely on trade, and I cannot afford to lose half my forces to The Brash."

He *had* known. The Brash, the tumultuous sea that crashed against their western borders, left Illija with few options. He had counted on it.

Elowren removed and unrolled a scroll from his breast pocket and shifted his hands with a willful concentration on the parchment. The lengthy parchment obeyed his Sway gesture: Cast by the firm hold he had on his kingdom's magick, his new treaty waved and rippled through the air like a lost bird.

She caught and crumpled it in a fist before stretching it to read. Elowren waited.

She tsk'd. "These terms are absurd." He didn't respond, Illija continued to shake her head. "Seasonal parties, Elowren? Peace summits?" She rapped her hand against the document, rattling it. "This is *pacifism*, this is a promise that I attend a ball and not slit Amarus' throat as he dances."

Elowren withheld his reply and tried not to imagine his friend with a dagger in hiss neck. Such a thought would only bring Illija satisfaction.

"While you and Amarus may wish for war," Elowren said, "I will no longer have it take place in my kingdom. I have been lenient with both of you, but—"

"Do you truly believe Amarus will behave any better?" Illija cut in. "He swore I wouldn't see my sons again. Do you know Amarus to go back on his word?"

No, Elowren did not know Amarus to go back on anything, let alone his word. But he did hope to persuade Amarus to a compromise: Elastor working as a proxy towards peace.

Illija shifted, as if sensing his hesitation, so he spoke quickly. "I will speak to Amarus. He will agree—"

"No," Illija recoiled. "No he will not. He'll feign agreement and then strike. I will not endanger one son for the false promise of seeing the other two." She tossed the scroll back at him. It bounced and rolled to his feet. "Throw your lavish parties. We will not attend."

"Then we are full circle," said Elowren. "Elastor's borders are closed to you. And, should he be more accepting, open to Amarus."

Illija's fine nose flared, fists grasping her throne to hold her in place.

Elowren ignored her bluff with his own, twisting in a turn to go, before looking back. He could only hope he did the right thing. "It was the town of Luka, you know," he said softly. "There was only one survivor."

Illija's eyes tightened, yet her mouth held less resolve.

"Whether your armies attacked or they were simply caught in the crossfire. People—good, kind-hearted people—are dead." His braids whipped back in chorus with his sharp turn towards the doors. He wouldn't stay here tonight. He would ride straight home.

"Wait."

Elowren couldn't help his immediate thoughts, *Thank the Summerlands, thank all of Thrice, thank—*

"Don't get ahead of yourself," Illija warned. "I offer an amendment."

He turned back to her, waiting.

"I will sign your treaty. There will be no skirmishes, battles, or bloodshed from Aloran troops on your land...but—" Illija pressed her lips together, distrust written across her features. "—I need a guarantee that Elastor will not join Xenkesh's side."

Elowren couldn't help himself, he was offended. He didn't like Amarus' treatment of Illija any more than Illija's treatment of Amarus. He knew and loved them both. Did she sincerely believe he would betray her?

"I would never do that to you, Illija."

She closed her eyes. "I'm sorry, Elowren. I need more than words. I require action, proof. I cannot risk Amarus whispering in your ear, and I cannot risk partaking in your parties with my enemy of war."

Elowren rolled his tongue to keep from voicing his aggravation. "What is it you need? Aside from my past and constant show of friendship?"

Illija released a labored breath. "You're not the only mind Amarus can poison. As you know, your paramour greatly favors him over me."

Elowren let his dislike for how Illija spoke of his queen show plainly across his face.

She ignored him. "I propose your heir, Kezerah, attend my court every time Amarus attends yours. Let my youngest, Ikaika, be given a chance at peace and for her to see I'm not the monster they make me out to be."

The idea shocked him. "The dangers of her leaving court are too great," said Elowren, solemnly. "You know this. It affects us all."

"Which is why you know she would be safe here," Illija countered.

"She is not to leave the Solstice Court, let alone Elastor—"

"—By old laws. Laws you can easily redraw, like the one you wish to write today."

"I can't—won't," Elowren caught himself. "It's not done."

"Then she is bound to favor Xenkesh over Alora in time, as I will not endanger my own, and your guarantees are only as permanent as your rule."

Elowren's brows neared his circlet. "She's only five. Do you intend for me to have a short rule?"

"With friends like Amarus? Who's to say?"

"Illija—"

"Don't say I'm being unreasonable. A counter to your fanciful elysium is perfectly fair."

Fair did not play a role in his daughter's safety, nor the well-being of his people. He crossed his arms, planting himself—stubborn roots and all—into her stone floor. "No."

She waited for him to back down, the challenge clear. He wouldn't. He studied her further. Her rigid posture as unyielding as her stare. How had she come to distrust him so deeply? Whatever the cause, he would do what he could to mend it.

"I can, however, promise to not only stay clear of this war, but to swear complete impartiality. My court will not speak of it. My daughter will only be given objective knowledge as needed to prepare her for her duties to the crown."

"Until Amarus—"

Elowren raised a hand to prevent her interruption. "As long as you are unwilling to attend my court, or feel unsafe doing so, his court, too, shall not be permitted. If either of you attend, my family —my heir—will treat all sides with impartiality and equal favor." He looked her in the eyes. "There will be no arranged pairings, no visits or meetings that the other is not also invited to. I vow, on behalf of my kingdom and the Soul Heir herself, the kingdom of Elastor will maintain complete neutrality in the present war between Xenkesh and Alora."

Illija frowned. Elowren kept his mind open and eyes on her. "And the consequences?"

Elowren suppressed a flinch at her sharp tone. He knew she intended the consequences for Amarus, but it didn't change how her words pierced him.

"The consequence is a broken treaty."

"War," Illija said, her words like thunder. "Break a treaty with me, Elowren, and there will be war."

Elowren squared his shoulders, weathering the threat like any storm at sea. "So be it," he said. "If any part of the treaty is broken, or anything like Luka happens again, you will find yourself at war not with one kingdom, but two."

This was a language Illija understood. She nodded, uncurling her hand. "Then I shall sign it."

Elowren loosed a breath and used his Sway. The paper leaped from the ground and cascaded through the air once more.

Illija scratched lines out, and wrote in new ones. He waited patiently at the bottom of her dais. The parchment he got back looked vastly different to his original agreement. But a successful settlement nonetheless. The swell of guilt and compassion for his daughter sank his victory. Kezerah already appeared to be growing out of their fortified castle; always a leap and climb away from falling, a constant need to dash and catch her before she reached the ground. Could he add one more condition to her exhaustive limitations? He stared at the curves in his own lettering as Illija answered his unsaid questions with uncharacteristic gentleness.

"As you said, she is not only the Soul Heir but will be queen someday. Better to quell her expectations for freedom now than allow her hope for something more."

His eyes left the parchment. Illija's face held an expression he hadn't seen in over a decade: eyes wide and doe-like, soft and unguarded in beauty. He fumbled. Then, as he at last spoke to a friend, he admitted. "I don't want this for her."

Illija lent a wan smile. "Well, you might not choose retirement until you're ancient."

Elowren scoffed. "Need I remind you who predicted my time would be cut short?"

"I'd never wish it, Elowren. I just—"

Elowren sensed the fresh hashing of a stale argument between them. "Twenty." She tilted her head and he clarified. "Kezerah will be crowned in her twentieth year. Elize and I decided. By then she will have matured in her magick but still possess an open mind. And I shall enjoy far less weight on my brow." He gestured to the all-too tight circlet about his head.

A phantom of a playful look crossed Illija's lips. "And to prove I wish you a long and prosperous rule, I implore you to stay here tonight. Please, use our hot springs and rejuvenate yourself after your wearying journey."

He tipped his chin in gratitude. "A good idea. I believe my soldiers and I would greatly appreciate it."

Elowren smiled in relief. This treaty needn't hinder Kezerah long. It was a temporary gauze on a wound bound to mend. It left plenty of time for Illija to come to her senses. For the war to end. Surely, they could resolve their conflict by then.

Yet, once more, the queen of Alora's tone had grown as cold as her kingdom. "Well, I am nothing if not *sensible*." Elowren realized his mistake but before he could respond she jabbed her chin in the direction of one of her servants. A servant came forward. Illija spoke with clipped efficiency. "Please, guide our guests to their rooms and baths and be sure King Elowren is not just treated as a monarch, but a friend." Her gaze did not return to his.

Elowren cursed himself for the blunder, but knew better than to try and assuage her any further that evening. Moreover, the zeal to barter had abandoned him at the mention of a hot bath. "Thank you for your hospitality."

The Aloran servant journeyed from the dais. Illija stayed seated.

For the best, Elowren thought, turning to follow the man. He needed time to recover after so much dreaded, staunch diplomacy.

Illija scoffed, calling out to him as he left. "Get plenty of rest Elowren, as I'm sure you still have one more *friend* to convince of your kingdom's supposed neutrality."

Dear Elowren

Elowren, it was not safe until now to tell you, as I believe my letters are being intercepted. We had no choice but to flee Alora. I must speak to you in person. Tonight. I am at your gate.
     -Your friend Illija.

Curious Minds

"Kez, move over—Ouch!"

"Shh!"

"Kez, it's not fair, I can't see!"

"Dar, shut up, they'll hear!"

"No, not till I can see!"

"Fine, here. Now, shh!"

Andarios shifted his cheek to press it firmly against Kezerah's. The sight of them must have looked ridiculous, heads squeezed together as if trying to form into one being, as they faced a wall: each with an eye shut, to see through a small hole, meticulously carved out of the wood, overlooking the Strategy Chambers below. Despite Andarios being twice her size, Kezerah managed to dominate most of the opening with one of her violet eyes.

There had been a time, when they were younger, that the two had fit easily into the secret passage. This was no longer the case. Andarios' yellow eyes narrowed at his friend as he debated whether or not to push her again, or pull her cloud of red hair that took up half the space in volume. The echo of voices in the chamber below diverted the desire.

"I do not think Illija needs to be seen tonight." Queen Elize clipped her words, not bothering to disguise her annoyance. "Almost ten years of isolation, without visits to even the largest court functions, only to call upon a king as if he were a steward. It's irregular—It's rude."

"If she were not herself a queen, my love, I would be inclined to agree," King Elowren said, from his seat by a glowing hearth. "As it happens she is not only a queen, but a dear friend. The only irregularity I see is that this does not align with Illija's typical diplomacy, and after so long, I admit, I'm eager to see her and hear her out."

Kezerah smiled at her father's words. Like the sun's warmth, his voice provoked a sense of serenity that bordered on cheerful. Half the reason she found herself listening to these meetings was to hear him. He spoke, acted, and carried himself like a monarch should, which both fascinated and terrified her, as she did none of those things to the necessary standard. A ruler required a discipline and control she found dull, if not impossible, to uphold for long periods.

Andarios nudged his face closer to the spy hole, digging his cheek painfully into hers. She nudged back, regaining her view of the chamber. Her mother, Elize, paced around the oak table, carved into the shape of The Thrice Kingdoms. The wood engravings had been stained to divide each border: indigo veneer leaked into a rich plum purple, then ruptured into vibrant mahogany.

Her mother picked up one of the small blue pieces that littered the top of the table; one of the miniature soldiers representing a part of the Northern armies of Alora. Most of the blue lay scattered across the red Southern kingdom of Xenkesh. Her home, Elastor, the immediate road to either battle ground held a deep black groove along The Edge. Like a line of ants, a small foot trail made of all three colors arched across the purple center of the map. Elastor's armies currently oversaw Xenkesh and Alora's traverse across their land, pressing them to the Western Coast of Elastor and away from small villages.

Elize inspected the blue piece in the same manner she inspected Kezerah's dresses for dirt, that was to say, meticulously. "Do you think this has anything to do with the skirmish outside of Sorrel?"

Kezerah bit her lip, anticipating the forbidden information. She had been asked to leave a mundane meeting earlier in the day due to news coming in of a possible breach in the treaty. The report had been passed around, person to person, until it reached her father, seated next to her, and its voyage came to an abrupt end.

'Perhaps this is...a bit graphic,' her father had said. *'Why don't you spend some more time with Andarios today.'*

The Strategy chamber's vaulted hearth crackled with firelight as autumn air blew in from the ornate double doors. Kezerah pressed her forehead into the wall in a desperate bid to attain the details withheld from her. Hanan, the steward, hurried in, interrupting the conversation. Kezerah grappled with her disappointment, one eye glowering at the steward. Hanan always appeared to need just a bit more sleep, but his unkempt disarray surprised her. A corner of his night tunic escaped formal breeches and his hair was still coiled in its usual bun, but loose as if rushed.

"Majesty, Queen Illija of Alora, and Crown Prince Ikaika of Alora."

Andarios and Kezerah's smushed faces turned towards each other, their citrine and amethyst eyes wide. The queen they had been expecting, having eavesdropped on Elize and Elowren's earlier conversation. Prince Ikaika, on the other hand, Kezerah hadn't expected to meet anytime soon. In order for Elastor to keep peace with both Alora and Xenkesh, no favoritism could be permitted between them. A painless task since she didn't know either of them well enough to hold favor.

Queen Illija was an exciting surprise, but Prince Ikaika's visit bordered on rule breaking—a favorite hobby of Kezerah. She rapidly tapped Andarios' leg, in case he hadn't been paying sufficient attention. He swatted her hand away but grinned, his teeth as brilliant a white as his hair. Even in the dimly lit wall they had crammed themselves into, Kezerah could see the mirrored mischief dance across his face.

Heavy footsteps and a chair creaking on stone brought them back to attention. Elowren stood, and Elize moved to stand stiffly by his side as the fiercest-looking woman Kezerah had ever seen entered the room.

Illija held an immediate presence in the chamber, not just physically, but energetically. Her walk embodied both a stomp and glide as she marched through the door frame in a deep rich velvet cloak with fur-lined trim. Her long ink-black hair was saturated and silken. Her skin reminded Kezerah of the pearly seashells she collected on the beaches of the Summer Quarters. A feline face with wide lips and eyes, bordered her beauty on strange. Hooded eyelids framed a never ending depth of dark brown. Kezerah knew if she had been closer, Illija's stare would have been impossible to look away from.

Though her frown cut deep into her features and anger smoldered in her eyes. Andarios shifted back ever so slightly from their hole. He had apparently had a similar reaction to the Queen of Alora's entrance.

Elowren approached despite her terrifying posture, arms wide in greeting. "Illija, welcome. It is always a pleasure to see you, no matter the hour."

Elize sniffed obtrusively behind him, unmoving.

Kezerah frowned, disappointed that the Prince of Alora lingered in the hall, out of her view. She shifted her position for a better angle and heard a tsk of annoyance to her right.

Illija seemed to warm slightly, and leaned into Elowren's embrace, but her eyes remained ignited. "Elowren." If Elowren's voice was the sun's warmth, Illija's was winter's night: clear, cool and deep. She continued after a pause. "I understand this violates many of the conditions understood by our treaty. I wrote to Elize of the danger Ikaika faced but received no answer. Please know that I would not put you in this position if given another path."

"And what has put you on this path, my friend?" prompted Elowren, concern coloring his words.

Illija looked back to the hall she had just marched in from, a sharp nod motioning another figure into the room to stand beside her. She then pulled him to her protectively. "You know of my youngest son, Ikaika," she said as introduction, holding him to her.

Ikaika appeared small in Illija's presence. As if sensing this, he shifted slightly out of her grasp. This only led to her holding him tighter, and her son finally giving in.

Ikaika shared his mother's dark hair, but where her hair lay straight, his curled faintly despite its short length, framing a serious face; a rich sand to compliment her seashell hands that gripped him tightly. He had his mother's eyes, set in a face more angled than hers; his jaw more pointed, and lips more stern than supple. Despite his mother's grasp he managed to look up at the king with an independent demeanor, pointed chin lifted, eyes fixed in an unyielding gaze.

Elowren, bowed to the boy. "Young Ikaika, it is a pleasure to finally meet you. Your mother speaks fondly of you in her letters."

Ikaika nodded, seeming unsure what to say. Elowren offered him an outstretched hand and he took it in his own, wordless, but firm.

"Amarus goes too far," Illija continued, her voice strained as she spoke. "He sends assassins. Not for me, but for my son, a child."

Kezerah raised a brow, at Illija's use of the word 'child.' Ikaika looked just as old as Kezerah, if not older and, at a fresh fourteen, she disliked the comparison. Andarios whispered the word *'assassin?'* under his breath and Kezerah refocused.

Elowren looked up from Ikaika sharply, but Elize broke her silence in answer. "What would you have us do? Break treaty and join your side? Where is the proof of this offense? Assuming you haven't also over-stepped in your petty squabble."

"*Petty. Squabble,*" Illija spit back, enunciating each word. "Elize, you wouldn't last a moment under what I've endured."

"Yes, I'm sure your life as queen of not one, but two kingdoms has been quite trying." Elize's words struck out quickly, and Illija's lip curled into a snarl.

Elowren reached his hands out, as if to prevent them from launching at one another. "Enough. Illija, I assume you understand my position on endangering my people is final. My army will not join your war. What is it you wish of me instead?"

"Haven."

"Haven for a queen at war is equal to harboring that queen's war!" Elize snapped.

Elowren's eyes patiently pleaded with his paramour, only one hand raised now, in her direction.

"Haven," Illija continued slowly. "Not for myself, but for my son. As I said, he is a child, and innocent. This war is not his, and if I can help it, he will not inherit it."

"It seems he won't inherit anything, based on how poorly you're able to protect him from his brothers and Amarus," Elize cut back in coolly.

Illija pulled back on her son to cover his ears.

"Elize!" Kezerah flinched. Her father used a stern tone so rarely it startled her.

"Ambrose and Rorrik would *never*." Illija asserted.

Elowren's voice warmed back up quickly, and he continued,

softer. "Of course not, but let's continue this conversation more cordially and with more privacy. I'm sure after your long journey the young prince is tired." Elowren motioned towards the idle steward. "Hanan, will you see that Ikaika placed in the Spring Quarter and made comfortable for the night?"

Hanan bowed and motioned for Ikaika to follow him.

Illija kissed the top of her son's head and detached herself long enough for him to follow Hanan out of the room. His stride had a soft grace about it that did not suffer from his mother's heavy steps, instead reminding Kezerah of the small foxes that slinked in and out of the Winter Woods: light on their feet and difficult to catch.

Illija's next words came out sounding wry. "Perhaps we may also venture to a more secure location."

"We assure you, our walls are not so easily breached," Elize answered, her pert nose lifting.

Illija's lips twitched into a grin, her gaze drifting up to stare in the direction of Andarios and Kezerah's hiding place.

"It's not your outer walls I fear have been breached, dear Elize." She said the queen's name as if it tasted badly on her tongue.

Kezerah and Andarios looked back at each other, unbelieving that they could have been seen from such a small hole at such a great height. But then she spoke again, directly at the hole that the children then scrambled away from, not bothering to be quiet.

"Your inner walls, however, seem to hold curious minds."

KEZERAH MADE it into the antechamber first. Andarios, directly behind her. He worked to situate the tapestry back into place, hiding the passageway.

She took his hand, and dragged him towards the door. "She might have already told them we're here. Come on, let's go!"

Once in the quiet Winter Quarter corridor, they slunk along the stone wall. The Solstice Court was the oldest standing structure in all of Elastor, and its moss covered walls were cool on Kezerah's back. Elongated arches gave a view of the surrounding halls that made up the castle boundaries. The Summer Quarters stood to the east, built along the sea. The adjacent Autumn Quarters, with its high glass ceilings and maple trees within, situated to the west. A high raised wall, both a stronghold and shield in the south. Winter, Autumn, and Summer all stood connected with one another, fortifying the Spring Quarters.

The circular stone tower sat in the center with only a small guard turret and stairs threading it to Summer. This protected the chamber of Elastor's Soul Heir in every way possible. Unfortunately, the Soul Heir herself needed to get back to her chambers, unnoticed.

"Summer to Spring?" Andarios offered.

Kezerah looked to the moon waxing into the west. "The Summer guards just switched. They'll be too alert." Kezerah worried her lip. "We can wait for the door guard rotation in the maze." At the moment, she could at least deny her and Andarios' whereabouts. Hanan or her night nurse catching them left little room for a lack of consequences. Her mother had recently moved Andarios' rooms farther from Kezerah's. She didn't want to see how far Elize would go to separate them further.

They hurried toward the sloping stairs that led to the main floor and outer courtyards.

Lined with multi-colored quartz stones indistinguishable from blown-out lanterns, the path led them to the edge of the Autumn hall. They stood parallel to Spring; only the meadow lay between them and the maze tucked against the southern wall and west training yards. Andarios began to cross, eyes fixed on the maze ahead, then stopped abruptly.

The glow of an oncoming lantern gave warning just before Hanan's concise voice floated through the air. He and the prince walked openly into the daisy-stained meadow, heading toward the Spring Quarter staircase.

Kezerah jerked Andarios back, hushing him when he grunted a curse in irritation. Once the steward and his charge were out of sight, she led them past prickly silhouettes of weaponry left outside the barracks, and a deserted training yard still sticky with mud. They reached high rows of hedges, and an archway of foliage. Once concealed behind the first corner of the entrance, Kezerah dipped her head out from behind the hedge. Andarios at her back. From her vantage point she could see Andarios' rooms, on the second floor of the Spring Quarters.

In the distance, Hanan and the prince disappeared into the enclosed staircase, the light of their lantern fading. Kezerah's fiery curls and Andarios' snowy hair snapped back behind the hedge and both let out a long awaited sigh. Andarios unwound his hand from hers, and pushed back a loose strand of white to better glare at his friend. Kezerah scuffed a foot in the grass. It had, admittedly, been her idea to spend their evening cramped behind a spy-hole.

"Do you think it's compromised?" she asked, easing the tension between them.

"Considering the Queen of Alora, notorious for violence, Mind Melded and heard our thoughts?" Andarios said. "Yeah, I'd say so. Though I'm not really willing to test the theory."

Kezerah tried to feel guilty, but it had partially been her curiosity in Aloran magick that had prompted her to eavesdrop in the first place. While the Sway language – used in Elastor for non-verbal communications – was common, she had not yet gained a Hold on Sway, the magick of her kingdom. She had played at acquiring her kingdom's ability to move objects and people—which required a strong will and effort to harness—for as long as she could remember. But the Aloran ability to effortlessly read another's thoughts had an irresistible pull.

"Wasn't she magnificent though?" Kezerah said, giving up on her pretended guilt. "Imagine, hearing everyone's thoughts, you'd never say the wrong thing, you'd always know the answer." She leaned back into a hedge, her own thoughts trailing. To never second guess if she said or did the wrong thing. To know what people wanted *before* they looked her over in disapproval.

Andarios grimaced. "I'll pass on that. People are messy enough without their minds getting in the way. Not to mention the headaches."

"The headaches pass," Kezerah said. "A few years of pain, and you could be as powerful as Illija."

He raised his brows at her. "Aren't you not supposed to show favoritism?"

"Pft. As if I actually make a difference in a decade-old war."

Kezerah rolled her eyes, waving the thought away like an errant fly. "But fine, King Amarus is magnificent and powerful too."

Andarios snorted. "Seems to me, powerful people get assassins sent after them."

"Do you think the prince fought off the assassin himself?" Kezerah grew excited at the thought. "Maybe they don't need Honorguards in Alora. Maybe they're trained to kill from the age of ten and he did away with the assassin before they even drew their blade."

Andarios shrugged, pulling and tearing a leaf from the shrubbery surrounding them. He had apparently decided not to humor her. The hedge rustled in protest, and Andarios smiled at Kezerah's agitation.

"I'm going to ask him tonight," she said, in a deliberate whisper. She then checked beyond the hedge once more.

"Kez," Andarios warned, ripping the leaf into smaller pieces to busy himself. "We've already been caught once. Don't you think your mother will be mad if she finds you out and about?"

"When isn't she mad?" The coast clear, she grabbed his hand. With Andarios back in bed, her mother had no leverage, and she could move more freely.

She didn't need to look back to know Andarios grinned. "Fair shot."

Kezerah giggled and they entered the Spring Quarter, and wound up the stairwell.

They grew quiet again before entering the hall with two guards at her door. A minor obstacle they were ready for. Andarios slipped through the door to the first set of unoccupied guest chambers. Kezerah's stomach tumbled as she imagined him having to make the double hop from the guest chambers' balconies to his own room across from hers.

She limbered up for the sprint to her door upon her guards' mid-moon shift rotation. She heard voices echo from the floor above, her cue to dash across as soon as her guards' backs turned. Their plum-dyed leather armor glowed in the ensconced light as they pivoted.

"Do you plan to go?" a low, calloused voice said behind her. "Or am I to guard His Majesty from the stairs?"

Kezerah jumped and stumbled back. Hours spent in nooks and crannies quieted the yelp that leaped and held in her throat. A shadow moved forward. A man stepped into the firelight and the orange gleam revealed a shaved head and plain black clothes. A fresh and irritated gash ran along his partially bandaged face.

'Am I being assassinated?' The thought crossed Kezerah's mind that she didn't know how to be assassinated. She should have run but her legs didn't budge. The man continued to stand there, then crossed his arms with a huff.

"Go on then," he said, with a gesture towards her door. "You look to be short on time." Her instincts caught up with her nerves. She dashed to the salvation of her door without care of her guards catching her. Hand on the knob, she glanced back to see the man take position at the door next to hers. Prince Ikaika's Kingsguard then. She would need to find another way into his rooms. The front door was no longer an option. He glanced at her sidelong, his eyes reflecting the torch light from a brazier on the wall. More light and muffled voices came from the stairs behind him. Kezerah slipped into her rooms.

Her door snicked closed just as another in the hall opened.

Hanan left the guest chambers, which now housed a sleeping prince. The Aloran guard startled him but Hanan quickly composed himself. Diplomacy held importance both high and low. He nodded in gesture, averting his eyes efficiently away from the red gap in the middle of the man's face where he assumed more facial features might be.

"His Majesty has settled in nicely," Hanan said. He had been relieved with how calm the boy had been. Hanan had overseen as maids tended to his needs. Fresh bed-clothes had been provided before the small prince had crawled into the large bed and immediately closed his eyes for what looked like the first time in days. Ikaika gave not a word of protest through it all; a welcome surprise, given the permanent residents of the Spring Quarters. The boy had rubbed at his forehead and brow in soothing, and Hanan made a mental note to make sure lavender oils would be dispersed into the chambers.

The guard only gave a nod in return. '*Oh good,*' Hanan thought, '*not a conversationalist.*' All the better. He had a list of tasks to do and knew, out of the three children he would need to check on tonight, he had just tackled the least difficult.

Andarios' room held nothing but heavily exaggerated snores and darkness. Hanan stepped out, bracing himself for the true challenge. The Princess of Elastor made no such performance. Kezerah sat up in bed, grinning expectantly at him. Light burst from every lit lantern in her room. Her nightgown backwards, as if donned in a rush to the bed. Her bright eyes watched him as he sighed and entered the space, somehow already messy despite the frequent tidying up the servants did.

"Hanan!" she said, whisper poorly contained. "Finally! What's he like? Does he get to stay?"

Hanan answered as he blew out each candle. "Much like myself, Princess, he's tired. As far as him staying, that will be up to your parents and Queen Illija to decide. But for the night, yes, he's staying."

"Do we get to meet him?" her voice remained upbeat despite the darkening room.

'*Did she have to light all the candles?*'

Hanan sighed. "That is also up to the many majesties I'm sure you have been eavesdropping on," he said dryly. "But," he added, "if the treaty is to be followed, no. It would be unwise for you to interact with Prince Ikaika."

Kezerah blew out air and seemed to deflate with the action, sinking into her pillow. "It's a stupid rule anyway. Why should we care if everyone's parents can't get along?"

While Hanan's job didn't formally include instructing Kezerah in history, he couldn't help but correct her; there was too much at stake for her to choose a new playmate in lieu of her duties. "Your parents have kept our kingdom safe by being impartial and fair despite Alora and Xenkesh not getting along. Elastor is a refuge, and the only neutral territory where both parties can safely speak in a move towards peace. As the future ruler of this kingdom, that responsibility extends to you—"

"Hanan," Kezerah groaned. "Forget I said anything. I'll go to bed if you stop, I promise."

Satisfied that his dry lecture had served its secondary purpose, Hanan nodded, then stepped out of the now darkened chamber and into the moon and flame lit corridor.

The night nurse, Nimah, turned the corner into the hall at that moment and Hanan gave another nod in her direction.

"Are they asleep yet?" she yawned.

"Your humor brightens the evening," Hanan responded dully. "I would start with the young lord of Luka. His snores were particularly vibrant. I might have bored the princess into slumber."

The nurse nodded. All fairly typical behavior of her charges.

"We have a guest child as well," he added. "He is not to be disturbed, and his personal guard shall remain posted at his door."

The nurse's brows raised in surprise as she took in the marred spector behind him. She opened her mouth to speak.

Hanan waved her off. "I can't say more at the moment, but I imagine we will have better instructions in the morning." The nurse raised eyebrows at him, but he gave her no more than stoicism. Finally she shrugged alongside a half curtsey. Hanan turned to go. He reached the stairs and heard her huff upon entering Lord Andarios' chamber.

"Enough of that," she chastised. "Not even a komodai snores so loud."

IKAIKA HAD BEEN asleep for what felt like a blink when his dreams shifted into a vivid picture.

Small bronze hands reached out over a stone balcony, elbows lifting, and dragging a petite body up and over the rail. A flash of copper obscured his vision briefly, and then a moment of triumph as whomever he Mind Melded with stood straight. The focus shifted from the climb to more specific thoughts.

'How should I wake him? I hope Nurse isn't in here, that would be

bad, or that man…' The excitement edged slightly into shyness as the adventure of the climb wore off.

Ikaika awoke, and his mind snapped back into his own. He turned and watched a small girl freeze in place on his balcony, as if trying to blend in with other non-existent sculptures. He snorted in amusement as he sat up, specks of light dancing across his vision as a mask of pain spread behind his eyes. He ignored it as best he could, grateful for the dark. Daylight always worsened his migraines.

"I'm awake," he said, figuring out the best way to transform the statue back into a princess.

She loosened into a willowy girl wearing a night shift much like his own. He recognized the copper he'd seen during his accidental Mind Meld as the shock of deep orange curls that framed a pretty, heart-shaped face. The strands cascaded down to her waist. The glow of a waning moon shone through the pink petals of a cherry blossom tree outside and backlit her silhouette. His one flickering candle gave her dark complexion an even warmer glow, and her purple eyes gleamed like gems. Ikaika straightened.

Intrigued by her vibrance he gestured to the end of his bed, and she loosened even further. She took confident steps as she bounced onto his bed.

"We're not supposed to meet, you know," he said, but he had a feeling she knew very well.

"And you're not supposed to be here," she countered, the grin never left her face as she looked around, her hands patting the coverlet as she tested the mattress' level of bounce.

He cocked his head to the side. The level of animation made her age difficult to gauge.

"How old are you?"

"Fourteen and three moons," she said, her voice daring him to denounce her for it.

'Only half a year younger than me,' he thought. She stared at him with open curiosity, so he allowed himself to stare back. He noticed now she had freckles sprinkled across her wide button nose. He didn't know what to say, but he soon found he didn't need to. She was perfectly capable of carrying the conversation.

"So, who tried to kill you?"

"The King of Xenkesh," he answered mildly, as if it hadn't been the most frightening night of his life.

"Why didn't he try and kill your mother?"

A question Ikaika had been asking himself. Why him? He didn't know the man that had once been his mother's paramour, nor had Ikaika met his brothers, who both resided alongside the King in Xenkesh. Ikaika in no way wanted his mother to be in danger, but it had stung to realize someone—many someones, his brothers even—hated him enough to want him dead.

"I think the King...and my brothers still want my mother to live with them. He hates her, but I don't know. It's confusing." He let his sentence drift off, uncertain how much to say or if he even understood enough to voice it properly.

"How did they do it?" Ikaika adjusted on the bed, confused by the question, still thinking of his mother and her complex past.

"Do...what?"

"Try and kill you," she said, as if that was the only obvious answer.

His head pulsed harder now, the pain wrapping around him like a mask. He rubbed the bridge of his nose. "You're kind of nosy aren't you?"

"A bit." She leaned in. "But I like to know things. What if they come here and, as my guest, I need to protect you?"

He laughed at this, and her eyes narrowed, lips twitched in a pucker to one side.

"I don't think it'll be your job to protect me," he informed her. "I'll have guards for that, and, eventually, enough training to protect myself."

If this had been a week earlier, he would have declared being perfectly capable of protecting himself *presently*. However, the man in the dark, striking as quick as hail in a storm, flashed through his memory. It had dashed away any illusions of bravery Ikaika had of himself.

The man's mind had been so cruel and vile it had woken Ikaika up moments before the attack, tumbling him from his bed. He had never made it to his feet, constantly scrambling and tripping across his floor. Hands had reached out for Ikaika where he had been just moments before.

Eriko had burst in as Ikaika curled up on the floor. His Kingsguard had repeatedly told Ikaika to run, but he couldn't move, having accidentally Mind Melded into the assassin. Until Eriko's sword had pierced his chest—*the assassin's chest*—and Ikaika had slipped into unconsciousness.

He returned to the conversation as the princess, Kezerah, rolled her eyes. "Well, until then, I'm the one that slipped into your room without anyone noticing, so perhaps I should get some credit."

She had a point. "How did you get in here?"

"Climbed."

It was Ikaika's turn to roll his eyes. "I mean, how did you not get caught?"

"Oh," she said, excited again. "Our courtyard is connected. It's only accessible through our balconies so it's not guarded from the inside. My balcony is next to yours. So, I just jumped to this one."

Jumped and almost fell to your death,' Ikaika thought, remembering through her eyes as she struggled to lift her dangling body up from the edge. "Well, you've proven yourself to be as adept as an assassin. Now what?"

She seemed to preen at the praise of being compared to a cold hearted killer. "Now, we sneak out."

Burning

Illija stood with her back to the King and Queen of Elastor. She trusted Elowren, but it felt unnatural to turn her back on a serpent such as Elize. Illija continued the pulse of Melding throughout the room. It kept her at ease, even if Elize's thoughts were violent in nature. She knew Illija had lied about the assassination, but Illija didn't understand how.

'She's been nothing but trouble her whole life. Even as a child she ruined everything.' Elize's mind continued to churn out her jealousies, remembering them all as children and misremembering Illija's want for the attention she had received. Elize had always been this way: frivolous thoughts, lavish parties, petty behaviors. When they were young she had chalked it up to Elize's humble background. A need to have nice things after going without. Well, Elize had obtained plenty of nice things since handfasting with Elowren, and she was still just as fussy, if not more so.

Illija had no patience for it, but her request was too great. She needed to keep calm in order to appeal to Elowren. She sighed, receding her Melding back into herself and turning to face the room.

This chamber was far more private. The density of books limited the amount of people that could cram in. Housed in the Winter Quarter, it overlooked dense forest and, in the distance, the mountain peaks of her homeland. Even seeing Alora from afar made her soul ache. Too often her time was spent away from those mountains. She blamed Amarus, which brought on a fresh steam of anger to her boiling heart.

'Ice Queen,' they called her. She scoffed without humor. How lazy some minds were; she was the antithesis of ice. Her rage moments from erupting. A flash of screams and fire entered her thoughts and she shuddered.

"Is this location more to your liking?" Elowren asked gently, closing the door.

Looking at Elowren now she needed no Melding to see that same kindness in his eyes, wide with concern. She saw in him a genuine heart not even she could begrudge.

"Yes, thank you," Illija said. "I'd prefer our children not suffer the same distaste for one another that their parents have so slowly acquired over time." Then added, "It saddens me that such resentment has grown between us."

She hoped she came off as heartfelt. She must have because Elize rolled her eyes at the same time Elowren's managed to soften further.

"I, too, am saddened by all our new formalities," he said. "So often I picture how it once was... all of us running through the gardens, enjoying the fire festivals in Trusol."

She couldn't help but see the images his open mind conjured there. *Herself, young and beautiful; Elize with a somewhat less puckered expression on her face; Ozule looked at Illija lovingly, while Amarus laughed and pulled her into the circle of dancers. The capital of Xenkesh thrummed around them.*

Her mind recoiled from the thought of Amarus and her face hardened as she tried to maintain her composure. "Yes, well, given that our ties are now so formal, I have an official request for you, Elowren."

Elowren's face fell but he remained listening.

"I ask that my son stay here until I have better fortified my lands from those who wish him harm. I am too often away in battle and cannot ensure his safety. Once he is trained to Meld properly I know he will be capable, but he is still just a child, and Amarus—" she gritted her teeth at the name, "—would see him dead before he is given a chance to rule in my stead."

Illija meant to Meld with Elowren but Elize spoke, breaking her concentration. "Perhaps this is yet another misunderstanding, and someone was merely sent to retrieve the boy. Amarus loves both of his sons dearly; your young Rorrik is rarely out of his sight. It seems natural to want all three brothers to be reunited."

Illija swallowed bile before responding. She summoned all the serenity she could muster. "Child thieves, while abhorrent, do not often carry ornate knives given to me during my handfasting ceremony." She managed to smile, a show of teeth.

Elize moved to touch her paramour's shoulder, a pout forming on her lips. "I suppose there's no way to know for certain, given that he was stabbed through the chest before being granted the chance to speak. Unfortunate that your tactics don't leave much room for the benefit of doubt."

Illija's teeth pressed together so firmly she thought they might crack. Though, the calm resolution of Elowren's thoughts allowed Illija to smile smugly at his queen. Elize's involvement always brought out a minor pettiness in her.

Elowren spoke moments after his thoughts. "The benefit of the doubt must indeed be granted; and as a child *was* at risk, either of kidnapping or something more insidious, I must place that benefit in your hands Illija."

Elize's pout slipped into a frown, dark blue eyes mimicking an ocean storm. Her rosy coloring looked blotchy next to Elowren's dark umber as it further reddened. The temptation to slip into Elize's mind hummed in Ilija, if only for the satisfaction, but Elowren's next thoughts caught her off-guard.

"Prince Ikaika will be granted Haven in Elastor as long as you wish. But his brothers will be extended the same invitation. Let them see how all parties may live in harmony here, and that not all moments need to be filled with strife." Elowren placed his hand on Elize's, still clenched at his shoulder. "In order to maintain the safety of our children however—" Illija did not like his next thought. "—I will not forbid Amarus alone from coming here. Neither yourself nor Amarus will attend court while each other's children seek haven in Elastor. Neither of you will be given access to poison each other's heirs against one another nor be given the chance to cause harm."

Illija stormed. "They are *all* my children, Elowren. Do you think I would do my own sons harm? That I would hurt all that I fight for?"

Elowren's eyes remained calm despite her wrath, his tone matched. "Not all harm is physical, Illija, and if you believe you fight solely for justice, perhaps you need to look at the villages burned in your wake, and the countless mothers who will not lay eyes on their children again." The line of his mouth hardened as he finished.

She entered his mind and found only stone resolve and pain: for her, for her children, for the casualties of war, and even for his absurd loyalty to the scab that sat upon the Xenkeshi throne. No, there would be no more reasoning with Elowren. Ikaika was safe and situated. Ambrose and Rorrik—pain shot through her as she pictured her elder sons, imagining them as small children despite knowing they were nearing their magick by now—they could come here, without Amarus' influence on them. They would not meet their brother on a battlefield. The thought loosened the tightness in her chest. She nodded, unwilling to glance in Elize's direction.

"So be it," she conceded.

Elowren clapped and smoothed his hands together, before quickly moving them as if to draw something toward his chest. A paper whirled through the air from a shelf, he caught and unraveled it.

His blasted treaty. He motioned for a quill and it too flew to his outstretched palm. He wrote in a line, demanding his terms in order to grant her son's haven. After scribbling his own signature, he motioned first to Elize, then Illija. Moving his thumb as if to wipe his cheek, he pressed an invisible seal to the paper and Illija watched as it shot out the window with the speed of an arrow.

While they waited, Illija wondered at the patience to learn every gesture needed in order to make Elastian's Hold on Sway work. Unlike her Mind Melding, which took great discipline for the mind, the people of Elastor, if gifted, needed to use their hands in order to bend magick to their will. To speak Sway was one thing, to Hold Sway quite another. While she found the idea of doing such mundane tasks just by twirling her finger intriguing, she could not imagine life without her ability to glean another's mind: the greatest defense imaginable. An even greater offense if one knew what to do beyond the monks' teachings.

A flash of light accompanied the crackling sound of burning (complete decoration on Amarus' part) and revealed the paper on the table from far-flung Xenkesh. Amarus had chosen to write his lengthy scrawl in red ink, instead of the trio's black. Illija's eyes rolled at his theatrics. Elowren nodded, rolling the scroll and placing it back on the shelf.

Overcome with exhaustion, and with her task completed, she left the table. "I shall retire and depart in the morning." She left it at that. She had no more to say.

Illija's walk from the Winter Quarter to Spring seemed to take mere moments, the little castle so much smaller than she remembered. Up a flight of stairs sat a sleeping nurse in a chair. The round little woman rocked to and fro outside a door heavily stationed with guards. Ikaika's personal guard, Eriko, motioned for her to pass. The Elastian guards did not stir to stop her. The new gash along Eriko's freshly bandaged face and gore-torn features left little room for argument. She would miss her sword master, but it reassured her to have him at Ikaika's side.

High-up, fogs of lavender fell into the silence of her son's well-guarded room. A bed with curtains made from intricate lace leaves caressed mussed sheets in the breeze of an open door. Empty. A spike of panic surged through her before she took a calming breath and closed her eyes. Illija reached outside herself, until she heard his quiet thoughts, peaceful in sleep. They came from the room across the hall. The nurse started up in attention as she opened the doors.

Feathers, torn cushions, ribbons, and overturned chairs were strewn across the floor. In a massive pile of blankets lay three sleeping children.

The image reminded Illija of the lions she had seen in Xenkesh, the cubs knotted together in a tangled heap. She picked her son's face from the pile and kissed him tenderly on his forehead. His mind reached, to dip into hers, and she allowed him to see just how much she loved him, and how much she would miss him.

The other two children lay undisturbed. She easily identified Elowren's child, her tawny fawn complexion dotted with his same freckles. While Elowren's face was longer, she recognized the stubborn set of his jaw. A far more playful smile tugged at the child's lips, but just as warm. Her stature was petite despite her long limbs. Illija had to smile at the girl's hair—a much more deeply striking shade of red than her mother's—heavily adorned with feathers, from a pillow that had been ripped to shreds.

The girl clasped hands tightly with a youth, his hair an astonishing white, with a heavily sun-kissed face from a summer outside. She suspected what family he hailed from. Unfortunately, Melding into his mind only brought up pictures of their past battle with overstuffed pillows, and an especially delicious cherry suncake he had recently eaten.

Illija smiled. Perhaps, while not as planned, this would do nicely. Ikaika deserved a childhood not wrought with danger and war. The Solstice Court had always felt like a dream, a shroud against the violence of the world. She would come back for him. She would make sure he didn't turn out too soft and coddled by this dream. She just needed to rip the beating heart from Amarus' chest before she did so.

Placing one last kiss upon her youngest son's brow, she left yet another one of her children behind.

AMBROSE STRUGGLED to both catch his breath and hold it. He scanned the crumbling village, and did all he could to combat the rising smell of charred flesh from entering his nostrils. Sand rose up with the heat, and he shut his eyes against it. The scene remained in vivid detail behind his closed eyelids. The amber that littered the shambles of the coastal town matched the skyline; a burnt red with ominous hues seared into its depths. Bits of broken doors lay splintered open in an array of colors. Ash and worse scorched the ruined homes.

Another gust of sand rushed at him. He raised a forearm to cover his face, and nearly vomited. He had forgotten the gore that smeared up his wrist from the woman he had not been able to save—and had hastily had to bury from sight.

"Where's my momma?"

"I don't know."

"Where is she? Where's my mommy!"

"I'm sorry," Ambrose said, trying to sound brave, trying to sound like Azalea. "I don't know."

The girl, covered in soot and ash, held his hand in her small grubby one. Ambrose tried to tell himself it was slick with sweat and not blood. Her eyes were wide and glazed. She couldn't be more than ten. Ambrose reminded himself he was seventeen, he was the adult here. He was part of the rescue party and wouldn't allow his father to regret the decision. The little girl repeated the question again, just as frantic, just as demanding.

"Where's my mommy?" Instead of grasping his hand tighter it slid from his. She collapsed in the pieces of her broken down door, blowing up the smell of ash and carrion as he took in a breath. Ambrose broke, coaxing her back off the ground with lies.

"We'll find her," he promised, letting go of her hand he raised her by the arms; her too-frail shoulders felt like bird bones as she wept. "It's going to be okay." He rocked her and again surveyed what used to be a prosperous Xenkeshi village situated along the Ambre Cove. He could hardly believe he stood in the village he'd eaten in yesterday. A woman had gifted him an amber studded sword belt because word had circled that he would be visiting. Her smile had been wide and genuine, feeling honored to present her crown prince with a gift. Her shop, now an unrecognizable rubble of charred stone, was trailed with blood, as if she had been dragged from her home before they burned it.

The girl in his arms weighed almost nothing, but each step felt as if it took all day, if it was day any longer. The smoke blotted out the sun, the light dim in the direction he needed to go. He faced south, and focused each step on leading them back to the small camp his father had raised in order to tend to survivors. The girl still murmured her question in his ear, a babble of fear and need for assurance. He kept lying to her.

In the distance glinted the black scaled armor of his father's battalion. The King of Xenkesh had sworn to personally protect the encampment. His elite force formed a ring around the makeshift tents filled with tears and screams. King Amarus had assured everyone that Alora had retreated, and would not return. But Ambrose's father had also assured Ambrose that Queen Illija would not attack in the night. "Even the ruthless Queen of Alora obeys the laws of honor in war." He'd assured him.

His father had been wrong.

"Where's my momma?"

"I don't know. We'll find her."

She wailed in his ear. Ambrose stopped, deciding to switch strategies. He patted her instead, like he'd seen his father do with Rorrik. He made small, desperate shushing sounds under his breath, until soon it was the only sound left.

"There now," he said. "Let's go find Mommy…"

"Is your momma here?" she asked. A tattered remnant of a red Xenkesh flag whipped with the wind. He couldn't tell if it was saturated by the wet coastal air, or spattered in blood. He closed his eyes, his lashes damp and eyes welled up from the smoke.

"No, it'll be okay. She's gone now." He assured her, hoping this time his father was right, and his mother wouldn't come back to finish the job.

"COME ON, Am! Snap out of it!" Ambrose broke free of his thoughts just as Rorrik's sword thwacked against his shoulder. The memory of Ravysh's soured smoke gave way to the fresh, balmy sea air of Trusol, his capital. The white baked bricks below his feet stretched out to high columns of bleached marble. The soft burble of the Lull chorused alongside the thick amber fabric of Xenkesh. It had been moons since the attack, but the memory still bit into him every time he entered the Trusol arena, lined with Xenkesh's flags.

He twisted his curved sword in a circular motion. While he preferred two curved blades, he knew his father wished Rorrik a victory today, not him. But Ambrose planned to make it fair, not easy. His one sword twirled around lazily in his right hand. He knew how much it would antagonize Rorrik's attack; counted on it, in fact.

His little brother's face conveyed every emotion he had in his arsenal as he ran forward, an absurdly ineffective battle cry cut short as Ambrose jabbed his hilt into Rorrik's gut, causing him to double over.

"Again."

His father's voice was apathetic. Ambrose forced himself not to look up at the King, and tried to give him what he wanted, which he supposed was Rorrik's progress. Ambrose allowed Rorrik to come at him again, ignoring the easy hit and allowing Rorrik's blade to clash with his. He moved slower, as if fighting underwater, to allow Rorrik to get his hits in.

Ambrose could feel the hum of anticipation from his sword's soul, the need for action. Rorrik's sword echoed the sentiment. It was like a siren song, a thread meant to be tugged, a question waiting to be answered. Ambrose answered it. His blade thrummed with excitement as he linked with it. His magick bridged the connection between his desires and that of the forged steel in his hand. It wanted action. It wanted the catharsis that only came from impact. It furiously wanted to win. Ambrose nudged at the magick within it. The magick that clung to all things with souls. His sword grew heavier, the hits more weighted. The next swing of impact ripped the sword from Rorrik's grip. It clattered to the ground a few paces away.

"Hey!" yelped Rorrik. "No magick!" He looked to his father, who merely raised his brows. "It's not fair. I haven't Bonded yet."

"An opponent will not wait for you to be ready," King Amarus said. "They will wait for you to be caught unaware." Their father nodded for Rorrik to pick up his blade, but gave Ambrose a stern look when his younger son's back turned.

Ambrose rolled his eyes. This time, when he felt the call of Bond magick, he reluctantly ignored it. Instead he raised his sword far too high, in an effort to end the fight more quickly.

Rorrik swung, the blade wobbled to feint Ambrose's opening. He waited – muscles tensed, arm slowed, sword screaming in agitation – as Rorrik finally got the hit in.

"Good, Rorrik, a beautiful strike!" exclaimed their father.

Warmth and praise radiated from Amarus. Ambrose reminded himself that his father knew his skills, and his pleased tone was for his efforts as well. King Amarus did not want Ambrose's best today, he wanted a warm body for Rorrik to swing at, to build his confidence that seemed to be so lacking with his sword master.

Ambrose dared a glance over to his father in the hopes the practice had ended but knew the king would rather Rorrik get a full morning of training in. Amarus sat cross legged on his shaded dais. Servants fanned his oiled bronze skin as he decided whether to push his sons further, his light green eyes stony, before glazing over into a smile that crinkled his face.

"Alright Ambrose, enough for the day. Rorrik–" He addressed his younger son in the same easy-going tone, but with a pinch more authority, to prevent one of Rorrik's outbursts. "Go wash up, and return your sword to Azalea."

"Can't I keep it with me? Ambrose gets to keep his!"

Ambrose attempted to keep the arrogance from his tone, unable to stop himself from poking his brother one more time. "You can't even keep it in your hand, how do you expect to walk around with it at your waist?"

"Because I wouldn't have you knocking it out of its sheath!"

"Enough," Amarus said lazily, eyeing Ambrose disapprovingly. "Rorrik, until you can keep your sword in your hand, it is not your sword, it is Azalea's. And until you can take it from her properly, it will stay in her possession."

It was no easy task to dislodge a sword from Sword Master Azalea of Trusol Court. Just the memory of trying made Ambrose grasp his blade's hilt.

Rorrik harrumphed, and walked off the small circle of the arena, mumbling as he went.

While his father appeared to be in good spirits, Ambrose approached, not making eye contact with the King as he poured himself a glass of honeydew-saturated water.

The relief of the sweet liquid was short lived as his father's voice spoke in a low murmur. "I have had word from your mother."

Ambrose tensed, then made sure his features were as bland as possible. '*Was she well? Had she laid siege to another harmless village?*' His mother's actions were a mystery to him. He could not reconcile the deep brown eyes of the woman promising him safety, and those of the ruthless queen who'd left him, only to return and burn his home to the ground. Village after village destroyed in her wake.

"She has left your youngest brother in Elastor. Elowren sent word that the treaty was being amended to accommodate the unusual circumstances. Apparently she arrived in the night and left him the very next morning."

Ambrose could see what his father had left out in order to allow his words time to sink in: His mother had abandoned Ikaika, too.

Was she incapable of loving them?

His father had once ventured to Alora to beg for her return. To remind her of the children she left behind. His gesture had been repaid with a siege on their borders, and the start of a war that had lasted Rorrik's entire life. Ambrose remembered the early days of war. When he had allowed himself to believe his mother had been stolen away. His father had been patient with him, and allowed him to first idolize, then resent her.

His last memory of her—his lasting memory—was a creature embodiment of butchery and blood. Sword raised. Eyes like embers, directed at him. Nothing short of Azalea and a swarm of guards had stopped the monster that broke down his door. It had taken years to understand that the monster had been his mother. Her return had been an act of brutality: a stormed castle, countless people massacred, including their uncle Ozule, and little to no understanding of why.

When Illija herself had led the raid on the village of Ravysh this past Summer, Ambrose had been forced to shift his perception of her. It allowed him to finally place the monster with the monstrous act. The pain of her leaving had scarred over, but now, this sudden abandonment of her youngest son made the wound feel fresh.

"Does that not violate the treaty?" Ambrose asked.

"Elowren, while foolish, is a kind man. He would never turn a friend away in the night. It was..." Amarus worked his jaw, trying to model diplomacy for his son, "—unkind to take such advantage of his generosity, but it's done now. He sent me an amendment to his terms last night and I accepted. You and your brother may also seek Haven in Elastor." He finished his drink, as if trying to wash down the absurdity of the statement.

Ambrose scoffed at his surroundings: the warm air, swaying palms, and turquoise ocean view. Seeking haven from paradise didn't interest him. However...

"Ikaika is there now? Can he not be brought here?"

Amarus' frown deepened and he looked down at his glass. "That was my first question as well. To be alone and not with family..." His father sighed. "But, I'm sorry, my son. Apparently, in the negotiations, it was made clear I may not be there while Ikaika is present. So inviting him to be alongside his brothers is not an option." Amarus spoke his next words with regret. "My one relief is that Illija, also, will not come to Elastor while you or Rorrik are there. I do not understand the reasons behind these dealings, but it is evident that Elowren has no intention of defying Illija's wishes where Ikaika is concerned."

"But she left him." Ambrose hated how childish he sounded, he looked down and away from his father.

Amarus shook his head. "We cannot afford Elowren to lean in favor of Alora's cause. His army would change the tiding of the war. I speak not as a father but as a king. Ikaika will remain in Elastor under Elowren's protection." Evident disdain coated the word 'protection.' After seeing the look on Ambrose's face he amended. "For now."

Ambrose's stomach turned. His mother refused to even enter the same room as him. But what had his brother done? Displeased her in some way? Perhaps, now older, he had spoken out on the atrocities that had taken place. Luka. The failed takeover of Broxen. The tragedy at Shyr had been enough to stop all formal dances in the capitol. No one who knew of Shyr could deny its brutality. He imagined a young boy, maybe someone like Rorrik, speaking out and being cast aside. Discarded like a ruined shield. Could his mother be so ruthless? He thought of Ravysh again and had his answer. *'Being discarded by Illija is merciful.'*

Like a sun dipping below the sands, he commanded his heart to cool. He didn't need her. He had a father and brother who loved him. He just needed his people to be safe, and for this war to end. Then he could mend ties with his stolen brother.

"You can tell King Elowren we have no immediate plans to travel to Elastor," Ambrose said. "Unless, of course, he decides that our brother belongs with his family." He hoped his voice sounded firm.

His father looked up at him with pride. "I shall send word that this is the outcome you desire. Maybe his heart will soften to your cause, instead of mine."

Ambrose nodded, and his father stood. "Come, you can help me write the letter yourself. You're good with a sword; let's sharpen your art of diplomacy as well." He guided his son through the palace threshold and out of the midday sun.

Years in Seasons

Ikaika struggled to describe Andarios' room as anything but plain. Sparse in decoration or elaborate furnishings, either an incredibly tidy person or a soldier lived there. The armchair had the appearance not of something new, but unused. Sun-faded fabric marked cushions frayed with time rather than late nights reading by lantern light. Pillows lay piled around the bed, but only a lone flat pillow rested at a low bannered headboard. A pale-wood wardrobe had all the fixings of something to hold clothes, but it was as if the carpenter had stopped there, just passionate enough to add round, unpainted knobs in decoration. The only grooves in the furniture lined the top drawer; where he imagined a single uniform was pulled out and put away each day without a need for style or trimmings. Ikaika noted that everything appeared crammed together. All the furniture situated itself around the walls and left space only for twin, glass balcony doors and an unmarked door he suspected led directly to the chamber pot. Without a tub in sight. Ikaika cringed at the possibility of bathing in such close proximity to where he relieved himself.

Fortunately, his own chambers had been large enough to accommodate a quartz bath in the alcove. Alorans took bathing seriously, with ample hot springs and bath houses along its streams. The foreignness of this room sunk in and reminded Ikaika how far from home he'd fled.

He thought of his rooms back home; curated to his liking. Shelves of books, a hot fire, and a balcony facing away from the rays of the sun. Would these two have found his room strange? He hadn't a clue. Only his mother, Castiel, and servants had been invited in. He'd had no one else to invite. Kezerah and Andarios moved around each other as if two stars in orbit, and suddenly he couldn't picture them apart. Or where he was meant to fit in.

The princess flopped herself onto Andarios' small bed with a huff, a mess of pillows sighing around her.

"It's nothing like the royal guest chambers," Andarios said, humbly.

Ikaika became aware he had been observing the space unabashedly and gulped down his nerves. "No, it's nice. Everything all in one place."

Andarios laughed. "That's one way of looking at it. I'll take my massive four post bed back then, if you please."

Ikaika tensed. Had they moved this burly boy's rooms to accommodate him? "Oh, I'm—"

His thoughts dashed away as a pillow flew past him, hitting Andarios square in his middle. "Shut it, Dar," Kezerah said. "Those haven't been your rooms for moons."

Andarios chucked the pillow back. "And I still dream about the bed."

So as to not interrupt their banter Ikaika shuffled back against the wall closest to the privy. Kezerah wound up to throw another pillow. She caught Ikaika's eye with an impish smile; the pillow's trajectory changed at the last moment to be thrown at him instead.

Ikaika moved easily out of the way, and Andarios nabbed up the pillow. His stock refilled, he threw it back at her in force. Feathers burst at the seams as the princess ducked down and it hit the wall instead. Andarios laughed at her.

Ikaika shifted away again. He attempted to distance himself from Andarios, the easier of the two targets. Kezerah wouldn't have it. Two more pillows were flung toward Ikaika. Light and fluffy, they too were easily evaded. Ikaika didn't know what to do besides refuse her further projectiles. Only, to his shock, for Andarios to turn coat and toss a pillow her way, which she caught and again threw at Ikaika. He surprised himself and smiled at her soured expression as yet another pillow hit the wall. Though he had tried to stifle the taunt, Kezerah and Andarios caught the softening of his facade and halted their own battle. A triumphant glance passed between them like words and they both angled their next pillows at him.

Cushion after cushion missed his head. When their pillow reserves were spent, Ikaika realized he had little option but to engage and found himself not just dodging pillows, but throwing them himself. The weight of the last few days eased with each burst of feathers.

When Andarios admitted defeat, the trio flopped to the ground. Battle plumage continued to fall around them and litter the floor.

"That was the best pillow fight I've ever had," Kezerah said, while she caught her breath. "Even if it did end in a draw."

Ikaika grunted, then attempted to blow a feather out of his hair. It stubbornly remained in a loose curl. "It's not a draw if you surrender."

"I didn't surrender!" Kezerah said. "Dar did!"

Andarios shrugged, then tossed a dispirited pillow her way. "Someone had to—look at my room."

He gestured to the ruined space of fabric and feather debris, as well as an overturned arm chair. The mattress had been stripped and the bedding lay heaped in the middle of the floor. Andarios caught the pillow as Kezerah threw it back his way, emptied of its contents. He yielded further by placing the deflated cushion behind his head as he lay in the nest of bedding.

Ikaika took in the space with fresh horror. "Sorry about the mess."

"Don't be," Andarios said. "It was nice that Kez lost for once."

"I didn't—"

"You were going to. You're lucky I surrendered before it got really embarrassing."

Kezerah rolled her eyes, as she face-planted next to Andarios. The two laid side by side.

Ikaika suddenly felt out of place again. Was he too meant to lay down? Or was he an intruder on a friendship and expected to find his own way back to his rooms? His earlier comfort now peculiar, silly, next to the friends' ease with one another.

He shuffled his feet and tried not to slip on the bedding.

Kezerah flung a hand out to reach him. "Where are you—oops!" she said, right as she grabbed his ankle and Ikaika slipped backwards onto the bedding and pillows.

Ikaika rubbed at the back of his head. This pain was altogether different from the usual pain of Mind Melding.

Kezerah's face peered over top of him, wide-eyed and worried. "Sorry, are you alright?" She asked meekly, at odds with the confident girl who had slipped into his bedroom.

He had the urge to soothe her, and he smiled despite the throb in his head. "I'm fine." He gave a small laugh. "Like I said, you've proven yourself an adept assassin."

He watched the tension ease from her features, lips parted in a relieved grin. "Well, that's what you get for trying to blow our cover." She laid back down, then rolled onto her stomach to better speak to him.

Andarios pushed her leg off his, as he made himself more comfortable; Kezerah kicked him. The two finally situated with Kezerah's legs pinned beneath Andarios', the two shaped into an L.

Kezerah continued her explanation, "We can't leave yet. We'll have to stay up until the nurse's switch."

Ikaika raised his brows. "Nurses? Like, for children?"

Kezerah's cheeks darkened, and she ripped apart a feather as she answered. "Well, just for the time being, while we're in the Spring Quarters." She picked the stem bare of down. "I'm supposed to move into the Summer Quarters any season now."

"The Queen already tried to move me to the barracks," Andarios added. "But Kezerah begged enough that King Elowren gave in."

"It wasn't begging," Kezerah assured Ikaika. "I negotiated."

"Father, please!" Andarios said, in a mockery of Kezerah's voice. "He's my only friend! I'll be all alone in the children's quarters— Ouch!"

"Well now I have two friends," Kezerah said, hitting him again. "So you'll have to be nicer to me—or I'll just sneak into Ikaika's rooms."

"Good, maybe I'll wake up in time for drills," Andarios said, with a shrug.

Ikaika didn't know what to say. The idea that he might already have friends hadn't occurred to him; just as quickly he realized he might not get to keep them.

"Erm—I don't know how long I'll get to stay," he admitted.

"You'll at least stay until you're not being assassinated, right?" asked Andarios.

"Dar, he's obviously not being assassinated, now."

"You know what I meant!"

"Right," Ikaika said, and hoped she was right and that time had very much already passed.

Kezerah inspected his face, and Ikaika tried to emit bravery, rather than his true unease.

She mistook his expression. "Maybe my mother's information was wrong, and it wasn't your father who tried to kill you. Maybe it was just a rogue bandit."

That jarred him. The King of Xenkesh did not get brought up without malice in his household. "Amarus is not my father. Ozule is —or, was. Amarus only fathered my brothers."

Andarios and Kezerah gave hushed "oohs" in understanding.

"Weren't King Amarus and your mother paramours?" Andarios asked. "I thought I read that the war started because Queen Illija ran —erm, left Xenkesh."

Ikaika lifted his chin. "The paramour ceremony was arranged, but my mother wasn't given a choice. You have to mean it for a pairing to work." He wasn't about to admit that by both Aloran and Xenkeshi law, despite the lack of intention, the ceremony still technically bound the monarchs by contract.

Kezerah looked at a feather with keen interest, and a moment of silence fell.

Ikaika, not wanting to continue the conversation further, didn't say more either. He knew what it would lead to. Ozule was only widely known for three things. Being Amarus' brother, his affair with Ikaika's mother—that led to Ikaika himself—and dying while trying to save her as she fled Xenkesh. None were comfortable topics for him.

Luckily, Andarios changed the subject, his voice tight. "Well, parents are complicated." He reached out and grasped Kezerah's hand. "So instead, let's assume you'll be here through the morning meal, and you can duel me in the training yards."

Relieved for the shift back to lighter subjects, Ikaika smiled.

"Excellent. It'll be nice to fight someone other than Eriko. I'm tired of losing."

Andarios snorted. "Well, then I'll be sorry to beat you—Kez, you in?"

Kezerah yawned, seemingly bored by the idea of duels with anything but pillows. "My mother has a meeting with the Lords of Heartsglove. She didn't invite me so it's probably actually interesting. I was going to listen in."

Andarios gave a groan, but his eyes were closed and remained so.

Kezerah yawned again, and Ikaika caught it as he sank further into the nest of down and silks.

"Don' fall aslee…" Kezerah murmured, twisting to lay on her side. She nestled into her pillow, propped up next to Ikaika's shoulder. "The nurses still…need to…"

Ikaika didn't bother with a response. Her head further slumped to the side, to rest against his arm. He wasn't sure if it was proper, or if he should wake her. The warmth and coziness of the room took root, and Ikaika instead scooted closer to provide himself as a more suitable pillow. His eyes fluttered closed, and before he knew or understood, the unwavering strength of his mother's love poured into his mind. Then, for the first time in his life, the assurance that he would be surrounded by friends.

YEAR ONE, AUTUMN

While it had taken Kezerah mere moments to realize how fun it was to pester Ikaika, each season brought about new opportunities to test her limits. And his. Unlike Andarios, who matched her beat for beat, Ikaika appeared unwavering in his stoic tolerance of her. He only ever reacted on a rule-of-three basis, where she taunted him enough to prompt a reaction. He always chose to first try and ignore her, as he apparently preferred to observe fun rather than have it himself.

Kezerah found throughout the Autumn season that the rule of three also applied to Ikaika's willingness to do her bidding.

As the apple trees came into harvest, she asked Andarios to lift her to a branch. Ikaika sat in the roots of the tree, reading a book with the most focus Kezerah had ever seen applied in her life. Andarios obliged, only to pretend she was too heavy, swaying back and forth until they fell into the pile of leaves. Bursts of red and orange flittered down around them. Untrusting of her friend, she asked Ikaika. He had continued reading as if he hadn't heard, though each plea quirked his mouth up ever so slightly.

On the third plea, she said, "I'll not sneak into your room for three nights, consecutively, and shall bow every time you enter the banquet hall for the next week, praising the ground you walk on—"

Ikaika wordlessly closed his book and stood up. He stretched out his lean limbs, pushed thick curls from his eyes, then crouched down below the branches, ready for her assent to his shoulders.

She picked every apple on the branch, tossing them at Andarios' head while he did his best to catch them. Ikaika lowered her back down. She bounded off of him to procure the stolen apples. In thanks, she handed him a large crisp apple hued with a swirl of red and green.

He tousled her curls. "The three night's sleep and bowing will do, thanks."

Kezerah beamed at him. His smile in answer; well worth the groveling as he sat back down with his book.

She bowed low. "Thank you, your most prestigious and malodorous majesty."

"Doesn't malodorous mean he stinks?" Andarios chimed in, mouth full of apple.

"Shh," Kezerah hushed, not breaking her low bow with downcast eyes. The picture of innocence.

After the trio had been thoroughly chastised for being out of their rooms, Andarios found his training regimen much changed. Sleep came for him far earlier and heavier than any of them liked. This chased Kezerah into Ikaika's rooms (Three nights of consecutive peace aside).

Ikaika reveled in the night and told Kezerah it eased his mind when more people were asleep rather than awake.

"It's like their mind's grow softer," he explained, as they lay head to head on his bed staring up at the ceiling. The balcony remained tossed open from Kezerah's entrance.

"Read my mind," Kezerah ordered, thinking of the most ridiculous thing she could, he groaned at her.

"You're imagining Hanan in your mother's dress, now you've changed it and it's Andarios—Kez," he whined, rubbing his temple.

Kezerah stopped, looking worried. "I'm sorry, does it always hurt?"

"Not so much when I'm dreaming. But if I hear one voice, I tend to hear all the voices around them as well. It's hard to shut them out."

"Sorry," she said again, meaning it.

He bumped his head against hers. "It's alright. It was worth the image of Hanan in a dress."

They giggled and continued looking up. Ikaika often fell asleep first, so Kezerah started another conversation to distract him. "What would you do if you weren't going to be king?"

"Be a guard."

Kezerah turned over onto her elbows, staring down at him. "Ikaika of Alora, that's the most boring answer you could have come up with."

He looked up at her, deep dark eyes wide. "Well, it's true. I remember wanting to be Eriko when I grew up. Uncle Castiel had to talk me out of it. What about you?" He lifted his mouth into a half smile. "I bet you want to be a pirate or something."

"A pirate would be nice," she mused. "But more realistically I would want to be a spymaster and get to travel around gathering information."

Ikaika snorted up at her. "Like your mother? That's surprising, you two don't often align on much. Though you already do spy on people."

Kezerah curved a brow. "How do you know my mother is Spymaster?"

Ikaika tapped his temple slowly. Kezerah grew more surprised. "She gave it away? What a terrible spymaster."

Ikaika laughed fully now, twisting himself around to face her.

"Actually, it was you. You thought about it right after I got here, and I caught it." His expression was chagrined. "Sorry."

Kezerah rolled again, and Ikaika mused at the fact that she couldn't still herself. "Ugh. So I'm a terrible spy too."

"I wouldn't say that, just maybe not the best secret keeper. Your thoughts are... loud."

"Sorry," she apologized again.

"Don't be," he assured her. "I like your thoughts, they're funny, and your dreams are all the better. Sometimes they're worth the migraines."

"You can see my dreams?" Kezerah looked horrified.

"They mix with other people's, but yeah, I can usually tell when it's yours."

"How?" she asked, urgent.

"Lots of heights, towers, and dangerous situations."

"Oh," she said, relieved.

"You dreamed of me once." Ikaika grinned wickedly, and enjoyed her reddening cheeks. She smashed her face into a pillow, and he laughed at her. "What? We were just sledding on the ice," he said innocently. "Did I miss a better one?"

"Shut up, Ikaika," she said, her voice heavily muffled through the pillow.

They lay there and talked for hours before Ikaika dozed off. Kezerah slipped back over to her rooms, joining him in sleep. She dreamt of them fishing for stars; the world flipped so the sky stretched out below them. The dream so mesmerizing that, when Ikaika woke up, he found himself trying to fall back asleep to Meld with her again.

Year Two, Winter

The Wheel of the Year turned, the Equinoxes drew nearer, and time sped by in Elastor. More young nobility and friends of Kezerah joined the Solstice Court during festivals, but never stayed for longer than a season. Kezerah, Andarios, and Ikaika were the only constant occupants of the Spring Quarters. By Kezerah's sixteenth Yuletide, however, she decided she had had enough of her childhood rooms.

"They're for children," she pleaded as she followed her mother into the Winter Quarters. The air matched the bite in her breath with the promise of snow. "I haven't been a child since—"

"Since last night?" Elize said, without a misstep in her stride. Her mother's posture and intricate braid into her large crown made Kezerah feel like a peasant begging for scraps. The Queen prompted further when Kezerah looked confused. "When you chose to make lewd jokes at evening meal?"

Kezerah tossed her head back and groaned. They passed through the threshold of her father's study. Warmth and cinnamon swirled in the space, mixed with the musty smell of books.

Elowren looked up from his stack of parchments, his eyes amused. "What's this? My heir has decided to grace me with her presence for a council meeting?"

"Hardly," Kezerah said, attention still on her mother. "As you said, it was a joke—a funny one. Even Kai laughed."

Indeed, Ikaika laughing had been the point. In the time he had joined the Solstice Court, she had found him somewhat immune to her humor. The only minor hit she had gotten in was during that evening's meal when her mother had asked her father if he thought the ground would be fertile for the Spring festival. Kezerah had quipped that everything was fertile during the festival. She was uncertain if it had been her wiggling her eyebrows up and down at him, or the joke itself, but his composure had broken as he spit into his cider, cheeks flushed despite regaining control soon after. Her mother had not been pleased. It had been a truly triumphant evening.

Elize's frown rivaled the look of disapproval in her eyes. "You say you're not a child, and in the same breath denounce a council meeting." Her expression turned toward Elowren. "A council meeting, I might add, that she is meant to attend."

"I have plans," Kezerah said. "Nobody asked me to attend the council meeting."

"Nobody asked because it's expected you attend," Elize said through her teeth.

Kezerah wanted to explain that *she—Kezerah*—had never been invited or expected to attend a meeting. Before she could speak or act or think for herself, her life had been decided: Her identity carved into stone. At what point had *she* said *yes* to never having a free afternoon? Or cramming away knowledge that didn't interest her? The person expected to show up to these meetings, present perfect proclamations, and give even keel answers without asking questions, didn't exist. Those were expectations of the Soul Heir, and why would she have ever agreed to that? Kezerah huffed. Centered between two people who had not only agreed to the role of ruler but volunteered for it she knew better than to bother.

"We're getting off point," she said instead.

Elowren came around the desk, looking between the two of them. Kezerah made sure to use every facet of her charm: eyes widened, lip pouted, and head cocked to one side. Elize crossed her arms in combat.

"And, if I dare enter the fray," Elowren said, "what *is* the point?"

"Responsibility," Elize declared.

At the same time Kezerah answered, "Freedom."

The two glared at one another, and Kezerah used her mother's pause to levy her position. "I want to move into the Summer Quarters."

Elowren's playful expression lessened to caution. "The heir— under even less uncertain circumstances—should not be stationed in our least protected quarters."

"All of the Solstice Court is protected, painfully so," said Kezerah. "I'm too old for Nurse, curfews, and being boxed in with no view. I'm ready."

"You have yet to Hold Sway, and Monk Biloba tells me your proficiency in the language is..."

"Lacking," Elize finished

"I'll take hold of my Sway any day now. Monk Biloba just has an infatuation with grammar."

Elowren shook his head. "There is also the Summer Quarters itself to consider. It has access to the Lull, the balconies are set on the cliffs, and with it the sea-trading routes between all three kingdoms. It's too much of a risk."

Kezerah couldn't argue the allure of the Summer Quarters being the most vulnerable wing of the castle. Every Summer, she eagerly climbed the stairs to eat the meals on the open terrace, with nothing but ocean to the east and fresh sea air swirling around her. The corridors were built with the heat in mind, and made of nothing but cool tiles and high pillars free to the elements. A spiral staircase escaped the Solstice Court's fortification to lead down to soft sand and a private shoreline.

"You say that as if mother doesn't travel each year, despite her illness," Kezerah said. "Do we only care about the future Queen? What of our current one, who just last year collapsed and had to return early––"

Her mother's voice held more threat than warning. "Don't speak on subjects you haven't the slightest ability to understand." Kezerah sensed the danger and retraced her steps.

"I just want to be given the same freedoms everyone else is granted. I'm tired of being the only one who doesn't get to choose their own rooms, or switch quarters with the seasons. I'm tired of being trapped in Spring!"

"That's hyperbole," Elize said. "You are not like everyone else, and both the Prince of Alora, and your low-born friend, reside in the Spring Quarters."

"As if you haven't tried to move them both!"

"Kezerah," Elowren said. His tone contrasted the animosity in the room, yet Kezerah could already see his resolve. He aimed to console. "While I understand your frustration—"

"But you *don't* understand my frustration," Kezerah cut in. "You weren't the Soul Heir! You don't know what it's like. You got to have fun growing up. Go on trips—get in trouble." She knew her father sympathized by the softness of his eyes. However, Kezerah could also see the hard set of his pointed chin, and the stubborn press of his lips. She grew all the more frustrated. "I'm not asking to see the world. I'm only asking for a room with a view other than one scrawny tree!"

"All young nobility start with rooms in the Spring Quarters," Elize said dismissively.

"Yes, Mother," Kezerah said, through her teeth, "and then they leave. How old were you when you got to choose your room?"

"The privilege of being raised in a palace didn't fall into my lap, nor was I the Soul Heir," Elize said. "I wasn't born to my position as queen. I fought for it. Earned it. You have an entire kingdom counting on you, and you can't be bothered to join a council meeting."

"Fine!" Kezerah snapped. "I'll go to the council meeting. Then, can I choose my own rooms? Not have the nurses and Hanan breathing down my neck?"

Elowren's face fell, and betrayed his answer. Anger towards her mother festered. She should have waited and tried to speak to him separately.

"Well, Perhaps..." Elize said, tentatively, "a compromise could be reached."

Elowren knit his brows together, but didn't add in.

Kezerah blinked. Her mother said yes to precisely nothing. She acted quickly. "Done—Yes," then added eagerly. "What is it?"

Elize spoke each word with well crafted deliberation. "If you were to continually join council meetings, and actually follow the guidelines of protection we have laid out for you, the topic could be broached once more."

Kezerah did not like the open-endedness of the statement. "That's cheating. You've only offered a conversation in barter for daily meetings and dull afternoons."

"This isn't a game Kezerah, there is no 'cheating,'" Elize said stiffly.

Kezerah soured, why did she ever think this shrew of a woman could be reasoned with? "All of your compromises are games, Mother. I just won't play them anymore."

Elize drew herself up. "Fine then. Conversation off the table. Enjoy your bountiful afternoon with your leech of a playmate. You can rule from there for all I care. With your lack of experience it will be fitting to have a childish queen serve from her childhood room."

"Elize, that's too—"

"Do we want the best for her or not, Elowren? If she doesn't try, what are we working towards?"

Her father's defeat came out in a breath.

Kezerah's lip trembled. She didn't dare look at him, his pity would only summon her tears. Yet another battle slipped through her fingers. "Okay," she choked out, subdued. "I'll attend meetings for a renewed conversation in...?"

"The following Spring," Elize said. "Ruling a kingdom is a slow affair. I expect it to have a steep learning curve for you. And your previous follow-through has been poor."

"I won't miss a single meeting."

"Or creep about the castle past hours," her mother added.

Kezerah withheld her retort. She did not *creep* and found this descriptor irritating, especially coming from a *Spymaster*. She worked her lips into a smile. Her response worded carefully, to ensure her trips to Ikaika's rooms remained uncompromised. "Alright. I shall not sneak out of the Spring Quarters, and will attend any and all meetings." She turned to her father.

Elowren was too quiet, too pensive for Kezerah to feel secure in the bargain. Her fingers intertwined in plea. Elowren sighed. "I shall follow your mother's wisdom in this." He looked to Elize. "Perhaps, when you have returned from The Edge, we can reconvene, privately. For now, let's welcome in the lieges that wait eagerly to join us."

Kezerah's shoulders slumped as she remembered the topic of this meeting. Every winter, around Yuletide, Elize traveled to the less fruitful areas of their kingdom. The Edge: the war torn area Alorans and Xenkeshi journeyed to in order to fight on each other's lands. While Elowren did everything in his power to keep their lands safe, skirmishes still occurred. Bandits often used this as an excuse to raid towns and travelers alike, blaming it on one side or the other. Elize visited these areas doing what she did best. She dispersed crops from less affected areas, turned small occasions into lavish celebrations, and lended aid to those affected. While exciting in practice, in preparation, the talks mostly consisted of budgeting and division of labor.

Kezerah groaned.

"Unless you'd rather go play in the snow?" Elize offered.

Kezerah rose to the challenge. "No, that's fine. Bring on the mathematics."

Hours later, after her mother's departure, Kezerah rolled fresh snow with numb fingertips. "I wish I could go."

A snowball whizzed past her head and she ducked as Andarios

rolled a new one. "Why would you go? You hate being around your mother."

"Yes, well," she said, tossing a snowball back at him, "in this fantasy, I'm going so she doesn't have to." It hit him in the shoulder.

"Ah yes, how noble of you," he acknowledged, launching one at her. It missed, and elicited a squeal from the visiting twins of Glassberry, who were making a snowman behind Kezerah. While friends of Kezerah, neither had ever quite warmed to her gruff best friend. The twins preferred rumors passed over hot cocoa and appraising the newest trends from coastal society. Kezerah loved to see the new blends of fabric they brought, and to hear the silly things lieges did when outside the eyes of the capitol. She just also enjoyed snowballs.

"Sorry!" Andarios called back. Whistle glared at him, and Willow stuck her tongue out. Ikaika appeared out of nowhere however, and charmed the sisters while he rebuilt their fallen creation.

Kezerah lobbed a snowball at Ikaika's head. He caught it, wordlessly adding it to the snowman's face.

"Show off!" Andarios and Kezerah called out in unison, comrades until Andarios shoved ice down the back of her coat. The snow war resumed. They flung flurries at one another and Ikaika eventually joined in after finishing with the twins. They chased each other into the Winter Quarters, Hanan shouting for them to dust the ice from their shoes as they slid into the hall. The only person who ever truly prevented Kezerah's happiness now away for the season, not a care was given.

Year Three, Spring

Dear Crown Prince Ambrose, I hope this letter finds you well—or, in the least, finds you—I write once more to invite you to the Solstice Court, the soul of Elastor and heart of Thrice. In times of war, we work to forge a semblance of peace. May you accept this invitation of Haven in an effort to work towards our treaty, and the future truce between Xenkesh and Alora. Let us put the notion of violence aside for an evening of silks and revelry this Spring. I, as your gracious host, look forward to your response and our better acquaintance.

Sincerely, Princess Kezerah,

Soul Heir of Elastor, Crown Heir of the Solstice throne, ally and friend of Xenkesh.

"What's this?" a light and lilting voice said. An arm, once draped across Ambrose's chest, reached beyond him to lift the thickly perfumed paper from his nightstand. He delayed the action, lacing his fingers in hers.

"Nothing." he leaned in for a kiss. "Politics."

His bedmate dodged the kiss, unfurled their clasped hands and applied her weight on him. His only option was either to watch her naked body cross over his, or push her off. He chose the show. Safeya took her time, red painted lips smiled at him keenly as she procured the letter. "You know I love politics."

"I know you love power."

She did not correct him. Safeya's golden brows arched scandalously as her eyes darted across the page. "Oh? A love letter to my dear prince?"

"Hardly," Ambrose said, reaching once more for the paper. "An invitation to the Elastian court." He shrugged, fingertips catching the edge of the paper. "One is sent every season."

Safeya jerked the letter out of reach. "This sounds less like an invitation to court, and more like an invitation to bed."

"Now you're projecting," he teased. "It's from the Soul Heir."

"Yes," Safeya said, checking the sheet again. "Soul Heir, ally, and 'friend' to Xenkesh."

He let out a huff of breath. "It's an expression, Saf. Elastor thinks everyone is a 'friend', that's why they're useless."

"And what do you send in reply to these perfectly innocent invitations of silken evenings and revels?"

Ambrose heard the subtle shift in tone, a build in tension indicating jealousy. In truth, he'd never bothered to respond. The letters were always hollow and dutiful; a sneer of superiority that insinuated that, by not attending, he somehow lacked good will. When was the last time the Soul Heir had to reduce rations for soldiers? To send a loved one to the Summerlands at the Bethync docks? Was she even aware of where her silk came from? Or that a portion of the silk-worm forest that produced her lavish fabric had been burned in a siege last moon? They had been lucky to salvage as much of the forest as they had, limiting the quantity greatly. Where was *that* mentioned in her invitation?

Safeya still held the letter out of reach. It didn't matter though. While paper was not kin to his Bond object, it had a soul—paper was also notoriously malleable—and that was enough.

'*Burn.*' he suggested to the amenable letter. The paper did not hesitate. It had been so many things before: a seed, a sapling, a tree. What was one more transformation?

"Ah! Ambrose!" Safeya waved her hand frantically before flinging it out and away from her. Ash scattered as it hit the white marble floor. She prepared to spit more venom his way, but he drew her close.

"What I send in reply isn't important. As far as what I do *now...*" His hand traveled from ample waist to thicker hips. "I grant you an invitation to find out."

He left her with the decision to either push him away, or wait to see what he'd do next. She chose the show. Fingernails dug into his dark hair, mussing it to fall in his face. He would show her just how little he gave a damn about some foreign princess' letter.

"XENKESH IS ASKING for a higher price on silk," drawled the newly appointed liege of Port Aveltra. "Three gold a yard, instead of the standard one."

Kezerah drummed her fingers on the table to the rhythm of the chirping sounds of Spring outside. The lords, ladies, and lieges of Elastor all sat around the Strategy Chambers. The fires remained dampened to combat the warm weather. It gave the room a hollowed out look. Plain stone walls stifled, rather than highlighted, the mulberry pigment of an armchair perched by the hearth and weighty library. Plush cushions left abandoned for more practical seating. The council's sturdy wooden chairs drawn up to the carved map table. The Lord of Larken coughed and Kezerah swore dust expelled from his thin lips. Elowren beckoned a servant and she compared the servant's velvet tunic to that of the armchair, wondering if they came from the same roll of fabric. Water poured in a drowsy trickle from a Glassberry pitcher enameled with jewelweed and a gilt lip. Someone droned on about something and the water drained slower.

Kezerah sat beside her mother who placed a hand next to Kezerah's to silence her finger tap. The window across from Kezerah appeared to shrink the longer the council meeting continued.

"I do not think—" her mother began, then shot Kezerah a scathing look at her returned drumbeat. Kezerah's hand froze in place. She had every intention of being on her best behavior this meeting. The time had come for the court to begin migrating feasts and guests to the Summer Quarters, just a moon before Kezerah's seventeenth birthday. She had been patient. She had bided her time and the time was now.

She gave her mother a smile that showed all her teeth.

Elize continued, "I don't think that's necessary. Sorrel is more than capable of providing our wardrobes and fabrics."

The Liege of Aveltra looked uncomfortable. "That is fair, Your High Majesty," they paused, treading carefully. "Though, Sorrel mostly supplies cotton and wool. Silk is—"

"A luxury most of Elastor cannot afford," Elize finished, casting her eyes toward Elowren who now drank from his newly refilled glass of water. "Tell King Amarus the answer is no."

Elowren set his water down and brought his folded hands up to rest his chin on. "Did Amarus' envoy provide a reason for the price increase?"

"Actually, it appears the Crown Prince, Ambrose, was the one to make the request."

Ah, Ambrose. Through trial and error—many errors—Kezerah understood the eggshells she trudged across shattered at a much faster rate when he became involved. Though he had become a less frequent subject of discussion after the announcement last year that he intended to take over as his father's chief war strategist: A title Elize had been quick to point out was not often gifted to someone of his age.

"See what happens when one applies themselves?" her mother had lectured.

Kezerah rolled her shoulders to sluff off her mother's disappointment. She watched a songbird out the window scuffle with a squirrel. She suspected the squabble to be a territorial dispute.

"Ambrose continues to refuse our invitations to court," Elize said tersely, "but has the nerve to request more coins for his silk? I must say after all of..." Her mother's cadence hinted at a soliloquy. Perhaps the bird-squirrel dispute involved a nest? Squirrels *were* known to threaten eggs from time to time. She chose to side with the bird on this one. Seeds and berries were one thing, but nests should be left out of it. What right did the squirrel have?

"That's quite the assumption."

Kezerah's heart lurched a little, thinking the comment directed at her. A lord of Heartsglove bickered with younger Lady Larken. Of course they hadn't been weighing in on her thoughts of a woodland war. They could have opinions on the real one. She shook out her hands, surprised they were moist and balled up into fists.

"You'd think Xenkeshi would be more compromising, given their magick," Heartsglove jested.

"It's bargaining that they're good at," said Lady Glassberry. "How's the saying go? A Xenkeshi only compromises once? From then on, they bargain."

Many chuckled at what Kezerah could only assume was the mustiest joke the room had to offer. Elastians speculated the deals made between Bond Wielders and souls were forged through compromise: a coaxing for the soul to do the wielder's bidding. Kezerah had been fascinated with the subject for a fortnight, sending her first letter to Prince Ambrose riddled with further questions on the subject and several spelling errors. She'd been instructed to rewrite it (four times).

She slumped further in her seat at the memory. Early on, it had been decided she would write to Ambrose each season. Many agreed it only fair to create a correspondence, since her interactions with Ikaika were so direct and frequent. Yet, it could hardly be called a correspondence, as Ambrose had never responded to a single one in three years. She had given up in the early onset of silence, and it had been left to Elize to take up the mantle. Kezerah assumed the slight had been marked down in a book somewhere to tally up her short-comings.

Her mother reigned in the meager chuckles being passed about the room. "Compromise is besides the point. It's simply rude to ask if you aren't willing to give anything in return."

"Nothing is simple in war, my sweet," Elowren reminded his paramour. "I'm sure he means no offense."

"I'm sure." Elize turned back to the Liege of Aveltra. "However, if he is trying to have Elastor pay for their war through proxy, he can think again." Lady Glassberry shared a smug look with the Lords of Heartsglove. Kezerah put a cheek in her clammy hand. She'd hear all about her mother's graceful competence from Whistle when the twin's mother relayed the exchange. She could practically hear her friend wistfully quoting her Queen, *'and then she said, 'he can think again.''* Kezerah rolled her eyes.

The Liege Aveltra nodded and stood. Discomfort lingered in the Liege's eyes as they looked from Queen to King. "If *both* Your High Majesties are in agreement then?"

Kezerah knew if she'd caught the slight, her mother definitely hadn't missed it. Technically, while co-rulers until they deemed Kezerah capable of the throne, Elowren's lineage directly descended from his parent Kleodore: The Soul Heir before Kezerah. When young, she often quipped about being her own grandparent, but then the reality of the joke set in and her humor on the matter receded.

Elowren and Elize made eyes at one another. Then he gave a definitive nod. "We are. If silk is at a higher price, it's just as well we support Sorrel and wear more cotton."

With the meeting adjourned, all stood. Both Lords of Heartsglove eagerly complimented the Queen on her concise decisions as they left. Kezerah heaved a sigh, only to realize everyone—including her parents—had begun filing from the room.

"Wait—" The chair she sat in scraped against the floor abruptly as she stood, startling both her mother and father at the threshold. Kezerah flattened her hands awkwardly across her skirts to appease her mother. "Erm... if I could have a word?"

They waited, Elize halfway out the door as Elowren held it open. A loud squawking emphasized the silence and announced the skirmish outside had turned ugly. Elize prompted Kezerah with a clearing of her throat.

"We'll be moving feasts into the Summer Quarters for the season soon," Kezerah began. "And I thought—" Her plea withered at her father's crestfallen expression and slackened posture. "I've been attending all the meetings..." she finished, half-heartedly, her shoulders slumped in disappointment to match his.

"I know you have." Elowren's hand slipped away from the door and he held it out in entreatment. "Perhaps when you Hold Sway," he said. "I had expected the manifestation by this time—"

"But I can communicate in Sway fluently now," Kezerah argued. "And some never Hold Sway!"

"Yes," Elowren agreed patiently. "But historically that has rarely been the case for the Ellas line, and never the Soul Heir."

"Well, this Soul Heir still hasn't," Kezerah snapped. "Maybe Ellas finally passed on to the Summerlands and you're just stuck with me instead."

"Lower your voice and think for one moment where your words go," her mother ordered as she looked out and down the hall. "The last thing we need is for courtiers to question your legitimacy!"

Elowren closed his eyes before opening them on Elize. The two stared at each other. Kezerah sent a silent invocation to the Summerlands to be granted with Mind Melding instead. Per usual, her pleas went unanswered and she remained magickless—while they fought an unspoken battle of wills.

Eventually, her father redirected his attention back to her. "Kezerah, I've known your soul since before you were born and will know you anywhere, in any form you take. Never doubt that." He brushed his braids back. "But, I cherish the person you are now and would like to delay endangering you in what ways I know how. That said, the Spring Quarters are much safer. Until you have some defense at your disposal, *I* believe it is wise to keep your current limitations in place."

"Dar is my defense. He could come with me," Kezerah tried.

"Oh?" Elize put a hand on her hip. "Does he Hold Sway now? Can he finally be moved into the barracks with the other soldiers?"

Yes, as a matter of fact Andarios *had* recently tripped Kezerah from across the room while they practiced. A fact they had both decided to keep to themselves. "No." Kezerah grasped for a new curve in the conversation. "Is that where you'll send Ikaika when he comes into his magick? The barracks?"

"Of course not," Elize said slowly. "He's our ward. Our ward which will inherit an entire third of the continent. Not some low-born—"

Kezerah couldn't help but bristle. "Dar isn't low-born. He'll inherit Luka when he comes of age."

"A fitting inheritance," Elize scoffed. "Luka being an excellent example of what happens when charity is unearned. Furthermore, I'm glad you've raised the issue of the Aloran heir again. Because I'm of the firm belief that it would be wise for you to be distanced—and measures put in place—from Prince Ikaika. We would hate for gossip to travel to Xenkesh that you favor their enemy of war."

"They don't even return your letters!" Kezerah's nails pierced her palm. "What does Ambrose of Xenkesh care who I spend my time with?"

"It is Amarus we need to show caution towards," said Elowren. "When backed into a corner...he is known to take regrettable actions."

"That sounds like Amarus' problem," Kezerah replied, vehemently. "Not mine or Kai's."

"No, it is *our* problem, Kezerah. *Your* Kingdom's problem," Elize said. "And it's exactly those kinds of statements that make it so obvious it is time for you and *Crown Prince* Ikaika *of Alora* to spend some much needed time apart."

Kezerah looked to her father, but he seemed uncomfortable, a frown both at his brow and lips. "Father!" Her heart picked up pace and her throat tightened. She fought to keep her composure but the conversation had taken a turn. Kezerah wanted more freedom, not for Ikaika to be moved out of reach.

"No," Elowren said, "as you have said my love, the princes of Xenkesh have an open invitation to visit our court and converge with our young allies. It should not be Kezerah nor Ikaika who are punished if Xenkesh chooses to remain distant."

Elize pursed her lips.

Kezerah exhaled in relief, briefly not caring that she remained in the Spring Quarters.

"If Prince Ikaika and Lord Andarios opt to stay in the Spring Quarters, I shall not prevent them," Elowren continued. "The rest we can discuss once you Hold Sway."

Kezerah nodded, not daring a glance in her mother's direction. "Yes, all the same curfews and rules in place."

Elowren smiled, seemingly pleased to grant her this small happiness despite her shackles.

"Good. I'm glad we could reach new terms then."

Kezerah went down one hall, her parents another. She managed to keep her smile intact until she descended the Winter corridor stairwell. Moss and fairy-wrens decorated a fountain in the center of a small and peaceful clearing. The fountain babbled as the birds bathed. The Spring Quarters loomed ahead; a wall of stone and pop of blush foliage. Her steps turned to stomps, prompting the birds to take flight. She watched their retreat with a mixture of vexation and guilt tangled up inside her.

They took refuge in the blossoms of her inner courtyard's tree. The branches boasted pink petals, dancing in celebration. She swore it mocked her. Kezerah kicked the stone wall of the fortress and enjoyed the throb in her toe. She had done everything asked of her, only to end up in the same conversation with worse results. More rules, more hurdles, no freedom. A few surrounding daisies had survived her burst into the clearing and she twisted her velveteen slipper into the grass, ruining both flora and shoe, in a satisfying squash of dirt.

"The meeting went well then?" Ikaika said kindly from behind her.

Kezerah sucked in air as she faced him, then expelled it out as she slumped against the wall. "Oh yes. Instead of moving to the Summer Quarters, I was given the option for you and Dar to be trapped with me."

Ikaika leaned next to her, and she looked up at him. Suddenly, the idea of him remaining in the Spring Quarters felt foolish. While Kezerah had hardly sprouted an inch since his arrival, Ikaika now stood a head taller. His build had remained lean, but his shoulders had broadened, and features sharpened. Ikaika looked and carried his age. Kezerah felt and acted no such number.

Sweat gathered at his temple and he wiped it away self-consciously, aware of her critical stare. "Dar and I were in drills all morning. He shouldn't be too far behind." Ikaika picked a bedraggled flower that Kezerah had smashed in her rage. "So, if you have some emotions you'd like to rid yourself of–" He smiled as he uncrumpled the petals. "—I'd be happy to lend you my sword to swing, at Andarios."

Kezerah laughed despite her mood. "Thank you, but after years of pretending to be competent during every boring council meeting. I'm finished humoring my parents with the idea that I'm useful."

Ikaika continued to fix the flower, but his brows scrunched together. "It couldn't have *all* been boring. Not with the war..." He trailed off, and sounded unsure.

Kezerah scoffed. "The war especially. I can't say anything in those meetings. We just sit there and nod while they give us the numbers, then I leave and the council talks about things that matter."

His eyes, which had been focused on his task, ignited with challenge. "Numbers of what? Victories?...Bodies?"

Kezerah shrank from both his words and the accusatory tone in which he said them.

Ikaika stopped himself. "Sorry," he said flatly.

"You know I can't—"

Ikaika's voice thawed, his expression following soon after. "I know. I just got a letter from Castiel this morning and it was...Well, really, I'm sorry I asked." He handed her the flower, pristine and dainty in his deft fingertips.

Her curiosity prickled and she stifled it, taking the flower instead and twirling the stem, uncertain of what she should or could say.

"I do believe your mother *had* intended to move my quarters soon, based on some errant thoughts I overheard," Ikaika said, a corner of his mouth twitched up at one side. "So, perhaps the meeting wasn't a complete waste of time."

"Oh?" she asked dryly. "All I managed to do was offer an extension to your sentence—which I understand you gracefully declining."

Ikaika took the pirouetting flower from her hands. Kezerah's pulse quickened as he placed the much less bedraggled flower in her hair. "Honestly Kez, for me, a few more seasons in the Spring Quarters really doesn't sound all that bad."

Kezerah tried to hold tight to her anger, but when she grasped for it, she found it replaced by a songbird fluttering about her ribcage. Her argument for a room, only a rock-skip away, sounded silly. "No," she breathed. "Maybe it isn't."

YEAR FOUR, SUMMER

Waves of heat drenched the Solstice castle, the guests and its occupants chased into the shade of trees and high archways. With summer on the horizon, the Solstice Court blazed in high celebration for Kezerah's eighteenth birthday. Elize had spared no expense: jugglers, artisans, and local Elastian dishes were brought in. Pink candied cherry petals were gathered and spread out on tables in abundance alongside music and entertainment. The festivities unfurled across the castle grounds, with both Elastian nobility and skilled commoners in attendance. Aerial dancers trapezed from colorful ribbons, hung throughout the meadow's branches, while a theater troupe did a stunningly realistic performance of Ellas commanding the earth with his Sway. The crowd cheered as both Sway and Bond magick amplified their applause by shaking tables and plates throughout the meadow lawn.

Kezerah could see exactly none of it, the noise of cheers drowned out by the lapping waves of the Lull. The moment her mother turned her back, she had retreated down the sandy steps to the secluded Solstice Bay shore with no intention of rejoining until coerced into that evening's feast.

The sun's shimmer high above promised plenty of sulking and sunbathing left to achieve. Her day nurse had pestered her into a cotton wrap dress, covering her neck to ankle, which Kezerah had hiked up to her thighs. Ample aloe and Xenkeshi coconut oils shone across her brown skin. She'd spent the majority of her birthday, and the days leading up to it, on the sands of the Summer Quarters in both an avoidance of pressure and the hopes of sparking inspiration to Hold Sway, to no avail.

Resigned to failure, she melted in the warmth of the sand, slippers cast aside and the twins lying beside her. She enjoyed the lack of pressure associated with Willow and Whistle. The twins rarely came to court but when they did, they were often content to lay out in the sun and complain about nothing of consequence. It was easy to pretend the sisters were merely here to visit her, and not witness 'The great Ellas reborn' come into her Sway abilities.

"I wish my birthday was in the Summer," Whistle said, round body turning to have warmth at her back. "But our mother would never put on a party for us like this."

"It's not for me," groaned Kezerah. "It's for people like you to think it's for me."

"Sometimes it can just be as simple as a summer party, Kezi."

"Technically," Willow said, "it's not Summer until the solstice. We still have another week of Spring."

"Don't use the 'S-word,'" Kezerah grumbled, pressing her cheek into the grains of sand.

"Both seasons begin with 'S,'" Whistle said, fed up with Kezerah's mood.

"I knew I'd find you here!" Andarios cast a shadow over the three limp forms lazing in the sun.

Kezerah pushed her face further into the sand. She reached a damp, cool, second layer just as her friend nudged her with his foot.

"Come on Kez, you've been sulking down here for weeks."

"She doesn't want to be bothered right now," Whistle said, with freshly-directed irritation. "We're sunbathing."

"*She's* sulking—*you're* enabling," Andarios said. "But thanks for the input."

Kezerah heard the harumph and rustle of sand as Whistle stood, Willow not far behind. "Well, she won't move. So enjoy your abling."

"That's not—"

"See you at the feast, Kezi," Whistle said. "Good luck."

Kezerah mumbled, turning onto her back to confront her

friend. Flecks of sand spilled from her face into her hair. Andarios' expression told her much of the sand had remained caked in patches to her skin. Stray kernels of sand threatened to fall into her eyes. She didn't bother to wipe them off. While Ikaika had grown taller than her, Andarios had grown in every direction imaginable. A head taller still, he towered over both of them. His tanned silhouette partially eclipsed her view. A light breeze, gifted by the phantom of a storm in the far off sea, rustled his mop of white hair.

She closed an eye, to better look at him. "Do you mind moving a little to the left?"

"Kez."

"Dar," she chimed back with the same level of annoyance.

"You can't Hold Sway if you don't try."

"I can't fail either," Kezerah said, then rolled her eyes at Andarios' expression. "You *know* I've been trying."

"I know you *were* trying."

He referred to the end of their practice sessions. Early on, when Andarios had gained his Hold on Sway, they had decided to conceal it. Elize would be swift in extracting him from the Spring Quarters, but if he taught her, they could move together. Each time Andarios had improved a pit of jealousy had rooted in her gut. That was until she'd seen the glimmer of elation cross his face and her jealousy dissolved. She couldn't begrudge him what so clearly made him feel more connected to his parents. She could begrudge herself however and soon it became evident she couldn't keep pace and quit trying all together.

Kezerah let out a long sigh. "I'm eighteen. That's it, Dar. Do you know how rare it is for magick to manifest after eighteen?"

"As rare as a recurring soul cycling through the same blood-line for generations?"

Kezerah glared up at him.

"Take a break then—Not just lying on the beach like driftwood. Distract yourself," Andarios urged. "There's an entire party waiting for you upstairs."

"Yes, I know. That's why I'm down here."

"Fine, then. Kai and I are about to go spar," Andarios offered.

"We'll go to the northern yards. They're less crowded and nobody would look for you there."

Kezerah pretended to deliberate. "Too hot. Can't move."

Andarios let out a huff of breath and, as his shadow shifted, Kezerah thought she might have won. Then she felt herself lifted into the air.

"Ahh—what—Dar!"

Andarios cradled her, before he rocked her back, then flung her forward—and tossed Kezerah into the Lull. A splash of tepid water erupted as she collided with its serene surface. Her shout was cut off by the taste of salt and the need to shut her eyes as she fully submerged.

Kezerah sputtered as she came up for air. She swore as she spit water, and trudged back towards shore, towards murder.

"Since you're up, and cooled off," Andarios shouted, and backed up towards the sand dusted stairs, "you should join us."

"When I get my hands on you—"

"You'll what?" Andarios taunted, a glint in his eyes bright enough to match the sun. "Complain to Kai? Have him avenge you?"

"Shut it," Kezerah said, each step closer to Andarios' hasty retreat up the stairs.

"In that case, it's only proper you watch—to ensure your honor is defended."

Kezerah sprang for him, and Andarios gave a whoop of laughter as she gave chase. Both of them ignored party guests and performers brought on her behalf. Music played on up-beat strings, and she heard the Lady Sorrel remark on the state of Kezerah's undress. Both she and Andarios raced into the northern practice yards.

Ikaika already stood there waiting, in padded leather armor. "Oh good, you're here—Kez, what happened to your dress?"

"Beat Dar into the mud," Kezerah said, her arms crossed and eyes on her friend, "and I'll tell you."

Ikaika's inquisitive expression broke into a grin, with a rare show of dimples. He looked over at Andarios, who latched bracers and shoulder pads onto his plain wool tunic. "If you insist."

The two friends dueled, mountain peaks framing the horizon.

Kezerah dried on the wooden fencing that surrounded the sparring yards as she watched. She knew her friends sparred now more to distract her than for real sport. Quiet footsteps approach behind her, barely audible under the thwack of practice swords. The light had dimmed into dusk before anyone had bothered to look for her. Without the spectacle of her gaining her Hold on Sway, she'd paled next to the theatrics and acrobats of the party. The *idea* of her had sufficed.

She twisted slightly on the fencing to look back. To her luck and joy, the steps belonged to her father.

After a shy smile at Elowren, she turned her attention back to the match, which had the added benefit of concealing her pleased expression at having been searched for.

Her father rested his forearms on the wooden post, next to where Kezerah perched. Elowren's close-cropped beard was no longer peppered, but a pure crisp silver. The metal clasps in his braids, to match his silver circlet, caught the light and drew her attention from Ikaika's swift parry. "Summerlands, I bet they'll start referring to Lord Andarios as the Bear soon, like his father," Elowren said in greeting.

Kezerah scooted closer to lean on his shoulder. Glad to see him outside of a dusty room, strewn with papers. "He's too friendly to be a bear."

Both friends gravitated their way and Kezerah tilted back instinctively, though neither were close enough. Elowren chuckled, his eyes on the match. "People grow unimaginative when there is something already established."

Andarios smiled as if he'd heard, then doubled back as Ikaika used the distraction to make a jab at his center. Both laughed as Ikaika pressed his advance.

Kezerah scoffed, but enjoyed watching them spar. She could see their personalities shine through each of their maneuvers. Andarios' movements were structured yet playful, his strict training in clash with his personality. Kezerah could never tell if he took a match seriously until he won. Ikaika's movements on the other hand always seemed methodical: calm and calculated, though mostly defensive, with small strikes towards Andarios' calves.

She soaked in the warmth of her father's shoulder and the waning sun. The two continued to watch, and Kezerah yawned as her stomach grumbled. This would be her last match of the evening.

Ikaika ducked under Andarios' practice blade, then swept quickly to the side. Suddenly behind Andarios, he didn't bother with the blade of his slim practice sword, but instead rapped a knuckle at a pressure point in Andarios' shoulder. Andarios dropped his large weapon with a curse. After a moment of sputtering, he yielded, and the two bowed.

Kezerah couldn't help but laugh at Andarios' grumbling.

"I told you doing something other than moping was a good idea," Andarios said, mud splattered into his floppy hair as he dabbed his brow with a sleeve.

Kezerah lifted her hands; two fingers walked then stumbled over an out-stretched pointer finger in the Sway to trip him. She sighed when Andarios' steps didn't fumble in the slightest. Her father looked at her with raised brows and a soft smile. She detected pity in his gaze.

"It was worth a try." She shrugged with no intention of ever attempting it again.

"That it was," Elowren agreed, pushing himself off the post in an altogether unkingly way, drumming hands on the wood in an upbeat rhythm. "On that topic, I was indeed sent to persuade you to attend your own birthday feast."

Kezerah rolled her eyes. Only one person could *send* the king anywhere. "It seems mother won't rest without me being in attendance to my own inadequacy. Wasn't the theater troupe enough for her?"

Kezerah expected a platitude but Elowren granted her a drawn out exhale. "Today wore me thin as well, if I'm honest." She blinked. Her father nudged her, a rare mischief in his smile. "One trapeze artist would have been excessive, but a dozen?"

Kezerah laughed, "How many servants do you think she ordered to dip those petals in sugar."

"Ugh," he groaned, "not nearly as many as I'll need to help us take the ribbons from the trees. Poor Hanan, we'll have to help."

"They're on every tree!"

"On every branch of every tree!"

Both father and daughter laughed at the absurdity of untangling each knot from each branch on each tree in the Solstice Court. Said streamers came into view as the two returned to the party, and the laughter they had both shared blew away in the breeze. Kezerah swore their camaraderie flew away with it.

"It won't be so bad," Elowren promised, a hand squeezing her shoulder as he led them towards the sparkling lights of the Summer Terrace.

In a sought-after return to their solidarity, she raised her eyebrows and bunched her lips in a knowing look. Elowren chuckled, but it no longer sounded playful, his eyes straight ahead at the crowd ascending the Summer terrace. Kezerah gazed up at him, and noticed he'd gained new wrinkles in his dark skin. "I wonder if you could help me with a new project I've begun working on."

Kezerah tilted her head, but didn't dare promise herself to yet more meetings.

"For now it's a bit of a secret, but it was actually seeing you wind through your maze the other day that began the idea."

Kezerah straightened. "Secret as in..."

"Nobody knows about it yet. I plan on unveiling it this Summer, but it needs more work before I make a fool of myself in front of old Larken and Ralven. Perhaps it could take place of the afternoon meetings?"

No council meetings, and hours spent with her father and secrets. "It has to do with mazes?"

Elowren tilted his head from side to side. "Of sorts. Waterways, really. I'll explain more, let's say..."

"I'm free tomorrow," Kezerah offered. "Dar has training after morning meal."

Elowren grinned. "Tomorrow it is then." They had arrived at the spiral stairwell leading up to the Summer Quarters. Elowren drew her close with an arm. "A quick announcement acknowledging that today is the day we celebrate you, and all your *future* accomplishments. Then, the feast will be underway." He lightly bumped her lowered chin. "With plenty of chances to try again."

Autumn Equinox

ELLAS LED HIS PARAMOUR AND THE EXILED REBELS TO where Sorrel[1] stands today. Bethync scholars hold records of Ellas' travels through the Banished Lands in order to find a permanent settlement. While away, a substantial earthquake devastated the foothills of his new home.[2] Ellas witness the very foundation crack beneath his loved one's feet.

While The Banished Lands were known for its perilous environment and frequent tremors, records indicate that never before had such quakes caused so much destruction. A seam[3] tore through the whole of the continent, modernly known as Thrice. Ellas plunged hands into the ground and, by means of sheer will, commanded the earth cease its violence. While the ravage of Thrice promised catastrophe, nature itself bent to Ellas's might, sparing countless lives. This led to border neighbors indebted to the newly founded Kingdom of Elastor.

In the years subsequent to establishing Heartsglove, Ellas further spread his teachings to others: The art of Holding Sway, developing in those without the Bond Magick. Elastians accomplished an adept ability to control their surroundings in one lifetime and allowed a non-verbal language to flourish in the Kingdom of Elastor. Ellas' life was cut short, yet, the loss extricated a layer of potentiality still being studied by modern scholars*

·   ·   ·

---

*   1. The Sorrel family is one of the last original founders [Ralven and Ellas aside] to still hold land titles as of this printing.

2. It is said Ellas stood on the grounds that later became the Solstice Court's Spring Quarters.

3. Modern name: The Strand

KEZERAH'S EYES skittered over the page once, twice, and on the third skim, she darted a glance from the library bench she sat at to her tutor, Monk Biloba. Their black cloak draped over them like a shroud. An unblinking gaze read a tome double the size of her own. The only sign of life marked by the slow scan of dull-gray eyes across the page. Kezerah shuddered at the possibility that it was for a future assignment.

Thick air and the smell of books stuffed the library. Rows of shelves sprung from each wall as if trying to take the place of pillars. She wondered how Bethync boasted the largest library in the world when every book ever imagined had already been shoved into the Winter Quarter. The idea was all the more unfathomable by Monk Biloba cutting their scholarhood short—give or take a century—to tutor Kezerah, of all people, in academics. Surely Bethync couldn't be all that grand if Kezerah was the tradeoff.

She held back a sneeze in an attempt to avoid her tutor's attention. Ikaika's book rustled as he turned the page. Kezerah scooted down the long bench, not stopping until she bumped into his portion of the elongated table.

Ikaika didn't budge, continuing to read undisturbed despite Kezerah doodling in the margins of his text, several pages ahead of her in the reading.

She drew a sun, moon, and stars, followed by a jutting tree with twinkling lights for leaves. Ikaika looked unbothered and she continued on, creating an obscenely large amount of curls atop a stick figure. Then, she worked on a lion, its jaws widely threatening to consume the curly person. Ikaika's lips lifted at the edges, and she suspected he now only pretended to read. She started on her second figure as she adorned herself with a sword.

He picked the graphite from her fingers, pressing his warm shoulder into hers, angling himself to draw. He gave himself a sword, smudging hers and replacing it with three circles.

Kezerah frowned, disliking this less heroic perspective, and took the pencil back, imbuing herself with the power to breathe fire. She crossed out the lion's eyes to make her menace clear. Ikaika rolled his eyes, before sketching a scaled lizard with sharp fangs. The addition of wings allowed it to hover over the lion; a new foe for them to conquer.

'**KOMODAI DON'T HAVE WINGS**!' Kezerah wrote, drawing an arrow toward the absurd bat-like additions.

'**YOU DON'T BREATHE FIRE,**' he wrote back before he set the graphite down quickly and shuffled himself away, just in time to leave Kezerah alone at the long bench without a book.

Monk Biloba looked up and spotted her. "Majesty Soul Heir?" they said, lifting a tuft of white hair above shrewd gray eyes. Their skin matched the aging parchment of their book. "Have you already finished the readings for today?"

"I—erm, I was assisting Prince Ikaika with the material," she blurted, and looked over to Ikaika, desperate for some such assistance. Kezerah remained uncertain if Ikaika intended to rescue her until he finally spoke, his volume low in comparison to hers.

"Right. Yes, as the reincarnation of Ellas, I thought she might be beneficial in helping me understand his history." He looked over at Kezerah. "Thank you, I understand much better now."

"You are most certainly welcome." Kezerah beamed at her tutor.

"And what did you have trouble understanding exactly?" Biloba challenged. "I, as your tutor, would like to know the areas you perhaps need more study."

Kezerah sensed this going poorly, but did not know how to prevent it. She gave Ikaika a look of apology as he scanned his page for answers, now decorated in chaotic doodles.

"I was confused at..." He deliberated, trying to find something she could easily explain to him. He apparently didn't have much faith in her Elastian history. A fair assessment, for this was her first lesson she hadn't escaped in weeks. "Why Ellas's soul never fully reaches the Summerlands, while the rest of our souls reside there until we choose to return."

Kezerah stared at him blankly.

His eyes widened, believing she should know.

The next prompting from Biloba was to her. "And what wisdom did the most recent reincarnation of our great land have to say about this mystery?"

"Yes well..." Kezerah began, trying to muster all of the scholarly words in her arsenal, "Undoubtedly, this question in a grand sense can be further broadened." She gulped. "As the Summerlands are already heavily ladened in mystery, and therefore... I surmised..." Ikaika subtly shook his head, his lips a quivering line as he held back his amusement. "The ethereal realm is not ours to bequeath a simple answer but instead... explore with—with vigor."

She finished, the monk's face now so scrunched with pain that Kezerah hoped they might pity her enough to not inquire further.

"Which I took to mean," Ikaika concluded, as if her nonsense had borne sense, "that Ellas's soul is of such strong will that he, instead of truly moving on, remains tethered to his bloodline in order to forever keep the earth at bay."

"Did you," Biloba stated flatly, it wasn't a question but Ikaika nodded in answer.

Kezerah chimed in after clearing her throat, "Precisely."

The tutor rubbed at their bushy temples. "Princess, I am assigning you the next one hundred pages of text with a ten page essay on the Elastian Famine following the Xenkeshi trade bans. Have it on my desk by the waning crescent or I shall have to report to the King and Queen that you are exactly three moons behind in your studies."

"Yes, Monk Biloba," she said with a drawl.

"That was terrible," Ikaika chuckled as they left the library, taking the large tome from her hands and carrying it back towards the Spring Quarters. "I can't believe you used 'bequeath' in a sentence."

"You gave me the most abstract question possible!" she accused, already grimacing at the amount of reading she would have to get done in order to avoid her mother's chastisement.

"I gave you a question about yourself! I wouldn't have imagined you could make such a long sentence out of, 'I don't know.'"

They climbed the stairs. Kezerah slumped against the threshold of Ikaika's door as he handed her the book back. He left his door ajar to continue the conversation while he changed. "I miss Dar coming to lessons," she admitted. "I didn't get in nearly as much trouble when Biloba had to keep him in line."

"I doubt he feels the same." Ikaika's voice carried through the crack in the door, the rustle of clothing and the clicking of belts fastened as he hurried. "Not to mention, there's not much use in Elastian governmental rule and history on a battlefield. He likes his tactics trainings with Rook too much to give it up."

Her nose wrinkled of its own accord. "Ugh, Rook."

"He's a good captain."

"He's my mother's Queensguard. He picks on him."

"With the assessment for *your* Queensguard coming up, he has to be hard on him. Dar doesn't mind," Ikaika assured.

Kezerah shrugged, forgetting he couldn't see it. He walked out the door, now sporting leather padding stained a deep purple with fastened bracers and a breastplate. An insignia on his shoulder pad stood out as the only sign of his Aloran heritage and the simple fact that, regardless of what Ikaika wore, he looked like a prince. He smiled down at her, his hair long enough now for thick inky curls to fall in his face. She scowled up at him as he tousled her hair. Then, to her surprise, he bumped her chin with his finger in familiarity before heading towards the stairwell. Kezerah brushed an absent minded hand below her chin.

"Come on. You can gawk at Dar and I from the training yards."

Kezerah dropped her silly, errant hand and tossed the large book through Ikaika's still open door. She hoped if she pleaded with enough charm, he would read it to her this evening.

"I can't," she said, catching up. "The Glassberry's are meant to arrive before mid meal, and I haven't seen the twins since my birthday."

Ikaika waited for her at the bottom of the stairs, and gave a nod of understanding. "I think I'll stick to training."

Kezerah skipped the last three steps, sticking her landing with an arch of her brow. "Oh? Are you sure? Whistle asked about you this summer."

"Is that the loud one, or the quiet one?"

Kezerah kicked at his shins, and Ikaika hopped back to avoid the attack. "She's the nice one—They both are," she chastised. "And how can you not tell them apart?"

"They're identical. Isn't that the point?"

One of Willow's blue eyes had a starburst of hazel at its center and Whistle walked with more purpose but Kezerah knew people didn't notice these details on first, or even forth, glances. "Only on the outside," Kezerah said, "and you have the ability to hear their insides."

Ikaika snorted at her word choice. "Well, one of their insides is loud—And with the feast coming up, I'd like to avoid unnecessary pain."

Kezerah had no argument for that, so she made her next retort a silent one, tossing her hair behind a shoulder.

Ikaika turned towards the Winter hall, his preferred training yards just beyond them, while Kezerah continued toward the Autumn Quarters and Solstice gate. The two friends' parting marked by a wave of hands.

Kezerah turned back to see Ikaika pad off through the grass. It had been just over four years since he had joined them at the Solstice Court. It posed a challenge to believe he hadn't always been there, his presence a constant since his arrival. Now, the crops once again grew in abundance; squash and apples ripened quickly on trees and vines. Kezerah could feel the tension build in Ikaika every time the season came about. As preparations were made for the Autumn Equinox, he grew quiet, more pensive, and often could be found training on the side of the castle with Alora as its view.

Admittedly, Kezerah hated the idea of Ikaika ever returning to Alora. The deepest, most selfish corner of her soul housed the idea that his mother might never return, deciding to rule without him. The thought crumpled in on itself any time Ikaika raced eagerly over to receive one of Queen Illija or Castiel's letters. Though the letters' likely inclusion of war and politics formed a palpable divide, deepening her frustration.

Kezerah dismissed the thought now, and distracted herself with the giggles and laughter that announced the twins' arrival. The Glassberry sisters exited their elk-drawn carriage at the Solstice Gate; both still sported peachy skin and fair hair brightened by this past summer's sun, their large blue eyes teary from unbridled laughter.

The two hugged Kezerah immediately, their thick bodies adorned with new curves and, to Kezerah's irritation, more height. The three walked and the twins told Kezerah about their trip to Heartsglove, the capital that surrounded the Solstice Court. Descriptions of food, jewelry, and dances in the night air began to take shape, but blurred like distant memories as the twins spoke more rapidly than a river left unchecked by dams.

"How did it taste?" Kezerah asked, grasping for details. "Did you bring it with you? What was it made of? Show me the steps."

Whistle gave her a loose twirl and giggled. "Sorry, I only remember that part, oh..." Her friend stopped; their pirouette had led them to the steps of the Spring Quarters. "Actually, Kezi...we're staying in the Autumn Quarters this time."

Kezerah fought a flinch. "Ah, right."

Willow's gaze turned troubled and she took up Kezerah's hand. "You didn't know?"

Kezerah ran her free hand through thick curls. "Of course I know. I just forgot." At the twins' unconvinced faces Kezerah pulled Willow toward the Autumn Hall. "Come on, tell me about where you stayed! Were there private baths, or just communal?"

"Communal," Whistle said, following with a grin. "Very, very communal."

Kezerah thought she had averted embarrassment until they settled in the twins' room to continue relaying their ventures.

"Oh, Kez, you wouldn't believe the inn keeper's daughter! An absolute dream!" Willow said.

"Willow was swooning!"

"So were you! Don't make it seem like I was some lovelorn fool!"

"Seem? Willow, you were."

"Well, if I'm a fool then why did she kiss me?"

"Liar!"

"She did! Right before we left. She put a flower in my hair. See?"

Willow summoned a flower that dashed through the air, displaying the ultimate proof. Kezerah looked from the flower to her friend. "You—you can Hold Sway?"

In answer, both Willow and Whistle raised their arms, looking as if they dropped an invisible ball from one hand to another, motioning to the left. Both girls' hairstyles shifted. Willow's swirled into an updo, just as Whistle's fell in waves at her shoulders.

"It came on right after the Summer Solstice!" Willow informed her eagerly.

"Nobody told you?" Whistle said with dismay. "We registered with your mother. That's why we can't stay in the Spring Quarters."

Kezerah wrinkled her nose. "She neglected to mention that part." *Any part.* She plastered a smile on. "So, how did it happen? Who got it first?"

"Well..." said Willow. "I was arguing with Whistle about Thrice-knows-what and accidentally flicked a vase at her from across the table."

"Accidentally? Flicked?" Whistle challenged.

"Well it got sort of thrown across the table—"

"—at my face."

"While I was thinking of throwing it."

They broke into giggles at their own story and Kezerah waited for it to subside. Her eyes cast down towards the twins' luggage, filled with ruffles and risque garments she would kill to try on (or die trying as her mother would certainly never allow it). Suddenly she felt weighed down, anchored in place and left behind. Her shoulders sagged. *'Don't think about it, don't think about it, don't think—'*

"Oh, Kezi, are you crying?" asked Whistle, coming closer.

Kezerah rubbed at the pricking sensation in the corner of her eye. Her chest felt hot, like a day spent on the Solstice Bay sand. "Of course not."

Willow rubbed at her back. Whistle sat close, dabbing at her cheek with a swatch of satin.

"We didn't mean to upset you!"

"We should have waited to register."

"Ours isn't even very strong."

"I bet yours will be much stronger if it comes!"

"*When*, Whistle, *when.*"

"Right of course, it's just a question of when. It could be any day!"

"It could be tonight!"

The words consumed Kezerah whole, cutting off her ability to breathe. She stood, too quickly, scattering the twins' hugs and rapid succession of kindnesses. The room went quiet. All of their expressions were a mix of guilt and hurt as they stood there.

Kezerah took a breath and swallowed the pity whole without bothering to chew. She grinned with a gulp, then picked up the flower that had fallen to the floor. "The real question is..." she twirled the dainty stem in her hands. "Can you Sway fast enough to catch this?"

Both twins gasped, the flower flung out of the open window and into the chorus of the training yard below. At the beginning of its descent however it ricocheted on seemingly nothing then shot back and into Willow's hands. Stunned, the twins watched Kezerah pick up a frilly piece of lace from Whistle's bag.

"Wouldn't it be so embarrassing if Dar suddenly saw this in the training yard?" Kezerah asked, impish now in her glee.

"Don't you d—"

Like a provocative butterfly, the stringy lace fluttered out the window. Whistle's screech turned into a frantic giggle as the first piece was returned—the négligée, narrowly saved by Willow—until the matching set was also thrown. By the time Kezerah reached Willow's corset both girls had launched themselves at her. They all toppled onto the bed. Grunts of resistance turned into squeals and cackles as the battle for undergarments grew more frazzled. In the end, they spilled across the bed in a fit of laughter that, this time, Kezerah could join in on.

"WE CAN ONLY SWAY what we can move ourselves," Willow explained, sometime later, after Kezerah requested a rearrangement of furniture to demonstrate her friends' new power. The question arose out of genuine curiosity, she assured herself, rather than masochistic fascination. Unable to raise the large canopied bed, Willow instead stacked pillows as tall as a tower. "It's not like Bond magick. We can't speak to the objects; just move them as we normally would."

"We can affect people though!" Whistle said. She Held Sway in Kezerah's direction. An unseen force pressed at Kezerah's back propelling her forward, she toppled into the tower of pillows. "So, it's kind of just like—" Whistle tapped her finger to her lips. "—A shortcut to moving."

"On the topic of Bond magick." Willow re-stacked the pillows as Kezerah raced to collect them quicker. "Did you hear a royal Xenkeshi ship docked at Port Aveltra?"

"No, I haven't heard much of anything since I stopped attending the meetings regularly," Kezerah admitted.

Whistle shrugged. "That's okay. Our cousin recently had her heart broken and all she did her whole visit was talk. I've got enough gossip to last three lifetimes of council meetings."

A knock came, and Kezerah stepped over the now mess of a bedroom to open the door.

Andarios smiled in greeting, "Hanan sent me to get you. Your mother wants us all to dine in the banquet hall because of the guests." His eyes darted to the twins and then quickly away at their giggles, which were poorly stifled.

Kezerah looked back and Willow giggled harder than Whistle. Whistle eyed Andarios appraisingly, a coy smile on her face. Kezerah searched his attire for something funny. He wore the dark purple colors of Elastor, his hair pushed back and formal. Apart from a blush that ran up his neck and into his cheeks, he looked decidedly un-amusing.

Puzzled, Kezerah shrugged. "Alright. Give me a minute and I'll go to my room to change." Andarios looked eager to leave the scene and nodded, slipping away before the door finished shutting.

"Speaking of swoon. Kezi, when did Andarios get so tall?" asked Whistle.

Kezerah cocked an eyebrow, confused by her friend's use of the word "swoon" in reference to Andarios. "Erm, I think he's always been tall?"

"Not that tall," Whistle said, their giggles a lot less endearing.

Kezerah didn't dignify that with a response. While magick often coincided with maturity, it seemed some of her friends had grown dappier rather than sensible. *'I guess at least I don't have to worry about regressing,'* Kezerah thought dryly, the sisters now whispering on their pushed together beds. Willow began talking about the tavern girl again, and Kezerah said her goodbyes, leaving her friends to their hysterical laughter.

IKAIKA FLIPPED THROUGH CHAPTERS, trying to find Kezerah's spot in her studies. He stopped on a heavily illustrated page. Lines, brackets and dots connected names to portraits of various monarchs, their family trees and past Kezerahs. Ikaika always found Kezerah's lack of interest in her reincarnations concerning. He himself found her reincarnation fascinating and keenly disconcerting. All souls reincarnated, but where Alorans found solace in the stars and the Summerlands housing those souls preparing to return, Elastians worshiped a soul that remained rooted to the earth. Kezerah's soul always passed on to the next in her line, never allowing her to be amongst those stars.

He passed over several images of Soul Heirs who looked varying degrees of alike, but all carried the same title, the same soul: Ellas.

SOUL HEIR ELLAS – ELLAS THE FIRST
BORN – BT(BEFORE THRICE), UNKNOWN
DEATH – WARRIOR ERA THIRTEEN
TITLE – KING
PARAMOUR – LILA OF JAI
SOUL HEIR RIVKA – ELLAS THE SECOND
BORN – IRON BEAR ERA ONE, ARCHER MOON
DEATH – IRON BEAR ERA TWENTY ONE
TITLE – QUEEN
PARAMOUR – SILL OF RALVEN

SOUL HEIR BASHA – ELLAS THE FIFTH
BORN – MONARCH ERA ONE, ZEPHYR BREEZE MOON
DEATH – MONARCH ERA EIGHTY SEVEN
TITLE – KING
PARAMOUR – EZIL OF ZELOS, JEM OF GLASSBERRY, NENYA OF ALORA

<u>Soul Heir Kleodore – Ellas the Eleventh</u>
Born – Whirlwind Era One, Gloam Sable moon
Death – Whirlwind Era Seventy Two
Title – Monarch
Paramour – Hikari of Alora

Ikaika let his finger slide down to the last picture. The illustration of Kezerah was not her most recent portrait painted this year, but a beaming ten year old with bright eyes. The purple of her irises, and the warmth of her skin and freckles erased by the black and white image. Still, her far less stoic posture made her easily recognizable, alongside the cascades of curls filling up the free space around her.

<u>Soul Heir Kezerah – Ellas the Twelfth</u>
Born – Silver Salmon Era One, Thunderstorm moon
Death – currently living
Title – Princess
Paramour –

Ikaika flexed his fingers as he looked at the blank space next to "paramour". He disliked that a space had been made, the presumption clear. His hand twitched towards his quill, absentmindedly he made the beginnings of an I in the empty space.

A knock at his door.

Ikaika stood, bolt upright. Ink tipped over and the book closed in haste. When Hanan walked in, the two stared at each other. Ikaika's change in posture, it appeared, was too abrupt to go unnoticed. "Yes?" Ikaika said in answer. He worked a smile into place with effort. Hanan warily looked around the room for what was amiss before he gave a smile to match. "I'm to instruct you in preparing for the Equinox Feast. There is to be a dress code this evening," Hanan said. "Unfortunately, due to our guest capacity, there are no extra servants to spare."

Ikaika looked down at his Elastian high-collared tunic. Meal dress codes were common, but Ikaika rarely fell short. He flattened a small crease in the fabric. Hanan shook his head.

"You're to wear Aloran formal attire for tonight."

Ikaika raised his eyebrows before shrugging his shoulders in concession. "Alright." He opened the doors to his wardrobe and looked back with a chuckle. "But there's no need for instruction. I know how to dress like an Aloran."

Hanan waited until Ikaika pulled out a tunic he liked and the steward clicked his tongue before moving forward. "My apologies, your majesty," Hanan said, "but I'm afraid that's only considered formal day wear." He continued slower, after a brief glance at Ikaika's now dubious expression. "Tonight, formal evening wear is required."

After a brief pause, Ikaika relented. "Perhaps your assistance is necessary after all." He took a step back, feeling abashed. Hanan stepped in front of the wardrobe and took control of the situation and Ikaika's clothes.

"Just you wait," promised Hanan. "You'll be the best dressed Aloran noble at the Solstice Court."

A weary loneliness creeped in. After all, the Solstice Court only housed one Aloran noble.

KEZERAH STOPPED in the threshold of her doorway to find her room far more bustling than she'd expected. Her day nurse readied a dress while two more servants set out oils and paints, another already prepping the hair oils she used when bathing.

"A bath?" she asked, then stopped, her jaw dropping open as she fully took in the extravagance of the dress the servant laid out atop her bed. Crafted from interwoven spider silk, it featured an embroidery of autumn leaves and foliage in shades of browns, blues, and deep purples. A corset that held its form upright sat beside it. "Is that for..." She didn't dare believe. "What is that?"

Her nurse looked at her either in pity for herself or Kezerah, the grueling preparations just beginning. "I'm sorry, Majesty Soul Heir. Her High Majesty has instructions for all nobility's evening wear for the Equinox feast. It will take some time to securely fasten." Kezerah continued to stare. The dress beckoned to her, its elegance surpassed beauty, it allured. The desire to lace herself into it and never take it off doubled. Then, she shook her head. "Wait. Did you say—my mother decided this?" Her same mother, who had taken down every shred of silk in sight out of spite last spring.

Her nurse nodded. "The dress was picked specifically by Her High Majesty."

Kezerah shut her mouth and swept her hair back with an airy shrug. "Yes, well, alright then. Do your worst."

Her day nurse brushed Kezerah's hair into submission, then defined her curls with oils. Each curl became its own thick strand that fell to her waist. Boning lined the corset embroidered with autumn colors to give her skin an even warmer hue. The figure in the mirror surprised her. Elastian style often placed her in high collars and thick linens. This fabric billowed out to slip down her shoulders, then clung to her shape before it spilled into a waterfall of fabric. Her throat and collarbone fully exposed, she stifled a shiver of excitement at her reflection.

She wanted to dash back to the twins to hear their squeals of glee, a sound she withheld remembering her mother had chosen it. Crimson ties at the back sealed her into an hourglass. Aware that her servants watched, she stole one last quick glance in the mirror before they began to paint her face.

Kezerah finally emerged from her room, several sun-spans later, freshly groomed. Despite his quick departure, Andarios stood bravely outside her door. The sight of him reminded her that, while visually pleasing, she could no longer climb trees, run freely, venture into dusty caverns amidst walls, or scale princes' balconies to pester them.

"Honestly, all of this, for the Equinox?" Andarios looked unbearably regular as she took up his hand.

Ikaika's door opened and they both whirled around to see him. She wondered how he might view her dress, her friend being somewhat practical when it came to clothes. She banished the thought as he stepped out into the hall.

Ikaika's hair had been given a similar treatment to her own— wavy black hair swept to the side and held by oils, his dark blue leather tunic trimmed with a silver-gray fur. Kezerah noticed his formal pants differed from the Elastian style and instead of hugging tightly like Andarios', they were loose from the waist down, before tapering at the knee to fit snuggly along his calves.

"You're staring, Kez," Andarios whispered, voice teasing.

"I must have picked it up from Whistle after seeing her gawk at you," she whispered back, much louder.

Andarios fell silent.

"Did anyone else not have a choice in dress this evening?" Ikaika asked, eyeing his attire.

"You mean you didn't dress like a peacock on purpose?" Kezerah said sweetly. Ikaika graced her with a glance and went still. His pupils seeped into the black of his irises, an unsaid word left on parted lips. Kezerah smiled and Ikaika quickly inspected the floor before returning to her eyes. Then one of his half smiles crept into place to return her expression, though she deducted a point due to his unease.

"I—yes. Erm, well no. That is, Hanan dressed me like a peacock." He cast a look at Andarios as if expecting his friend to step in. Andarios' smile took up his entire face. Ikaika rolled his eyes and finally addressed Kezerah again. "Let's go. Before your dress gets dirty."

She scowled and Andarios barked a laugh. The trio began their slow procession down the hallway, dodging dust as they went. Plans immediately fell apart along their walk. Kezerah tripped Andarios and he took revenge, pushing her into a pile of fire willow leaves.

Kezerah brushed the last traces of leaves from her dress, and they entered the Autumn Banquet Hall side by side. Dinners and guests had officially moved into the Autumn Quarters. Whenever entering Autumn, guests consistently remarked upon the contrast. Fragile, fractured glass dyed the ceiling with colors and mosaics. Elk, sea nymphs, and tree dryads circled each other. Winged horses and a hawk, mid-metamorphosis into a man, flew above a bear. Folklore spiraled between the moons and stars of the Summerlands. Forged into a high dome, the glass depictions accommodated the protruding trees that lined the dark stone walls. Tangles of roots fought with the craggy floor for dominance while the trees flaunted vibrant red leaves, with lanterns that hung from the branches to give off a glow of fire light. Between mason and timber, high-arched hearths heated fervent conversations; their pyres lit in rows across the immense space.

Kezerah counted the table set for forty or fifty guests: several more than she had originally imagined. An abundance of food and finery lathered the table in purposeful disarray. Elize's fine tuned aesthetic showed in every perfectly placed copper candelabra and deceptively random arrangement of decaying wildflowers. A series of natural elements set just so, to appear effortless. Children poured decanters of spiced milk with maple. Parents ladled marionberry mulled wine simmering with oranges and cinnamon on the surface into goblets. Grapes spilled off of cheese plates and piles of oat and cranberry dented muffins threatened to topple. The mess situated itself atop a glittering midnight-teal satin, that mimicked the bed of stars above.

Elowren sat at the double head of the table, Elize to his left. He leaned in, speaking to the Lord and Lady of Glassberry, the twins' parents. Next to Elize was the Lord of Ralven. Kezerah let out an impolite groan upon seeing him.

"What?" Ikaika asked.

"Dyllian is probably here." Kezerah relented no more information. Her mother darted a glare towards her, both in warning and greeting, as she sat down (as far from her mother as she could muster).

Ikaika tilted his head to one side. "Who is Dyllian?"

"Oh right," Kezerah said. "You came after the whole Yuletide debacle."

Ikaika sighed and tried again. "Ah yes, the 'Yuletide debacle' in which Dyllian...?"

Andarios picked up her slack. "Dyllian of Ralven is Kez's mortal foe. Every time he's here he goes out of his way to make Kez's life a nightmare."

Already, scenarios flashed through her mind of being expected to hold her composure—and the trouble she would be in after failing to do so—with Dyllian of Ralven skulking around. She wrinkled her nose. "Ugh. Stop saying his name. You'll summon him, like a poltergeist."

Ikaika cocked an eyebrow, turning to look at Kezerah. "I didn't know it was possible to actually get under your skin."

"That's because you're no good at it. All Ralven has to do is breathe—Oh Thrice, he's coming over. I told you, a *poltergeist.*"

IKAIKA FOUND himself overtly amused at Kezerah's change in demeanor, intrigued to see just what type of person could make such an easy-going creature such as Kezerah so wound up. Apart from her impatience with her mother's overprotective and admittedly over-bearing nature, Kezerah consistently managed to charm everyone she encountered. Ikaika himself had been immediately smitten. He had witnessed her dodge chores, homework, swordplay, and other duties with a playful smile and endearing demeanor. She only ever truly became cross with Andarios or her mother, for opposing reasons. It also served as a wonderful distraction from her *dress*, which he had not allowed himself to comment or look upon again. Upon seeing her, every thought in his head had been the wrong one. The only ability he'd been graced with was the competence to keep it to himself.

He took pity on her now curdled expression, and nudged her. "Just watch. I'm sure he's not half as bad as you remember. He'll take one look at your ferocious expression and rue the day he crossed you."

While her body remained poised to pounce with her fork, her eyes shone toward him with an affectation of appreciation. "Yes, I suppose I am far more ferocious than when I was twelve."

Andarios made a sound of disagreement next to her but her eyes remained on Ikaika. He basked in her singular focus until the twins appeared, showering her dress with compliments and pulling her attention away. Kezerah's attention, momentary as it was, had been enough to lift his spirits tenfold however, and he cheerfully grabbed a handful of shucked sunflower seeds, eager for the night to unfold.

WITH IKAIKA to her right and Andarios to her left, Kezerah knew she could keep her cool around Dyllian. The twins sat across from the three of them, solidifying what Kezerah now considered her impenetrable circle. She hadn't seen him since she was a child. Surely Ikaika was right, and he must not be as bad as she remembered.

"Princess Kezerah, are you aware you've got a twig in your hair?"

A ghostly pale boy, with dark golden hair and eyes to match, slid into the chair next to Whistle, who scooted away in solidarity. Kezerah surveyed him and realized just how wrong she had been. Dyllian had the most punchable face she had ever laid eyes on.

"Hello, Dyllian," she said, forcing her tone to sound nonchalant.

"Here, allow me." Dyllian got up from the chair he had just sat down in, made the long walk around to the other side of the table, and plucked a small bit of foliage from her curl. He handed it to her as if it were a flower.

"There, now you don't look quite so wild. A beauty revealed beneath the leaves." Dyllian winked, and Kezerah heard Andarios stifle laughter behind her. She gritted her teeth, intent on not being removed from the Autumn Hall before the first course. She snatched the leaf from his hands and tossed him a smile to sharpen a blade on.

"I hardly recognized you, Dyllian, you've grown so pale. Have the Ralven crops failed to get sun?"

Dyllian bowed low, as one would in a formal throne room. "It has been some time hasn't it? I was sorry to miss your birthday feast, but it sounds like I didn't miss much. I'm pleased to see you remain... unchanged and charming as ever." Before Kezerah had time to push Dyllian into the hearth, using his found foliage as kindling, his gaze shifted to her right. "Oh! Hello!" he said, addressing Ikaika before turning back to Kezerah. "You neglected to introduce me to your table partner." He offered Ikaika a low bow and hand. "My sincerest apologies. I'm afraid our future queen can be quite informal at times. We have every hope however that, one day, she will gain enough decorum to lead us."

Kezerah looked over to see Ikaika's lips twitch. Was he trying to hold in a laugh? Ikaika rose and bowed in return, clasping the outstretched hand.

"Ikaika of Alora," he said, voice velvet, looking sidelong at Kezerah before adding. "A pleasure. Truly."

Dyllian looked taken aback, recognizing either Ikaika's name, or connecting what he had heard about the prince of Alora's continued residence at the Solstice Court. "Then I'm all the more apologetic for the neglect. I am Lord Dyllian of Ralven. I'm sure you're familiar, as my lands are the majority source of your diet here. It is my greatest pleasure to make your acquaintance."

"A simple oversight I'm sure," Ikaika said with delight. "Kezerah is so often distracted by her queenly duties."

Dyllian nodded, accepting the excuse graciously. "As I'm sure is the case."

Kezerah's teeth clenched. Dyllian made his way back around the lengthy table.

Ikaika leaned over, his voice filled with amusement. "I should have guessed your mortal foe would be manners."

Andarios snickered, but cut the sound off abruptly as Dyllian sat back down, remaining loyal to his future mannerless queen.

DYLLIAN SPOKE ANIMATEDLY throughout the entire first course. Kezerah slumped in her seat after his third or fourth story of how he solved a tax debate in his mother's absence over the summer.

"...And Aveltra told me we *shouldn't* try to tax people based on their harvest. That if we did that, they'd only make the minimum. Easy to say when your coin is made on the upcharge of exports."

"Not to mention the access to a never-ending water supply."

"Well," Dyllian pointed to Lord Larken with a waggling finger, "the Ralven Province has ample rivers in that regard. Though... I suppose First Thaw we'll be expected to *share*, reducing our production."

"Ah yes, 'land irrigation', how could I forget. From castle chamber pots to your crops."

Everyone at the table chortled to their finest extent. Kezerah thought about bashing her face into her plate to elicit a reaction; a messy venture, as she was served a pumpkin stuffed with rice, mushrooms, and perhaps a tad too much butter.

Dyllian cleaned his fork with a cloth before beginning on his pumpkin. "Prince Ikaika, is it true Alora has no tax penalty? That many pay for wares through labor?"

Ikaika looked up from his plate in surprise. "Oh erm, yes. They all do...or, we do. I currently get allowances converted to coin from my mother..." Ikaika trailed off awkwardly to stir his rice.

"Fascinating," Dyllian said, as Kezerah put an elbow on the table. Bored. "Oh—Princess Kezerah, did you know, you're slouching."

About to exchange slouching for lunging, the creak of the Autumn Hall door stole her attention, and Kezerah looked over as Hanan entered the banquet hall.

"Your High Majesties, our guests send their deepest apologies for their late arrival. Their ship found difficulty docking in Port Aveltra."

Kezerah perked up. Guests? Mid-meal? She looked around the table, realizing for the first time that there were two empty seats next to Dyllian. She had been too distracted, in an effort to avoid his face —which she still very much wanted to strike—to notice.

"No apologies necessary, of course," her father said, looking over at Elize with mild puzzlement. "Please, permit our guests' entry." Hanan bowed and everyone stood to greet the newcomers customarily.

"Presenting their royal majesties, Crown Prince Ambrose and Prince Rorrik of Xenkesh."

THE DIN of minds already blathered in indiscernible excitement. After the announcement of Ikaika's brothers gasps and murmurs echoed through the room. Brothers who served a throne that had imprisoned, then nearly killed his mother and had succeeded in killing his father. These brothers were all his mother fought for. His whole life had revolved around these larger-than-life entities and yet he'd never laid eyes on them before. Hanan moved to the side and then, there they were. A notable contrast in height separated the two of them. Ikaika assumed the taller one to be his eldest brother, Ambrose, and the shorter, leaner one to be Rorrik. He realized then that he had always pictured his brothers looking like him.

This was not the case.

Ambrose's chest and shoulders were broad, muscle showed on his exposed russet arms adorned in thin gold bands and crimson silks, ill-suited for the change in season. Swords hung on either side of loose-fitted pants, with oddly paired boots.

Ikaika searched for his mother in this stranger's features and only managed to perhaps find resemblance in the fullness of their lips. Though that thought became uncertain as those lips parted into an unfamiliar, wolfish grin.

He imagined that grin in the council meeting as Amarus hired an assassin to kill him. These brothers—this family—were the root cause of his presence here, and why he did not learn to rule on his own throne. The odd urge to entice their thoughts from their heads surprised him. What did he care about their opinions of him? Ikaika's face became marbled and cold. He didn't intend for them to get a read on him either.

The younger of the two brothers—*'my older brother,'* Ikaika amended—trailed behind. Though smaller and leaner than Ambrose, Prince Rorrik attempted to carry his feet in the same easy fashion, missing what Ikaika could only describe as a strut, by strides. They looked like, well, like brothers. Ikaika wondered how his mother had created a set so similar yet so far from him.

Ambrose's voice, deep and smooth, exuded confidence that swirled around him like warmth to a fire. "You would not believe how many ships were trying to dock in that fish port, Your Majesty. We thought we'd have to swim ashore." He sauntered over to the chair next to Dyllian and sat down unceremoniously, causing everyone else to quickly take their seats and Rorrik to speedily catch up and sit down next to him.

"Prince Ambrose, Prince Rorrik, welcome," King Elowren greeted, sounding truly pleased if not a bit surprised to see Alora's natural enemy arrive late to a dinner party, "I must admit, I was not aware you would be dining with us tonight. But there, I now see I overlooked that my lovely Queen saved you a seat all along."

"A surprise," Elize said sweetly. "I thought perhaps to avoid any unwanted anxiety for yourselves or Prince Ikaika."

At the sound of his name, Ikaika snapped his gaze from his brothers to the Queen, her lips upturned in a pleased expression.

When his eyes traveled back to his brothers, the stare was returned. An uneasy silence filled the space as all three siblings examined one another. He realized he hadn't moved since their entrance.

Whatever Ambrose found seemed to unnerve him and he looked away quickly, his voice a bit gruffer than his previous tone. "Well, I'd say he's surprised." Ambrose smiled and raised his brows, beetle green eyes sharp and focused on Queen Elize momentarily, before adding, "And here I thought we were rude just for being late, when we're altogether unexpected intruders."

"Not at all," Elowren said, then raised his glass. "But hungry guests you must be. So, let's eat." And with that, the meal, though somewhat stilted, resumed.

KEZERAH SAT STUNNED in her chair for several moments before she remembered Ikaika and assessed him. He looked truly rattled. She felt the need to pat his shoulder or offer him part of her baked brie and apple, but he looked like he might be ill, and she figured it probably wouldn't stay down. Unable to assist him, she chose instead to not antagonize him, going out of her way to keep her elbows down instead of jabbing him as she ate.

Neither Rorrik nor Ikaika said a word, but Ambrose grew even more lively, giving a vivid picture of what weeks at sea were like. At first, she tried to only steal small glances his way, but the crown prince held a captivating appearance, somehow embodying both menace and vibrance. His shaggy hair reached his shoulders, partially pulled into a disheveled knot at the back of his head. The coloring appeared a rich dark brown she would have called black if she'd never laid eyes on Ikaika's hair.

She picked at similarities, trying to make them match. All three brothers had similar jaws, she decided, but Ikaika's was a bit more pointed, and Ambrose's more squared. Their noses were all identically straight like Illija's, but Ikaika definitely had the highest cheekbones. Despite these attributes, though, they looked...dissimilar. Almost opposites, which given the war, she supposed in some ways they were.

While the exhilaration of their arrival kept her entranced, guilt soon followed when she laughed along with the rest of the table, save Ikaika, at a joke he told. What would be worse? To laugh and offend Ikaika, or to withhold her mirth and risk coming off as rude to the Xenkeshi heirs? She shouldn't hold exclusive loyalty to Ikaika, yet... this situation muddled her regular tendencies.

Ambrose's stories of foreign fruits and unusual plants filled the table. He drew every discussion in. Instead of individual conversation, it seemed everyone wanted to engage in the excitement. Elowren and Elize both chimed in with stories from their youth that she had never heard before. Dyllian's platform stolen, he mostly ate and eyed Ambrose nervously, as if afraid he might attack. Ambrose stabbed his bits of venison to demonstrate and conclude his story. Satisfaction took shape when Dyllian flinched.

But the glee once again dissipated when she felt Ikaika jolt next to her as well. Though, when she looked up at him, his face registered as indifferent, practically bored while watching his long-lost eldest brother talk about stabbing a terrifying scaled creature. She began to give her friend words of encouragement, then stopped herself. What if she worded it wrong? Kezerah bit her lip and did her best to focus on her dessert.

"I hope the gifts we brought survived the trip," Ambrose said. "Some of our sweeter fruits are also the most fleeting."

"Kezerah, did you hear that?" Kezerah startled at her name and looked over at her mother, who addressed her with a smile. "Were you not just saying to me how interested you are in possibly furthering our fruit trade?"

Kezerah's mind rushed to the memory of her, weeks prior, complaining about a bruised banana at breakfast. This was not just a leap, but a hurdle. The table stared at her expectedly. Then, Ambrose turned and cocked his head. His eyes widened as he studied her.

She hurdled.

"Yes," she said, wishing her mother indigestion. "We were speaking about how brilliant it would be to enjoy our fruit...within the same season it was grown."

Ambrose laughed or rather let out a short, quick breath. Kezerah bristled. "Of course, we'd be pleased to send it to you precisely when it's picked. However, given our current shipping routes, I'm afraid we can only send what survives twice a harvest."

"Survives?"

Kezerah knew by Ambrose's expression he had baited her. "Crops are the first thing to be burned in a war, Princess."

Kezerah's cheeks burned hot. While not initially caring about stupid moldy bananas, she found herself determined now to navigate bartering for them, while carefully skirting the issue of war. "Perhaps on the fabric shipment then, which comes more frequently."

"Less now–" Ambrose's gaze was steady. "– Due to the silk. Which looks lovely on you, by the way."

The silk. *The silk.* Twice baited, she thought back. By luck, she recalled her last council meeting, then winced. It had been the meeting where they had denied his export in exchange for her mother's home province, Sorrel.

She glared down the table at her mother, then smiled sweetly at Ambrose. "Thank you. But you know, I truly do love bananas. Three gold a yard was it?" She shrugged. "That's worth the price of fresh bananas for me."

"Kezerah—" her father warned from the far end of the table.

Ambrose was faster. "Done. I'll be sure to write to my father's council in the morning." He turned to the head of the table, where Kezerah did not dare look. "If your heir's word can be stood by, of course."

"Of course," she heard her father say, somewhat sternly. "We trust Kezerah would only speak a fully formed idea. Which I'm sure this is. I look forward to hearing all about her rationale in our next meeting." Kezerah deliberated how to justify a banana worth three gold when her father continued. "But for now, we usually save politics for our evening salons, Ambrose, which I'm sure you'll find invigorating."

A tremendous sense of inadequacy sagged Kezerah's shoulders. A familiar companion. She usually found relief in not being forced into the after-dinner salons. The politics so often turning to conversations of war. Now, she didn't know where to look but down and her attention fell to her hands as the conversation continued without her.

Dar nudged his chair closer to hers and she clung to the comfort of his warmth. Once the meal finished, she would need to make it clear to him that she needed a meeting. She glanced over at Ikaika who still pushed food around from two courses ago. Yes, a meeting was definitely in order.

JUST AS IKAIKA thought he couldn't bear any more of Ambrose's loud and boisterous voice, Elowren stood. Ikaika's tension ebbed with relief at the feast's conclusion, so much so that when everyone followed Elowren and stood, Ikaika remained seated, eyes trained on his untouched dessert.

"My friends, while this was a fantastic Equinox feast, it must reach its end. As the night grows nearer and we light our fires sooner, I hope you will all join us for our pending Nighttide celebration. For now, I regret to say my queen and I are tired and shall forgo attending the late-hour socializing. But please, continue to enjoy your evening." He lifted his glass.

All raised their glasses in answer and the feast, finally, ended. Guests groaned about full bellies and long nights. Elize's voice rose like a bell. "Hanan, will you please escort our new guests to the Spring Quarter. Perhaps there they can become better acquainted with Prince Ikaika."

Ikaika stood. Spring Quarters? His brothers? He balked at this further invasion into his oasis. Although he missed his home, his mother, and his culture, here in the Solstice Court, with its high walls and jovial conversations, he could easily forget what lay just beyond it. His reminder now stood right across from him.

Ikaika took a reflexive step back while Rorrik looked to Ambrose, alarmed. Ambrose merely appeared inquisitive; a look cast over Elize in slow assessment.

Relief cooled Ikaika's nerves at the sound of Elowren's stern voice, the one he used when he decided to be a stubborn boulder instead of a man. "No, I think not, my sweet. That might be a bit much for this reunion. Prince Ambrose and Prince Rorrik can stay in the Autumn Quarter with the rest of our guests." He turned to them and explained warmly, "It's in this wing of the castle. The trees planted along the western wall are at their best this time of year, and the view of the harvest crops is magnificent."

Ambrose bowed cordially, then he and Rorrik followed Hanan; his dark eyes looked pained before his expression changed back into a grin. Ikaika turned from them and chose the double-doored exit toward the meadows rather than running the risk of gracing the same halls as his brothers again.

Meetings

"What in Bethync was that?" Rorrik paced alongside a stationary Ambrose alone in their room. "Nobody knew we were coming?" He continued to create a trail in the wood floor.

Ambrose fought to keep his eyes open. The dinner had drained him, like a candle burned down to the end of its wick. Another emotion crept along the edges but he stamped it out, unwilling to acknowledge it just yet. A fire crackled in the hearth between two grand beds and he let the heat of it revitalize his mind.

Rorrik made his seventh round through the small space. "Ikaika definitely didn't see us coming. I told you we shouldn't have stayed at that tavern. If we hadn't been late we could have—"

"Ror," Ambrose snapped, holding his brother's narrow shoulders to prevent another circle. "Enough. I know. This night didn't go how I expected either. But it's done."

"Done? It's far from done. Did you see how he looked at us? Like we were going to jump on the table and demand his head in front of everyone. And that pompous expression? I wanted to wipe that look right off his face."

His face. Unwelcome, unbidden, Ambrose couldn't fight the memory of seeing his youngest brother's face for the first time. The joke was immediate, and on him. He had looked right into his mother's face. Her eyes, her stare, her features. Here he had thought he'd come seeking an ally, to rescue his brother. But from what? His mother?

Rorrik continued, "She obviously has her claws in him. That's not our brother, just some underling she created to serve her."

Ambrose's feelings about his mother often conflicted; Rorrik had no such memories to taint his perception of her. His younger brother had looked at Ikaika and seen a cold Aloran youth bearing the Queen of Alora's descriptors. While Ikaika's complexion stood as beige against Illija's ivory, the finer details were there: icy, distant, callous. Ambrose had tried to look, tried to see past her, but finally his true feelings emerged: disappointment and pain.

He had thought maybe his mother had not come back for Ikaika because, like Ambrose, he represented a life she did not want, away from her cloud coated mountains and desolate tundras. But this ruined that narrative for him. Alternatively, he had imagined coming here and rescuing Ikaika, and Ikaika wanting to be reunited with them. Instead the truth struck him. Ikaika wasn't some wounded child. He stood as his mother's vassal, looking at his kingdom's enemies, positioned here with a purpose: a purpose Ambrose needed to figure out.

Ambrose collapsed onto his bed and sunk into the stuffed mattress, trying to find the angle. What could be gained from Illija's only heir seeking haven in a neutral kingdom, away from the battles, and fires and screams, surrounded by festivals, dances, and court games? It seemed a useless tactic if raising a king.

"Did you see the Elastian Princess looking over at him? She's obviously smitten," Rorrik said, disgusted.

Ambrose had most certainly seen the princess. He had caught her glittering purple eyes watching him more than once. If not for being seated next to Ikaika, she would have been impossible to look away from: Warm brown skin, and curls upon fiery curls cascading down around bare shoulders. In Xenkesh, her dress would be considered modest, but here the cut defied Elastian fashion in an appealing way. If she hadn't been the Soul Heir...

The epiphany came to him like a slow fog. "The Princess," Ambrose said, "that's going to inherit the throne."

Rorrik had resumed pacing, not yet catching up to his own accidental revelation. "Yeah, that's what princesses usually do."

"No, this particular princess is going to be inheriting the incredibly neutral, potentially war-ending throne."

Rorrik paused in his pacing. Eventually catching up. "Oh, you think—But the treaty—"

"Is only as good as those upholding it. If she falls madly in love with a dashing prince? Her father's promises are not going to sound so appealing. Elastians also have to handfast by choice, not politically. If she chooses him..."

"If she chooses him, father will definitely invade Elastor."

"We don't want to invade Elastor."

"Speak for yourself. With Elastor out of the way we don't have to tiptoe around treaty lines. Sorrel for instance! Is that a Xenkeshi village or an Elastian one?"

Ambrose found himself without patience for his younger brother's babbling. He rolled over. His eyes adjusted to the dim-lit view. Outside, his glass doors overlooked what he suspected were fields of crops. In the darkness of night, they looked like nothing but hills and shadows. His head spun through different ideas, determining the bounds of his control. He needed sleep. When he stayed up like this his brain frayed at the edges. His consciousness drifted.

Rorrik eventually laid down on his own bed with a huff. "Well, Father will want us to act fast."

Ambrose didn't reply. Rorrik's own wants often ended up cast out as their father's. Yet admittedly, Ambrose and his father's conversation had served as an undeniable catalyst. It had been his father who had finally persuaded Ambrose to make this journey. After a difficult law had been passed, his father had spoken the words so simply, so casually.

"Perhaps it is time you seek Haven in Elastor. Ikaika has been there for some time now. Maybe the years with Elowren have softened his heart, or possibly the young princess can be reasoned with."

It had not been Amarus' words, but his willingness to say them that had persuaded Ambrose to go. His father carried a lot of pride, but above all, he prided himself as a caring father. He'd always respected Ambrose's decisions and never pushed him to make a choice he didn't want to make. Amarus had sculpted independence into his children even when Ambrose's own pride had gotten in the way.

Ambrose still remembered how fool-hearty he had been in his first war meeting. His advisors had spoken up against him, but Ambrose had been so sure his plan would work. Until he had lost his entire battalion. Copper pieces merely slid off the board.

.   .   .

"I IF I HAD STOPPED YOU, you wouldn't have learned anything," his father had said.

Ambrose had continued to stare at the empty space on the map. "People died because of my mistake…"

"And now you know what power feels like," his father agreed. "A king without power is not a king. I'm not a father who raises followers."

For Amarus to even suggest Ambrose change his mind about journeying to Elastor, after years of not intervening in his decision, Ambrose had understood the time had come for him to set aside his own pride and do what was right for his kingdom. He just wished, for once, his father—his king—had told him exactly what to do. Instead, Ambrose pondered his next step with apprehension, until fatigue overtook his mind.

LANTERN LIGHT SPILLED in from the hall of Kezerah's room. The Night Nurse opened the door once more to check on Kezerah. Kezerah did her best impression of a dead person until the room grew dark once more.

The next task presented a tricky situation. While Andarios possessed many useful traits, stealth eluded him. However, tonight's plan relied on Andarios reading her mind, which despite him not being a Mind Melder, was probable.

Her sultry dress traded out for a nightgown, she climbed easily into Ikaika's room. Already awake, he lay on his side, facing the balcony. His cheek leaned on his palm in expectation. She hid a smile, pleased he'd obviously been waiting for her.

She beckoned him towards the balcony. "Come on, tonight you're coming to my chambers."

His face flushed a little and she rolled her eyes at his sudden propriety.

"Don't start thinking of my virtue now. We still need to break Dar out."

Ikaika chuckled and rose, his mood seeming to follow. "My dearest Princess Kezerah, I just hope, one day, you gain enough decorum to lead us."

She winced at his Dyllian impression, then shuddered. "Should I be worried? Because that wasn't half bad."

Ikaika smiled, despite the stress etched into his face. "Maybe he's rubbing off on me."

"Maybe I should find a new friend."

He shrugged and followed her to the opposite side of the railing. "Sounds like a good night's sleep to me."

The moon cast more shadows than light through the cherry blossom tree as both hopped over to her balcony and slid through her doors.

Once inside, Ikaika stood awkwardly at the threshold. "Now what?"

"Mid-moon shift," Kezerah answered, a rock now in hand. "For the next breath and a half, there're no guards. And if Dar is who I know he is–" She cracked open her door and smiled. "– Then neither is Nurse."

"There's not a chance," Ikaika said under his breath.

"That," Kezerah whispered, "sounds like a bet." She tossed the rock. It hit Andarios' door with force, and then they waited.

Nimah closed the Lower Lord Andarios' doors. His snores still sounded a bit off, but eventually, they'd smooth into his actual ones. She let out a sigh. At least she didn't have to attend to the Xenkesh boys. 'Boys,' she laughed to herself. The brawnier prince had looked older than Terryn, her eldest and a new recruit in the Elastian guard. She had not thought of him as a boy in years. She shook her head, hardly able to believe she would see yet another set of children grow out of the Spring Quarters.

After this brood, she was done. Prince Ikaika might be well-behaved enough, but the King treated his daughter too softly. Nimah would never have allowed her children to sneak about at night without consequence. Only a little over a year, she told herself. She could manage that.

A moment from sitting down in her corridor chair a crash sounded. She froze mid-sit and looked from the Ralven Lordling's door to Andarios', the more rational option. Yet, the sound had definitely come from the former... *'He seems like such a good boy, hard to believe—'*

Another clatter—glass by the sound of it—from inside the room. Nimah lifted her skirts and ran over to the guest rooms. She shielded her eyes, surprised by the lantern light as she entered. Nimah stepped back to avoid shards of vases shattered and scattered across the floor. Water and flowers spilled out around soggy slippers. Dyllian stood in the center of the room and mess. More peculiar still, he tightly grasped an empty chamber pot. At least, she hoped it was empty.

"Lord Dyllian," she paused, lost for words. "What are you doing? And that chamber pot needs to stay in place. It flows to the pipes."

"I—" More than half asleep, he tried again. "The lights were lit, and I went to blow them out, and then the chamber pot moved towards the balcony, and then there was a crash and..."

He seemed to lose steam as he spoke, questioning each event as he said them.

Nimah thought of Kezerah, but neither she nor Andarios Held Sway. Did Dyllian? Had he Swayed in his sleep? But no, Hanan would have placed him in the Autumn Quarters if that were the case. Magick marked adulthood. Dyllian looked anything but as he stared around the room in confusion. She blew out the candles, removing the chamber pot from his tight grip, then ushered him towards his bed.

"Maybe a bit of sleepwalking?" she assured him, his pale face looking peakish.

He nodded. A small clink sounded from the corridor and he jumped and yelped loudly, eyes frantic as they searched the room.

"It's fine, my Lord, just the guards changing watch in the hall," she appeased, hoping to not wake the others. Despite her reassurances, he searched the room, eyes wide. Nimah decided she had best stay close to prevent further outbursts, and pulled up a chair. She sat down next to his warm fire and pulled out her knitting needles.

. . .

KEZERAH THREW a smug glance at Ikaika the moment Andarios leaped through the door and shut it with haste behind him. They had debated on Andarios getting the signal that the hall was clear in time. When their friend's large frame had barreled across the hall to her ajar door, nothing but triumph coursed through her. Andarios now panted against her wall, catching his breath.

Ikaika, graceful in defeat, nodded. "Nice timing, Dar."

"I heard the rock." He winked over at Kezerah as he tossed the credit right back her way. "A bit of chaotic Sway from my balcony and both Dyllian and Nimah had their hands full."

"You know this will go straight to her head, right? She'll be insufferable." Ikaika said, smiling and gesturing to Kezerah.

"It would have gone to my head regardless," said Kezerah. "It was timed perfectly."

Ikaika rolled his eyes. "*More* insufferable, I mean." After a pause, he began. "Well, now that you've summoned us, are we going to talk about what my brothers are doing here?"

Kezerah moved to sit on her bed. If she stayed standing she knew she'd fidget and she wanted to appear more in control than she felt.

"Erm, actually, I wanted to talk about why we didn't know about them coming sooner."

"What?" Ikaika's tone held a sharpness she wasn't accustomed to. "I mean, yes, we should have been told, but their reasons for being here can't be good."

Andarios stayed quiet, so Kezerah decided she couldn't be completely in the wrong. She pushed past Ikaika's agitation. "Well... we don't know that for certain." Their arrival had been jarring but benign, if not a bit intense. She had rolled the conversation she'd had with Ambrose around in her head since it ended. It had been her that asserted herself (albeit for bananas). Ambrose hadn't argued or coerced her into the outlandish price.

"They strutted into the hall, mid-meal, like a couple of Xenkeshi warlords," said Ikaika.

Kezerah couldn't pinpoint how his comparison sounded offensive, or if to say so would be considered defending Xenkesh... against Alora—or Ikaika? She floundered, brow scrunched with words she couldn't say. Finally, she answered tentatively. "That's sort of what they are Kai—or at least will be. You walk around like an Aloran prince."

Ikaika balked. "And what does an Aloran walk like? You know, never mind."

"Don't get upset with me," Kezerah huffed. "It's my mother who sprung them on you."

"Maybe your mother just didn't know, and tried to save face."

Kezerah scowled. "And since when does my mother not know things?"

Ikaika shrugged. "She doesn't know everything, or she'd be breaking up this most improper slumber party."

"Ugh," Kezerah pressed fingers into her scalp. "I'm trying to navigate this and you've suddenly decided to be so—so—uncompromising."

"*Decided*?"

"I think maybe we're getting off both of your topics here," Andarios said, taking a step into the conversation. "Let's start with Kez. Why do you think they were a 'surprise', as your mother called it?"

Grateful to be back on track, Kezerah thought through her response. This had been the oddest part of the night for her. Her mother encompassed nothing but meetings, planning, and unceasing orders. Yet, the evening had clearly ended in disaster and not even her father had known.

"I think perhaps my mother is meddling. She always gets what she wants, and if she wanted tonight to have gone smoothly, it would have. She had... a look."

"A look?" Ikaika, dear friend and current pest, caught her uncertainty. "If she were meddling, don't you think there might be a reason for it? Maybe she felt protective for a purpose."

Kezerah glared, fed up. "You're going to write off strangers but defend my mother?"

Ikaika tossed his hands up. "Oh yes, the strangers that may or may not have been involved in my assassination. Good point. I'm sure your stuck-up mother is truly the greater threat here."

"Assassination *attempt*," she said, now standing.

Andarios—who must have sensed Kezerah's growing pettiness

and need for assistance—tried to follow. "He has a point. While your mother is... a handful and it's odd that she didn't mention it to anyone, what does she gain? Besides the look on Ikaika's face when they walked in," he added, tossing an apologetic smile Ikaika's way.

Ikaika caught and accepted it with a nod. Then returned to Kezerah.

"She..." Both looked at her, expecting an enhancement to her argument. One she didn't have. Outnumbered, the pillars of Kezerah's argument crumbled. It had been over a decade since Xenkeshi royalty had entered the Solstice Court. The event had been momentous, historic, and she had focused on her mother fouling up the dinner arrangements.

"Maybe she just didn't want the King to be angry with her?" Andarios offered.

Kezerah shook her head. "He wouldn't be angry. Anyone is welcome at the Solstice court, and their visit falls within the treaty."

"Anyone? Should I expect the pirate Skulldragger to join us for breakfast then?" Ikaika asked.

She rolled her eyes. "You know your brothers aren't pirates." Her tone matched his now. She didn't like it, but couldn't stop it.

"No, I don't," said Ikaika. "And neither do you. We don't know them. At all..." Ikaika covered his eyes with a hand. A common sign that he fought off a Melding migraine. The silence stretched as they allowed him to compose his thoughts. "Alright, alright. I don't like our tones either. I'm sorry it got heated. I just...I know your mother is snobbish and definitely over controlling. But it's because of that I think she's far too busy to dabble in the family drama of her paramour's ward," he blew through his nose. "Family drama we should be wary of. They might not be pirates, but they're not our friends. They arrived out of nowhere."

Kezerah contemplated where to go from here. She couldn't show favoritism, but was undoubtedly friends with Ikaika. That left her with two options. Either befriend Ambrose and Rorrik or lose her friendship with Ikaika. So, one option then. Kezerah finally nodded.

"Fine. But the only way to know that for certain is to get to know them." Ikaika did not look mollified, so she pushed. "If they're pirates—or something more insidious—they won't be able to hide it for long. The Solstice Court is too small and too boring."

"It *used* to be boring," Ikaika grumbled. "Nice, and quiet, and boring."

"You're right," agreed Kezerah. "*You* were the last exciting thing to happen here." Ikaika looked pointedly away. "And I wouldn't trade that for anything. So, let's try."

Ikaika continued his pensive stare at the ground a moment longer, then his shoulders sagged along with a sigh. He inclined his head then he glanced towards her glass doors, to his room. "I'm tired. See you for breakfast?"

Kezerah tried not to let the abrupt dismissal sting. His migraines always made him surly. Rest and eliminating the looming mystery of his brothers would help. A discovery simply laid the truth bare. Maybe they would realize that everyone could get along. Then no more tension, no more need for neutrality. Perhaps... no more need for a treaty either. A sense of certainty grasped her.

"Breakfast then," she said, grounded by her new plan. "I wanted to sneak over to the twins anyway. Dar, you in?"

Andarios looked panicked. "To the twins' rooms? Erm, no that's alright. I've got early drills." He took a step towards the doors that lead into the hall. "I'd better just go to bed."

Kezerah swerved in front of him. "You know you can't go out that way yet!" He contemplated the door with a weighted expression. The door that would most certainly get him caught by the guards he had narrowly avoided when getting in. Kezerah reeled. "This is ridiculous. You stay over with me all the time."

"You're not the twins."

Before Kezerah could process this, Ikaika, who'd lifted himself across the balcony railing, paused. "Dar, do you want to sleep in my room tonight? As to not be caught and beheaded for putting the princess' safety in question?"

"We don't behead people!"

Andarios looked overcome with relief. "Yes, yes I would."

"Fine. Jump a balcony rather than stay the night then," Kezerah said crossly. "We'll get more gossiping done without you."

Both Ikaika and Andarios spoke over one another.

"Excellent."

"Sounds great."

"Have fun."

They shared a grin and laughed at Kezerah's expressions. Then hopped over and disappeared into Ikaika's room.

ANDARIOS LET OUT A SIGH, and looked back at Ikaika, radiating gratitude. "I owe you."

Ikaika's curiosity piqued, Andarios' thoughts rarely did the spiraling plummet he'd witnessed in Kezerah's rooms. Images of Whistle's appraising eyes had led to false conversations he couldn't quite parse. He ventured further. "Twins not your type?"

Andarios shook his head, in better spirits now that he'd escaped. "Not even remotely."

Ikaika thought of Willow and Whistle. They were pretty enough, both round-faced and with plenty of curves. Willow, he knew, preferred a more feminine form. Whistle recently seemed to prefer anything that breathed. He had seen himself featured in her thoughts on more than one occasion. "They're a bit talkative," he tried. *'Though, so is Kezerah.'*

"It's not that." Andarios tested Ikaika's mattress for bounce, reminding Ikaika of Kezerah. He forced a frown. Not everything needed to return back to her. "It's just... she never really liked me, you know?" Andarios lay down and Ikaika followed. "So what changed? I've been me this whole time."

Ikaika received flashed snippets of Andarios; *training, growing, his face still boyish but jawline filing, a worried tinge to the reflection as his body continued to shape itself outside of boyhood.* Ikaika squinted in the dark, trying to hear his friends present words past the swirl of thoughts. "You think she just finds you attractive?"

"I know she does. And I've heard enough to know what that means of late." Andarios fluffed then flattened his pillow. "And I don't know how I feel about that." *'Yet,'* his thoughts chorused with a curious uncertainty. Ikaika skirted the omission carefully, and instead used the momentum to press Andarios on a subject he'd often wondered about.

"Not even Kezerah?" Her name felt forbidden. He wanted to take it back but instead his mind betrayed him further, conjuring her instead. Her body taut with muscle from scaling balconies, warm light brown skin, and yes, she also had curves and, although much less of them, they did flatter her figure. The intensity of the moment broke when Andarios let out a rough laugh.

"Kez? No, definitely not."

Ikaika had to admit the dismissal surprised him. He found himself offended on her behalf. "What... I mean, she's pretty enough." That wording had been poor, and his head continued to ache, he needed sleep.

Andarios nodded. "Sure, she's beautiful really, but..." He trailed off and to Ikaika's horror he was graced with Andarios awkwardly trying to give Kezerah a dandelion, the two standing there with nothing to say for the first time in their lives. Romance appeared off the table then.

Ikaika felt like an idiot. "Oh, are girls not interesting to you?" He couldn't help but tease. "Dyllian, perhaps? Or another liege catch your eye?"

Andarios laughed again but his face grew a bit more thoughtful. "I'd kiss Kez before I laid a finger on Dyllian. But no, I don't think anyone has ever appealed to me. At least thus far. I just... I don't know, maybe no one's quite right, but there's no way to know without mucking it all up in the end, you know?"

'Kissing? When did we start talking about kissing?' Color rose to Ikaika's cheeks. He hoped it was too dark for Andarios to notice. Ikaika nodded in response to his friend's admission, thinking it over to see if it applied to him. He imagined Kezerah's terrorizing grin and untamed laugh. It sent a pleasant shiver down him. No, Andarios' preferences, or lack thereof, definitely did not apply to him. "Right yeah. Kissing Kez is definitely a bad idea. I get that." Ikaika decided to cut off the conversation before it got out of hand.

"Well, night, Dar." He used the nickname more out of an aim for casualty than familiarity this time.

Andarios chuckled but allowed the quick dismissal. "Night, Kai." He sounded a tad bit mocking. Ikaika appreciated his friend's willingness to let it go. He fell asleep, his dreams thankfully did not drift but remained firmly planted in his own mind.

Honeydew

Kezerah waited outside Ikaika's doors, her stomach growling. Nimah left Dyllian's rooms with a yawn. "Go to breakfast, Princess. Prince Ikaika, I'm sure, can find his own way down."

Kezerah had meant to argue that she always waited for both Ikaika and Andarios. However, she refused to look like a pining girl, unable to get breakfast without him, and couldn't mention Andarios slept in the chambers as well. Her stomach growled once more. The decision made for her, she left the Spring Quarter in search of food. Up late last night with Willow and Whistle, she knew better than to see them before midday.

Breakfast did not hold the same intensity as last night's dinner, but Kezerah noticed the Autumn Hall seemed quieter than usual. The King and Queen would not dine with the guests until the evening, leaving it an open breakfast. She piled her plate high with bacon and observed a few other interesting dishes added. A long slab of food littered the back table to grab what you wanted and sit leisurely where you wished.

She scooped eggs baked into a tomato sauce and olives that came in every color. The sight of extra fruit amidst the squashes surprised her; this time of year it was rare. She picked up a vibrant, green sweet-smelling fruit and inspected it. It smelled like the sweets passed around during Yuletide.

"Honeydew," a warm, deep voice said just behind her ear.

She jumped as the warmth tickled her neck. Then, she placed the voice and turned around slowly, calming herself. Ambrose stood close beside her, filling his own plate with the crisp sweet melon. She had thought his eyes dark before, possibly like Ikaika's, but now she discerned they were a deep rich green, catching color like sea glass.

He didn't seem to notice or care that she inspected him and he continued speaking, tone easy. "We brought some with us. Silly, since it will probably not last much longer, but it's a favorite of mine."

She added two more slices to her plate. "Thanks for the tip. Now I can stock up before it's gone." She pointed to the rainbow of olives. "A favorite of yours as well?"

His nose crinkled and she thought it made him look younger, boyish even. "If I fed them to my enemy, sure."

She laughed, trying a large one. The flavor carried a bitter saltiness, followed by an acidic aftertaste. Her expression must have conveyed her emotions because Ambrose let loose a laugh, his face uncontrolled in his bout of amusement. It continued as she spit the large olive back onto her plate and scraped the rest back into the bowl on the table.

"It seems we have similar taste, though I've never actually been allowed to spit my food out before." He seemed overjoyed by her reaction, and she started to respond when Dyllian's high strung voice sounded behind her.

"Did you just—put your food back, after it's been in your mouth?"

Kezerah sighed and turned to Dyllian, who squirmed in place.

"I didn't put the chewed up one back," she said, gesturing to her large, gnarled, purple olive. "Just the ones I wouldn't eat."

"They were still on your plate! They might have touched that one," he said.

"Fine, Dyllian, would you like me to take them back?"

"Princess," he said slowly, as if unsure if she would comprehend, "they've all touched now. The entire plate is tainted."

A few other guests who milled about the hall looked over, curious as to what caused the young lord distress.

Kezerah examined the large bowl of olives, wanting to shove them all in her mouth from spite and shuddering at the idea of it.

Ambrose's reply interrupted her thought, "Tainted is an interesting descriptor for your princess." His mild tone managed to sound chastising.

"Well no—she's not tainted," Dyllian said. "Just the olive she—"

"She put it in her mouth, blessing it with her lips. I'm unaware how lips such as hers could do anything but better its flavor."

Kezerah snorted. Ambrose's words dripped mockery but he delivered each word with so much offended sincerity she couldn't stifle her laugh.

Dyllian left his mouth partially ajar, perplexed on how to continue after the proclamation that Kezerah's lips were a blessing, he tried regardless. "I don't see you with blessed olives on your plate."

Kezerah rolled her eyes. He was so childish. "Dyllian, if you'd like me to eat an entire bowl of olives in front of you, just say so."

Before Dyllian could respond, Ambrose plucked her chewed up olive off her plate and popped it in his mouth. Now she and Dyllian stared with matching expressions. His jaw gave the motion of chewing, and he tossed his head back, eyes closed as if savoring it. Then he gulped, opened his wide mouth and stuck his tongue out for Dyllian to assess. When Dyllian did nothing but cringe, Ambrose smiled back at the still-gaping Kezerah.

"Truly, the sweetest food I've ever tasted. Kezerah, my dear, you must chew my food for me more often." He looked back at Dyllian, his tone colored with sympathy. "Unfortunately, I've taken the best one, but you and the Princess' other subjects may take the remnants." He gestured to the bowl of olives like one showcased a prize, then twisted his hand out to Kezerah in offering. "Please do me the pleasure of accompanying me and my food out in the courtyard? I wish to look upon the leaves."

She took it; his hand, warm and rough, enveloped her fingertips entirely. She savored Dyllian's dumbfounded expression one more time, etching it into her memory, and followed Ambrose out into the crisp air of the Autumn Courtyard.

"Would you like me to start with your honeydew?" Kezerah teased as they sat down on a stone bench under a fire willow. Its long dripping branches shrouded their table, giving the feel of being in a private room rather than right outside the Autumn Hall.

He smiled and took a bite of the melon in question. "Despite my bold words, I'm afraid honeydew cannot be improved upon. I shall have to eat it all myself."

"Probably for the best. My ego was becoming unbearable."

She took a bite of her own food; the eggs cooked perfect, she mixed them in with her bacon. They ate in a comfortable silence, natural even, but she realized after a moment he looked her over, examining her face much like she had done his.

"I assure you, my lips are the only part of my face that's blessed."

He smiled, not even remotely abashed by being caught staring. "Your eyes are an unusual shade."

She nodded. Her eyes were often what people first noticed about her, once they got past her hair. "A 'family' trait, apparently," Kezerah said, disliking the conversation's direction towards her status as Soul Heir. "An inheritance from the first of our line." She gestured to the dark purple banners donning the hall. "Thus the Elastor colors."

Ambrose surprised her. "I'm relieved that's not how Xenkesh came about its colors. Bloodshot eyes are not a charming look. Amber stones are much more appealing."

She thought of the dark crimson and gold of the Xenkesh flag. The Ambre Cove ranked high on her must-see list that she'd never reach. It was said that the amber stones washed up and littered the cove so densely that the entirety of it glimmered red. Willow and Whistle had described it to her once. The image in her mind painted something beautiful. It was also said Ambrose himself had been named after the cove.

"Nonsense," she said, "you wouldn't catch me fighting a man with blood red eyes. Perfect for intimidation."

"Oh yes, just what Xenkesh is known for," Ambrose said with a chuckle. "Our menace."

He said the words as if he thought them funny. Though 'menacing,' she remembered, had been one of the words she had thought to describe Ambrose upon first seeing him. She reassessed him now, lazily consuming a plate of fruit, his posture relaxed against the tree as if planning a nap. How had she gotten him so wrong? She trailed her eyes up to the hanging branches, not wanting to be caught staring again.

"Are you not ordinarily flocked by friends?" he asked, extracting her from her thoughts.

"Oh, yes, but they all slept in. We were up quite late, but after last night's exciting events—" she nodded giving him his due. "—I didn't want to miss anything today might bring." This wasn't entirely true, as she had duties with her father to attend to, but she wanted to give him space to explain. He did not.

"We?" He had caught her plural and she wondered why she hadn't thought to correct it.

"Mm." She nodded, feigning nonchalance. "Some of us have rooms close to one another, so we mingle after the lanterns are snuffed out."

"One of those 'some' being my brother."

Kezerah weighed what to do with his directness. Often she and Ikaika would skirt past the awkwardness between them. Ambrose appeared to prefer to bash into the truth headlong.

She tried it herself. "Yes, his room is next to mine. So, we've become friends." It felt nice, freeing.

He grinned, thrilled by the idea. "It seems you're not one for rules then?"

"I have been known to leave my quarters past hours," she announced regally. "Late night activities and such."

"Oh? Where do you go for these 'late night activities'?"

His question sounded like a challenge but she spoke honestly. "Just to different bedchambers, depending on where the nurse is least likely to look."

His scowl bore a hint of teasing, but his eyes glinted in a dare. "Just to your rooms? With all of that brilliant city surrounding you?"

Kezerah blushed, seldom the least daring in the conversation. "I'm not allowed in the city. I'm the Soul Heir... without a successor." This last part left her unsettled. Kezerah would never have a successor—or, at least, not while she lived. Her soul would abandon her the instant her life faced mortal peril and tether itself to the next in her line. Her parents had bore no more children, and Elize had experienced great complications before Kezerah. Her uncle, on the Ellas side, had left no heirs behind, meaning the Ellas line only continued one way. Of all the topics meant to be avoided, Kezerah actively chose to steer clear of childbirth.

Ambrose seemed unaware of her dread, and mulled over her

words. "Shame. Rorrik and I stayed in your capital on our way in. Heartsglove is quite the sight to see."

"Ambrose of Xenkesh, are you trying to coax me into breaking the law?"

He taunted a mischievous smile. "Princess, you told me of your interest in rule breaking. I merely offered an experience worth breaking the rules for."

Kezerah could see he toyed with her, thinking she was too timid to do anything worth his notice. But the idea of going into Heartsglove had always delighted her. The conversation had gone in an unexpected direction. She followed its course, hungry for the dare.

"A fair shot, if you can actually deliver. Do you happen to know a place in the city worth my mother's wrath?"

He gave a wide, but dismissive, grin. Clearly, he didn't believe she would follow through with her bluff. "That I do. If you find yourself curious, feel free to fetch me in the Autumn Quarters. At any span of the day, or night."

Kezerah fumbled her fork. Was he...flirting? The very idea felt as foreign as the food she had on her plate. Romantic notions weren't beyond her; in fact, the idea thrilled her. However, no advances had ever emerged nor been returned (at twelve, she'd batted her eyes at Whistle, once, and it had gone unnoticed). All of her friends treated her as simply that: a friend. And all visiting nobility treated her as much less, or as an unapproachable figure of sorts.

She looked at Ambrose's cocky expression; eyes alighted on her with unfettered interest. Kezerah gulped and suppressed her reaction. Just her luck that the only person to show any real interest she could have no real interest in. She reminded herself of her task to form a friendship. So instead, she planned on how to best wipe the arrogant smile off her new friend's pretty face.

IKAIKA STRETCHED as he quietly padded out of bed. A milky, pink glow peaked through the branches outside his window, and he wondered at the time. Andarios snored louder than his footsteps so he dressed and shut the door behind him with ease.

Eriko wished him a gruff good morning. "Does your lordling friend need guarding, or is my rest permissible?" The trio had found out early on it was near impossible to get past Eriko, but, trained more as a warrior rather than a guard, they had also discovered Eriko much more lenient. *'I answer to your mother, and your mother directed I answer to you. Don't do anything stupid,'* had been the extent of Ikaika's chastisement following the realization Kezerah had been in his rooms.

"If Dar finds you at my door he'll just use it as an excuse to get extra training in. Better take the nap."

Eriko gave a lazy salute as he walked away. "Don't be late to our drills, or I'll make you train with a claymore." Ikaika shivered at the thought.

Once down the stairs and in the meadow, to Ikaika's surprise, he noticed the sun had risen well beyond the eastern hills. Many courtiers had already finished with their breakfast and looked upon the reddened trees. A row of children jumped and stomped in a pile of saffron brown leaves. Ikaika urged time to jump back with longing. After standing there a moment he forced his feet forward.

In the Autumn Hall he moved to the open table, eyeing the egg medley with caution. He extracted some open-face trout, pickled plums, and saw, to his surprise, plenty of olives left over despite them being imported. Not wanting to waste them he heaped several on his plate, before turning to find a seat.

While he had teased Kezerah, he had no intention of sitting next to Dyllian by choice and continued to scan the space. Rorrik sat at the opposite end of the table, eliminating either side as an option. He followed Rorrik's surly expression out to the courtyard where two silhouettes sat obscured under the large yellow, orange, and deep red canopy of leaves. Another stone table stood empty next to it. Sure to not make eye contact with Rorrik, he moved purposefully to the table outside and sat down.

The air had some bite to it, but Ikaika never minded. Next to Alora's frigid Winters, Elastor lived in eternal Spring. Kezerah's laugh rang out, echoing through the courtyard, and Ikaika looked around him to find the source.

Her voice edged into a lilt she used for some of her more wicked jokes and he managed to catch the end of it as he got up and walked towards the overhanging branches.

"I was moments from making him as ghostly as he appears." She finished, leaned in close to—Ikaika took a moment to register Ambrose, after only seeing him once in the banquet hall. Not expecting to see him here, it felt like placing a completely unfamiliar face.

The lack of recognition might have also been because Ambrose's face had transformed. While last night he had spoken with non-stop high energy, he now had a more easy grin: dark eyes fixed on Kezerah, his muscles relaxed. He had an elbow on the table, palm propping up his chin, leaning forward as if to hear her better. Considering how close she too leaned in on the small table, Ikaika guessed that Ambrose could hear her just fine.

The glow of the leaves around them created an odd intimacy. Suddenly, Ikaika felt like an intruder. He stepped back and both occupants turned at the movement.

Ambrose registered him with a moment of surprise, eyes widening and then narrowing.

In contrast, Kezerah's expression at first showed polite confusion, followed by an all-encompassing grin; his entrance seemed to light up her whole face. He felt a peculiar magnetic pull in opposite directions as her smile shifted him forward.

"Kai! You're up!" she greeted him.

"Andarios' snores ensured a later night than I intended." He hated that he rambled.

"Well, sit!" She gestured to the smidgen of space between the two of them, Ambrose taking up a third of it. "I was just explaining how Dyllian and I first met."

Ikaika edged further back, meaning to say no, but only managing a small shake of his head. Kezerah could give his brother all the benefit of the doubt she wanted. Ambrose didn't hide his displeasure at Ikaika's arrival. He now showed remarkable focus on a slimy pale green food that he supposedly intended to ingest. Kezerah bolted upright to pull on Ikaika's arm, before dragging him to the table.

Ambrose shifted, eyes wide while looking Kezerah over, reassessing her. "Oh, this is actually happening."

"Apparently," Ikaika managed, hollowly, before seeing Kezerah's face and trying to calm himself. He knew what a bind she'd been placed in. But he'd never really had to put the treaty into practice.

It had been easy with Ambrose in Xenkesh with an open but unused invitation to court. With his presence, the nuances of the rules grew tricky. Would she have to start scaling Ambrose and Rorrik's balcony? The idea made him ill and he twirled his utensils on his plate. He knew fighting with Kezerah would simply make her more stubborn, but he couldn't pretend to be amiable with the people who had so affected his own life, as well as his mother's.

"I have no intention of making your life more difficult," Ikaika finally said. He could not apologize for his feelings towards his brothers, but he could try to be decent for Kezerah's sake.

Ambrose scoffed instead of responding in turn, then shoved the slimy fruit in his mouth. It looked revolting. Ikaika could do nothing but stare, wondering how long he could sit here before making an escape.

KEZERAH WATCHED Ikaika watching his brother warily. The expression on his face held little promise. She had been happy to see her friend upon his arrival. Now, she wondered if she had made the right choice in combining the two of them so early.

Ikaika looked at Ambrose in disgust; the simple act of chewing seemed to send him over. The space weighed heavily in silence. She wracked her mind for a topic they might have mutual interest in. While she didn't intend to bring up their mother, she thought perhaps their shared lineage might interest them.

"Ambrose was explaining some of the foods we don't often have imported," she began, assessing the situation for outbursts. Neither seemed to be particularly upset, so Kezerah continued. "I had yet to taste a honeydew before. Have you tried one, Ikaika?"

Ikaika looked down at the fruit as if he believed it might crawl off the plate. "I have not." He spoke without interest and she kicked him under the table. He looked at her with exasperation and she met him with pleading eyes. "But, I'm sure, they're...an experience."

Ambrose grunted, looking down at Ikaika's fish and olive

medley. "I wouldn't be surprised if they weren't to your liking. I hear palates up north are sensitive to more complex flavors."

Kezerah assessed if she felt comfortable enough kicking Ambrose when Ikaika bit back. "Perhaps, if Xenkesh hadn't cut exports in order to blackmail our grandmother into a political alliance that led to a plague, our palates would be more sophisticated."

Kezerah's eyes widened. She had not seen *that* coming. She felt herself losing the room. "It's honeydew. The flavor really isn't that involved," she insisted, having tried some earlier and finding it to be sweet, and not much else. "Besides, Ikaika has spent years here in Elastor. He has tasted plenty of our complex flavors."

Ambrose's expression became unkind, as he surveyed the lack of distance between herself and Ikaika. He met Ikaika's eyes with a knowing look. "Oh, I'm sure he has."

The charming would-be-friend had disappeared, and a stranger now sat in his place. Kezerah drew herself up. All progress of their conversation tossed away for his petty jibe in Ikaika's direction.

"Follow that thought one step further, Xenkeshi, and you can eat your honeydew off the floor," said Ikaika, a chill to his voice.

Ambrose barked out a laugh that didn't meet his eyes. Kezerah had officially deemed the moment a disaster, yet couldn't pinpoint just where she'd gone wrong.

"Enough," she said finally. "Honeydew is off the list of topics for conversation."

"Good," Ambrose said, "because I just lost my appetite." He slid the remaining fruit over to her. "I think I'll take a walk through the city, and see what else Elastor has to offer." He stood up, bowed in Kezerah's direction, and then strode off.

Kezerah put her head in her hands. "That went terribly." She emphasized each word. She looked over at Ikaika as he shifted the food on his plate. "The Xenkeshi export ban *and* the Bane Harvest Plague?"

Ikaika looked insulted. "Only after he said my entire Kingdom has no taste," he insisted. "Kez, he's awful. You should have heard what he accused you of in his mind."

She put up a hand. "I don't want to know."

Ikaika mumbled something that sounded like, "Yeah well, me neither."

Kezerah stood up. "Alright, I'm sorry. It most certainly wasn't *all* your fault. I'll talk to him."

Ikaika's mood seemed to plummet further, but he said nothing, letting her leave the table and follow after Ambrose.

SHE CAUGHT up to Ambrose as he neared the stables. He took flinching steps towards an elk that skittered back and forth at his approach, riled by his own nervous behavior. He jumped when she called out to him before crossing his arms. "Decided to break the rules after all?"

It had been easy to talk to Ambrose upon their first meeting. Effortless even. It took effort now, not only to speak to him, but to do so kindly. While her tone stayed sweet and formal, her words held a new edge of irritation she didn't like. "Not just yet. I still have responsibilities to attend to this morning," she said, "but, unless you'd like to be bitten by that elk, perhaps you'll walk with me instead."

He backed away from the animal, then threw her an easy smile that didn't quite meet his eyes. "If you insist."

"I do."

She led him up the nearest tower, bypassing her maze. She had no desire to share it with him, not with his haughty, amused glances at her. Instead they took the steps up to the guard tower gates with the best view of Elastor's capital.

Vast and sprawling, clustered and stacked stone buildings and thatched roofs defined Heartsglove. In the night it sparkled with lantern light, but with the sun high and proud, her city shone at its best. The houses wore a lively coat of rich green moss. The dots of moving villagers appeared to look like distant fields of flowers, tangling among one another in the breeze. She imagined it smelled of raised loaves of bread and herbs dried along window sills. A river of opals snaked under an arched bridge. She was imbued with an all encompassing urge to see it up close.

"It's amazing how many people fit, despite its size," Ambrose said, appreciating the view alongside her.

"Its size?" she gestured at the never-ending view. "Is Trusol filled with giants then?" She regretted the jibe, her eye level just below Ambrose's shoulder. His smile said he'd had the same thought.

"I meant no offense. Elastor and its capital are lovely—" Violet flags stitched with silver hung loosely around them at each turret, a reminder of which kingdom he stood in. "The people I have met, just as equally so," he said with belated diplomacy.

Kezerah wanted to ask for more details, but refused to appear too eager. Instead, she kept walking, his long strides slow to keep pace with hers.

His tone, while not unkind, carried a bit of impatience. "I am assuming this leisure stroll is due to you disliking your prince's taste buds insulted."

"At least that assumption of me is correct," she replied, still looking at the city as they walked.

He caught on, and asked with faux innocence, "Are there other assumptions I've made of you that are incorrect?"

Kezerah turned to him, meeting his gaze with her own. "You tell me. I can't read minds."

She did not need Ikaika to explain what he had seen in Ambrose's mind, his veiled vulgarity had been clear. She watched as he sized her up, finding nothing playful in her expression. His face became thoughtful.

She gave him a knowing look, and he nodded, admitting to his earlier accusation. "I had meant to make a disparaging comment towards my brother, but I realize it was also an unfair assumption of you. My apologies."

Kezerah brushed the words away, caring less about his assumption of her sex life and took a page out of his book, getting to the crux of the issue. "It's not the assumption I take offense to, but the debasing of what I *believed* to be the beginning of a friendship."

Ambrose's brows rose into thick strands of hair. His lips lightly parted, as if he meant to speak immediately but held back. He tried his apology again. "I admit, I feel like I'm coming into this friendship at a disadvantage. But I didn't handle myself gracefully. I truly do apologize."

While he definitely handled himself gracefully now, there lingered an uncertainty in how sincere he was. She needed to make her point clear. "I enjoyed our conversation earlier, and I think I very much want to be your friend." His smile flashed with charm, but she pressed on. "However, that is not possible if you intend to antagonize the friends I've already made."

The smile held but she inspected the differences in the effort it took to hold it in place.

"The Solstice Court is only so large. Believe me, I've explored every inch of it. As you pointed out earlier, my options are limited. And, as I'm not allowed to show favor to either of you, the disagreements between you and Ikaika limit my options further. If you fight in one room, I shall be forced to leave it in search of another." She looked at him, stance firm. "So I'd prefer if we can all remain in the same room."

His grin fell away, eyes serious and contemplative. He rubbed his lips together in thought and she found it interesting that he couldn't seem to keep his mouth from moving.

He nodded. "I think I want to be your friend as well." He sounded too surprised for her liking. "I also think I may have created a false image of you in my mind." He smiled down at her apologetically, offering her an elbow to walk less formally. She wound her arm through, allowing him to guide their walk. "Can we talk like friends once more? I admit, diplomacy gives me a headache." She sensed the sincerity, and gave one sharp nod in acceptance. Her mouth pulled at the sides, drawn to return his smile. "Excellent. Now, how much do I need to behave in order to be your friend?" he asked, wanting to know his bare minimum for manners.

"Enough to keep you both from fighting." Let him determine his own limits; he seemed clever enough to find them.

He ran a hand through his dark hair, and she noticed it had chestnut undertones in the sun. He let out a long sigh. "I'll do my best then," he said, his glance less brief and voice more teasing. "I think it might be worth it."

A flutter stirred in the pit of her stomach and she ignored it. If she was going to enjoy their easy banter, it would need to remain just that. Like what she had with Ikaika. She could do that.

Balance restored between them, Kezerah tossed her hair to the side with a smile. "I think you'll find *your* worth, Ambrose, is being equally weighed."

Ambrose's laugh was what she imagined the sound of thunder to be, deep and unrestrained. "Then I'll do my best to measure up." His features flashed a moment later in levity. "On that topic, as your friend, how may I steal more of your *uninterrupted* company?"

Kezerah scoffed. "A mystery I've yet to solve." She drew her attention back to the sun, nearing midday. She had yet to miss a meeting with her father, and now she ran late. "I actually have been shirking many of my duties in trade of friends." She began to unwrap her arm from his, and he drew closer.

"Are you sure you can't be persuaded to bend a few more rules?"

Reminded of his playful dares from earlier, she quelled her need to match him. "Unfortunately, not. But," she added, at his poorly concealed disappointment, "like you said, I know which quarters to find you in." She let her hand slip from his arm, and continued forward to leave Ambrose on the tower with nothing but the view.

Responsibilities

A dent formed in Kezerah's cheek as she propped her head up on a fist. She stared longingly out the window of her father's study. Thankfully, it faced north and, speckled off in the distance, her Winter Woods. She had been sitting in the clustered room with her father for the first half of the day while he instructed her on their new style of irrigation system set to go in after First Thaw.

"Kezerah, this is very important," her father chided, tapping the map of the surrounding crops.

"I know. I swear I'm listening." A bird trilled and she noticed the cascading mountains were already capped with snow.

"I'd say you are window gazing more than listening," he said, his tone was soft but he raised a dark gray brow in warning.

"No, I am," she insisted. "We use Sway to push the water through the path, just like we move the herbal oils and water through the walls of the castle."

Her father nodded, pleased. "Right, but what of those on the Aloran border? Many in Luka and Western Larken provinces have families without magick, or they are Melders. Do we only have our farmers who can Hold Sway reap the benefits? Or do we bring people in specifically for the job? In both cases, they will need to be compensated, which will require a cut from the lieges' pay."

Kezerah thought for a moment, happier with a puzzle rather than a lecture. "If the channels are put here—" she pointed, "—and here, then the farmers without Sway will be in the path as the water is moved down to the next farmers with it."

"If the village agrees to it," he corrected.

She nodded. "Right, those who don't agree we can deviate from the path."

"Sounds reasonable," he said, beaming and adjusting the map with her corrections. "The Ralvens showed pushback on their largest channel. Did you want to make an adjustment?"

Kezerah studied the graphite squiggle made to represent the largest water supply outside of the Strand. "...If we do that..." She tried to think how far back they'd be required to go in the planning for such a reduction. "We're down half the resources needed to make this route work. I think the Ralven province can learn to share."

"Well then, we've reached this project's conclusion." Elowren withdrew a dab of wax from a drawer, then pressed his crest into the right hand corner of the plans. He slid the documents across to her. Kezerah tilted her head in curiosity.

"These are your plans, Kezerah. They must bear my seal, but it's the maker who signs them into action." He handed her a feather quill. Kezerah looked at the maps again, wondering if they were correct or ready. She'd been looking at that bird for a long time.

"Someone's best is not a request for perfection," said Elowren. "The element of care is the key. Do you care about this project you've worked on?" Kezerah nodded. "Do you feel you've tried your best?" Kezerah hesitated. Then nodded again, slower. "Then this Kingdom has been given all it can ask of you."

She looked back down at the plans, smears of work and hours of thought from the past three moons poured across it. She signed. Each letter in her name energized her as they appeared. When finished, she handed Elowren back his quill, and he smiled.

"Now, go before you jump out my window."

She kissed her father on the cheek and raced out the door before he remembered she was supposed to scribe his council meeting.

KEZERAH GRAZED her hand along rough-hewn stone walls. The damp sponge of moss interrupted the coarse texture of the bumps and grooves that slid across her fingertips. The distant hum of water through pipes led her as she skipped foot to foot. Her ear followed the path of oils that connected the castle through waterways. The corridor from Winter to Summer chilled as the archways parted their walls to open air.

She passed guards who wore helms with steel visors to block out the afternoon sun. Slowing her pace, to appear more innocent, she made her way towards the Spring Quarters.

Water rushed through stone and she pictured the irrigation map again. The relief of work finished returned the skip to her step. Every canal impressed onto the page, she'd helped add to the new map. The closer each province's map was magnified the nearer she felt to exploring Elastor. She'd imagined visits to small villages never mentioned on travel-ogs, looked into local holidays and the best times to start and stop building within seasons. A few extra troughs she'd admittedly added along the border, just to roam the boundaries of her home a bit longer.

The Lull's gentle chant eclipsed the trickle of water as she reached the Summer terrace, with views of Spring. She scouted out the towers and parapets surrounding her rooms, as her first order of business. From afar, three sets of guards on the tower greeted one another before slipping into each other's places. Step for step. Easy enough to slip past, if only a tad more time threatening.

The guards on the terrace eyed her warily. She grinned and wished them a pleasant midday. Only the smallest twinge of guilt pulled at her smile. They'd only be in trouble if she got caught. She cast her eyes to the towers again. The burst of pink petals in the middle of her confines stirred in an errant breeze. She watched the tree dance in its cage. She had no intention of joining in its compla-cency. Not with a dare in her heart and all of that brilliant city surrounding her.

Satisfied with her surveillance of the guards, she crept down to the maze. It twisted about in a tangle until she reached the clearing pressed against the Eastern Wall. She set to work where the wall met the grass and dug into the cold ground. Dirt thickened beneath her nails. A stone in the wall's base shifted. She used the gap to widen the hole further. The gurgling of water rejoiced behind the wall. Two more stones shifted. She gave a triumphant pull at one stone and it jostled free to reveal a hollow foundation. Without their brethren the next two stones fell away easily. A loud kerplunk below announced a narrow waterway: the castle's irrigation system. If the maps she'd reviewed could be believed, then a large drain spilled down the hill to the crops outside of the castle walls. The hole below her now gaped wide enough for a Kezerah-sized person to crawl into.

A test undoubtedly required, she eagerly began to lower herself into the hole. Hanan's voice carried over the hedges. "Princess? Princess Kezerah? Your mother is asking for you."

She clambered out of the hole, placing herself awkwardly in front of it. "Yes, Hanan! I'll be right there!" She shouted back, as he came around the corner. She looked a mess, arms covered in dirt, her dress no better. Her skirts fanned out around her to obscure the newly dug up earth.

The stress and exhaustion on Hanan's face, upon seeing her, made it appear as if he too might like to escape.

"We have no time to properly prepare you," he said after a moment of staring at her. "You can explain to your mother why it looks like you've been wading through sewers."

She stifled her smile at his assessment but inclined her head. "Yes, sorry, Hanan. I shall wash my hands and be right up."

He looked down at her hands, probably doubting anything she did at this point to be sufficient. He shrugged. "I shall let her know you will be with her momentarily." He stalked off in the direction he had come. Kezerah stood, uselessly brushing off her stained dress. A stone bench lingered in a corner of the hedges and she dragged it forward, concealing the evidence. Then rushed to the fountain to wash away the most noticeable grime from her arms and under her fingertips.

KEZERAH'S EFFORTS were wasted on Elize. The queen sat in one of the many meeting chambers, wearing a dress of gold brocade with dark jewels to match her autumn crown. Her mother always dressed fashionably for the season, but today Kezerah thought she looked more like a bumblebee. Elize looked her over and seemed to think Kezerah resembled something far worse.

"Honestly," she began, already tired of her. "How did you get that dirty in a council meeting?"

"Father let me miss it, to—" she fumbled to find a responsible reason, "—to look over the irrigation we're planning. I tripped."

They both looked down at her muddy form, neither believing her.

"Fine. I asked you here to talk about your responsibilities to Prince Ambrose and Prince Rorrik. I do not wish to make them feel unwelcome."

"Ambrose and I ate breakfast together and took a walk," Kezerah assured. "I already know my duties."

"I believe Prince Ikaika, too, joined you for breakfast, did he not?" her mother challenged. Having a Spymaster for a mother was sometimes incredibly irritating. Kezerah rolled her eyes. "Briefly. It was fine." *Sort of.*

Elize assessed her once more, still upset with her state of dress. "Nimah gave you your monthly Preventions?"

"Yes, nights ago." Kezerah wrinkled her nose at the conversation's turn. "What does that have to do with anything?"

"You tell me," Elize said. "You're the one with a torn dress, covered in mud."

"I was checking the irrigation!" Kezerah said, aghast. "Alone. I don't even need the stupid concoction."

"Of course you do," Her mother protested. "You know how dangerous it is. Think of Soul Heir Rivka, Ayla, Ioni, Adol—"

"Alright, I get it—"

"All of their souls transferred during childbirth, Kezerah. All of them; reincarnated."

"I said, I get it." She sounded bitter and hated it.

Her mother studied her clinically. Kezerah looked about for something to distract her attention. Not a notebook or dust speck out of line. With limited options she reluctantly returned her gaze.

Elize pursed her lips. "Good. In addition, I'm instructing you to spend time with Ambrose and Rorrik, separately from Ikaika. We don't want Ikaika and his brothers fighting."

"I'm already working on that," Kezerah said, her one success under siege. "They've agreed to try and—"

"Enough," her mother cut her off, voice filled with authority. Kezerah felt herself quiet. "I have told you to spend time with them separately. I did not ask for your input. I will say this again: it is not worth the risk of us becoming involved. You've had years to build relations with our Aloran allies. Give our Xenkeshi allies the same reception."

Kezerah nodded, finding herself still unable to speak.

"Go. But be cleaned up and ready for tonight's dinner by late afternoon. A dress will be laid out."

Kezerah made it down the hall before she released a roar of outrage. Too late she noticed a pair of servants passing by. *'Oh excellent,'* she thought. That was sure to get back to her mother. Even when following the rules, she couldn't do anything right.

She saw Ikaika in the distant practice yards and moved to vent out her vexations, but felt tugged away from him. She didn't want to fail. She wanted there to be peace. But every move she made was a misstep on a stage: careless, clumsy, and ill-prepared. Even the idea of small talk with Ambrose or Rorrik seemed too impossible to manage right now. Whirling away from the Winter Hall she stomped off towards the barracks to find the one person she was allowed to speak to, without strings dangling from her arms.

SHE FOUND Andarios receiving instructions in the stables. A large, cloudy gray mare pawed hooves beside him while Rook, the captain of the guard, directed her friend on the horse's care. The fact that Andarios had been deemed worthy of his own horse boded well for him. Horses were rare, Elastor's main mounts being elk.

"She's not skittish around komodai or iron wolves, but you'll need to start combat training with her, or she won't stand a chance against either," Rook said, tone stern and back facing Kezerah.

She picked up some stones next to a pile of straw and juggled them behind the instructions. Andarios spotted her and pinched his face into a forced frown. He tried to look as if he concentrated—and failed upon one of the stray stones falling out of sequence, smacking her on the head.

Andarios snorted, and Kezerah dove.

The captain turned sharply, yet found nothing behind him but an empty bale of hay.

ONCE HIS LESSON HAD COMPLETED, Andarios helped Kezerah pick loose straw from her hair. "So, is she yours then?" Kezerah asked, as she saddled up on her dark pony, Soot. She loved Soot but had to admit she felt childish riding next to Andarios' large mare. Soot, however, was *safe*, so Soot was the mount she rode.

"As long as I'm serving in the Queen's Army," he said cheerfully. "Good thing," he added. "I'm pretty sure Daffodil would keel over if I tried riding her again."

Daffodil, the dappled white pony three sizes too small for Andarios, snorted her agreement from her stable. Both friends laughed as they rode out towards the Northern Gate. The sham of a gate led to a larger cage; the western perimeter, encircled by high, uninviting walls, which housed a large field for riding and the royal hunting grounds situated in the Winter Woods. The forest had been named due to its backdrop of snowy mountain peaks, but on this autumnal day, it burst with reds, browns and yellows, mixed in with the vibrant smell and color of pine.

"So," Kezerah began. "How is..." She wracked her brain for a taboo subject. Something with the tangy taste of rebellion she craved. "The war?"

Andarios, who rode ahead, nearly swung himself fully around on his horse. "War-ish. Why do you ask?"

She glared. "Can't I ask? Do I need to be docile with you too?"

"Of course not, you've just never seemed to care much. At all, really."

She tried not to let the accusation rumple her mood further. Reminded of her dinner conversation with Ambrose, she admitted, "Well, with both sides at court I just don't want to come off as ignorant. Impartiality doesn't have to be ignorance, does it?"

Andarios made the face of someone thinking very hard on a subject. "I don't know."

"Well, I say it doesn't. I want to know, and you're the only person I can ask without the information being strained like rice."

He passed her over with quizzical eyes. "Last I heard there was a skirmish on Alora's Tiertyde coast. A ground troop is based in Fort Thistle—on our border. King Amarus once again sent an overture to negotiate, once again ignored by Queen Illija. And, her battalion rode without her along the Xenkeshi Strand."

Kezerah bit back the annoyance, understanding little of what information he'd given her. "Why without her?"

"Officially? Because they have an auxilia and Fort Thistle doesn't have a Melder." Kezerah clung to the hint of gossip amidst the military jargon.

"Unofficially?"

"Unofficially, people are saying this is as close as she can get to all three of her sons at once." Andarios gave a glance to the open field. "And we've been on high alert patrols since she stationed herself there."

"People think she would attack Elastor?" The idea seemed ludicrous. A treaty was a treaty, peace was peace.

Andarios shifted in his seat a little. "Not if she doesn't have cause."

"What makes people think—" Kezerah stopped to read Andarios' weighted expression. "People think I'll be the cause. That I'll do something wrong with everyone all in one place."

"People are just cautious. If it can stop an attack, why not do a few extra patrols. Just to show we're at attention."

"People?"

"People," Andarios agreed.

"So, everyone."

Andarios didn't deny it. "Since when do you care what anyone thinks? Let alone everyone."

She didn't answer. Everyone expected her to fail. Nobody expected her to do this right. No wonder her mother had been on edge. Elastor might have Illija on their doorstep, but Elize had a much larger risk to manage. Kezerah, ruining everything. The pressure made her feel expanded, vulnerable, like a bubble easily popped.

"Alright, out with it," Andarios said. "What did she do?"

Kezerah huffed, "Oh, the usual. Reminded me of what I'm not

doing and implied I'm not doing enough," she fiddled with Soot's reins. "She also reminded me to take my Preventions."

Andarios cocked his head to one side. "What for?"

"Dar," Kezerah begged. "What do you think?"

Andarios rolled his eyes. "I know what the potion is for. I meant, why ask? It's not like you're—" He studied her. "Are you?"

"Obviously not. You would be the first to know."

Andarios snorted. "I sincerely doubt that."

"I meant the first person outside of the act, Dar." Again, a bitterness chewed at her, but this time, her mother wasn't there.

He slowed his horse. "What's bothering you? Is that something you want? You want to..." He left his sentence incomplete with a tossing twist of his hand.

Kezerah tried to untangle her feelings. "Not necessarily. I just want the choice. And for it not to be silly for me to take them." She fought embarrassment. "I want to feel, you know, desirable."

Andarios shook his head. "Desire isn't just one way. There are dozens of ways to want. Home, family, experiences, fun. You're plenty desirable."

Kezerah bit her lip, understanding but wanting more. She didn't know if she trusted anyone save Andarios to give her the answers. "What about pleasure?"

Andarios tsk'd as they entered the shadow of trees. "We can have one of life's simplest pleasures, right now." He clicked his tongue and pulled at his reins. "Race you to the falls!" Then he and his horse rushed forward.

Kezerah cursed, and nudged Soot into a full-forced wobbling gallop. Bramble creaked, and small animals darted past the oncoming horse and pony, their riders loud with laughter. A tight ball of tension unfurled in Kezerah's stomach, and she knew she'd made the right choice in seeking out Andarios.

By the time she reached the clearing, where Andarios waited for her, she was ready to trample him. He stood near the falls, at the cliff base of the mountain. The jagged edges of amethyst deposits glimmered behind the splash and roar of water as he dismounted and bent over the pool to drink alongside his horse.

"About time. I thought maybe you'd gone back to the castle to practice boring desirability," he teased. She kneeled next to him, pretending to get water herself. The water's temperature was a cold shock in her hands. Andarios let out a yelp as she flung the water at him and soaked the side of his tunic and face. Her laugh turned into a shriek as a much larger scoop of water drenched her stained wool dress.

She splashed back, then scooped newly made mud into her hands, threatening him with it. He lazily outstretched a long arm and pushed it back on her, and she tossed the remaining slop at him. Mud splattered everywhere; the horse and pony inched back from the crazed animals flinging icy water and soil sludge at each other.

Someone slipped, or was pushed—the story changed later between them several times—and both had to drag themselves out of the chilled pool. Teeth clattered as they looked at one another, then laughed, and mounted their horses to head back to the castle, the sky darkening into dusk.

SHOUTS ECHOED through the empty Autumn corridor, unintelligible as they bounced from wall to wall. Ambrose liked to think he wasn't often surprised, but doubled back at a shrill sound coming from a grand door. A grand *locked* door. He looked about once more. Not a soul in sight. A patterned rug ran the length of the passage with nothing but lanterns hooked on spiraled iron, leading to the main feasting hall. So the door must not be regularly locked or guarded. Which meant someone had locked it for privacy.

"Hello," Ambrose cooed at the ornate lock. The metal mechanism inside clicked in reply. "What a flirt," he chuckled, and allowed the door to slowly yawn ajar. A large foyer stretched forth, making the residents inside look small by comparison. Princess Kezerah—if he could even be sure, she was so caked in mud—stood shivering near the tall youth she'd sat next to at last night's feast. Though perhaps Ambrose was mistaken, as the amount of mud rendered his white hair nearly invisible beneath it all.

The boy stood with his head bowed in submission, the opposite of Kezerah who towered beside him, despite her petite stature. Arms crossed and poised in defense, she aimed herself at a bell of gold and onyx. Then Ambrose understood the shrill sound from before had belonged to Queen Elize, her elaborate ball gown as stiff as her posture.

"Were you expecting to just waltz into the dining hall like some wild animal?" the queen demanded. "Accompanied solely by an unpaired suitor?"

Kezerah seemed unbothered. "Andarios isn't a suitor. He's my friend, and training to be my personal guard, meaning he will one day have to accompany me solely, everywhere."

"Your guard is undecided," the queen said, exasperated. "Did you not once think how this would look?" Ambrose himself pondered how it looked for a moment and wondered if these had been the 'responsibilities' he'd been jilted for. He shifted his position, uncomfortable with the idea that someone might not have chosen him over *mud*. Kezerah harrumphed.

"Who would care? If anything, it keeps me out of your way."

"Kezerah, you're ridiculous. Everyone would care. You're supposed to be our next queen. I have a guest quarter filled with nobility and I will either need to explain your absence, or walk a bog monster into my banquet hall, claiming she's related to me."

"I'll make the decision for you, *Mother*." The word mother seemed to replaced a much nastier word. "I'll skip dinner. No need for you to conduct two nights worth of late entrances."

"Then your friend can miss his meal, too." Queen Elize turned her attention towards the boy. "If you expect to be a personal guard to a princess, I suggest you start acting like it. If you prefer dalliances in the mud you can return to Luka where you belong."

Kezerah moved in front of her friend, her posture changed to one more optimal for combat rather than a conversation. "He goes nowhere."

Ambrose only registered Elize's steps toward Kezerah after she took them. In a blink she'd caught her daughter's jaw between her fingers. Ambrose straightened, thinking perhaps he should intervene. Her voice grew low, and he strained to hear, deciding his next move. "Continue to defy me and you'll have no idea where he goes."

Kezerah jerked her face from her mother's grasp and Ambrose released his breath. She remained silent and still, eyes glittering with violence. Queen Elize turned without another word—towards the door Ambrose lurked in. Not bothering with the lock, he backed up and rushed a retreat to the banquet hall.

He found his place next to Rorrik, already consuming the appetizers strewn across the long wooden slab of a table. Rorrik had luckily seated them closer to one of the crackling fires. Ambrose hadn't wanted to admit it, but the climate here proved far colder than he was used to. He kept wanting to remove the boots he'd bought upon entering Heartsglove. He preferred bare feet to leather, but the floors stung with early winter frost. The hall also featured high vaulted rafters to accommodate the large trees and glass domed ceiling, making it somewhat drafty.

Ikaika sat far down the table. Dyllian, the lord Ambrose had antagonized this morning, spoke to him out of earshot. Ikaika's calm demeanor seemed ruthlessly polite, and Ambrose wondered what he actually thought. He probably enjoyed Dyllian; they could be boring and remote together.

Rorrik stabbed a boiled egg with too much force. "Where's your princess?"

"Either committing matricide or bathing." The queen sat herself at the table, her composure regained. "I suppose the latter."

Rorrik sighed at his brother's cryptic answer. "Well at least you can't abandon me again to sit alone, while you flirt."

Ambrose shrugged. "You could have joined us."

"Ugh, and listen to you tell her what other body parts of hers you find to be a blessing? Yeah, no thanks." Rorrik reached for bread now being passed around. "Not to mention Ikaika joining you. Isn't she supposed to prevent wars?"

That part of the morning had not been particularly fun. While Kezerah had become more interesting, the mood of the moment had definitely suffered from his brother's stiff postured presence.

"We need to attempt to get along with him," Ambrose answered finally, and he cut off Rorrik's response before he could start. "Not befriend him, not bring him home and ask father if we can keep him, just not antagonize him. It creates the wrong narrative."

"It makes you look bad in front of the Princess you mean."

"The Princess that could lead us to our ruin, yes."

Rorrik groaned. "Fine. I'll attempt to not kill him."

"Thank you."

"What are the chances I get a dance with one of those twins?" Apparently bored by his inability to fight his brother, Rorrik nodded at the two giggling blondes.

"I'd say about half."

"Half? What, now you want a princess *and* a twin?"

Ambrose rolled his eyes. "Half because I definitely saw the one on the left kissing one of the noble ladies in the garden earlier today."

"Ah. Half a chance it is then."

"Careful though," Ambrose said, "they're Glassberrys."

Rorrik raised brows then looked them over once more, his face spread into a grin. "I should have known."

"Yes," Ambrose agreed, amused by the resemblance. "At least your taste in women is consistent."

"My taste?" Rorrik argued. "Safeya of Jai was your—"

"Shh, not here." Ambrose eyed the princess' friends to make sure they were not overheard. "I don't know if that particular fact will be useful to have spread right now."

Rorrik squashed a hand to his cheek, properly chastised and prickly. Impressed by his brother's attempt at good behavior, Ambrose tried for peace. "I'll ask after the other twin's availability. Maybe you can work on your diplomacy by honing a bit more charm."

"I'm plenty charming!" Rorrik said, the irony of his tone making even him laugh.

Ambrose took a long sip of his cider. "As you say. I'll stay out of it then."

"Well…" Rorrik said with uncertainty, looking back over at the sisters. "If given the chance, put in a good word for me."

Ambrose nodded, watching as Ikaika, for a fourth time, looked over at the two empty seats to his left, where the princess and her friend had sat the previous night. Ikaika then looked their way, as if assessing him to see if Ambrose had stored his friends somewhere. The blatant suspicion astounded him. Ambrose smiled back at Ikaika to combat his irritation, hoping it looked feral, before remembering he had just told Rorrik not to taunt him. Ikaika's expression didn't change, instead he simply turned back to his conversation with Dyllian as if he'd never left it.

"Easier said than done, isn't it?" Rorrik said.

Ambrose didn't need to look over; he could hear the smug smile. "Well," he said, pleased as the main courses finally made an appearance, "perhaps distance is the better route traveled."

Dress for Stealth

Kezerah pulled on black hide leggings and searched around her wardrobe for a top, while Andarios stood outside her door.

"What are you looking for?" he groaned.

"Something black, something so I can't be easily seen."

"I wish I could go," he said, let down.

"I know. Me too."

Once washed, they had deliberated on whether or not Andarios accompanying her on her late night adventure was worth the risk. They decided, if caught so close to this recent offense, the risk was too high. Kezerah enjoyed taunting her mother, but not at the expense of her friend. She fumed at the threat of sending him away. However, it had also fueled her desire to sneak into the city. Appearing less soft to Ambrose wouldn't hurt either; she preferred to be the most trouble in the room and sensed her crown threatened.

"You could borrow one of my shirts?" Andarios suggested from the hall.

"That would be the same as me wearing a dress."

He chuckled. "Ugh, don't make me laugh, it makes my stomach hurt."

Guilt washed over her and she promised herself she would smuggle back food tonight. Maybe she could ask Ikaika to bring some? That sparked a different idea. "Oh! I'll be right back."

She ignored her friend's complaints as she darted to her balcony door and flung it open, expertly making the jump to the adjacent terrace. Ikaika's doors were unlocked and she stepped into the dark space. The smell of lavender wafted through her nose as she opened his wardrobe and rifled through. She found a smaller leather jerkin regularly worn with a tunic, but she liked the way it hugged her figure as she laced the front, navel to chest. She crept back to her side of the courtyard as nothing but a whisper.

"Whoa, I'm pretty sure that top was not in your closet." Andarios said, taking her in as she joined him in the hallway.

"I'm pretty sure I'll be keeping it in order to remedy my wardrobe's ailment."

Andarios laughed as Kezerah did an over-dramatic spin.

"Something tells me you won't have to persuade Ikaika to keep it." His words sounded like a joke she wasn't in on, which baffled her. Footsteps interrupted them from down the hall and they separated. Kezerah tossed a nightgown over her attire, hastily laid down, and waited.

The door opened, then after a pause, shut again.

Kezerah flung the large gown off and slipped into her supple riding boots the moment her night nurse had done her last round of check-ins (muttering to herself as she settled in front of the door). Kezerah returned to Ikaika's balcony, looking up at the climb she had before her.

A shadowy silhouette stood in Ikaika's threshold. She scrambled back, intaking a breath before realizing it was Ikaika himself in the doorframe.

"Since when do you sneak up on me?" She asked, trying to steady her heart and breathing.

He seemed unbothered, movements agile as he came towards her. "Since you decided to sneak out with my brother, who may or may not be a murderer, after just meeting him," he said the words matter of factly, but Kezerah caught the iron in his tone.

"I didn't think you'd want to come. And how did you even find out?"

"Andarios' mouth is as big as his appetite. When he didn't show at dinner I brought him my left overs. He mentioned it immediately. As for wanting to come, I don't, but I also don't trust him. So I'm coming with you."

He walked over to his bed, pulling a neatly folded outfit from under his pillow.

"Turn around," he commanded.

She whirled to let him change, immensely relieved Andarios had gotten to eat before her return.

"Wait, how did you get past Nurse?" she asked, turning in surprise as the thought occurred to her.

Ikaika pulled at the shirt half over his head. The moonlight shone to expose honed muscles defining his lithe frame. He glared at her, dragging a long-sleeved tunic the rest of the way down. She blushed and looked away. "Oops, sorry."

"You can turn around now," he said sardonically. "The damage is done, and I didn't have to 'get past' Nimah. I asked her."

"Oh," she said, still trying to shake Ikaika's muscles from her head.

"So, how are we getting out of here?" he asked, surveying his balcony.

They looked down together; the ground below a sharp drop to a stone floor, the cherry blossom tree thick and gnarled but too far away to be useful. The courtyard was completely walled in from the ground up, and just above it was the night sky and a guard's parapet.

She pointed. "See up there? There's a blind spot at that turret. If we keep low, the guards on the main towers won't see us and we can sneak from Summer to Winter." She went on, ignoring the slow shake of Ikaika's head. "If we time it right, the grounds near the Autumn Quarter should be fairly quiet, seeing as it's just a whole bunch of old people who have to get their beauty sleep in order to write tax plans in the morning."

Ikaika eyed the parapet, looming half an oak's length above them. "Alright, let's go—wait, is that my shirt?" Ikaika truly looked her over for the first time, no longer distracted by their escape plans. He kept looking.

Kezerah grinned at him. "It was. Did you want it back?" She pretended to untie the front to see what he'd do next.

"No, keep it," he sputtered, averting his eyes. Mauve undertones tinged his neck and face.

"I was hoping you would say that," she chimed, pleased they were back on even footing. She jumped onto the ledge and grabbed a jutting stone.

Her arms ached from pulling her weight. The idea of plummeting to the ground assured she tested her footholds a bit more carefully than she normally would. After she reached the ledge of the battlement, she turned to wait for Ikaika, hand outstretched. Yet, as soon as she moved out of his way, he bounded to the top. Kezerah inspected him for sweat, and wiped away her own furiously.

Sentries moved in regimented steps across the towers surrounding their own. They ducked low. Steps light. Once in the corridor at the bottom of the stairs, they ran along the hall. Twice they escaped into rooms to dodge servants until the path cleared. Kezerah motioned for Ikaika to follow her into a small antechamber, bone cold from the open window and unlit fire. She ducked behind a tapestry and they were inside an inclosed space, inner walls pressing against them.

"Where in Thrice..." Ikaika said under his breath. They slid, shoulder to shoulder. His arm brushed hers and she focused on answering him.

"It's the Strategy Chambers," she whispered. She paused in her lead and looked down. Then she crouched, and Ikaika joined her. With a nil amount of arm span, she nudged into him. Her cheek grew feverishly hot against his as she guided him to look through the small hole. "See? It's actually where Dar and I first saw you."

Ikaika didn't respond at first, taking his time to cast an eye through the spyhole. "First impressions?"

His breath added to the warmth around them. Her legs ached from crouching too long. She shifted and her knee bumped his. "Warm," she said, "erm—nice, I mean. You seemed nice." She couldn't look at him, the close quarters would force their noses to brush. She scooted away and stood. "Come on, we'd better keep going."

The spy wall led to a similar space to the first. They raced across the abandoned Winter Quarter's corridors and scurried down the stairs.

"We'll go around the back side of the Autumn Quarters, to the outer verandas and balconies." Kezerah noted that Ikaika's mouth had firmed into a straight line. He wordlessly followed her as she inched along the castle wall, dodging windows and servants doing late night tasks. Then a riot of light, sound and people boomed into view. Music drifted as guests mingled on lantern lit terraces. Cool night air accompanied chimes of laughter. Most of the Solstice Court was awake in the Autumn Salon.

"So much for the beauty sleep and tax plans."

Kezerah nodded. "I bet the tax plans still happen. They'll just look terrible while they're writing them." She changed course and dove behind one of four pillars leading out to the cobbled veranda and footpath to the Solstice Gate.

She heard Ambrose's deep laugh, and risked a peek from behind the pillar. He was formally dressed, talking to Rorrik, Dyllian, and Yara Sorrel. Dyllian bobbed his head eagerly, listening to Ambrose's every word. After a moment more, Ambrose excused himself towards the drink table, and his eyes met Kezerah's. She was pleased to see shock amongst the depths of green. Good. He had underestimated her. He grabbed a glass goblet of rich crimson and in three strides made it to her pillar, leaning against it as if relaxing from socializing. "Alright, I admit, I was not expecting to see you tonight."

"Was it not you who invited me here just this morning?" she asked prettily. "Something about seeking you out if I grew curious?"

He smiled and swirled his wine. "Yes, thank you for the reminder, how foolish of me." He risked a glance at her. "Though after your mother's wrath this evening, I'll really have to show you the best of your city to make it worthwhile." He finished what was in his glass. "A moment while I grab my cloak."

Before she could respond he pushed himself off the pillar and sauntered towards the stairs. Ikaika remained quiet by her side, giving her a puzzled look.

"What?" she asked.

He cocked an eyebrow. "You don't think it's odd he knew what happened with your mother this evening?"

Kezerah paused for a moment, realizing she hadn't caught the remark. "Well, you knew about it, and I hadn't told you yet."

Ikaika narrowed his eyes. "Yes, we'll just ask Dar if he was chitchatting with the crown Prince of Xenkesh. I'm sure that checks out."

"My mother probably just complained about it. Lady Sorrel is her cousin and an absolute gossip."

Ikaika didn't answer, his mind made up to be untrusting of Ambrose.

Kezerah peeked back around the pillar. Ambrose now wore a black cloak over his otherwise colorful attire. He bowed to the crowd. The Lady Sorrel pouted in a way that Kezerah thought made her chin retract like a turtle, but Ambrose didn't catch it as he turned to speak in Rorrik's ear. Rorrik's expression soured, then he looked beyond Ambrose towards her pillar. Kezerah withdrew too late, sure that their eyes had met.

"Alright, let's go," Ambrose said as he rejoined them.

"I think Rorrik might have spotted me," Kezerah apologized.

Ambrose looked back, but Rorrik had already charged off, Dyllian not far behind. "I wouldn't worry about him. He won't say anything." He cast his eyes Ikaika's way and frowned. But instead of something snide, he let out a shiver, pulling his cloak closer to him.

"Cold?" Ikaika asked mildly.

"The sun actually bothers to grace my kingdom," Ambrose said, rolling his shoulders in irritation. "I'm ill-accustomed to harsh climates."

"So, you're cold then."

"Yes, Ikaika of Alora, I'm cold," Ambrose snapped.

Kezerah gave Ikaika an irritated stare but he pointedly inspected the pebbled path. She cut them off before they began arguing about the weather.

"Shall we attempt to get to Heartsglove tonight?"

Ambrose moved his arm in a sweeping gesture as he answered with grandeur. "The lead is yours."

She took the lead and guided them towards her maze. The escape hatch she'd created stirred up a giddy satisfaction inside her and she wanted to see their expressions. However, upon reaching the hedges, Ambrose pulled her back, a hand on her shoulder. "Where are you going?"

"To the maze," Kezerah said. "There's a break in the wall, by the barracks." His expression remained confused. She explained further. "They won't just let me through."

Ikaika's attention fixed itself onto the hand at her shoulder, he moved closer.

Ambrose exhaled through his nose. "You didn't bring anything to disguise yourself?"

She gestured down at her outfit. "I dressed for stealth."

Ambrose's gaze slowly followed her hands down her neck, chest, torso, and legs. He grunted, clearing his throat. "Very stealthy, Princess. If we ever need to escape a brothel, you're our girl."

Kezerah glared, pointing at her hair. "It's not like this—" then to her eyes. "—nor these don't instantly give me away."

Ambrose sighed, removing his cloak and draping it across her shoulders, it was warm, heavy, and had a rich scent, peppered and savory. He pushed her hair back so it didn't fall from the opening. This extracted a blush from her and she tried to keep her face even.

Ambrose turned to Ikaika. "You're not Bonded? You can't Mirage?" It sounded more like an accusation than a question.

Ikaika looked confused, then annoyed. "No, I'm not Bonded—and I'm only eighteen this past Winter, so I've not trained my *Melding* yet."

Ambrose's face soured. "Mind Melding. I should have guessed." A person had an equal chance of either parent's magickal gifts, or none at all if neither parent held enough magick. Ambrose's exhale seemed to let go of some vestige of hope they might still have common ground. He turned away from Ikaika and scrunched his brow in concentration, palm raised to Kezerah's face. Kezerah took an involuntary step back. Nobody had used Bond magick on her before. She braced herself, unsure what she braced for.

"There," Ambrose said, finished. "Problem solved, but stay close." He walked ahead.

Kezerah followed after him. "Wait, what did you do? I feel the same." She whirled around. "Am I invisible?" Ikaika gave an uncharacteristic snort from behind her, and she turned to him. "Am I?"

He studied her, then caught the difference. "No, he's not that powerful it would seem, or inventive."

Ambrose stopped in his tracks. "I'll have you know Mirages are not easy. Most can't accomplish more than sparks in the air."

Mirages were, in Kezerah's opinion, an unfair perk that other magick users had no equivalent for. She loved when traveling circuses hosting Bonded performers came to visit. They always had at least one capable of both commanding objects and creating the fabulous displays that lit the sky with color and light. This element of Bond magick still stumped the great scholars of Bethync, though Kezerah hadn't cared much about the mechanics.

She looked down at herself again, trying to find the difference and imagining how bursts of color could make her less noticeable.

Ikaika took pity on her. "It's your eyes, he changed them."

Her mouth dropped open. "Changed them?" She looked over at Ambrose. His expression grew less offended at her awe. "To what?" she asked, with excitement. "What color are they?"

Ambrose's smile was bright, showing all his teeth. "The second best color to your own, of course." Before she could ask, he continued walking.

Ikaika caught up with Ambrose's stride easily, his own cloak's hood up now as to not be recognized. Kezerah trotted behind. The gate loomed closer, and she was glad for the distraction as Ambrose explained, slowing his pace.

"My father is a master of Mirages. He can create impeccable details with color and light to facade images across one's face." He gave Ikaika a pointed look. "It's incredibly difficult, and only those with a powerful Bond can manage even the simplest mirage."

Kezerah opened her mouth, stuffed with questions, but the gate grew nearer, and she kept silent. Guards stood high up on the watchtowers, and Kezerah's heart pitter-pattered. She recognized many of them. This was it, they would ask her to drop her hood and they'd all be caught.

"Names?" The guards demanded.

Ambrose spoke in a confident voice that she now associated with strangers; it was friendly and upbeat. "Ambrose and Rorrik of Xenkesh, and Sword Master Azalea of Xenkesh."

He walked as if the gates would simply open for him regardless of their masters. He was right, the guards didn't even bother a glance. The large steel and wood gates groaned open to allow them to exit.

Kezerah lifted her foot to take her first step outside the Solstice Court. Her pulse quickened and palms dampened as she clenched them. Her parents would be furious. She couldn't even picture their reactions, the idea was so unprecedented. It had been drilled into her head again and again. Their words rang in her ears: she was the heir, her life was precious, Elastor would be lost without her. *They* would be lost without her. It was why she had tried swordplay, in the hopes of showing her parents she could look after herself. If only swordplay hadn't been *boring*. Everything she was meant to be was boring. How had she managed it so well in her past lives, when now it was as if she had been hand-crafted to ruin it all?

"We don't have to go. We can go back to our rooms." Ikaika's expression was earnest. His voice sounded so reasonable, so—safe.

Kezerah planted her boot on the hard packed earth. She looked past Ikaika, to Ambrose, who was ahead once more. She made her next step more deliberate.

Ambrose's smile quirked up on one side. Her next step summoned a full-on grin.

She grinned back, and walked with ease. "No, I'm alright. I just want to make sure each step counts."

Heartsglove

THE WALK INTO HEARTSGLOVE FOLLOWED A LONG TRAIL down hills of crops, with the moon hidden behind clouds high above. Kezerah shivered as they reached the Lunar Channel. She had never seen it up close. The arch of the bridge exaggerated in order to allow for small boats to pass through. Lunar lilies were planted along the sides, snaking across the railings with closed bulbs, while muted stones clung to the river bottom.

They passed over the bridge, clouds spooled away like wisps of incense and the moon unveiled itself. Moonlight spread to brighten the river rocks below, revealing them as ice opals that glittered and brightened the Lunar Channel's pathway. The river, a mirror reflection of the night sky, stretched endlessly in either direction. Petals unfurled, their movements fragile; the bridge brightened, giving the scene a milky, luminescent glow as blooming lilies sparkled like stars.

Ambrose jumped at the unexpected shimmer of light, inspecting both the flowers and the twinkling opals. He appeared enraptured, and none of them spoke. A light zinged through the open sky. All three took in the sight before continuing slowly across the bridge. Kezerah used the time to steady her pulse. How many times had she looked out across the channel as others hurried on by, never appreciating what it was to be able to take in the sight? Soon, the moonlight was no longer necessary for visibility, as vibrant lights from wooden houses, lantern-strewn streets, and colorful glowing orbs lit their path. The futility of steadying her heart rang in her ears as they approached. Sounds roared around them as if the great hall had been intensified tenfold. Kezerah picked up bits of yelling, conversation, and laughter from every direction. Anxiety probed at her excitement as they drew nearer to the Heartsglove estate and the crowds beyond.

The Heartsglove estate house stood at the entrance to the city. While twice the size of the rest of the stacked buildings, it was manicured to match the rest of the city in style: wood brushed with yellow, featuring criss-crossing slats and ivy trellises up its sides. Hydrangea bushes lined the stone gates, giving the manor a welcoming appearance. It was a relief to know the Lords of Heartsglove were not in residence tonight, but in the Solstice Court. As her mother's closest friends, Kezerah was unable to believe—disguised though she was—that they would not recognize her upon close inspection and report back to their queen.

Kezerah shrugged off the shackles that bound her to the castle walls in a rush of freedom. The feeling surpassed any exhilaration possible by cider or wine.

Music played in several pockets and side alleys, the jumble creating an out-of-tune cacophony. She was all at once alive and incredibly overwhelmed. Crowds pushed past her, and she grabbed Ikaika's hand in order to not lose her companions among the masses.

A sultry, high voice coming from a bearded merchant caught her off guard, as they flung large jewels in her face. "My dear, you're practically naked without this necklace! Would you like to try it on?"

Before she could answer she was dragged forward, and a man cut a fish's head off and jammed a stick in its decapitated body. "Fresh fish! Just in from Aveltra today!" While the abrupt assassination of the fish had not been alluring, the salt and herbs pressed into it were, and her stomach protested her rejection. She grasped Ikaika's hand tighter. His hand squeezed back in return; his head turned away from her as he trailed Ambrose's easy gait.

She watched as Ikaika nudged Ambrose's shoulder and she tensed, fearing an altercation, but then he said something to Ambrose she couldn't hear over the noise. Ikaika's other hand pinched the stem of his nose in pain. He must be Melding by accident. She asked him if he was okay, but her voice was drowned out by the crowd. Whatever he said, Ambrose nodded, and they turned a corner, the noise muffled by the walls of the two buildings. They kept walking until a dimly lit tapestry doorway came into view. It seemed too small to be their destination, but Ambrose ducked inside. The air that greeted them past the threshold was thick and warm with the smells of well-spiced foods. Kezerah's stomach shuddered in response. Relief flooded her when they took a seat at a back table, her ears still ringing from the loud streets.

"Ikaika reminded me that you skipped dinner and might want to eat before exploring," Ambrose said, expression mildly guilty. "I apologize, I forgot."

A tavern server came over and poured pitchers of water. Kezerah drank gratefully, although it was a tad warm. The server turned, and looked brightly over at Ambrose. "You're back!"

Ambrose smiled. "I said I would be."

Kezerah cataloged the smile as a true one. She looked between the two of them. "You... know each other?"

"I stopped here on the way into court," he answered. "Kofi's family serves curry just as good as home."

The server, Kofi, beamed. "I'll add the extra spice, just how you like it!" They winked, then left the table before taking the rest of their orders.

"I thought you were late because your ships couldn't dock?" Kezerah reminded him, catching the lie.

Ambrose shrugged. "I wasn't about to show up late to a feast announcing I'd already eaten."

Kezerah looked back at the server, hoping to catch their attention again to order.

"Food is coming," Ambrose assured. "They only serve one thing here. That's how you know they serve it well." He grinned over at Ikaika, neither a stranger's nor a friend's smile. "Impressive since Kofi is half Aloran."

While the words were clearly a taunt, Kezerah sensed Ambrose attempting humor and let it slide. She turned to Ikaika, "Are you alright?"

He had his hand still pinched at the bridge of his nose, but he nodded. "It's easing. I just need a moment."

She chose not to distract him further. Ambrose looked across the table and eyed his brother's condition. "What's wrong with him?" he stage-whispered.

"Mind Melding," she explained. "It used to only happen when he slept, but it's gotten harder to control as we've gotten older." She looked back over at Ikaika, hoping for permission to continue. He was as still as stone, and she decided to explain vaguely as a compromise.

"His mind has natural... barriers," she tried. "When he's ready, he'll go to the monks in the mountains of Estora and they'll help him control the barriers so he can weaken and strengthen them as needed. Right now they're going through a bit of a—" Kezerah whirled her hand in the air, seeking a kind description for Ikaika's intermittent agony, "—growth spurt, so he's trying to control them himself."

Ambrose nodded, eyes concentrated on Ikaika. "He seems pretty ready right now. Is it not possible to go to the mountains earlier?"

Kezerah shook her head, now uncertain if she should explain further. The reason he was unable to enter Alora, where the monks lived, was due to seeking Haven... from Xenkesh. "Not currently."

The food arrived. The smell of spices consumed Kezerah. The thick sauce reminded her of the color of changing leaves, with bits of butter roasted chicken mixed into rice and peppers. Her first bite of the robust stew dazzled her senses. She tossed her head back, *Mmming* in approval. Her nose ignited with a flare of heat, and she grabbed for her water. Ambrose laughed and prevented her, instead handing her a thick milk.

"Water will make the heat worse, drink this." The sweet cream extinguished the blaze in her throat. Then, she dove back in for more. Ikaika ate some, but surrendered his portion over to her—along with his half smile—when she gave it a look of longing. He seemed to be better, though his eyes looked glazed from rubbing them. Kofi came back over, pleased with their clean bowls.

"If you plan to do some exploring, watch out for radicals," they warned. "Especially you Alorans."

"Aloran," Ambrose corrected the plural and handed over a silver piece.

Kofi giggled. "Sure, well whatever you are, just make sure you use coin." They turned to Kezerah and Ikaika. "It's just three coppers for newcomers."

Kezerah stared. "I—I forgot coins." Who came to a city without coin? Someone who never had to use them, she supposed. She blushed at her foolishness.

Ikaika reached into his pockets and put a medley of silver and gold coins down in front of her. She looked over at him to object, but he raised a hand. "You can pay me back later. I'm not shopping tonight."

Kezerah smiled, not sure if she would buy anything, but liking the option. Kofi handed her back the change.

"Shall we explore then?" Ambrose said, rising as if it had already been decided.

Ikaika and Kezerah stood, but Ikaika winced upon getting up. His skin appeared chalky, sweat dewed at his forehead.

"Kai?"

He shook his head, eyes tightly shut. "I'm fine."

He didn't look fine. Kezerah bit her lip, conflicted on what to do.

He gave a pained smile. "I know how badly you want to see the shops." He tapped his temple grimacing. "It's okay. It's not like I'm not used to it."

She felt all the more guilty for him hearing her thoughts on shopping but not on the concern for his health. He seemed to notice his admission had made it worse and tried to give his smirk, which was dampened by the pain in his dark eyes. "We should go back."

"No," Ikaika breathed. "Not through the crowds again—" He clenched his teeth. "I mean, maybe I just need a moment."

"Perhaps staying behind is an option?" Ambrose offered. While friendly on the surface, it was his stranger's grin.

Ikaika didn't buy it either. "If you think I'm leaving her alone in a city—"

Ambrose rolled his eyes, crossing his large arms. "Alone? That's a bit dramatic. And it's her city. She'll come back in one piece. Or she can sit here and drink lassis all night, since she obviously won't let you wreck your mind for a night out."

"She is also standing here," Kezerah said, annoyed. "And unless you can actually make her invisible, you can address her directly."

Ambrose looked abashed and tried again. "Kezerah, would you like me to safely escort you through the city, while my brother recovers from his headache?"

"Migraine," she amended automatically.

"Migraine," he corrected amiably.

She looked back at Ikaika. "I can't stop you from coming with us, but I saw how much pain you were in. It's either you stay here, or we both do. Or," she added as a third option, "we can go back to the castle."

Ikaika kept his eyes closed for a long time. He looked up at Ambrose, then back to Kezerah.

Kezerah squared her shoulders. Friends were one thing, chaperones another. She could do this, she *wanted* this.

He gave a sharp nod. "Then I'll stay here."

"I'll be quick," she promised, and he sat back down, covering his eyes with his cloak once more.

AMBROSE DID NOT TAKE Kezerah's hand but slowed his pace to stay with her as she moved through the streets. People swerved and shoved as they passed by. Children rushed around Kezerah's legs, eager to obtain a front row seat to a nearby puppet show. Aloran symbols covered the puppeteers' caravan, but a Sway translator enticed the children into a story as they all sat down. Everyone talked and moved with ease, in element with the chaos all around them. Her people, her city. She straightened, mimicking the confidence that swirled around her until her illusion of mettle eased into a shaky self-assurance. *'My people, my city, my people, my—'*

A streak of heat brushed against her cheek, followed by a whoosh and sound of applause. Ambrose drew her back. Her eyes adjusted, and she watched a man juggle—in a far more complex routine than Kezerah was capable of—sticks set ablaze. The fire swung in wild movements as he entertained a crowd in the middle of the road.

Ambrose's body was close, an arm secured around her. She tried to pretend his hold was normal, that the hand at her waist didn't make her want to lean closer. His scent was heady, like the smoke of the fires that spun around them. They watched the performance a moment longer, and Kezerah knew she did so from greed. She angled her head to speak. He bent low to hear. "Is it always this crowded?"

He shook his head. "Right now they have Night Markets once a week, earlier and earlier leading up to the Nighttide festival." Drums started up nearby. He pulled her in closer to hear him. "Kofi also mentioned it grows less tame as the night goes on."

A flash and flurry of colorful scarves caught Kezerah's eye, and she looked over to see dancers intrude on the crowd, dividing their attention further. They moved and twisted to the rhythm played, hypnotizing Kezerah although she didn't recognize the steps. A few of the dancers were clearly Xenkeshi, as they summoned sparks and rolled their hips—laid bare despite the chill—but many, Kezerah could tell, were Elastian. Their hands Swayed sensually up high-collared necks, summoning spectators forward. She felt a sting of otherness. Ambrose had stated that this was her city, but it was all completely new to her. She didn't even know what type of dances they did. She asked Ambrose, who despite just getting here, seemed to know Heartsglove better than she did.

"The dances have no steps, but perhaps another time I can show you how they're done." His eyes twinkled. She could sense he was having far too much fun seeing her out of her element. She unraveled herself from his arms—and warmth—patches of cold circling her skin from the absence of his touch.

Then, two figures hopped onto the roof of the caravan. Entranced by the dancers, Kezerah paid them no mind until they began shouting over the music.

"Fair wages for fair work!"

"No coin, no crops!"

Kezerah tilted her head. She knew farmers were paid for their crops. She had the hour long dronings of Monk Biloba in her head to prove it.

"I don't know why they'd say that," she told Ambrose, almost embarrassed at the admission. "We have a system." She did not mention she hadn't a clue how it worked, but it existed.

Ambrose opened and closed his mouth. He spoke slowly. "I don't believe they are referring to Elastians paying unfairly." Kezerah's mind buzzed. She'd already botched the banana to silk trade, and now feared saying something to disgrace herself further. Ambrose rushed on after noting what must have been vivid panic across her face.

"Alorans. They pay through trade. I'm no master of coin but I can see how it might cause...tension."

"Oh, I—" Kezerah stumbled over her words, she had a million but the treaty swiftly diminished them down to three. "We should go." Gratefully, Ambrose didn't press her. They continued on, speaking of anything but the continuous riot building behind them.

Despite his vague answer from earlier, Ambrose, as a guide, proved to be quite useful. His stride through the streets marked the confidence of someone used to exploring. She glanced up at him while he spoke familiarly with a textile merchant. Unsure if he knew them or had started up conversation to allow her time to peruse, she did so.

She admired the patterns woven into the tapestries and blankets. She detested weaving, giving it up first among her many hobbies, but these stunning sharp lines and intricate motifs made her wish she had been more interested—before she remembered just how tedious the act was.

"My father loves weaving," Ambrose stated, joining her in her perusal. "Every Yuletide he makes my brother and I something new. So we hang it in our rooms for the year to show how much we like it."

Kezerah would not have guessed this gesture from her image of the King of Xenkesh. "Is he quite skilled then?" she asked, running a hand down a tightly woven basket.

"Summerlands no, not at all." Ambrose laughed, spinning a hanging plant in a yellow and red sling. "He just likes making us things and getting them in return. Though I'd rather just buy him something, as the sight of a loom makes me cringe." He paused at a memory, and the thought quirked his lips. "Better not bring that up, though. Ror and I haven't gotten around to mentioning it."

Kezerah laughed, the idea of three Xenkeshi warlords exchanging Yuletide gifts and hiding poorly made loom crafts a humanizing image. She realized that, until this point, she wouldn't have been able to picture it, and decided that needed to change.

She took his arm, guiding him out of the shop. "Well, then we best find different souvenirs for you to bring home. We wouldn't want him to think you believe Elastian weaving superior."

A stall hosted an array of portraits. Kezerah rolled her eyes, seeing her image in varying sizes. Each one holding the same expression. Bored, with lips slanted in an attempt to smile after hours of sitting in the stagnant throne room. A young man at the entrance, not much older than herself, held a large framed painting up to sell.

"Get a real portrait of the Soul Heir! No imitations! Painted in person at the Solstice Court!"

Ambrose paused, his grin grew wide at her expression.

"Don't you dare."

He moved past the boy and into the open-air shop.

"Hello there! Welcome! Welcome!" Came the shopkeeper, an older man, his slicked-back hair and sharp beard both as oiled as his paintings. He looked vaguely familiar and Kezerah realized he must be the same artist who had come to court. She withheld a groan. He had been both cranky and persistent. "See anything you like?"

Ambrose gave Kezerah a sly look as he took up a smaller version of her portrait. "That I do. How much for this lovely piece?"

"Ah, you have good taste," said the artist turned merchant. "Ten gold."

Ambrose arched his brow. "Ten?"

Kezerah stared at the picture of herself, pocket-sized and smirking. Her cheeks flushed as Ambrose examined it further. He looked over at her before turning back to the man and answered. "Would you take five?"

"Five!" Both Kezerah and the artist chorused. Quick to parry, Kezerah added. "I think ten is perfectly fair."

"It's very small," Ambrose said nonchalantly. "Not to mention, it's simply a bust. You don't happen to have a full-figure portrait do you?"

The artist and Kezerah looked at one another, equally exasperated. "I'm afraid not," the man said. "The princess is..." Kezerah raised a brow, curious as to what she was. The artist looked her over, lost for words, then she watched as recognition lit his eyes. "You..."

Kezerah grabbed Ambrose's hand. "We best be going."

"But I haven't—" Ambrose started.

"You're right," Kezerah said, "she's only worth about five. Thank you!" She pulled at Ambrose's arm. She might as well have tried to drag a castle wall. He looked down at her, bewildered. "I was joking. I'll pay the ten." He grinned down at her. "Twenty if it were that outfit—"

"I—I know you," the man said, his voice unbelieving of his own words.

"You must be mistaken," Kezerah said, and was relieved to find Ambrose also took a step back as he came to terms with the situation.

"I painted your every freckle, the curve of your jaw, the light of your eyes." His face turned from awe to something akin to fear. Panic. "What are you *doing* here?" His voice became urgent. "You—You can't be out here. You could be harmed, killed." The last word brought his true fear to his lips. "You could kill us all!"

"Da," the young man from outside the stall came in, clearly embarrassed, "what are you talking about?"

"Arth, get the guards. She's the Soul Heir," the artist demanded. "She needs proper protection." The look given to Ambrose inferred that he had been deemed ill-suited for the role. The son merely stared at his father, wide eyed, and the artist shouted out to the street wildly. "Guards, she needs guards!"

His son tried to be heard over top of him. "Da, stop it! The Soul Heir is safely behind the walls of the Solstice Court," he soothed. "There is not a Soul Heir—past or present—who would risk her people by leaving it."

Shame ran along Kezerah's cheeks, coiled along her neck and shivered down her spine. The guilt nestled in her stomach like a snake.

The artist squared up against his son, and pointed a narrow finger in the direction Kezerah had been. "Then tell me why she's standing in my shop."

But Kezerah was now no longer in his shop. She backed up into the market crowd. Then, she ran. The shame she had felt in the shop curdled into dread. She took a sharp left onto a side street, then right, weaving through alleyways and roads devoid of sounds or people. What would her father say? What would her mother *do*?

A trio of men stood at a corner, eyeing her rattled state with curiosity. She studied them right back, recognizing the two protestors from the market. At first glance she thought she saw Ambrose among them, until she heard his shout from behind her. "Ke—I mean, hey, wait!" Eyes averted and hoods drawn, the men further retreated into a tavern. Ambrose muttered a curse under his breath as he caught up with her. He shuffled in front of her, cutting off her path. "Are you trying to get us lost?"

"I'm trying not to disgrace my entire kingdom by getting caught," she snapped.

"What? Back there?" Ambrose waved a lazy hand in dismissal. "He's an artist, they just have a knack for the dramatic."

The man's words had not been dramatized however, and Kezerah knew it. She bit her lip, thinking back to his accusation. *You could kill us all.'* Yes, the protection was never truly for her, was it? The reasons always differed when she had begged to leave the court. The danger to herself was expressed first in her father's list of reasons, but Kezerah knew—mostly from her patchwork of studies—the greater reason had nothing to do with *her*, and everything to do with her soul. Her precious soul, and her body encasing the reincarnation of their kingdom's founder. To lose her without an heir was to end that line and release her soul from its lineage loop, allowing it to return to the Summerlands, with no promise of when or if it would choose to return. Nor what form it would take. She was sacred, a symbol, and she loathed it. *'There is not a Soul Heir—past or present —who would risk her people...'*

"If you're finished dwelling," Ambrose said, looking around the empty side street, "I think you really have gotten us lost."

Kezerah cocked her head to the side. "I thought you knew the city."

Ambrose rolled his eyes. "I knew a good curry spot, and the main road. This—" He gestured at the deserted high walls, dimmed lanterns and uneven cobblestones, "—is not the main road." Whatever face Kezerah made softened his annoyance into a wry smile. "But not to worry. The first rule of traveling: when at a loss, ask a local." Kezerah trailed behind him as he followed distant chatter and laughter. The noise of crowds exchanged for intimate whispers, hushed secrets, and hums of pleasure. All the buildings had closed doors and windows, many with scarlet silks draped over the entrances.

"Ambrose—"

"Don't worry," he said, "we're not staying. Just cutting through."

A willowy man stood near a tattered, silk draped entrance. The shimmery gold that lined his eyes widened at Ambrose's approach, and he looked him up and down hungrily.

"Why hello, you look new." His voice was husky, like smoke, and Kezerah raised a brow as he extracted a sash from his waist. She raised the other brow as the sash fell at the back of Ambrose's neck, drawing him in closer. Ambrose did not balk, but looked at ease, bits of his tied back hair fell forward as he tilted his head. Something in Kezerah's chest constricted. Her teeth ground together.

"New, and lost. I'm looking for the Emerald Scarab. Do you happen to know the way?" The smile that poured across Ambrose's face brought a deep blush to Kezerah's cheeks. She both wanted to look away from the intimacy of it, and shove the courtesan, or Ambrose, to break the trance.

"If it's an inn you're looking for, we've got plenty of beds in here," the courtesan said.

Ambrose chuckled low. "Unfortunately, I'm traveling with my companion here."

The man looked Kezerah up and down with disinterest, then shrugged, turning his smile back onto Ambrose. "She can come too."

The laugh Ambrose gave only drew the courtesan closer, but Ambrose turned towards her. "What do you think, love, will these beds do?"

Kezerah stood stunned for a moment, thinking him serious. Then the mocking gleam of his eyes caught the lamp light, the dare from their breakfast together, *'come on, play with me.'*

Kezerah sauntered forward, following the man's example and adding a bit more swing to her hips. *"Unfortunately,"* she said, without an ounce of sincerity, "we seek beds less...occupied." She grabbed both ends of the scarf about Ambrose's neck, tugging him toward her. Ambrose nearly toppled over to meet her eyes. "And you've already paid for *our* lodgings."

Ambrose threw apologetic eyes at the courtesan. "I'm afraid it's true. My coins are already spent."

The man peered at her, then Ambrose with the remorse of a missed sale. With a flourished wave of his hand, he gave up. "Follow this road to the dead end, then take a left. You'll hear the main road. But it's a long way down to the Emerald Scarab." He shrugged. "Good luck." The sentiment was equal parts insincere and a dismissal.

Kezerah slid the sash off Ambrose's shoulders, and tied it about her own waist. "Thank you."

The instructions did indeed lead back to the main road, though the Solstice Court blurred far off in the distance like an apparition. They re-emerged into frenzied commotion. Many townspeople now held wooden goblets that sloshed golden liquid; the laughter more fevered, the bodies closer. Dice jumbled and clattered on overturned barrels, followed by whoops and boos as cards slid in and out of thin air.

"Stay close." Ambrose moved to stand beside her. "It looks to be a...fun area, but a bit rough around the edges." He winked. "Just the place you'd never think to find the Soul Heir."

People draped over one another, many sporting low-cut blouses or vests opened to reveal bare skin. Hands led hands into the alley they'd departed from. Rowdier music played, the townsfolk singing along, out of tune. Kezerah had the thought that, were she not the Soul Heir, this was just such the sort of place she would find herself. Everything about it was untamed, filled with secrets and laughter. Nothing felt shameful here. If she screamed or danced in the middle of the streets nobody would bat an eye. They might even join in.

"The prices will be good here," Ambrose said over the din of sin that surrounded them. "I've found, through time spent in my own city, it's also the place to spend your coin."

This sounded right to Kezerah, but she didn't understand it. "Why is that?"

"Because your city is only as rich as its poorest district," Ambrose said, returning a wink from another courtesan that fluttered by him. The woman's pants dipped so low the divots of her hips showed. "Your city center, and up, have plenty of wealth to spill between each other. These are the areas where the masses live, where loyalty is bred and songs are made." His words sounded sure, kingly even, and Kezerah tried to piece together what the winking prince and Ambrose—a king—might look like. He continued, either not noticing or not acknowledging her eyes on him. "You want to rule a kingdom, you feed your court. You want to *lead* your people, show them what you're worth." Ambrose laughed, jostling the coins at her waist purse. "And tonight you're worth about five gold, and three silver. So let's put it to use."

They found another pocket full of shops, many inside homes, and she gladly entered one to give her ears a rest. A round woman greeted her at the counter that doubled as a dining table. The stairs at her back led to the sound of rambunctious children, muffled by a creaking ceiling.

Kezerah browsed about the shop. Swords, leathers, and armor covered the walls. Ambrose took up the doorframe, legs crossed and shoulder pressed against the trim, subtly blocking the entrance from passersby. He watched her as she admired a saddle with yellow garnets embedded in it. It was by far the finest-made item in the store. She thought of Andarios, and how much he would have enjoyed the Night Market.

The woman came over, holding out green-glass earrings. "To compliment your eyes."

Ambrose stifled a laugh from the entrance. The woman ignored him, holding up a mirror to showcase her point. Kezerah gaped at her appearance. She had forgotten Ambrose's magick from earlier. Her creamy brown complexion dotted with freckles remained unchanged, but the eyes that stared back at her were dark green, identical to the chuckling boy behind her. They were his eyes exactly, down to the emerald flecks and shadowy depths.

She turned away from the woman, an eyebrow raised in his direction. "Thanks," she said to the storekeeper, "but I'll take the saddle."

Ambrose shrugged the saddle onto his shoulder, then followed her uncertain trail as she forged their path back to the tavern and Ikaika. They started down a side street, and a voice called out.

"You two! Halt. In the name of King Elowren, you are commanded to stop!"

It was the artist from earlier, now accompanied by a royal guard. Ambrose cursed under his breath, before he looked up with his stranger's smile, set the saddle down, and took a step in front of her. "Blessed Equinox. Is there something I, or my companion, can help you with?"

"I told you," said the artist. "Listen to how he speaks, they're nobles."

"Is nobility a crime in Elastor?" Ambrose asked, his hand swept out ostentatiously, Kezerah noticed, quite close to her face.

The guard, a captain by her green stained leather armor, looked them both over, brow furrowed. If she spoke, Kezerah didn't hear over the buzz of fear in her ears. She looked over at the artist, his words a sting needling deep into her skin. *'You can't be out here.'* But she *was* out here, and everything about it had felt right. Intoxicating. Freeing. Kezerah hugged her cloak a bit tighter about her face and took a deep gulp of air. *No.* She would not let this ruin the bit of freedom she'd crafted for herself. She just needed to craft a bit more.

"No, but kidnapping the Soul Heir would be a criminal offense," said the captain.

"Punishable by death!" spat the artist.

"Well," said the captain, "it's actually unprecedented. But, there would be a trial and a very strong possibility of death..."

Kezerah looked up at Ambrose, who already stared at her. His face concentrated on hers, jaw clenched. Time. She needed to buy time. Kezerah hoped she hadn't misread him, or her plan—still forming—would go badly, *rapidly.*

She took center stage. She remembered and mimicked the way the courtesan had moved in the alley, a bit more swing to her hips than usual. She adjusted the crimson sash at her waist, accentuating herself, then lifted an arm languidly, and placed a hand on Ambrose's shoulder. "Excuse me," she said, interrupting the argument between the guard and artist over the severity of their punishment. "Do you know who you are attempting to detain?"

She gazed up at Ambrose with a melting appreciation. "This is Prince Ambrose, Heir to Xenkesh."

Ambrose's green eyes went wide in question. Not a good sign for her plan. Kezerah admired him, unabashed. She leaned in closer, and hoped he'd get the hint as her gaze simmered into his. He cleared his throat. Then, like ice in sunlight, his movements thawed. Warmth enveloped Kezerah, as he crushed her to him. His hand rested firmly at her hip.

"That's *Crown* Heir," Ambrose said, and cocked a brow in the guard's direction. "And I ask you again. Is there something my companion or I can help you with? You mentioned something about the Soul Heir? If you have some sort of pamphlet, we'll just take that and be on our way."

The captain directed herself towards Ambrose. "Your Majesty, I apologize for the interruption to your evening, but I must ask you just who your companion is. He—" she gestured toward the artist. "—seems to believe he recognizes her."

Kezerah giggled, startling the group. "I'm sure he does—though, I can't say it's easy for me to keep track of all the...faces I come in contact with." She finished with a flourishing wink in the artist's direction.

He sputtered. "That's not—I have a paramour thank you very much! The only place I've seen you is in the throne room as I painted your portrait! I would recognize the Soul Heir anywhere."

Kezerah, caught up in her role, reached her other hand out and traced the smooth line of Ambrose's jaw and brought his eyes toward hers. "Well, that's flattering. At least now you know you're getting your coins worth."

Ambrose let out a strained laugh, closer to a broken cough. His pulse raised under her fingertips. Kezerah pretended to lean in more, nudging him with her hip. "Yes," he said, voice dry. He tore his eyes from hers, to address the guards properly. "Coin I've already spent for the evening. So, we must be going." Ambrose stepped forward and scooped up the saddle with one hand. A possessive arm pulled Kezerah along with him.

"If you're in such a hurry," urged the artist, "then why are you traipsing around shopping?"

"Is this because he didn't buy your overpriced painting?" Kezerah asked, irritated. "I bought this saddle for a quarter of the price by the way."

"And what reason would a courtesan require a saddle?"

"I can think of at least three reasons," Ambrose said wickedly, his grin daring the artist to press him further.

The artist stared at him aghast. The captain rubbed at her eyes.

Ambrose raised his chin high. "Now, if you will excuse us. I'm sure our room is ready."

"I'm sorry, but without any definitive proof..." The captain seemed torn between protocol and common sense. Kezerah couldn't tell if Ambrose's heart or hers thumped louder than the music. This was it, the moment of truth. Ambrose had either had the same thought as her, or she was about to make herself look incredibly foolish, and not just betray her identity, but her Kingdom.

"You said the Soul Heir has freckles?"

"Yes," said the artist with indignance. "You—The Soul Heir—have freckles all over your—" He stopped and examined her with a building confusion.

"That is something the Soul Heir and I differ on, unfortunately," Kezerah said. "In fact, while I am flattered, I'm afraid I don't have much in common with that portrait at all." She let her hood slip back, to reveal what she *hoped* was anything other than her cinnamon red curls. She let out a stifled breath as smoky brown ringlets were tossed into her peripheral view.

The artist beheld her, flustered now. "I—she—"

"Is obviously not the Soul Heir," Ambrose finished, impatient and breathless.

The captain looked from Ambrose to Kezerah, her lips a hard line. Then the tension eased from her jaw, and Kezerah had to withhold a sigh of relief. "I'll file a report in the morning. No need to keep you. Ma'am, Majesty, have a nice evening. Come on," she said sternly to the artist. "I'll take you back to your district." The artist cast one last look Kezerah's way before he followed the guard into the crowd. Kezerah fought the urge to taunt him with a smile.

She turned back to Ambrose and their eyes met once more. The charge from earlier passed like static from his gaze to hers. A heavy breath escaped Kezerah's lips, and then bubbled into laughter. Ambrose, a stunned moment behind her, also laughed. They stood laughing with unbridled relief.

"Like I said," Kezerah beamed up at him, "I dressed for stealth."

"I shan't question your choice of evening wear again," Ambrose said, before letting out a ragged breath. Kezerah noticed sweat beaded at his neck and temple.

"Are you alright?"

He nodded, closing his eyes. "I don't practice my Mirages enough. In Xenkesh, I just go out as, well, as myself." When he opened his eyes again, they looked tired. "And you have a *lot* of freckles and hair."

Kezerah pulled her hood back up, obscuring herself once more. "If we rush back, we shouldn't need the disguise anymore."

Ambrose nodded. "Good idea."

Though Kezerah knew her concern for him only accounted for a portion of her need to bring the night to an end. This had been a close call, and she had no desire for people to find out just how terrible of a Soul Heir she was.

Ambrose turned them east, towards the castle. She remained fitted against him as they walked.

"Where are we going?" she asked.

His smile was jovial. "I thought you said you were ready to go back."

Kezerah pushed away and smacked his arm. "Nice try. We're not leaving Ikaika at a tavern in the slums of Heartsglove."

Ambrose laughed. "Oh right. *Him.*" He tried to recapture her waist, but she pranced back and away. Aware it wasn't him she didn't trust at the moment, but herself. She still felt a flutter of warmth in her belly, the jolt of his pulse under her fingertips. She didn't know what she'd do if it continued, she just knew she was not allowed to find out. He heaved his shoulders in a dramatic sigh, making a turn down a well-lit street. "Alright, fine, if you insist. We'll first retrieve my brother."

The idea of Ikaika's presence relieved her, he always cleared her mind. Ambrose appeared to fog it.

He guided her over several streets until they reached the familiar glow, behind the cloth tapestry. She noticed a green beetle etched into the fabric of the sign. Ikaika sat right where they'd left him, politely listening to a story that Kofi told him, wildly flinging their arms.

Kofi broke off the story as Ikaika abruptly stood. He examined Kezerah, as if to make sure she wasn't missing any limbs. Then, satisfied, he bowed to Kofi. "Thank you for sharing your stories and food. It was lovely. I'll be sure to be back with the oils."

Kofi laughed. "You sure he's your brother?" they asked Ambrose, pointing a thumb in Ikaika's direction.

Ambrose's eyes still sparked from his earlier laughter, his frown forced. "That's what I'm told."

Ikaika walked past them towards the door, he looked exhausted. "Let's go. It'll be dawn by the time we make it back. We'll need to be down at breakfast before Nimah realizes we're gone."

"Ladies Glassberry," Nimah said, frantic. "Have you seen Princess Kezerah this morning?"

Day had not yet saturated the air with color in the guest quarters. It left the twins, exiting their room, a soft pastel in the dawn light. Both sets of eyes went wide.

"Yes."

"No."

One jabbed the other. "Willow!"

"I meant yes?"

Nimah looked past them into their room. "Thank Thrice, where?" The room was in no way tidy, but also princessless. Nimah spun back, all pretense of status fleeing her. "Well?"

The sisters looked at one another. "Oh well, not recently."

"But she's here—"

"Around..." assured and nodded the one that Nimah now knew full-well fibbed. Probably covering for her missing friend. *Missing. Missing Princess, Missing Soul Heir.*

Nimah swirled in place. She had no time for this. She dashed away without so much as a parting word. Where were they? She'd only slept for a blink, and both Prince Ikaika and Princess Kezerah were gone. She'd checked Lord Andarios' room and now the Glassberry's. Nimah let out a rattling sob. She had been so stupid. So comfortable in her routine with Kezerah's late night antics. It would cost her everything. Her job, her way of supporting her sons, possibly her life. If Kezerah had left the castle walls—But no, she just liked hiding sometimes, Nimah told herself. She only needed reinforcements. She ran down the steps that led through to the banquet hall and onward to the Winter Quarters. She would tell Hanan, he would know what to do, he—then Nimah stopped dead in her tracks.

Through the frosted glass of the Autumn Quarter, she could see the banquet hall set for an open breakfast, and Kezerah and Ikaika casually eating by a fire.

She marched up to them.

"Where have you been?" she bellowed, both looked up at her with large eyes, dark circles under each pair.

"Nurse, what do you mean?" Kezerah asked.

"Don't try that tone with me, Princess. I've watched over you since before you were potty trained."

Kezerah appeared horrified, and glanced at Prince Ikaika. '*Good,*' Nimah thought, let her be embarrassed for once.

Ikaika spoke calm and slow, as if to a wild animal. "Nimah, I'm sorry if we scared you. Kezerah and I awoke early this morning, and we saw you asleep. We didn't want to disturb you so we left to get breakfast."

Nimah thought back, how long had she slept? It was hard to say. Harder to say what would happen if word got back.

Ikaika continued, "You can see we tried to dress ourselves. Kezerah especially seems ill-equipped without you," he said, filled with sincerity as he gestured to Kezerah's clothes.

A new wave of panic seized Nimah as she looked down at Kezerah for the first time. She stared in terror at a scantily clad pairing of black leggings that hugged her hips until it met with a tightly bound bodice resembling an overshirt. Leather ties tugged at either side to expose much of her chest. She might as well have been naked in the banquet hall.

"Summerlands!" she cried, grabbing Kezerah's arm, and dragging her away from the table. "Up, up, up! Before your mother sees you! Up!"

Nimah's shoulders slumped in relief when Kezerah obeyed, with only minor objections as Nimah led her back up the stairs. Once in her room, Nimah drew a bath and further groomed her. Her hair was especially tangled and Nimah insisted Kezerah brush it while she looked for a dress. When she turned, Kezerah laid lolled out on her bed sound asleep, hair still wet from her bath. Nimah dropped the dress, confused.

The day nurse, Gili, knocked and Nimah scrambled over to shush her. "If you'd like an easy morning, I suggest you be quiet," she whispered.

The nurse nodded and backed out of the double doors with her.

"Strange, Prince Ikaika was also asleep in bed," said Gili. Nimah twisted at her apron. She was getting too old for this. *Kezerah* was too old for this.

Beyond tired, Nimah fumed. Kezerah had done what she always did: rebelled and sought out the company of friends. "I'm going to bed." Without another word or look back at Gili, Nimah trudged off to her rooms.

Aloran Interlude

Regent Castiel of Dawnscar hated being on land. If given the choice between stagnant ground (pollen polluted with tickling breezes), or the violence of the Brash Sea (salt rich and prideful), the choice was easy. He had promised himself, upon becoming Lord of Port Tiertyde, that he would only do so if he needn't step foot on Thrice. Lord Castiel of Storms solely ruled from the sea. So, once ordered to act as King Regent in Queen Illija's absence, he'd said no —twice. Then, Illija herself had ridden in to persuade him (she'd also beaten him in a duel, but Castiel didn't like to dwell). One winter as regent, and he could return to his briny home. He had agreed. That had been three winters ago.

He hated breaking promises—especially to himself.

Fort Thistle nestled itself between the smallest of Alora's mountains on the Elastor-Aloran border. The Strand, a crevasse that tore from Dawnscar all the way to Xenkesh's Zelos, served to divide the mountain into a pass. The cracked earth brimmed with sulfuric steam that wafted off heated water—courtesy of Dawnscar's natural hot springs—which meant Fort Thistle smelled like rotten eggs. Castiel spit on the fresh grass, still vibrant and growing. Mud sloshed at his boots from a sprinkle of rain that the earth soaked up like a porous sponge. Disgusting.

River docks and bath houses lined what was meant to be anything but a permanent encampment. Elk stables, wolf dens, merchant stalls and tents staked into the ground proved otherwise. Fort Thistle verged on establishing itself as a village. It also teetered on the border. A border town would become complicated if Elastor ever ceased to be Alora's ally. Castiel believed it to be just a matter of time. Illija remained more hopeful.

She leaned over a makeshift table, a map speckled with darts beneath her. Loose black hair hid her features, but Castiel knew his queen and friend anywhere. She held the title as the second most beautiful creature on Thrice (first place, when Castiel himself was at sea). Castiel couldn't help that vanity embedded his cornerstone: steel silver hair, smooth skin, an hourglass worth of curves, and a lifetime of being told he was beautiful had done it. The soul chose the body, and his soul had impeccable taste. Illija, however, rivaled him in just about every category. He had known from a young age, he could either be her friend, her lover, or her enemy. Witnessing Illija lodge an arrow into her ward's throat and spend twenty years trying to slay her paramour had made the decision for him. Illija wasn't a magnificent friend, but it served as the best of the three options.

"Give me the letter from Ikaika first," she said, hearing his thoughts as he neared.

"You want a summary?" Castiel offered, after assessing the gray-blue under her eyes from lack of sleep.

"Give it here, Castiel." An impatient hand outstretched. "Ikaika doesn't write unless he believes it's worth reading."

Castiel gave her the first letter. The seal broke twice over as it leapt from spy to spy before reaching its destination. Castiel had also read it himself. As the boy's guardian—should anything happen—he too liked to know how his pseudo-nephew fared. Until recently, it had been well. Illija's eyes scanned the too-short letter, devoid of emotions; it wasn't much more than a sheet of facts, and a rare request. Ikaika's Mind Melding had manifested, and in earnest. It wasn't unusual for the odd loud thought, or errant dream to get in at a young age, but no longer a child, Ikaika was in agony.

"I need to get him to the Temples of Estora," Illija said. "If he says he's in pain, it's double what's written here."

"Eriko could—"

"No." Illija's tone was sharp, and Castiel didn't bother finishing the thought. This was an old argument. "I'm not risking him leaving Elastor's Haven without a full escort or myself accompanying him." It hadn't mattered that they had gained the Brash advantage, or that there had been no assassination attempts since the young prince had gone to the Solstice Court. The night Ikaika had been attacked, Illija had been rattled and, in Castiel's opinion, had not recovered. The joke had landed on Amarus however. The tides of war had turned in their favor; Illija now freed up for more personalized attacks and Castiel left to nanny Alora while she did it.

Castiel shrugged. "Did you read the bit about Ambrose and Rorrik attending the Solstice Court? After ignoring four years of invitations, that can't be for nothing."

"What of it?" Illija's chin raised, eyes daring him to speak ill of her sons.

"You know very well 'what of it'. Amarus would not send them without a scheme in place. And with the princess coming of age..."

"She is not of age. She holds no Sway, and Elowren made it clear there would be no bias in our arrangement." At Castiel's unchanged expression, she continued, "The princess has also made a habit of entering Ikaika's rooms, which I've encouraged in my letters." Castiel raised his brows. Illija tossed her hair behind a shoulder, the closest she came to bragging these days. "I can only assume Alora to be well established in the Solstice Court."

"Alright, fine. What about the small detail where neither you nor Amarus may attend while the other's heirs are in attendance?" He had her there, and he knew it. "How are you meant to swoop in and procure Ikaika for the Temples when you can't pass through the Solstice Gate?"

"You just want to go," she said with an eye roll.

"I just want to *do* something," Castiel said with a raise of his hands. "You've been away from Dawnscar a long time, Illija, and being your regent is *killing* me, to put it lightly. The most interesting thing I've had to do all week was read a letter about pirates poaching wild animals and selling them to idiots. It's Alora. It looks after itself."

The Queen's lips pursed. Castiel saw her mulling his offer over. "I'm sorry, Cas. I'll be taking my personal battalion at first light."

Castiel narrowed his eyes. She had always been stubborn but 'relentless' better described Illija with her children. He let a moment of tension pass before responding. "Perhaps you are ready to read your second letter."

This letter was sealed, hand delivered by Illija's eye in Xenkesh.

The slight girl had rode a komodai through the night to get it to them, which meant whatever this letter contained was time sensitive. Castiel also knew this eye in particular had been stationed within Trusol palace. Only one thing kept Illija from her sons.

Illija split the seal with a knife, and opened the small-folded parchment. She let out a hiss. "Amarus." Her eyes darted from one parchment to the other. "Amarus would attack Tiertyde himself? He would brave The Brash?" She sounded disbelieving. She also sounded tempted. With the knowledge that Amarus' fleet would attempt an assault on Tiertyde, Illija's forces could flank him from Fort Thistle: An attack that cornered him in Aloran territory.

All Illija needed was her sons returned to her. All Illija desired was to rip out Amarus' beating heart. She had lost everything to this man. Her freedom, her love, her sons, herself—

"Stop it," Illija said in Castiel's direction. "I'm trying to think." She rubbed a thumb across her bottom lip. Her eyes danced across Ikaika's letter, and the note that promised vengeance. She hardened with her resolve.

"I will write Ikaika and explain. I never trained with the monks in Estora, and while I do not wish that upon my son, I know he is strong."

Castiel nodded. Then, for Ikaika's sake, tried yet another compromise. "If you wrote to your sister, she—"

"I have no sister, Castiel." Illija folded the letter into sharp, crisp lines. "And if you bring her up again, I'll ask someone else to accompany me on the Brash."

The Brash. The Brash. The Brash. The home and heart he longed for. He didn't dare hope.

"Which would be unfortunate," Illija continued, "because if I'm to meet Amarus in battle at sea, you're my guarantee to end this war."

Friend or Fool

AMBROSE LAID IN BED, THE SUN WELL UP IN THE SKY. HE'D been unable to sleep, despite returning to a quiet and empty room. Instead he replayed his second night in the capital through, again. His plans plundered by Kezerah. He had intended to court her further, then whisk her away for a night out in the city as part of an elaborate evening. Well-made plans didn't appear to mesh favorably with the Soul Heir.

He'd first believed she possessed a coy demeanor. Her poor handling of trade had validated that; the enticing yet empty invitations he'd received made flesh. After their conversation on the turrets however, he'd conceded she was intriguing, clever even. Now, he didn't know what she was. He just knew he wanted more of it, which complicated things.

Ambrose closed his eyes. The way she'd grabbed him, and bore her gaze into his. No Mirage could have hidden the heat in that stare. Then she had just turned it off, like blowing out a candle, to weave a ruse together in order for them to escape. All before he carried a gift she had bought for another man through the streets. He pushed his hair back just as the door groaned open.

Rorrik skulked in, movements slow and purposeful. "Ror?" Ambrose asked, and raised an eyebrow as his brother jumped like an antsy antelope.

"Oh good, you're up." Rorrik cleared his throat. Sweat spiked his shorn hair, his cloak's hood damp and stuck to the nape of his neck. He must have been in the practice yards, Ambrose thought, making a mental note to seek them out again himself.

"I've been up," he said, continuing to survey his brother.

"You were out late. I assumed you'd sleep in." Rorrik's tone begged for more information. Ambrose didn't take the bait. Rorrik had his skillset, albeit a bit focused, and subtlety did not make the cut.

He looked his brother over again. "Where's your sword?"

Rorrik gritted his teeth. "Oh, yeah, I forgot it..." The pause lasted too long for Ambrose's scattered thoughts.

"I told you, you shouldn't just huff off the field like that. That's how you lose it."

"I didn't! And I didn't lose it. They make us use dulled blades or practice swords."

Ambrose thought a faux sword prepared you for nothing but a faux sword fight. "Well, it looks sloppy, and makes you look irrational."

Rorrik didn't respond and tossed his armor on his neatly made bed. He looked tired, almost delirious. Had he slept? Ambrose knew if he asked he'd just be accused of nagging.

"Anyone formidable?"

After a petulant pause, Rorrik relented. "That Aloran, Eriko, is good. You should fight him if you have the chance, you might be outmatched for once."

Ambrose perked up. "The blue eyed one with the scar?" Scars were not a feature that stood out on a warrior, but Eriko's cut cleanly across his face.

Rorrik spoke rapidly now that he'd piqued his brother's attention. "Yeah, amazing isn't it? He's part of the rankings they're doing for the princess' Queensguard, but anyone can join. He's quick, caught me from behind before I knew it."

"Isn't he Alora's Sword Master?"

Rorrik busied himself by removing his boots. "Well, yes. Or, Ikaika's Kingsguard now, I suppose."

Ambrose nodded, tucking away the information that Ikaika had a guard, a Sword Master no less, skilled enough to elude his brother's bias. He would definitely make more effort to get down to the yards today.

"So, you were with the princess last night?"

Round two it would seem.

"I was in the city," Ambrose dodged, then distracted. "I went back to the Emerald Scarab, from our first night." He could practically hear Rorrik's scowl.

"Flirting either way then. I don't know what you saw in that tavern server."

"I don't know what you have against tavern servers," Ambrose countered lazily. "Some of my best experiences have been with people who bring me food."

"You know you're the heir to the throne, right?"

Ambrose rolled his eyes, giving up on his peace, he got up to dress. "Yes, I've been informed. But as long as they don't know that, there's no harm. And since when did you become so prudish? Are the Elastian's stuffy talks of virtue rubbing off on you?"

"I meant that tavern servers are beneath you, not that your virtues needed to remain intact."

Ambrose looked at his brother, disappointed and tired of the conversation. "Princesses are too much; servers, too little. I pity the person who tries to please you."

Rorrik frowned, angry now. "I don't need to be pleased. I just refuse to have our time wasted."

Mood soured, Ambrose pushed past Rorrik and opened the door. This is why he couldn't tell Rorrik things. He was too impatient. "Right, good. Just keep swinging that sword around, maybe you'll hit something." He looked down pointedly. "If you can remember where you left it."

The door slammed shut on Rorrik's muffled comeback.

The hallway remained quiet for only a moment, then either Lady Willow or Whistle stepped out to join him. Her blonde hair mimicked a style many other lieges here wore; braids spun atop her head in a circle. He summoned his charm and smiled her way.

She hid a smile with pressed together lips. Pink colored her cheeks as she inclined her head and looked around as if not sure she should or could walk his way. Finally, familiar territory.

"Good morning, Lady Glassberry."

"A pleasant *midday* to you, Your Majesty."

He offered an arm as she reached him. "Ambrose will do."

"I couldn't possibly," she giggled. "But you can call me Whistle."

"Lady Whistle, where shall I escort you today?" To Kezerah he hoped.

"Well, Queen Elize reads poetry to the children in the meadow midday. I'd hoped to listen in—" Ambrose tried to picture the Kezerah he'd met last night listening to poetry and fell short. He calculated his own aversion to poetry against the possibility of learning more about her from a close friend. Whistle decided for him. "—You must come! She reads beautifully, and they're all originals. Many of us think some of the prose pieces have hidden meanings. One year she had a line that read 'Amber winds spark the day, Saffron skies never fade away.' Which, since she's from Sorrel, you *know* must be a euphemism about the Bane Harvest."

Whistle looked up to see if he listened and he picked at the monologue for something he could respond to. A plague—that his kingdom may or may not have played a part in—he decidedly steered away from. "Sounds lovely. Nearly as lovely as your hairstyle. Your queen wears it similarly, doesn't she?"

Whistle brushed a flaxen strand from her forehead. "Yes, but mine's much less extravagant of course." She blushed and smiled regardless. "Most my age wear it this way though, it's not very original."

"Princess Kezerah notably doesn't."

Whistle laughed as they stepped into the Autumn foyer. "Kezi? I can't imagine. She never follows trends. Especially ones Her High Majesty sets."

"Not overly close with her mother then?" He'd guessed as much from the foyer incident but it was unfortunate news given how accommodating the queen had been since their arrival. He couldn't exactly begrudge complicated maternal relationships though.

Whistle waved to a passing pair of lieges, both giving her pointed expressions. Whistle answered with a firmer hold on Ambrose's arm. "Erm, no, or that is...It would be difficult, wouldn't it? With a mother like Queen Elize? I know I'd perish from the excessive success. But Kezi does her best."

Ambrose knew what it was like to have a larger than life parent. His father had always inspired him, but the weight of one day trying to live up to that standard? The active effort to keep the pressure from crushing him ran him ragged at times. *'Enough,'* he told himself. *'You're strategizing not empathizing.'*

The meadow buzzed with giggling children teetering on the roots of a broad tree swollen with apples. Queen Elize sat atop a wooden toadstool; her maroon dress swished to pool along one side of the stalk. Ambrose blinked away the overwhelming sensation that this wasn't real. That his mind had conjured the scene in some elaborate waking dream. Whistle pulled him down, awakening him. His reality fully grounded as the small child next to him began to dig in the dirt. She offered him a worm and he declined politely with a shake of his head.

"They are a liege, and I but a lady fair,
Our love forbidden, yet we dare declare."

Ambrose withheld a huff of breath, and leaned into whisper to Whistle. She brought a finger to her lips, gaze riveted on the queen. He wondered if he'd ever been shushed before. Swords clambered in the distance, mocking his surroundings. The queen shuffled through a hefty stack of parchment. The dirt digger began crafting him a bracelet made of clover stems while plucking off and eating the heads.

"In labyrinths of castles, 'neath the moonlit sky,
Our love story blossoms, nary seen by enemy eye..."

With no dignified escape, Ambrose sighed and settled in to hear fairy tales not afforded to him in his shortened childhood.

"Dar," Kezerah groaned, elongating his name in a plea. "It's been hours. I'm tired, let's go." She stood at the back entrance to the Autumn Hall, at the mouth of the West training yard.

"And who's fault is it you're tired?" Andarios circled his eighth opponent. Kezerah tried to remember his name. *Tamoran? Terry? Tim?* "Two more," Andarios promised over a loud clack. "Next is Fennel, then Eriko, then—" he cursed as a sword hit his shoulder.

"Point!" called Rook, from the sidelines.

"You're just lucky Prince Rorrik chose to go shopping this morning," taunted Tamoran.

"Thank Thrice for that!" huffed Andarios, blocking. "He's a terror in drills."

Kezerah was surprised. "Oh, is he good?"

Andarios chuckled. "No, just a terror."

Tim slapped Andarios' other arm.

Andarios tossed his head back and sagged his shoulders.

"End match. Win goes to Terryn. You're out, Luka."

Kezerah clapped her hands together. "That's it—Terryn!"

Andarios walked over, side-eyeing her as he removed his padding. Kezerah gave him a guilty grin. "I guess that means you finished early."

He didn't smile back.

"Hey," she said, "I'm sorry. You came in third though, that's good."

He shrugged. "I need to be better than good."

"Andarios," Kezerah said, trying to gauge his agitation, "you're not going back to Luka, if that's what you're worried about."

He shook his head but didn't look at her, eyes trained on Fennel and Eriko. She imagined he might be remembering his past and she knew how much he hated to think of it. Andarios' village, Luka, was on The Edge. When he had been a small child it had been burned to the ground, his parents along with it. He'd been the one to confirm to the king's riding party that they were gone.

She touched a hand to his cheek. He allowed her to guide his face towards hers.

"It won't happen. You're not going anywhere." She made her gaze intense and sure, willing the promise into being.

He nodded, but this time he seemed more assured.

She nudged him with her elbow, eyeing his arms. "Since when are you so muscular?"

He fought a smile, being brought back despite himself. "Since it became my unfortunate and impossible task to keep you in line." He lifted and tossed her over his large shoulder as she shrieked with laughter, carrying her into the Autumn Quarter.

. . .

SUNLIGHT SPILLED down through the glass ceiling, giving the illusion of warmth despite the chill outside. On one of Andarios' many whirls she spotted Ikaika leaning against one of the large trees. Not far away, Whistle and Ambrose sat by a hearth drinking tea.

Andarios set her down, seeming to realize the impropriety of carrying a screaming princess over his shoulder. Ikaika looked unbothered, reading a worn book in his downtime. Ambrose studied them, eyes drifting away from the conversation he had with Whistle, who seemed unperturbed and continued talking.

Kezerah refused to change her behavior with Andarios for anyone's sake. She grabbed his hand, pulling him toward their friends.

A tug of resistance made her turn back.

Andarios looked at her apologetically. "Actually, Kez, I've got to get back to training. I just knew you'd get bored watching everyone be pummeled by Eriko."

Kezerah tried to rein in her disappointment. "Fine. Go beat him so everyone shuts up about it then."

His hand slipped from hers. "As you command." He saluted, trotting off the way he'd come.

"Kezi, come sit!" Whistle trilled. "I was just explaining to Prince Ambrose how we celebrate the solstice!"

"Which one?" Kezerah grabbed a bowl of dried berries and candied rose petals from the large table. She took the seat closest to Ikaika in order to try and make him part of the conversation.

"The Winter Solstice of course, Summer is too far away to think about," Whistle said, impatient with Kezerah to keep up.

"Yes, but that's also the boring one."

Whistle looked offended. "How can you say that with all of the pretty snow, and the Yule Tree lighting? The candle making! The cinnamon mulled cider!"

Kezerah shrugged, unconvinced. "Everyone stays indoors, and there's always more council meetings for rations and supplies..." She realized how old she sounded and grimaced. "The sledding and snowball fights are fun though."

Whistle turned back to Ambrose, giving up on her friend. "Well,

don't listen to her. It's gorgeous. Queen Elize always decorates lavishly as well. It's my favorite part."

Kezerah rolled her eyes. Whistle was a staunch Elize supporter. ('Elizist,' Dar had often mocked). It was, in Kezerah's opinion, her friend's greatest flaw. She turned to Ikaika. "What do you think, Kai? Is Winter Solstice worth the fuss?"

"Well," he said, not looking up from his book, "it *is* the only way to get to my birthday."

She grabbed a dried berry and tossed it at him, commanding his attention. On the third toss of fruit, he sighed before folding a page in.

"I also like the snow," he said lamely. She threw another berry. He caught it, smiling as he walked over. He leaned forward to stand behind her chair, unwilling to commit to sitting down with her current choice of company.

"My favorite holiday by far is Nighttide Eve."

"The eve?" Whistle said, wrinkling her nose. "But that's the day of silence where everyone naps."

Ikaika nodded. "Precisely."

Ambrose blew out a long breath. "I can't believe you have an entire holiday dedicated to silence and napping."

Something in his tone made Kezerah feel protective over their traditions. "We have plenty of exciting holidays. Our customs just better appreciate the reveal. After all, your celebrations may celebrate the living, but many of ours celebrate the flesh."

Ambrose's eyes locked on hers. "You have my undivided attention."

She heard Ikaika make a sound behind her but, whatever his retort, he held it in.

"Our Spring Rites for one, are about fertility and the body. The day is spent planting, sewing, and growing." Kezerah allowed her eyes to hold the dual meaning of her words but added for emphasis, "In bedrooms, just as much as gardens."

"It seems I've come during the wrong time of year," Ambrose said low, holding her gaze.

Ikaika sighed, rubbing his eyes. Kezerah looked up at him, concerned.

"Ikaika?" she started to ask, but his expression brought her up short. He had a smile that she didn't recognize, it made his dark eyes look unkind.

"Yes, it's a shame you can't stay for The Unity Rites this Winter," he said, coming around the side of Kezerah's chair to sit on the arm, his own arm draped across its back.

"And what do you do for that one?" Ambrose mused. "Unite hands and hope for the snow to melt?"

"Not quite," Ikaika said, sounding pleased Ambrose had taken his bait. "There are often bonfires, and hunts, much like your Fire Festivals, but instead of giving chase to animals, they chase each other to find lovers to jump the fires with. Then join together for a night." He looked over at Kezerah. "Were you not saying the other evening you hoped to participate this year?"

His tone and words were conversational, but unrecognizable. Ikaika had always shown a panicked aversion to the Unity Rites. He'd even hinted that he found the Elastian Wild Hunts predatory in nature, despite the participants willingness to join in. When she had mentioned last year she thought it looked fun, he'd looked mortified.

"Erm," she said, trying to remember what the question had been, his eyes on her, expectant. "Yes, yes I did." She looked over to Ambrose to clarify. "Obviously only adults participate," she scoffed. "The 'children' just run around with ribbons."

Ambrose didn't look half as amused, instead focusing above her head. She looked up at Ikaika's arm and sensed the shift in atmosphere.

Whistle, always one for small talk, also sensed it. "Yes well, Willow and I joined last year." She shrugged. "It wasn't anything so special."

While not what she'd had in mind, the admission allowed her to redirect. "I didn't know that. You paired with someone?"

Whistle blushed. "It wasn't a true pairing. I didn't even catch their name."

"Names aren't necessary in knitting two souls together," said Ikaika. "All a soul needs is intent; a festival has more than enough of that."

"Ha," Ambrose laughed. "If my soul knitted together with every —" He stopped himself at Kezerah's quirked brows.

Ikaika picked up where he'd left off. "Go on, don't be modest."

Ambrose shrugged, and took a sip of his tea. "You need more than a festival for souls to become involved, that's all I'm saying. Dalliances are another matter."

"How romantic," Ikaika said. "I'm sure your re-admittance into the Summerlands will be quite the party."

"Invitations are exclusive, I assure you," Ambrose said, "when souls are in play."

Kezerah resituated herself in her chair, and hugged her legs closer. There would be no party in the Summerlands she'd ever be invited to, friendship or more. Her soul remained bound here, to the earth. Even if she did pair herself to another soul (plenty of her reincarnations had paramours) breaking the ties that tethered her in the cycle proved as futile as thwarting nature.

Whistle tsk'd. "You sound like Willow. She's determined to sample every Elastian in the kingdom to find her soulmate."

Ambrose leaned back in his chair, expression dubious. "Aren't *you* most likely her soulmate?"

Whistle blinked in quick succession. "What?"

"You're twins: Two twigs from the same branch, paired by birth." Ambrose looked around for allies. "Do Elastian's really believe twin souls—or soulmates as you say—need to be a romantic connection?"

Kezerah grew more interested. "Is that not what Xenkeshi believe?"

Ambrose leaned back, aghast. "Certainly not. A paramour is chosen, a pairing of two souls. A soul-twin is innate. They aren't necessarily lovers, but one and the same. One—"

"One star split into two. A starburst," Ikaika finished begrudgingly. "Alorans believe similarly."

Ambrose cast a relieved look at his brother before he caught himself and waved an errant hand. "Alorans and their stories of stars."

"Xenkeshi and their condescension over souls," Ikaika said with a veiled temper.

"Well," said Ambrose, "we do speak to them."

"From your endeavors, it sounds as if you also personally collect them."

Ambrose rolled his eyes. "Like I said, if I want my soul woven into anyone else's, they'll know." His tone was sardonic, but Ikaika's hand tightened on the back of Kezerah's chair.

"Consent. Such a novelty in Xenkesh—"

"Well, isn't this cozy?"

Kezerah startled as her mother came to stand by their gathering of chairs. She'd heard a bout of illness had struck the queen last night. She'd hoped that meant a day's reprieve. Apparently not. Kezerah realized that this looked a lot like a direct defiance of her mother's earlier orders. Mostly because it was. "Mother, we were just—"

"Discussing Xenkesh, I heard," said Elize. She smiled at the group but didn't look at Kezerah. "Whistle, Prince Ambrose, it was nice to see you in the meadow today."

Kezerah scrunched her nose, imagining Ambrose as an Elizist had a bad aftertaste. She inspected him for the common traits to those lost: eagerness, rapt eye contact, vigorous loyalty. He adjusted a bedraggled green bracelet on his wrist, mildly bored. Relief flooded Kezerah in a downpour as her mother continued.

"I'm sorry to interrupt, but I spotted Prince Ikaika and knew Hanan was looking for you. Something about oils?"

Ikaika straightened, his arm drawn back from Kezerah's chair in a hurry. "Oh, right. Yes, I'd asked for some."

Elize kept her smile plastered on and blinked expectantly.

"Erm, well," Ikaika said, backing up to retrieve his book, "I'd better go find him then."

"He'll be so pleased," Elize said. "You know how he likes to check off his lists."

Ikaika nodded, then looked at Kezerah with a last-ditch effort at bravery. "Maybe we can study after, get some of that text read?"

Studying, a perfect excuse to save face and flee her mother. Kezerah pushed herself off the chair. "That's a great idea I'll just—"

"Oh, Kezerah, did you forget?" Elize gave her a pitying look.

"Nimah mentioned you took a nap, perhaps it slipped your mind, the council meeting that runs until late midday?"

Kezerah slumped back into the chair. "No, I didn't forget. I'll be there." She gave Ikaika an apologetic look.

"That's alright, I'm expecting a letter from my mother anyway."

Her mood up ticked. "Oh, that's good! She's back in Thistle then?"

Ikaika's eyes left hers and, on their return, smoldered. "You're mistaken, she's in Tiertyde."

Aware of her audience, a deep tingle of embarrassment ran up her neck. Then her brows pinched together. "No... it must be Fort Thistle. Dar said—"

"Kezerah—" Ikaika caught himself in a calming breath. "She's in Tiertyde." This time she followed his quick glance. Ambrose studied the grooves in his chair, his blatant disinterest masking nothing. Kezerah turned back to apologize. Ikaika had already retrieved his book.

He bowed, expression unreadable. "See you tonight."

She didn't know what to say. An apology only made the farce more obvious. She frowned at his steady retreat.

Elize lightly clapped her hands together, commanding Kezerah's attention. "Well, it's been a pleasure to see our guests all getting along. But I'm afraid we'll run late for our meeting if we lag much longer. Kezerah, did you want to walk together?"

Kezerah tightened her hold on her chair arms. Her mother actually appeared giddy at her failure. Rejoicing in Kezerah's blunder with a broad grin. She'd rather kiss a pig than walk with her.

Kezerah's lack of response smoothed Elize's smile into a sullen pout. "Or I suppose, I can walk by myself, if you wish to stay behind with your friends." Kezerah knew she looked brutish, leaving her mother to linger beside her unanswered invitation.

Whistle's eyes widened. "Kezi..." *Treachery in the ranks.* "If you need to go..." *Eager, enraptured, loyal, lost.*

"Time must have gotten away from us." Ambrose stood and stretched, his dark auburn hair coming loose from its partial knot to fall to his chin. "Princess, if you need to postpone escorting me to the

Northern Yards, I understand. But, I admit, I had been looking forward to it."

Kezerah knew her face didn't hide her relief. "No, that would be rude. I can take you, it's on the way."

"What a coincidence. If you allow me a moment to grab a practice blade from the barracks, we can be on our way." Ambrose swept a bow the queen's way. "But please, don't feel the need to wait, Your Majesty. I'd hate to make you late."

Kezerah had never seen anyone come so close to dismissing her mother. She watched to see what Elize would do. It was well worth it.

Her mother took on the twitching qualities of a bird; studying whether to catalog something as predator or prey. The stillness that proceeded didn't allow for breathing. Then, Elize gave a dazzling smile. "Kind of you. Kezerah, I expect you on time." Her eyes glittered. "Once the meeting is concluded you can resume your time with our guests. I'm sure they'd love it if you joined us in the drawing rooms for once." With her orders made clear she gave a final smile to Whistle and marched off towards the Winter Hall.

Silence ensued. "Hey, ow!"

"Keep siding with my mother," Kezerah said, tossing the last candied rose petal at Whistle, "and I'll get the grapes next."

"She just looked so disappointed! Didn't she?"

The question had been directed at Ambrose, but he didn't listen. Instead, he cast a mournful gaze at the crackling fire. Kezerah dashed a foot against the ground. "Erm, thank you. You don't actually have to go to the Northern Yards. You can enjoy the hearths longer, if you want."

The fire's splendor shone in Ambrose's eyes as they alighted on her. "No, I'm afraid I have a few duties of my own. But we can reconvene after your meeting?"

"Sure." Kezerah shrugged. "Which of the Solstice courts' seven wonders would you like to see?"

Ambrose's laugh rumbled as he held it in. He moved past her, finishing what must have been cold tea. "Surprise me."

He sauntered off, and Kezerah hated that she found herself aligned with her mother; unsure if he wanted her as his friend or a fool.

Letter from the Solstice Court

Thistle.

—A

Expectations

"Alorans use our muddied borderlines to literally build, and reap, and sow our lands: tax free."

Kezerah sneezed, ruining Dyllian's punctuation. He'd taken over his father's drawling mantle for stronger border control that had been a mainstay in meetings since last Spring. He glared at her, as if she'd chosen to be attacked by dust, before continuing. "When we come to collect, the borders appear more and more blurred. Adding the additional resources will only further the problem." Sunlight leaked away into the threat of dusk, moonrise well on its way. If she could just get out of this meeting, she could still catch it glitter on the waves of the Lull. If Dyllian stopped talking, for once.

Twilight hung low on the horizon, her world painted in fuchsia and lavender by the time Kezerah was set free. Like a well-practiced pickpocket, the meeting had looted her of both time and patience.

"Find the princes, flee the scene," she repeated under her breath as she moved towards the Autumn Quarter drawing rooms.

In order to get her mother off her back, she'd decided to skip a stone and spend time with both Xenkeshi princes at once. She only needed to endure political prattlings for a blink, then she knew exactly where she'd take her guests.

The room moved with the rhythm of a hive. Both opulent and open, the little-to-no furnishings allowed the nobility to stand and mingle, never staying in one conversation too long. Servers passed along bright colored drinks in blown glass shaped like roses; Glassberry made, naturally. Most of the guests gathered near the fires, pockets of people trading gossip and laughter. Elize could hardly believe she'd crafted something so perfect.

People believed she accomplished excellence effortlessly. She never corrected them, but the endeavor far surpassed effort. The room simmered like an elaborate meal; hearty topics spiked with the aftertaste of gossip. It shifted like a well choreographed ensemble; dancers in each station before fluttering to the next. A poem with well situated prose; years of lines crossed out until she knew just what to do. By tonight, Elize not only knew what her courtiers wanted, but when and in what way they needed it.

Everyone wanted to feel important, but if the party grew too pompous then it edged into garish. A room should be prosperous, but not lavish. She didn't want people to attend her parties yet be too humble to mention them in front of their lessers. She wanted her subjects to idolize what they did here. To know that doting and altruistic hands carefully swaddled the kingdom of Elastor. Her parties, her people, her hands.

Her orchestra of conversation began to play out of tune. Words grew more hushed like curtains drawn back from the main stage. Elize followed the flaw, and her eyes landed—without surprise—on Kezerah. Her off-key melody. Elastor's future, and the future of Elize's domain; all that she'd built. Kezerah did not want to be here. Elize watched as she trudged in, head down and mumbling to herself. Well, at least she'd bothered to show up, albeit late. Elize tried to guide her way. She spotted and stepped closer to Prince Ambrose. All she'd asked for was a show of maturity, to balance the time spent with their visiting guests.

As to appear natural, Elize grabbed a flute of Xenkeshi red wine just as Ambrose did. "I must admit." She took a sip. "Your wines age nicely."

"A trait both Xenkesh and Elastor share." Ambrose beamed. "How do you foster such an opal-like sparkle in yours?"

"One of Ralven's many secrets I'm afraid." She checked on Kezerah and was granted a keen pinch of pain in her gut. Her daughter's eyes met then averted hers, as if she'd seen Elize and hadn't wanted to. Elize hummed with agitation. One of the many perils that plagued this kingdom's future: Kezerah's inability to face even the smallest obstacle head on. And why must Elize *be* an obstacle? If she only tried, only listened to her, Kezerah could be the most powerful instrument ever played. The lead in the ballet.

She and Ambrose continued their niceties, and her daughter marched over to the younger prince of Xenkesh. The one with no political power or crown to inherit. Worse yet, she seemed to interrupt the conversation Prince Rorrik had with his Sword Master. A few words passed and Kezerah crossed her arms and raised a brow. What kind of lively conversation—no, confrontation was she having? Elize stared. Rorrik frowned and stamped a foot. Really, how impossible was it for her to be diplomatic?

'Be good,' she urged, *'be a queen—'* Elize recognized the folly as she thought it. Her daughter could never painlessly fall into that role. She'd need to be molded into it, guided, forced mayhaps. Unfortunately, Elize had been trying all the above. If Kezerah continued on this way, Elize would need to find another way. A way for Kezerah to be much more useful and much less involved. She hoped it wouldn't come to that. Elize wanted nothing more than a smooth performance.

KEZERAH AWAITED RORRIK'S ATTENTION. The prince had been easy enough to find, as he stood in full regalia: a pearly scaled breastplate, flashy with golden trim to match his cloak. His hands flew wildly while speaking with his guard or Sword Master. Elastor held no Sword Master, so Kezerah only had Eriko to compare to. This woman could not have been further from Eriko. While Eriko stood dense and broad, this woman had been drawn with nothing but sharp angles and harsh lines. Fair in skin, eyes, and hair, everything about her appeared as cold and remote as her expression. Kezerah approached cautiously.

"I'm telling you, Azalea, if there's anyone who could beat—" Rorrik cut off abruptly, noticing her.

Kezerah hadn't expected to end the conversation. The sudden silence overwhelmed her prepared invitation. "Sorry, please go on," she said, not wanting to annoy him. When he did not, but continued to wait for her to speak, she tried again. "I was just looking for your brother and—"

"He's over there," Rorrik said, rolling his eyes. "Talking to your mother." He jerked his chin in gesture, practically dismissing her.

Whatever she'd said had somehow offended him. She attempted to fix it. "I was looking for you too, actually."

His frown remained but his eyebrows raised. "What for?"

"I meant to invite you both down for a walk along the Summer Quarter beaches."

Rorrik grunted. "Yeah, no thanks. Strolls along the sand aren't really my thing." He paused, palming a side belt loop. "It shouldn't be yours either. The coast is dangerous. Why don't you go lunar lily picking or something? I'm *sure* Ambrose would join you for that."

Azalea looked down at him in disapproval, but did not contradict his behavior. Annoyance prickled at the back of Kezerah's neck. "I think I can manage the Lull. But I imagine with all that armor on, you'd sink right in. Better stay up here where it's safe."

His frown deepened. "Make fun all you want. If pirates decide to abduct you off of your elite beach—"

"If only there were someone with us to ensure the safety of our stroll," she said with feigned innocence.

Rorrik looked more exasperated now than angry. He seemed to understand she worked to trap him in the argument but didn't have the stamina to fight it. "Lovely," he drawled. "Another quick wit. Fine, Princess, if you truly believe my brother isn't adequate protection, I'll accompany you." He turned to Azalea. "Think on it," he insisted, almost pleading, and took down his drink in full.

Rorrik ungracefully approached his brother, and Kezerah followed close behind. The queen spoke animatedly with Ambrose who appeared engrossed in her story. While she didn't wish to be around her mother, Kezerah found herself next to her anyway: a pendulum swung forward.

"Ah, Kezerah!" Elize said with a wide smile, caught mid laugh. "It's so nice to see you in the social halls for once. And look, you're not dressed in dirt." Kezerah bared her teeth, envying that pendulums, while striking a cold, hard force, were promised the release of being blown back. Instead, Elize hammered her in place; Her hand on Kezerah's shoulder weighed her down before she turned back to Ambrose conspiratorially. "She often sneaks off to run through the mud. You must be leaving a good impression on her."

Ambrose's grin could have lit kindling. "I've been told I leave an impression." His smile grew private as his eyes slid to Kezerah's. "Whether it's a good impression or not is still up for debate."

Elize laughed. "Well then, I'll leave you to it. At this point I believe any impression will do." Her smile held as she leaned in close. "Do not leave their side." She still felt the pinch at her jaw from the last time she'd defied her mother. Kezerah tugged away, freeing herself with a disguised bow and stiffly moving to stand by Ambrose. Her mother looked satiated. "Have fun." Then she joined a crowd who cooed at her in welcome.

Ambrose tilted his head and squinted at Kezerah. "You look—" She expected a compliment. "—ill. Are you in pain?"

A laugh escaped Rorrik. Ambrose glared at his brother then grimaced, rubbing the back of his neck. He tried again. "I only mean, you pull off a person being tortured quite well."

'Oh, excellent.' She'd asked to feel desirable and gotten this instead. Elize still glanced at her from across the room. Kezerah rolled her neck and tried to shake off a headache that probed at her temple. The princes had been found, she could leave. "Right, fine. Let's go." She grabbed Ambrose's hand and his breath caught as she dragged him from the party, Rorrik trailing behind.

Outside, crisp eventide air refreshed Kezerah's senses, the warmth of Ambrose's hand being the first to return. They had shared a physical closeness in Heartsglove, but she wasn't so sure if that was a safe habit to establish. Her pulse quickened as she remembered last night, which now held an illicit quality. She released him.

"Sorry, I think it just got a bit hot in there with the fires," she said, before adding more honestly, "and my mother makes me feel like a bird in a cage."

Ambrose looked down at her, nodding, green eyes concerned. This wasn't right, she was supposed to feel self-possessed and in control. Instead she felt strange in her own skin, like she didn't own, but borrowed it.

She smiled at him. "I thought we'd walk the Summer beaches," she said in invitation. "Rorrik, of course, joining us to make sure we're not procured by pirates." Ambrose seemed to notice his brother for the first time. Rorrik appeared less haughty now that the presumption of protecting his older brother had been announced in front of him.

A slow smile slid across Ambrose's face. "I feel safer already."

THEY TOOK the spiral stairs from the outdoor seating of the Summer Quarters. Ambrose imagined this would be his favorite place to frequent if it were several seasons warmer. He appreciated the Xenkesh-inspired tile design and the familiar sound of The Lull as it smoothly caressed the coast. He had seen both oceans, on either side of Thrice, and much preferred The Lull's placid waters to The Brash's rocky shores. Although both suffered from storms, The Brash itself churned like a tempest, while The Lull offered nothing but vast tranquility, with shots of distant lighting that skittered across bruised clouds.

From the Elastian vantage point, he was surprised to see the Isle of Bethync, far closer than he'd imagined it would be. Nothing but spindled black trees rose into the crackling storm. Many in Xenkesh said the island kept the storms at bay, from ever coming to land, but Ambrose knew that to be untrue. The island was powerful, awe-striking and ancient, but it did not harbor a sanctuary from the storms; it bridged to them. Bethync was a conduit to the afterlife, the Summerlands: a place of reverence and respect, not worship. He also knew, long ago, Elastor had been known for its earthquakes and tremors. Until the first incarnation of the girl before him had put them to an end.

Now that girl made lazy twirls in the sand with her bare feet, the fresh air seeming to have cured her peculiar behavior from before. The salt that curled into his nose smelled like home and regardless of the chill, he couldn't help but remove his boots to press his feet into the brisk sand. It was soft, and he nestled his feet in further, enjoying the sensation between his toes. Rorrik looked around, antsy and cautious while Kezerah watched him with an amused expression. In the dim dusk, stray glows of light could be seen streaking across the sky. Ambrose moved forward, feeling a bit homesick.

"This is nice," he told Kezerah, appreciating the gesture.

"Sorry," she said. "I know it's not exactly the right time of year, or hour."

"A kind thought all the same."

Her smile disarmed him. He thought of taking up her hand again, his palm still feeling the absence of her palm's warmth. He suddenly wanted his brother to be nowhere near him. Rorrik looked as if he wanted the same thing. He eyed the coast with skittish distrust. He must be taking the job of protector very seriously, Ambrose thought. Why did Kezerah continuously invite his younger brothers along? Perhaps she'd asked him to be a chaperone of sorts?

Or perhaps not, as she struck up a conversation with him. "So, how close have you come to beating Eriko?"

"Closer than most." Rorrik attempted to sound stiff, but it was obviously a topic he wanted to speak more on. "Andarios of Luka has lasted just as long as me, but I'd also just eaten, so it's fairly even."

Kezerah looked captivated as they walked. Ambrose decided not to interrupt and instead take the moment to watch her. He realized, outside of her friends, he hadn't seen her interact with others at court. He wished to see what she did with someone as obnoxious as Rorrik.

"Have you fought Andarios as well?"

"Oh yeah, plenty of times. He's brutal, but I'm definitely faster."

Kezerah smiled in encouragement. "Oh, how many times have you beat him?"

Ambrose smiled, knowing the answer to this one. Rorrik had defeated the large soldier precisely zero times.

"It's hard to say," Rorrik stalled. "There's a lot that goes into a match. Points and such."

"Rorrik," Ambrose warned, his brother's ego bordering on defiling another soldier's name.

"Fine, I haven't beat him yet, technically, but I've pretty much figured out all of his weaknesses," Rorrik admitted, sounding as vain as he was.

Ambrose let his cheeks fill with air before blowing it out in irritation.

Kezerah did not appear bothered however, smile still dazzling. She walked close to Ambrose, but he wanted her to turn that smile on him, instead of humoring his brother. "Oh, what weaknesses have you noticed?"

Rorrik grew energetic. "Well, he favors his left for certain. He also pulls back on his final blow, almost as if he doesn't want to end the fight. You can tell he doesn't Hold Sway yet either because, while we're not really allowed to use magick in drills, everyone slips it in now and then. But he'll start the Sway, then hesitate, and nothing happens. So after the first time you know a surprise hit isn't coming."

Kezerah nodded, seeming to catalog the information like a scholar on Bethync.

Ambrose could take no more of his brother's over confident voice. "I'd like to see how the Lull temperatures differ from Xenkesh," he said, using the excuse to grab Kezerah's hand. He cursed his treacherous pulse as it quickened upon the touch and escorted her towards the waters that lapped lazily next to them. *'Focus,'* he told himself for the hundredth time since his arrival. She'd given away his mother's location in candid conversation. The advantage was his.

She seemed dazed for a moment, looking at her hand in his. He wondered if he'd made a mistake. The thought made his palm clammy. Then she moved towards him, her kindred sly smile in place. "I think curiosity may get the better of you. The Bastian icebergs seep down this way, and while refreshing in the Summer—"

"Princess, if you're frightened, I remind you that Rorrik is here to save us," he injected his words with as much mockery as he could manage.

His dare worked, her face grew determined and she began tying her dress in a knot between her legs and about her waist. Frigid water licked his heels, and he tried and failed to hold back a wince.

She smiled predatorily, and his breath caught as she took the lead, dragging him into the water up to his knees. "Prince Ambrose," she crooned, before deepening her voice in an outlandish mockery of his, "if you're too frightened to swim you can join your brother on the beach."

She let his hand go, and dipped down, fully submerging herself in the biting tide.

Unwilling to be beaten at his own game, he pressed his teeth together, marching into the water like a prisoner to his death. His body numbed with the cold, the salt of the sea tasted less potent and familiar in these chilly depths.

Cascades of crimson hair rose from the water as Kezerah came up for air, appearing delighted to see he had joined her. Rorrik sat sullenly on the sand, useless in his armor. Guilt took hold for a heartbeat. Then, Kezerah arched back, floating atop the water, completely indifferent to its harsh temperature. All thoughts of his brother banished from his mind. He tried to control his shivering to enjoy the moment.

"Is the Lull that much different in Xenkesh?" she asked. He wondered if she could hear him, her ears still underwater and voice carrying.

"Vastly," he said. "Though, the Brash is so frigid I could hardly stick a toe in."

Kezerah bobbed up to stand, her full attention gained. "You've seen the Brash Sea?"

Ambrose tried not to warm himself with his arms and nodded. "One of our fishing cities, Broxen, is on its coastline." He paused, wondering how the subject of war was meant to be handled. He erred on the side of recklessly. "It's also where our ocean fleets depart, and enemy ships dock. It used to be beautiful."

Kezerah glanced towards the shore, where Rorrik stacked rocks. "Used to be."

Ambrose noticed she restated rather than asked further. It felt like a workaround, a way to continue the conversation. He took it. "The houses are painted black to beckon the sun. Then, at night, they're covered in luminescent algae of sorts, so the houses glow. From Pluvia, our mountain—"

"Volcano, you mean," Rorrik said from the beach. Ambrose slapped the water up on shore, his brother silenced after a yelp.

"From Zelos, it looks like starlit lanterns floating in the sea," he finished, a little more irritated than when he'd started.

"I'd love to see it."

"Unfortunately," Ambrose said, "Broxen has...changed. Most of the homes are abandoned, and the western half of Zelos is often plagued by skirmishes or rogue Aloran forces."

Kezerah looked down, a hand skirting across the water's tranquil surface. "Sorry, I meant... It wouldn't be possible for me to see it regardless." Stars winked into her reflection as she stirred, more orbs of light passed above them. "But I'll be sorry to have missed it."

"Right, of course. In the next lifetime—" Ambrose caught himself as she winced. It was a common phrase said in Xenkesh, but with Bethync looming behind her—a stretch of storm and afterlife she'd never reach—he felt like a fool. "However," he said, braving a lower depth of the cold water to move towards her. "You also weren't permitted in Heartsglove, so let's not give in just yet."

"Wow." She floated back and circled him. "Nobody has ever offered to smuggle me into a war zone before."

He liked how her voice let out the words, like a playful purr.

"Say the word and I'd gladly whisk you away. Though, I'm pretty sure that would be considered a war crime."

She floated closer, eyes bright at the prospect of being kidnapped. Her trust enticed but worried him. A sense of protectiveness intruded his thoughts. The idea of someone hurting or trying to take advantage of her suddenly appalled him. He caught his own reflection near hers and drew away, fighting the action. What could really be said about what he was doing? Could he not gain her favor and have interest? It wasn't as if the battle could only be won if he were miserable. He relaxed his shoulders, before they stiffened again in a shiver.

She gazed up from dark lashes, her smile as bright as her eyes. "If we leave now, we can get hot baths before dinner."

He regretted cutting their time short, but the promise of hot water overwhelmed him. "A singular bath will be fine. No need to spoil us with bathing separately."

"Come on," she said, amused. "Your words lose their allure when your lips are blue."

He tried to laugh, but it came out as a tremble and they waded back to the beach. He took his time with the straps of his boots in order to admire her, her dress clinging tightly to her body, every curve on display.

Rorrik kicked him, and he looked up, for once embarrassed at being caught. "Can you at least pretend to care that I'm standing here?" Ambrose attempted to look confused. Rorrik would have none of it. "The next time you need a chaperone, bring Azalea so she can at least beat you properly." He lingered as Ambrose moved to follow Kezerah up the stairs.

"I think I'll stay here a bit longer."

"A fan of moon gazing now?" Ambrose teased.

Rorrik rolled his eyes. "See you for evening meal."

At the top of the stairs Ambrose caught Kezerah mid-altercation with Dyllian. "You don't own the ocean, Princess," the lordling harrumphed.

"Just all your land and the surrounding area," she chimed. Ambrose found this an unorthodox way to speak to subjects, but Kezerah had proven to be a rather unorthodox person. She caught him watching her then blushed and muttered. "I told you, he's a menace."

Ambrose allowed Dyllian to move past him before leaning down to her ear. "Would you rather me smuggle him into a war zone?"

She laughed too loud to be subtle. "Ha, don't tempt me."

ONCE BATHED, Ambrose rushed to meet Kezerah at her door. She'd given him an inquisitive stare in greeting that he could've gotten lost in, but he broke her spell by offering his arm. "I thought we might sit together?" Relief eased his chest when she—finally— smiled and agreed.

He sat himself beside Rorrik and Kezerah took the seat to his left.

"Behave," he mumbled to his brother.

Rorrik scoffed. "I'm not the one who's wasted an afternoon fawning instead of wooing."

"Convenient, since you lack the skill."

"What are we whispering about?" Kezerah whispered, her lips twitched in amusement. A small dimple dotted the corner of her cheek. Ambrose noticed when she arched her brow in confusion, her freckles followed, like twinkling stars.

"We heard The Edge expanded due to Aloran raids," Rorrik said brazenly. "Care to cut in?"

Stupid, stupid, stupid. Ambrose kicked his brother under the table, but it was too late. Kezerah's expression fell from a grin to grimace. A night sky devoid of stars. She turned away, towards her plate. "No, I'd rather not. Thank you."

"That's fine," Ambrose said quickly. Pain bit at the back of his ankle.

"Sure," Rorrik said, "it's dandy. I bet it will all sort itself out. Anyway, let's talk about...what's left to talk about with our ally, Am, the weather?"

Kezerah's head dipped low, as if to scry into her stew, but her hand gripped into a tight fist in her lap. She was agitated; she held back. Ambrose wondered what opinions she held in. Tactically, allowing Rorrik to continue to prod her might lead to results. Ambrose warred with himself. Her shoulders curved in, her hair draped around her like a curtain of fire willow leaves. This was not an offensive posture; this was the posture of someone miserable. Kezerah miserable reared up something horrible inside of him.

He turned his attention first to his Bond, then Rorrik's fork. He focused on heating the metal. It obliged him cheerily.

"Ouch! Hey!" Rorrik said, dropping the now searing hot fork.

Kezerah looked up in alarm, and Ambrose caught her gaze and held it. "I believe the weather to be an excellent topic." He nodded towards her. "Do you have a favorite season?"

While the levity from earlier didn't return, she gave a little smile. "I'm partial to Summer."

He bumped his elbow into hers as he picked up his own fork. "It must be all that 'planting, sewing, and growing', you Elastians do." He punctuated his joke with a wink.

"That," Kezerah agreed, "and the cherry suncakes."

Rorrik grumbled behind him, but didn't dare interfere.

"Thanks," Kezerah muttered and took a bite of stew.

"What are allies for?" His smile fell, disappointed to see she now solely focused on her food.

The rest of the meal sped by. It seemed when not one of the grander feasts, guests left as their bellies filled. Kezerah only managed to answer questions he asked between mouthfuls of what Ambrose considered a bland simmered pumpkin and salmon dish. Due to her sudden ferocious appetite, she finished with her food much quicker than he. With a yawn, and a misty-eyed farewell, she disappeared from his side as quick as her curtsey.

Disquiet maddened his thoughts as she walked away. What if she'd only sat next to him out of obligation? The idea made him feel uneasy. He thought back to the beach, picking apart their conversation. Now she moved around the table, her steps leading her to Ikaika. Ambrose remembered her stating that she often visited her friends' bedchambers at night. He felt a flash of envy that he had to steal time away, while Ikaika simply waited for her to tiptoe into his bed.

Ambrose groaned. How many times had his father emphasized the necessity of border relations? Inviting the Sorrels, keeping in contact with Elowren and Elize, and constantly allowing trade deals to lapse without a rise in tax; all for Ambrose to not seek Haven out of pride, allowing Illija and Ikaika to seek it out of grand strategy. Foolish.

Ambrose stood fast enough that he felt Rorrik startle next to him.

"Where are you—oh, don't," Rorrik begged. "Let it go."

"Not a chance." Ambrose caught up to Kezerah and Ikaika, exiting the hall. Arm in arm. Ambrose attempted to calm himself, remembering Ikaika had the unnerving ability to sometimes hear his thoughts. *'Drum, sand, honeydew, sea breeze...'* he listed off to himself, emptying his mind to leave Ikaika at a disadvantage.

"Prin—" He stopped himself. Not allies, friends. "Kezerah."

Her hair swished like soft clouds in a storm as she turned to him. She waited, her open and curious face contrasting Ikaika's masked hostility. Ambrose began to invite her to do something, and realized he didn't know what she liked to do. He thought back to their time on the beach.

"Would you want to join me in the training yards tomorrow morning?"

"Oh…" Her face scrunched in thought. Ikaika choked a laugh next to her. Wrong. Wrong. He'd been wrong. She nudged Ikaika and seemed to come back to herself. "Yes, that sounds… nice."

Nice.

Ambrose wanted nothing more than to submerge himself in the Lull, and stay there. He stood awkwardly for a moment, then backed up. Retreat. Ikaika saw the easy kill.

"I have lessons with Biloba in the morning, but Eriko will be in the Northern yards," he nudged Kezerah playfully. "Maybe you can watch him finally meet his match."

Ambrose's desire to drown his brother dethroned his wish to sink into the Lull. "Maybe she will," he said, with more bravado than he currently owned. "A shame you can't join in."

"Really." Ikaika smiled at Ambrose for what felt like the first time. "I'll be sad to have missed it."

Kezerah looked marginally more intrigued. "Alright, the Northern Yards it is then." Her smile bemused at the edges. "I'll be there."

A Bit a Fool

AMBROSE DIDN'T MIND LOSING A FIGHT, NOT IF HE COULD learn from it. However, after being thrown on his ass in the mud for a fifth time—bones rattling on impact and a practice sword at his throat—it was getting a bit ridiculous. He told himself it was fine, and that he didn't care that Kezerah watched.

She perched on the wood fencing, legs lazily dangling down towards the mud he lay in. The practice yards themselves were small compared to home; nothing more than a corral for horses or mounts. Kezerah's presence made him feel as if he were in an arena, a warrior fighting for favor, as she observed Eriko pummel him to the ground. Her pretty, heart-shaped face gazed down at him with concern, positioned above his fall. Her slender brows knitted together, and lips pinched. Ambrose couldn't tell if she held back laughter or a cry of concern. Either way, she held back.

Ambrose let loose a huff of breath, not able to handle any more of her poor facade of pity. Eriko reached out a hand. Ambrose pressed his teeth together to gain enough dignity to be lifted up by the scarred soldier. A clean shaven head and face made Eriko's scar standout like a badge of honor. Ambrose wondered who had dared to cleave this man's face in two, and how dead they were. Based on Ambrose's abysmal performance, he guessed they were very dead.

"Another round?" Eriko offered, his voice friendlier than one would expect from a well-sharpened blade.

Ambrose gave a sidelong look at Kezerah, who now seemed so bored by his continual failures that she instead inspected individual strands of her hair. He couldn't blame her. Her hair was beautiful and, while Ambrose bested many of his own soldiers, Eriko had made a mess of him.

Azalea would be livid if she found out, and he took solace in the fact that all the other fighters in the practice yards were covered in mud and bruises too.

"I think I've learned my lesson for the day," Ambrose conceded.

The man nodded. "Good."

Ambrose detected the barest edge in the Sword Master's voice. Fair enough. The two of them had been cordial, considering Eriko had personally trained most of the warriors now invading Xenkesh's borders. That was, until, on Queen Illija's orders, Eriko had become a glorified babysitter, guarding her most precious son.

'*Kingsguard*,' Ambrose sneered. He went to put his practice blade away, wishing he could use the real blades at his sides. He felt for them in reassurance while trying to manicure his features. With the war so vastly out of their control, Amarus hadn't been able to assign Ambrose a Kingsguard. Despite him being crown prince, they couldn't afford a soldier of that skill to stand by Ambrose.

Azalea going with them had been risky, a privilege his Kingdom probably paid for in blood, while Illija sent Eriko away to wipe the floor with them in a dingy practice yard like it was nothing. No wonder Xenkesh was losing. He returned the practice blade to the line up.

"Are you alright?" Kezerah asked. Ambrose realized she no longer looked at her hair, all attention on his face. He felt the nasty bruise purpling on his cheekbone and pressed on it, wincing.

"Nothing a Mirage and some time can't fix," he assured, the smile he gave her deepened the pain of the wound.

"I meant your mood," she said, frowning a little. "You looked... angry."

"Oh." Well, that was unfortunate. Angry people were not appealing, and he didn't want her to believe he was a sore loser. Rorrik's sputtering from earlier had given her face a soured expression. Kezerah waited patiently for him to come up with more words. He walked over to her, the ground still soft from the day's practice.

"I just know my sword master will have a thing or two to say if she finds out all her training resulted in her pupil being tossed in the mud." Ambrose leaned against the wooden fence she sat on, making sure their shoulders touched, then regretted it as mud smudged her velvet blue dress. "Sorry," he said, and leaned away, digging in his pocket for cloth to Bind into a kerchief.

But Kezerah scooted over to reclaim the spot at his arm. "It's fine," she snorted, ungracefully. "It's just mud." Ambrose took the moment to admire her, something about this expression delighting him differently than her others. She seemed at ease, a bundle of mischief and keen eyes emerging despite her finely oiled ringlets and crisply ironed gown.

"Do you ever spar?" he asked, knowing he had stared too long by the arch of her brow. "You seem the type with pent up energy."

"I tried swordplay for a time," she admitted, a flash of teeth clamping down lightly on alluring lips. Ambrose made an active effort to meet her eyes. "But it's so—" her head tilted side to side, neck lovely and elongated, "—regimented. I had to train at dawn in order to have time to properly dress for meals. It took up all of my free time. Then I wanted to learn hand to hand combat instead. So, I did that for a while and..." She trailed off with a shrug. "I've done a bit of it all and not enough to do anything with it."

That potential felt wasted, but telling her so would probably lead to violence, regardless of how poor her form might be. He switched tactics. "I'm sure your words are clever enough that you need no blade."

Her smile spread to reveal a falsely coy expression. Her eyes danced with his flirtation. "I've been told I can be quite sharp of tongue when left unchecked."

"A duel I'd gladly challenge you to."

"I thought you'd finished for the day." Her tone was playful, but her expression seemed greedy for more. She expected him to up their stakes.

He obliged. Hands caked in mud, he leaned in, a hand alighted to cup her jaw and brush a thumb across her full bottom lip. Soft and plush, he tried not to imagine opening them in a kiss. Possibly grazing his teeth there, and moving closer, to muddy her dress further.

Instead he locked onto her eyes; flashing gems of starlight that smoldered upon widening. He withheld a gulp, focusing on trying to keep the rasp from his voice, as her lips slightly parted for him.

"If your tongue is involved, I'm happy to make an exception."

Color bloomed high on her cheeks and, for one full blink of her thick, dark lashes, he heard her voice catch.

Ambrose pushed off the fencing, jarring her further, and his smile turned lupine. "However, I have indeed worked up an appetite, and should change before I enter the Autumn Hall."

The true hunger in him had more to do with her mouth—now lightly speckled with mud—and the quickening rise and fall of her chest as she tried to recover her composure. He ignored the coil of tension that built up in him. She had bewitched him several times now, and he needed to regain a semblance of control over the situation. Fawning over her wouldn't do that.

So instead, he offered a hand. A trill budded in his ribcage as her delicate fingers placed themselves in the fold of his muddy ones. He walked her toward the Autumn Hall and then quickly excused himself to change.

ANDARIOS' gray mare blew her warm and pleasantly rancid breath into his face. She dug at the mud beneath them, impatient to leave the corral. Soldiers fought as he waited for his sparring partner to finish his morning break.

"I know, girl," Andarios cooed. "Drills, guard duty, then we're off to frolic until evening meal."

"Alright, enough flirting with your sweetheart." Fennel, his sparring partner, took another swig of water from his deerskin and wiped the dribble from his chin. His body looked too narrow for his height, like he stood on stilts about to topple over. Too bad he moved like a fresh sprung arrow. "Let's go another round."

Andarios planted a kiss on his horse's snout good naturedly, and turned to face his friend. "We'll be married at the rate you take water breaks."

Fennel smirked, then lifted his sword in response, and struck out towards Andarios' thigh. The two sparred for several minutes before Andarios went to block Fennel and found his opponent no longer attacking. Fennel looked past him, and Andarios turned before letting a groan escape.

"Looks like our fight's over," Fennel said, sardonically.

Prince Rorrik of Xenkesh, rested, washed, and dressed head to toe—not in training gear, but full-fledged battle armor—sauntered into the training yards. His expression looked like he was already in a foul mood and required someone to take it out on. In the last week of practices, that had been Andarios.

"Maybe he won't pick me today," Andarios said.

Fennel scoffed. "Maybe if you'd let him beat you on day one, that'd be true."

He knew Fennel was right. The first time Rorrik had joined them (after a hearty breakfast, good night's sleep and bath) he'd walked in like he had something to prove. Andarios' size had obviously played a role in picking him but Andarios hadn't minded, at first. Until he'd won and Rorrik demanded a rematch, again, and again, and again. It had consumed his entire practice.

When the prince showed up the next day with his elder brother, Andarios had made the mistake of ending the fight too early. Almost slipping up and using Sway at the last moment before calming himself. Then he'd seen an opening, catching Rorrik in a winning strike. Ambrose had laughed, far too loud to be kind, and the mud around Rorrik's feet practically boiled with his rage. Instead of lifting his practice sword, Rorrik had flung it into the dirt and hurled insults until his brother dragged him from the field. Andarios had thought that would be that, but Rorrik continued to show up, as he pleased, using drills like his own personalized training grounds.

Fennel wandered off, in search of a new sparring partner before Rorrik came over. Aware that Rook, his captain, continued to survey him, Andarios bowed stiffly. Rorrik responded by lifting his wooden blade higher, and charging forward. Andarios gritted his teeth. Rorrik wasn't a bad fighter by a stretch but he seemed to fight under a self-inflicted pressure, and that pressure crushed his restraint rather than honing it. He fought each battle as if cornered; sporadic strikes with power behind them. Andarios needed nothing more than to pay attention and use brute strength to fend him off. It irked him that each match did little but reinforce the idea that his strength relied on nothing more than his size. If he could beat Eriko, that would change. But to do that, he needed to get this over with.

Rorrik had obviously grown flustered because he jeered. "That's all you've got!"

Andarios blocked, and had enough time to glance Rook's way. His captain needed to know he fought better than this, that he took training seriously. The captain's eyes were as gray as the overcast clouds, and as unreadable as the stars hidden behind them.

Rorrik tried another taunt. "Still slow! You must be training with those Alorans. Did you get a nice little meditation in before stretching?"

Andarios suspected that there laid the real reason Rorrik showed up with a puffed out chest and venom to spew. While Rorrik might not be able to attack Ikaika, or Alora directly, he could fight Andarios without consequence. Andarios did not intend to give him the satisfaction, not when he too had something to prove: something far more important than Rorrik's fragile ego.

"Yeah, but don't worry. Kai beats me half the time," Andarios said. "So you're halfway to being half as good as him."

Rorrik's laugh was acidic. "Elastor really loves letting low-borns believe themselves high. You think because you've won a few brawls you can speak to me like that?" Andarios' practice sword diminished in weight, it felt like he now fought with a dandelion. It clashed against a sword so heavy it sent a shock wave up his arm. He clamped down for a tighter hold on his feeble flower of a blade. Rorrik was using his Bond magick to cheat.

'Kai, your brother is a prick.' Out loud, Andarios huffed, as impatient as his horse to get this over with. "Rorrik, less whinging, more fighting."

"That's *Prince* Rorrik to you, Edge scum!" Rorrik raised his sword far too high to be anything but a wild swing in Andarios' direction. Block, block, block.

Kezerah had told Andarios just what Rorrik thought of his fighting style. Andarios hadn't wanted to play unfair, but his sword felt as empty as his stomach. Andarios made a small swipe, just a smidge of his Hold on Sway, and watched Rorrik ignore a blow he assumed would never come. Rorrik stumbled. Andarios used the moment of shock to dislodge the opposing sword, breaking his own sword in two. Rorrik, further off balance, lost his footing and fell to the ground alongside Andarios' splintered sword. He pointed the shattered hilt at Rorrik's throat. Andarios half expected the prince to rise like a snake and strike out. Instead Rorrik's chest rose and fell, as his lungs tried to regain their lost air through his flared nostrils.

Andarios laughed, real and hearty. "I have but one monarch I serve, and she doesn't go by prince."

"'Queen', I'm sure, is the word you find most appropriate, as a member of the Queen's army, *Lower* Lord of Luka." Queen Elize appeared like a wraith at Rook's side, her posture as severe as her eyes while she surveyed him. Suddenly, the midday frost didn't have much bite to it. Andarios didn't dare answer her. He wasn't a liar, nor a fool. His loyalty would always be with Kezerah, and Kezerah alone. Instead he bowed, making sure it fell marginally lower than what he'd given Rorrik.

Elize watched him a moment longer, and a wave of unease passed over him. Her gaze shifted, landing on Rook to his relief. "A ship was spotted last night too close to our coast for comfort."

Rook bowed. "I'll have a coastal perimeter check at dawn."

"I'd like our very best to also check the Winter Woods. As Kezerah most often frequents it."

"Done." Rook surveyed the gathering of soldiers.

Andarios straightened and tried to catch his captain's eye.

"Fennel, take an elk along the coast and wood tomorrow. Pack a meal, that's half a day's ride."

Well, that stung.

"Did the Lower Lord of Luka not win this last bout?" Queen Elize asked, the admission disfigured her mouth in a soured frown. Andarios' mouth gaped open.

"He did," Rook agreed, then gave Andarios a hard look. "But Luka hardly makes it to drills on time and can be regularly found in the feasting hall with Her Majesty Soul Heir."

"Captain." Andarios couldn't help himself. "I haven't missed a drill since—"

"Since last week, when the Soul Heir's Queensguard position was announced," Rook finished. "It takes more than a week to build discipline."

"Come on, I've been training since I could hold a sword,"

Andarios said, a glance thrown at Rorrik. "And I finish at the top of the bracket in every tournament."

Rorrik pushed himself up. "And you cheat to do it! I felt you Hold Sway!"

Andarios tensed. This was an honor code not broken amongst soldiers. Apart from Rook, (who held no Sway) people commonly agreed, if casting magick, that it stayed between the two fighters. This would have been a minor inconvenience if...

"Unregistered magick is a punishable offense," said Queen Elize, "and he holds no such registration."

"Then punish him," Rorrik said, "for an undiplomatic victory."

'Undiplomatic victory?' Andarios resisted the urge to spit, but surprised himself when he spoke instead. He turned his attention to Elize. "It's true. I Hold Sway." Andarios wished a fond farewell to his room with an exhale. "I'm sorry I didn't mention it before. I feared us being separated and 'diplomats' aren't going to protect your daughter."

"Luka!" Rook scolded.

Elize pointed her chin high, and Andarios hated how much of a Kezerah-like gesture it was. "And you will?" she challenged. "You think you're better than every warrior in my battalion, the best of what Elastor has to offer?" She gave a grand sweeping gesture to all the soldiers that watched, forcing Andarios to meet their eyes. He saw challenges in several of their expressions, but he kept his gaze steady.

When his stare landed on hers again he made sure not to blink. "The best for her, yes."

Rorrik made a disgusted sound, but Andarios didn't dare break away from Elize's attention, even though the longer he held it, the dizzier he became. When she turned towards Rook, she looked tired, as if fatigued from the exertion of hating him.

"Register the Lower Lord of Luka with Holding Sway and put him on the forest route tomorrow."

Andarios' head spun. He had known this woman close to his entire life. Not once had she sided with him, let alone avoided the opportunity to punish him.

Rook bristled at the contradiction. "Alright, Luka. Let's see how that discipline has settled in. Be here by dawn, or I'm putting Fennel on scout duty."

"Yes, Captain." Andarios saluted, then as a forgotten gesture he bowed to his queen. "Thank you, Your High Majesty."

"Just be thorough," she said, and pivoted with skirts drawn up high to avoid the mud, towards the Autumn Hall.

Andarios tried to piece together his queen's change of heart. Kezerah definitely would've thrown a fit if his rooms had been moved, but those spats were typical between those two.

When the queen's silhouette had disappeared behind a doorway, Rorrik scoffed. "It's amazing Elastor has survived so long with Edge scum guarding its gates, let alone its royalty."

Edge scum. In the heat of battle, this had been a taunt easily ignored. But as Rorrik stood there, draped in gaudy finery that could feed an entire village suffering from Xenkesh and Alora's war, Andarios could only muster false sympathy. "It must have been embarrassing, sitting there, covered in mud, knowing you weren't even considered, let alone the best."

The soldiers around them in-took a breath. Perhaps he was a *bit* a fool.

"As if I care I wasn't put on some Elastian scouting mission. I'm a prince."

Andarios laughed. "You think it's because you're a prince? You weren't considered because losing to me is as close as you'll ever get to winning."

Rorrik marched towards the spike of dulled blades. "Again then!"

Andarios turned away. "That's alright, big day tomorrow." He exaggerated a stretch. "But enjoy sleeping in."

"Fight me, you overgrown dolt!"

Name calling: the middling hobby of the uninspired. Andarios rolled his eyes and looked over his shoulder. "You can fight me at dawn, I'll be the one too busy for your blustering. Or come along if you'd like. See how us Elastians survived so long without you."

Rorrik looked like he fought an internal battle with himself, and was losing.

"Enough of this," Rook said. "Sentinels, at your posts. Reconvene at dawn. Your Majesty—"

He addressed Rorrik now, and Andarios took pleasure in how delicately Rook spoke to this foreign flower who thought himself a soldier. "—Tomorrow, perhaps it's best to practice in the Northern yard. Our morning will be a bit full for swordplay."

Andarios made sure he snickered loud enough to be heard, and climbed onto his mare. Thank Thrice it was just the Solstice Gate post today, maybe he could catch Kezerah on her way to evening meal and do some whinging of his own.

Kezerah groaned as her muscles loosened in a stretch on the Summer Quarter's veranda. Ikaika and Ambrose followed suit, ending the most intense boardgame of Wolves and Rabbits she'd ever played.

She'd found Ikaika reading alongside the ocean view and begged him for a game. Like fog to sea, Ambrose hadn't been far behind, and it had resulted in warm and cool fingers moving the pieces across the board with a bit more fervor than Wolves and Rabbits required. Rabbits slowly disappeared, slammed down on the side of the table. Ambrose had succeeded in taking Ikaika's last remaining opal rabbit and both brothers had stood the moment she did, no words spoken between them.

She hadn't noticed how tense her body had gotten until she heard several cracks sound off in her shoulders and back. She looked up to see the clouds dotted with stars in between their wisps.

"Evening meal will be well underway," Ikaika winced. "I hadn't realized the time."

Ambrose waved his hand, towering over the both of them as he stood. "I'm sure they've saved us food. A perk of being a house guest is that they don't starve you."

Ikaika scoffed, seeming too drained from the match for much snark. "You really don't know Queen Elize. An unkempt guest is an unwelcome one. We'll have to eat in our rooms."

Ambrose turned to Kezerah for confirmation, which she gave willingly. "My mother is... particular. Once the meal begins, the doors are locked." She shrugged. "Your late entrance on the Equinox was remarkable for more than one reason."

Ambrose's face looked delighted as he turned from Ikaika, offering his arm. "Was it so remarkable? I hadn't known."

"It was certainly loud." Ikaika's hand glanced off of hers then, tentatively, it returned. Warmth bloomed in Kezerah's palm as their fingers intertwined. The touch felt as if it held its own spark of life. Her stomach made a small dip. Suddenly, their past casual holding of hands became just that: in the past. Momentarily distracted by his touch, she had to remind herself what Ambrose had said.

"Yes, you made quite the entrance."

Ambrose eyed her interlocked hand with a frown. To combat the look, she took his waiting arm, adding, "Not to mention you shut Dyllian up, leaving me in your debt."

Kezerah pretended not to notice that Ambrose appeared only partially mollified, or that Ikaika held her hand with a new sort of strength in the grip. She laughed, her balancing act made literal by her cattywampus posture.

"A debt paid in full if you join me this evening in the drawing rooms," Ambrose enticed, the odd trio taking deliberate steps down the stairs in order not to fall.

"Actually, I'm not supposed to attend those." Kezerah looked up at him in apology. "Or rather, it usually goes badly if I do."

Ambrose remained undaunted. "All the better. My remarkable entrance can be rewarded with yours."

"Kezerah isn't fond of the after-hours bickering. I'm sure she would prefer to eat in our rooms," Ikaika said.

"I recall you also aren't fond of being spoken of as if you aren't present?" Ambrose inclined his head toward her, a sly grin offered in hopes of reward.

Kezerah also didn't like the sensation of being pulled in either direction. She disentangled herself from both of them as they reached the bottom of the stairs, entering the Spring Quarters.

Luck was on her side and Andarios lingered in her doorway, a bored look on his face until their eyes locked. His expression became heavily amused as he took in both princes on either side. She held her chin up. Despite what she'd been warned, this had not been a disaster and she intended on proving it further.

"Since neither option is much appealing, I shall compromise with a third," she said, answering Andarios' smile as she met him halfway. "We can procure our own dishes, and feast among the stars."

"THANK the Summerlands we're getting food," Andarios said as the four of them crept along the back of the Winter Quarter, towards the kitchens. "One session with Rorrik and I could eat an elk."

"Rorrik?" Kezerah asked in surprise.

Andarios gave a sideways glance in Ambrose's direction, then gave an easy smile as they rounded the final corner. "Yeah, just some sword bouts. Thrice, that smells amazing! What is that, sage?"

The kitchen's air thickened with the hot, rich smells of the final course's preparations: a peppered pork tenderloin with splashes of spinach and legumes.

She heard Ambrose hum in approval behind her and she stifled a laugh, the growling of her own stomach keeping her focused. With the kitchen in full mayhem to present the final dishes, nobody paid any attention to the group that filled their own plates, all four treating the rows of dishes like a personal spread.

That was, until a young kitchen boy spotted them and dashed off, replaced with an irritated Hanan.

"My many young majesties," the steward greeted them flatly. "How kind of you to join us more than a third of the way through our meal."

"Hanan," Kezerah begged. "We're famished, and the sky finally cleared up. We thought we would eat in the maze."

"Famished," Hanan repeated, looking over at Andarios. "I believe I witnessed the young Lord of Luka eating his fill before abruptly leaving, without being excused."

Andarios rubbed at the nape of his neck, his smile guilty. "Well, when Kez and Kai didn't show…"

Ambrose shifted Hanan's attention away. "Perhaps, if we could get permission from the Queen? Would you be willing to send my apologies and formal request that I dine with Kezerah in the maze this evening?"

Kezerah shot Ambrose a look, as that was exactly how not to get out of this situation unscathed, but Hanan looked at Kezerah. "As the Queen resides over all social gatherings, I believe that may be the only proper way to go about this." He looked down the length of his nose at Kezerah. "Would you prefer I ask permission of Her High Majesty? Or do you concede to eating in your *individual* rooms this evening?"

Kezerah rolled her eyes, prepared to be sent to her chambers. "Yes, fine. Ask my mother." The outcome would be the same regardless. Ikaika looked over at her pityingly as Hanan bowed and turned, leaving them in the crowded kitchens.

Andarios nudged her. "Maybe if we run now, he won't bother to find us."

"We'll be hunted like animals," said Kezerah.

"If you stay awake until after the last lantern, I'll join you afterwards," Ikaika offered.

Kezerah nodded, but her hopes had sank. She looked up at Ambrose. "What part of, 'my mother is particular and locks all the doors', made it seem like she could be reasoned with?"

Ambrose shrugged. "While your mother and you may clash, she's seemed inclined to be hospitable for me."

"And why is that?" Ikaika asked, his question layered with suspicion.

Ambrose popped a brussel sprout, heavily laden with butter, into his mouth. "Because I'm a guest?"

"As am I," Ikaika countered. "You don't see me being given special treatment."

"Perhaps I'm a guest who hasn't overstayed his welcome," Ambrose said. "I'm sure you and Kezerah are practically seen as siblings now."

Ikaika's face heated and Kezerah sensed another argument. She cleared her throat, in a reminder of their promise to attempt civility. While Ikaika looked close to hissing, she was grateful he said nothing.

Hanan returned, his eyes a bit wide. "The queen has granted you permission to eat in the maze before you return, *and remain,* in your rooms for the last lantern."

Kezerah's head tilted back in surprise. "Are you—are you sure?"

Hanan did not respond to her, instead addressing Ikaika and Andarios. "She has also granted remaining Spring Quarter residents permission to re-enter the feast, or you may eat your *pillaged* courses in your rooms—as social etiquette requires."

Her jaw dropped at the blatant rudeness of the statement. "What? But that's not fair!"

Andarios looked unsurprised, but Ikaika's jaw clenched.

She turned to Ambrose who now seemed to be engaged with an invisible speck on his silken tunic. "Make your request more clear. All of us are to eat in the maze."

He gave her a slow sidelong glance, as if it took effort to pull his focus from the thread. "I don't want to be too forward with my host."

"Hanan!" She might as well be protesting to a withered tree, asking for it to produce apples past the harvest.

The steward looked impatient, his services needed elsewhere. "Soul Heir Kezerah, you have been granted permission to eat outside of your rooms. I suggest you act on them before she changes her mind—and, I remind you, the queen is not the only one expected to be gracious here."

Kezerah pressed her lips firmly together, trying to find a way out of this newly crafted scenario.

Ikaika saved her the trouble, and relieved her of the burden. "It's alright. We eat together every evening." His voice was soft, reassuring. He looked over at Ambrose who waited for the situation to sort itself, amidst the chaos of the kitchens. "And we have the privilege of your company often. We'll see you tomorrow."

Kezerah searched Ikaika for anything that might tell her to fight harder, to make a stand. All she found was unwavering assurance and care. Cool calm next to Ambrose's smug satisfaction. Her temper flared. She'd attempted balance and Ambrose had answered it with a dishonest tip of the scales.

She stiffly crossed her arms, turning towards Hanan. "No. As a Spring Quarter resident, I too will be eating in my rooms." She watched Ambrose's attention finally leave his tunic, and shock replaced his apathy. She averted her eyes, knowing any expression she gave him now would be rude. She sent acid in a direction more familiar to her. "But you can tell my mother I appreciate her...lapse in rigidity."

"I shall tell her no such thing," Hanan said, "but I suggest you make your way to your various destinations now while she allows this lapse in your own decorum."

Kezerah spun on her heel, Ikaika and Andarios muttered their usual platitudes the steward's way. She challenged Ambrose with a look. He recovered with a smile that didn't meet his eyes. "Another time then," he said, setting his plate down. Then he stalked off towards the Autumn Hall to take his belated seat at the table.

She didn't care. *'Let him pout,'* she thought, and handed her plate to Andarios, her appetite ruined. *'He can sit next to my mother and they can plan how to make me miserable together.'* She imagined her mother's expression, when he entered the dining hall late and alone. The image fed her all the way to her rooms.

"So, just to be clear," Rorrik said, as he and Ambrose made their way back from dinner. The corridor was nothing but empty stone, and warm lantern light. The walls were taken up by either windows overlooking the court, or doors to guest chambers. Rorrik's voice filled the sparse space. "All you did today was flirt and play board games? Do I have that right?"

"I trained in the practice yards this morning." *'Probably tomorrow morning as well,'* Ambrose thought bitterly. He didn't think his pride could handle speaking to Kezerah again so soon. He'd been so sure she'd be in on the joke. That the two of them would have mischievously left the others for some hard won time alone together. He grimaced.

"Which you could have done at home."

"Better that both enemies and allies see Xenkesh's ability with a sword," Ambrose said, irked by his little brother's tone.

Rorrik blustered. "I've been doing that just fine, thank you. I nearly had Luka on his back today."

"Nearly." Ambrose held back a crude joke. "Xenkesh's honor has been restored."

Rorrik marched ahead and spun to face him. "And what efforts have you made? Apart from admiring the princess' backside—as she walks *away*, mind you."

"Lower your voice," Ambrose growled, shoving past Rorrik and yanking open their door. Rorrik followed closely behind. The objects in the room shimmered in greeting as Ambrose's Bond magick rose to kindle the fire. The bone-dry logs obliged, tired by their withered existence. He next asked his Bond to converse with the stone walls that surrounded them. Each stone's soul listened avidly to he and Rorrik's argument: apparently, the most interesting conversation this evening. Nobody listened in then. He turned to his brother while closing the door firmly. "I already explained to you. We need allies. Kezerah is the future ruler here, warming her to us—"

"Father told *me* to look out for opportunities," Rorrik said. "I've done that, but all I've watched you do is waste them."

This was new information to Ambrose. Why give Rorrik instructions and not him? Uncertainty would not help stop Rorrik's posturing. "Opportunities for what? To make a fool out of yourself?"

"Opportunities to—" Rorrik sputtered and stamped a foot. "Ugh, I can't talk to you about anything right now. You're so distracted. You had her alone in the city, and on a private beach. How hard is it? Get her alone and make it clear Xenkesh is not to be toyed with. She either gets in line or gets out of the way."

Ambrose cocked his head to the side, his nerves crackling alongside the fire. "What are you getting at? Your brilliant idea is to—" he checked the walls again, voice lowering, "—is to what, intimidate her? *Bully* the Soul Heir?"

Rorrik rolled his eyes at the honorific. "Oh please, she's harmless. She doesn't even Hold Sway. It's said she's the weakest reincarnation of Ellas yet."

"So that means we should force her to our side?" Ambrose said, incredulous. "Because you believe that won't go over badly?"

"I believe Father is expecting us to do what is necessary. We just need to find out what's important to her and let her know she either has allies, or nightmares."

"Then you don't know Father as well as you think." Ambrose towered close, seething. If Rorrik wanted intimidation, he'd give it to him. "All of those rumors? All of that slander and you want to prove them right? Prove Xenkesh is just as treacherous as Illija says we are?"

Rorrik's shoulders folded in, a wolf with its tail between its legs. "We're losing, Ambrose," he finally said, cowed.

"We'll have lost more than the war if we feed into her lies," said Ambrose. "We have each other, we have Father, and I have a plan. Trust me, alright?"

His brother nodded but Ambrose could see he was restless. Rorrik did poorly without purpose, and he needed that energy in check. Ambrose forced calm. "You're right about what you said earlier." Rorrik perked up. It reminded Ambrose of when they were younger and he'd agree to play with his little brother. He softened further. "Win or lose, your swordplay is helping. You're creating connections and making up for lost time. It helps our case, and fosters sympathy for our people. Let Elastor see for themselves that we are not what our mother claims us to be."

Rorrik scowled again, his mood like the tide. "Fostering sympathy is proclaiming weakness. Their Sword Master throws me in the dirt each day, and Elastor's pet tries to shame me during drills, all the while you're getting turned down for late night picnics."

Ambrose tightened his jaw, reigning in his pride. He'd never hear the end of that.

Rorrik took his charged silence as an invitation to finish. "I'll keep fighting, but I fight for Xenkesh, and I fight to win. I suggest you do the same, because if we lose, we lose everything. It's time Elastor shares a bit of that fear."

Ambrose thought back to the boldness Ikaika had shown when he'd taken up Kezerah's hand. Ambrose *was* losing, and his enemy knew it. The knowledge spurred Ambrose's injured pride. He couldn't afford to divert his time. He had gotten a lay of the battlefield. He needed to stop acting like he was on a trip of leisure, and more like what his family expected. Like he aimed to win.

The Bear

"Psst—Dar."

Andarios rubbed at the sleep built-up in the corner of each eye, and forced heavy blinks to better see his pre-dawn assailant. He was unsurprised to find Kezerah inches from his face, nothing but freckles and violet this close. He groaned.

"I swear, if that moon isn't at least at the bell tower, I'll reincarnate you myself."

She gave a rushed glance out the window and her soft curls tickled at his nose, then she turned back with an impish grin. "It's *exactly* at the bell tower."

A half an hour early then. Not her worst offense. If he hurried he could get breakfast at the barracks before riding the perimeter.

Andarios rose, back cracking in protest as he did so. Kezerah switched places with him, flopping onto his still warm bed. Her body was far smaller than the impression he had left behind in the mattress. He grabbed for his breeches, dragging them up under his nightshirt.

"Couldn't sleep?" he asked. It had been some time since Kezerah had snuck into his chambers, their schedules always a miss with his training regime. A light sleeper, he'd felt her come in, but hadn't had the energy to ask her.

"I was thinking about last night," Kezerah said, twisting to lay on her side, cheek in hand. "Do you think I should have gone with him?" 'Him' he knew to be Ambrose; Kezerah's every third thought since his arrival.

"Tch. You were angry. That plate of food would have ended up in his face."

Kezerah drew invisible lines into his mattress. "Hmm. Maybe."

"You aren't mad anymore, are you?" This was what made their friendship so easy. A moment's annoyance, gone in a blink.

"I should be, shouldn't I?" Kezerah tossed her legs against the wall. Her head now hung suspended off the bed, hair sweeping his floor.

"You shouldn't be anything you're not." Andarios quickened his pace in getting ready. "Besides, pretending to be angry just for the sake of it sounds exhausting." *'Like Rorrik,'* he thought with a roll of his eyes.

Kezerah sighed and there was a thump as she slumped to the floor. "It really is."

Andarios could tell she was in one of her whimsical moods that led to mischief. He looked at the moon. It now crested in the first lights of dawn. Early enough to get breakfast, not early enough for a Kezerah-filled shenanigan.

"Then why don't you go back to sleep?" he asked. "You look half dead."

"Because *someone* ate the majority of my pork chop last night, and I'm hungry."

Andarios' stomach growled. "You gave it to me. Come on, we can get leftovers in the barracks." The cooks often turned leftover meals into morning stews for the soldiers.

Kezerah got up, her smile curving into one he knew all too well. "I was thinking we'd sneak over to the kitchens. They're making egg tarts for breakfast, and you always miss them."

Andarios finished buckling his belt, and tossed his leather padding over his shoulder. "That'll take too long."

"Only if you're slow."

"I am slow." Andarios thought back to yesterday's training. He needed to show up today. It was clear by the assignment that Rook saw his potential, but Andarios needed to show him he could reach it. Elize backing him was a fluke he could not rely on, nor mention to Kezerah.

"Dar, hello?" Kezerah nudged him, it was playful but from the look on her face he could tell she felt ignored. He must have missed what she'd said.

"Yeah, exactly. Sorry. Still tired, let's go." He started then stopped. Kezerah walked towards his balcony door, and Andarios made a snap decision, wishing his chance at breakfast farewell. "Should we shadow?" he asked. "It's still pretty dark." It meant it would take longer to get downstairs, but it also meant Kezerah wouldn't try to clamber down his balcony.

Kezerah pirouetted with a smile to stand behind him, angling her body to match his. It wasn't a true shadow, more of a mirror, but they had been doing this prank ever since Andarios had grown taller than her. Andarios walked out of his room. Kezerah's two guards on duty at her door, unaware that their ward was in front of them, and behind Andarios. He saluted, knowing behind him, Kezerah did the same, her arm blocked by his. He made his movements casual, if not a bit too languid to allow for any delays Kezerah might have. He needn't have worried. He stepped, she stepped. When he turned to ask the guards what the morning stew was, Kezerah pivoted to stand behind him, allowing them both to back up onto the stairs as he made conversation. Once the guards were out of sight, Andarios and Kezerah turned to look at one another. A mistake, since he'd been able to hold in his laughter until he watched hers burst forth.

"That was perfect," she praised, and skipped the last few steps of the spiral stairs. Her voice echoed through the walls loud enough to give their game away. "We should shadow all the way to the kitchens!" Andarios stopped and looked over at Kezerah, who assessed his posture. "What?"

"I thought we decided on the barracks."

Kezerah rolled her eyes, and a huff of breath misted out in the chilled morning air. "*You* said you were too slow. *I* said I was fast enough for the both of us, and *you* said—" Kezerah made her voice absurdly deep, "—Yeah exactly, let's shadow."

Andarios winced, knowing where it had gone wrong. "I might have missed that last part."

"Dar!" Kezerah's shoulders slumped, and Andarios started walking. If he didn't act fast they'd be arguing until midday. They stepped onto the frosted meadow grass, the crunch under his boots satisfying. The sound of Kezerah complaining, less so.

"Come on, you love egg tarts! It will only take a minute or two, and you can eat them along the way."

Andarios could see soldiers gathering in the distance. He couldn't be late. He picked up pace, knowing Kezerah could keep up if she wanted to. She did.

"Besides, you're one of the best soldiers Rook has, and he adores you." Using the word 'adore' for Rook was like using 'adore' to describe a chef's favorite knife: exclusively appreciated because it was sharp, and useful. A late and hungry Andarios was neither of those.

"One of the best is not the best."

He heard Kezerah snort beside him and didn't dare look down at her expression. Finally another cloud of air puffed up, as Kezerah admitted defeat. "Fine, to the barracks it is then."

Elk were being taken from the stables and saddled, he just needed to get in position, before Rook showed up. He picked up pace. "I'll head to the barracks, you can still nab us some of those egg tarts for later."

Kezerah stopped abruptly, Andarios paused a few steps ahead and turned around. Her arms were already crossed. She had sensed his dismissal. "Sorry. I'm just trying to be on time."

Kezerah's posture tightened, and her words left her lips in a frown. "What does that have to do with me? I've watched your drills plenty of times before."

Andarios' arm raised up to clasp the back of his neck. He needed to say this delicately, but with haste. "Well, I'm trying to take it seriously and well, you're not very—"

"You don't think I take your training seriously?"

Annoyance prickled at him. "You don't take *anything* seriously." He winced as she did. They needled at one another constantly, but never about the other's character. "Kez—I didn't mean it like that. Come on. You can come."

But Kezerah had already lifted her chin, most likely in an effort to keep her lip from trembling.

Andarios looked back towards the barracks with a sigh. Normally, this would be the moment he would offer his time in a truce, missing drills to accompany her instead. He couldn't do that. Not so close to Kezerah's Queensguard being announced. He needed it to be him.

"I've got to go, or I'm going to be late." It sounded like the apology that it was.

"Right, responsibilities and such."

Andarios inhaled through his nose until his chest barreled out. Protecting her didn't matter if he was the one hurting her. He exhaled. In two strides he reached her, and he took her hand in his. He'd heard many people describe Kezerah's hands. Courtiers grasped her fingertips for polite kisses, or guards 'helped' her from her pony. *'Soft,'* they'd say, *'as dainty as a rose petal.'* Those people had never held Kezerah's whole hand. They had the wrong end of the rose. Andarios laced his hand through hers, his calluses rubbed against the grooves in her palms made from climbing, and the knick between her thumb and pointer from slipping on the ice, the small bump at the base of her pinky where she had fractured bone upon attempting to lift his blade and promptly dropping it. They had bandaged the wound themselves—for fear she wouldn't be allowed in the training yard anymore—and watched as it healed crooked. He had been there for all of her imperfections, his small failures in exchange for her small freedoms.

He looked at her, and waited until her eyes met his with reluctance. "You *are* my responsibility. You're why I'm here. I don't care about fighting, or honor to one's kingdom, or anything silly like that." He swung his free hand back towards the soldier halls and stables. "One of those soldiers is going to take up position as your personal guard, your Queensguard. They'll be in charge of making sure you're safe, protected, that you're never in danger, that no one even thinks of putting you in harm's way."

"That sounds horrible," Kezerah mumbled. "More like a personal cage."

Andarios squeezed her palm, calluses digging in. "Which is why it has to be me. I don't just want you to be safe. I want you to be happy."

Kezerah's wintery expression melted into summer and her hand squeezed his back, before she gave in entirely and threw her arms up and around him in a hug.

Andarios laughed into her hair. "I'm also the only one who

knows half your stupid ideas before you have them. So I'm sort of made for the job."

"Luka!" a gravelly voice called. "Two minutes, let's go!"

Andarios pulled away. "See you for evening meal!" He jogged backwards and away. "Save me one of those egg tarts!"

Andarios wasted no time getting in line with everyone else. Rook gave detailed instructions and described the ship as possibly being pirated down south from the Bastians. The Winter Woods were just a precaution; the majority of the troop would take small ships from the Solstice Bay while others combed the beach.

"As a show of goodwill to Elastor, I too will join the patrol," announced Rorrik as he sauntered up.

"Ugh," Andarios groaned. "I was joking."

"That's really not necessary," Rook said, taken aback.

Rorrik addressed Andarios first. "Alliances are no joke, not that you would understand the politics behind it." He turned to Rook. "Sir, I insist."

Rook frowned. "As our ally, your safety is—"

"Of top priority, I agree," Rorrik said. "But as your queen said, you have your best and brightest here." Andarios ground his teeth at Rorrik's gesture. "So I'm sure if I go with Andarios it won't be more than a day of sightseeing."

Andarios turned pleading eyes towards Rook. He didn't like what he saw there. His captain looked trapped and running out of excuses. "Can you ride an elk?"

"Captain, we ride venomous drakes with impenetrable scales in Xenkesh. I can handle an elk."

Rook grunted his no-nonsense grunt. Andarios felt the end of the battle. He tried to bolster his captain's resolve, which appeared to be draining fast.

"Well, I ride a horse," Andarios said, crossing his arms. "So it'd be hard to keep up."

"I'm sure you could ride an elk," Rorrik sneered, "to accommodate your guest."

"I'll accommodate your—"

"Luka," Rook said, "whatever you're about to say, don't say it.

Just go grab an elk, and someone grab the Prince of Xenkesh an extra sword from the barracks!"

Andarios looked back at his horse, who hoofed in her stable expectantly. "Captain, I'm supposed to—"

"You're supposed to follow orders," Rook snapped.

Jaw tight, Andarios marched over, snatching an elk's reins from a stablehand. A smug smile tugged on the prince's face as he followed behind. Andarios slipped his boot into the saddle, knowing exactly where he'd like to place it next.

Each step Kezerah took was quicker than the last. Blurs of high arched hearths and tree roots lined her focal point: A back table, carved of yew and marbled with jasper, piled with platters of squash, and mid-harvest vegetation, but most importantly: the waning tower of egg tarts. Servants floated through the hall, attending to guests who had braved pre-dawn. She spotted Ambrose in an armchair next to one of the large stone hearths. He blew into his closed hands then rubbed them together. A servant interrupted the action to give him a bowl with steam rising from the top. Kezerah hesitated, unsure how to approach him then decided it was too soon. She would grab her meal and hold out until she could talk to the twins.

However, after dishing up her plate, she found an obstacle to her swift exit.

"Good morning, Hanan," she said, trying to keep pep in her step. "If you've come for the egg tarts I'm afraid I've taken the last one."

Hanan blocked the archway doors and only gave the dozen egg tarts on her plate a cursory glance. "Unfortunately, no. I am attending to your father in the throne room."

"Ah," Kezerah said, taking a step towards the still blocked archway. "Perhaps next time then."

"Perhaps," Hanan agreed. He didn't smile, though the look of sympathy he gave her came close. "Did you plan on sitting down to eat your meal by the hearth this morning?" He gave a meaningful look towards a specific hearth and the prince that sat there. "Or did you wish to accompany me back to the throne room to assist in your father's audience?"

Kezerah groaned and swung her head in Ambrose's direction. He sat peacefully, stirring steam. *'Too peacefully.'* She thought. Her anger from last night rekindled, she casted a glare at him, before placing it on Hanan.

"I suppose I'll stay here."

"Very good, Soul Heir Kezerah," Hanan said, and continued towards the Solstice Gates.

Kezerah slumped into the armchair next to Ambrose. He didn't look up but seemed quite pleased with himself; all Xenkeshi arrogance as he sipped his soup from a wooden bowl, without a ladle or spoon.

"Who eats soup for breakfast?" she said in greeting.

"Plenty of people," he said, smiling up at her as if she'd said good morning. "Xenkeshi to start, and Alorans to finish, if I'm not mistaken. Although—" he tapped his bottom lip in thought, "—I believe they only do so with broth, and we'll eat any dish at any time of day—as long as it's delicious."

Kezerah crossed her arms, making her mood more clear.

Ambrose registered her posture, eyes dancing as he took another sip. "You're angry with me."

"Of course I am!"

"Why?" he inquired, lazily setting his bowl down on a side table. "I wasn't the one who sent your friends away last night."

"You didn't prevent it. If you knew my mother would say yes, you could have requested us all come."

"I didn't know she would say yes," he said. "I merely observed that she seemed inclined to show me hospitality. How was I to know your mother was a djinn, in need of *exact phrasing* to see my wishes granted."

Kezerah dismissed his sly reasoning. "I refuse to believe you didn't want it to work out that way." She looked at him, irritated that he didn't seem apologetic in the slightest. "I don't like feeling like I'm being handled." She pointed to the empty archway where Hanan had stood. "At all."

Ambrose rolled his eyes. "I wasn't handling you. I created a situation which led to our mutual benefit. I wanted time with you, and you wanted time outside your rooms."

Kezerah shook her head in disbelief. "You trapped me," she said. "You thought I couldn't publicly decline you, but you were wrong." She took in her surroundings, the large hall suddenly grew airtight. "Then you threw a tantrum for your damaged ego, and sicked Hanan on me."

Ambrose's eyes sharpened into shards of emerald as they met hers, all playfulness gone. "I have no intention of holding you here against your will, nor would I expect you to agree to something in order to spare my ego," he urged. "I assumed you wanted to be here. You hesitated due to the treaty, so I made the treaty work for you."

"Well, that teaches you to make assumptions then, doesn't it." Kezerah stood, her grip on her plate so tight it wobbled and shook in her grasp. "I hesitated because of the treaty. I declined because of *you*."

Ambrose glared up at her, then stood up himself. His size made no bearing on her stance, as she followed him up with her eyes. "Fine," he said, "then consider yourself released from my clutches. I'm perfectly capable of stroking my own ego."

Kezerah gave him the slow once-over she had seen him give. "I'm sure you are." Ambrose's eyes widened, but she spun in place and stormed out of the hall before he could say another word.

WHEN IKAIKA AWOKE, shouting filled his head. Incoherent anger, with or without context, was usually an unpleasant way to begin a day. However, as servants looped buttons through eyelets of his tunic, he found the ire of this morning to be due to Kezerah berating Ambrose, and his mood improved substantially. His good humor continued throughout the day, as he watched Ambrose flounder to recover the situation.

The two of them sat in the meadow, Ikaika with a book, Kezerah practicing a daisy chain with wild blue cornflowers. Shade eclipsed Ikaika's chapter. He rolled his eyes and did not bother a look at Ambrose as his brother interrupted the quiet.

"Kezerah, can we talk?"

Kezerah stood abruptly, abandoning her flowers. "I need to study. Kai, you were going to help me with those chapters, right?"

Ikaika snapped his book shut.

He followed her to the library, and repeated the action when, mid-studying, a vibrant crown of blue and dashes of magenta was placed on their table. Ikaika rolled his eyes, seeing Ambrose had laced the flower crown with beautyberries. "Just a few moments, and I'll leave."

"No need," Kezerah said, pushing past him. "The library is yours."

The midday meal attempt gave Ikaika pause however. Ambrose sat next to her, appropriating Andarios' empty seat. His elbow rested on the table as he leaned in, and Kezerah spoke to the twins without acknowledging him.

He tried regardless. "Princess Kezerah, I'm truly sorry for my words and actions last night and this morning. They were inexcusable, and I'll be more mindful, in the future, of our friendship."

"Ah, assumptions about our future once more," Kezerah said. "That's very refreshing. Thank you, Prince Ambrose."

Ikaika snickered into his glass, his sip of cool water longer than needed to hide his grin.

"Alright," Ambrose said, with a nod. "More time then. Not a problem, I'd gladly spend a scholarhood on Bethync if it meant our friendship resumed."

Kezerah smiled. "Excellent, I'm sure black suits you."

"If that is you subtly requesting I wear black, consider your wish granted."

"Now who's the djinn?" she asked, and Ikaika tilted his head, not understanding. He didn't like where this banter was leading, and nudged her with his elbow.

"You up for apple picking?" he asked. "Dar isn't here yet, but we can still keep up the tradition."

Her lips spread into a bright smile, amethyst eyes rewarding him with a quickened heartbeat. "Sure, we can make spiced cider too."

They both stood and Kezerah addressed Ambrose formally. "Thank you for your thoughtful apology. I hope to make you some of Elastor's famous cider in my appreciation. For you to take *back* to

Xenkesh." Kezerah made an un-Kezerah like curtsey as they left the hall.

The orchard on the meadow's edge veered into a sharp drop to the Summer Quarter beach. Salt mingled with sweet in the breeze from ripened apples. "Are we really going to make this cider for my brother?" Ikaika asked, as he held the woven basket out. An apple fell from above and nearly missed his head. Kezerah's lean legs dangled, her torso and hair obscured by leaves as she climbed higher.

"Brothers," Kezerah corrected from up high. "Rorrik will get some too. It's only fair, since you're picking them with me."

Ikaika could practically see her winking, gleeful with her own clever take on the treaty. "Honorable of you," he said with a smile. Then, Ambrose's voice pushed at his temple, and Ikaika groaned. He turned, seeing his brother, still several strides away.

"What?" Kezerah said, hearing him.

He didn't bother to answer, instead he formulated a response to Ambrose's upcoming ruse.

"Ikaika!" Ikaika withheld a cringe, his own name sounding foreign coming from his brother's mouth. "Just who I was looking for."

Ikaika cut Ambrose a glare, knowing full-well why he was here. He glanced up at Kezerah, who now climbed down from the tree, her curiosity getting the better of her. Ambrose's grin grew, gifting Ikaika with the disorienting image of Kezerah not beside him but in front of him: Ambrose's view far more lingering. Ikaika side-stepped closer, watching himself do so. He closed his eyes, trying to push back against the vertigo. He needed to be present.

"That's right, I forgot the princess would be with you." Ambrose's mock surprise nauseated Ikaika more than his migraine. "How is my famous Elastian cider coming along?"

Kezerah snickered next to him, and dismay creeped in. "Get on with it, Ambrose." Ikaika resisted pinching the bridge of his nose.

"Well, I needed to go on a quick errand into the city. Ror is with the Lord Andarios, so I'm down a brother, if you'd like to join me."

Ikaika's answer was rehearsed and concise. "Thank you, but no. Unfortunately I have things I must attend to today."

"Dar is with Rorrik?" Kezerah asked, derailing the swift exchange.

Ambrose smiled, and Ikaika realized he'd missed a layered purpose to this conversation. "Yes, Ror has been joining morning drills, and the two of them rode out together this morning. I think I even saw Rorrik learning to ride an elk."

Kezerah cocked her head to one side, voice a bit wistful. "I didn't know that."

Ikaika rolled his eyes, hearing Kezerah reassess the brothers in her mind, adding complexities and nuances to their character. Always trusting Dar's opinion and stumbling through an argument they'd had earlier.

"Kai, maybe you should go," she said tentatively. "Maybe you'd have fun?" *'Maybe you can both give each other a chance at peace.'*

"There's no way in Thrice I'm going," Ikaika said. He'd read enough books to see where this was headed and found himself irritated by her gullibility. "At best, he'll get me lost, at worst I'll be dead in a gutter."

Ambrose scooped up a stray apple that had rolled down the roots of the tree. He took a bite, the crisp crunch grating as he watched the show.

"Ikaika," Kezerah said, "don't be—"

"If you say 'silly'," Ikaika said, rubbing his eyes, "I'll lose my mind."

"You look half there," Ambrose muttered.

"Ambrose," Kezerah warned.

"It's alright," Ambrose said, indifferent now. His posture was nonchalant while he admired his half eaten apple. "I'll go alone then. I don't mind." He set the marred apple in the basket and cast a smile Ikaika's way. "Enjoy making my cider."

Ikaika envisioned throwing the apple at the back of his brother's head, as he wandered off, back towards the Solstice Gates.

Kezerah sighed, her look weary. Ikaika set down the basket, the simple act of leaning down causing a fresh burst of auras and pain. "I need to lie down."

"Kai, I'm—"

"It's fine," Ikaika said, feeling anything but. "See you tonight."

He stumbled away, unable to hear her reply as it echoed out of sequence in his mind.

"DON'T you ever get tired of the same view?" Rorrik asked, atop an elk beside Andarios' own. Andarios looked out at the creamy yellow rows of meadow and the late-blooming, plumy fountain grass. While not in sight, he could smell sweet alyssum as it caught the wind in the late afternoon breeze. The air chilled enough to pink his nose but make him better appreciate the sun at his shoulder. The Winter Wood—farther off—beckoned with saturating hues of fire and promised warmth in contrast to Estora's sharp and icy peaks at the distant Aloran border.

"Yeah, Rorrik, it's exhausting to look at," Andarios said, trying to ignore the prince's constant needling at anything that wasn't himself. Despite Rorrik's brazen statements from earlier, as it turned out, elk did differ enough from komodai to warrant a riding lesson. The prince had been bucked off immediately. Andarios had first needed to calm Rorrik down enough to try again, then calm the elk down enough to allow Rorrik back on. Both elk and rider had come to the conclusion that it was this or nothing, and they settled into a bumpy trot that had them an hour or more behind schedule. If Andarios was lucky, he'd have enough time to bathe before the evening meal.

"I just mean, are you forced to stay here because of the princess? I've been all over Xenkesh and I can't imagine just being trapped on a beach."

"I'm not trapped." Andarios stared straight ahead. "There's just no point in seeing the world without her." A part of him wanted to take the words back, or to better explain the safety and love his friend gave him. That he didn't *not* want to see the world, but that the idea of doing so without Kezerah's hand clasped in his terrified him. He'd seen the world, and it had burned down around him.

When he let yet another conversation lapse into a silent reprieve, Rorrik tried again. "So, you and the princess ever..." He let the question linger.

Andarios threw his head back and looked up at the sky, wishing there were clouds to distract him. "Wow. You are not subtle—at all."

"Well, you do seem rather cozy together, don't you? Bit unusual for an outgrown playmate."

"We're not playmates," Andarios answered, flatly.

"That's obvious," Rorrik said. "I think we both know you two look like far more."

"It doesn't matter what you think," Andarios snapped. "I know who and what I am. We know what we are."

"And what's that?"

Andarios had endured these sorts of questions before. The discomfort gnawed at him. To say he and Kezerah were *not* something always felt wrong; they were everything. Yet, they also didn't seem to fit what people thought of them. Nothing he said on the subject ever made a bit of difference, it only confused everyone involved, including him. He chose not to respond in the hopes that Rorrik would give up. It almost worked.

"Do you think Ikaika and the princess have slept together?"

Andarios pulled at his elk's reins. The bull didn't resist but turned in an easy semi-circle.

"Hey!" Rorrik shouted. "Where are you going?"

"Back," Andarios said. "I'd rather have a staring contest with the queen than continue this poorly done interrogation."

"Alright! Alright!" A chaotic jostling sounded as Rorrik attempted to turn his reluctant mount around. "Something else then." Andarios gave Rorrik a look of suspicion. The prince gestured to the swell of trees before them. "Come on, we're nearly there."

Andarios turned back around, and attempted to enjoy the stagnant silence once more.

"The queen doesn't seem to like you much."

Andarios sighed. It was better than Kezerah's love-life, he supposed. "No. She doesn't like me at all."

"Why is that? Or is it because of the aforementioned subject we're not allowed to talk about?"

Andarios wished he knew the answer. The queen, at first, had scared him: a looming figure, cool glares, masked disdain, and his seat at the table moving farther, and farther down the line. One of his oldest memories showed Elize hissing his name when she had caught the two of them holding hands. Andarios had pulled away, afraid of what might happen next. Only for Kezerah to hold on tighter, drawing him close and pushing the fear away. The farther his seat moved, the farther Kezerah's did. The closer their friendship knitted together, the more Elize seemed to ebb away. Now, Andarios was at best tolerated and at worst ignored. Elize's flare-ups happened as a result of not getting her way, which was rare, when excluding him.

Leaves left star-shaped shadows on their faces as they entered the forest. "I don't know," Andarios finally answered.

"Maybe it's because you're low-born, a threat to her family line."

Andarios doubted it, Elize herself being low-born. Though she did like to spin it as if that were not the case. "It's more like...my very existence is a threat to her."

"Well, you do look rather threatening," Rorrik said, giving Andarios a head to toe appraisal.

Andarios inspected patterns of bark on passing trees. "Do I? I assumed you fought me first because I looked friendly."

Rorrik let out a genuine guffaw and Andarios couldn't help but be pleased. His gaze tracked down towards the earth, and he pulled his elk to a stop.

"What—" Rorrik began.

"Shh." Andarios got off his elk. His boots landed heavily in the leaf-rich soil and he drew closer to the deep stamp left in the earth.

"That's not possible," Andarios said, more to himself than to the impatient Rorrik that huffed behind him. He lifted his large hand, and spread his fingers wide. It fit into the paw print he'd found, with a lot of room to spare. Each perfect circle indicated a toe the size of a ripe, fat plum. He heard the soft thud and tread of Rorrik coming closer, and he began to rise.

"Get back on that—"

Both elks bolted. The thump of their hooves matched the pace of Andarios' quickening pulse. He cursed as he watched them go.

Rorrik blurred in his peripheral as he pointed. "What is that?"

Andarios exhaled loudly. "Bear tracks, bigger than I've ever seen. We need to go."

"No," Rorrik said, more rasp than whisper. "That."

Andarios turned and his muscles groaned to a halt as a gigantic white bear lumbered into the clearing.

Andarios felt the roar more than heard it, as if it were not loud in volume but vast in strength. The sound rattled him from within and dragged his heart from his chest. Rorrik leaned back as if his body meant to run but his feet remained rooted in place.

"Don't move," Andarios commanded. "We don't stand a chance running out in an open field." They didn't stand a chance at all, but Andarios wasn't ready to admit that.

"Are you joking?" Rorrik said, his voice two octaves higher than before. "We don't stand a chance *standing* here. What do we do— fight it?"

"If it were smaller, a black bear maybe, yes," Andarios said, "or at least we could scare it off, if it were brown."

"Yes, well." Rorrik gulped. "This one's white."

"It's an iron bear." Andarios didn't dare lift a hand to point at it, but his eyes tracked the bear's slow, laborious steps all the same.

"That...*that* is an iron bear?" Rorrik sounded disbelieving.

Andarios withheld a nod. "See the claws, and the erm—fangs?" he said. "They're not marrow and bone, they're something harder, sharper. Like the iron wolves that Aloran's ride. It's what they make their swords out of." Andarios closed his eyes for a moment, and tried to calm his breathing and collect his thoughts. "They can slice through steel, and can only be melted down in the volcanic pools of Dawnscar."

"That's lovely," Rorrik hissed. "I don't suppose you have a vat of lava or an Aloran blade around, do you?"

The bear let out another growl, the hard chuffing breath so hot it rose into steam.

"Stop moving!" Andarios said through teeth. "No, my sword is steel," he admitted. "It might as well be wood."

"Then how do we survive this?"

Ah. Rorrik had finally asked the question Andarios had been dreading. He tasted the answer as he tested his resolve to say it aloud and was impressed with himself. "We're not. You are."

"What?"

Both of them flinched as the bear reacted to Rorrik's voice. It lunged forward before it took a step back and pawed at the ground. The hard earth gave way without a fight.

"I told you I knew who I was," Andarios said. "Think about it. If we fight, we both die. If you die, and I survive, I'm executed—and Elastor goes to war after explaining to *both* neighboring monarchs that their son is dead." Andarios sucked in another gulp of air, and was relieved by the soothing calm the cold gave his lungs. "I die, the bear is satiated enough that it seeks food elsewhere, leaving you time to escape the tree you're about to climb up."

"I have to climb a tree?"

Andarios glared. "I have to fight a bear."

That shut Rorrik up. They looked at one another. Andarios noticed Rorrik's eyes were green, like the edges of sea foam along the Solstice bay shore, his skin bronzed by birth rather than the sun. Andarios tried to admire his own decision. He was saving a prince. He'd possibly be more renowned than his father—but still most likely nicknamed The Bear. He closed his eyes again, not wanting to look at Rorrik's any longer. He didn't care about glory, or fame. He didn't even *like* the epithet. If Rorrik died, war would come to Elastor. War would come to Kez. *Kez.* His best friend would be so furious and lost without him. He wished he hadn't hurried off this morning. He wished he'd gone and eaten egg tarts.

When he opened his eyes again, he faced the bear. Both stood their ground. Andarios moved his mouth as little as possible. "Slowly climb the tree to your left. It has low branches." He didn't need to look to know Rorrik followed orders.

Who wouldn't.

Andarios weathered a surreal moment. It felt endless, as if his mind had trapped him in a loop to save him from death. He stared at the fierce creature before him. His downfall. He was grateful to be given infinite seconds to gaze at it. Frosted silver claws dug into the earth. The bear rooted in place as if it had been planted, fostered in his mother's garden, especially to kill him. The fur was ill-tempered, vexed by being stained brown from soil. It flared in disheveled tuffs until grooming itself into a white so iridescent it yellowed pearls. Time picked up in tempo as he met the bear's eyes. A heavy black that demanded stillness locked him in place. Was it the bear's fear, or Andarios' reflected back at him? Andarios managed a swallow and watched the bear's eyes shift to his jugular. His knuckles cracked as they involuntarily curled.

The bear's ears followed suit and folded back.

Time snapped forward with furious force.

So did the bear.

Andarios surprised himself when his fist wrapped around cold metal, and he found the strength to lift his sword. The tanging clash of metal on metal surged through him as the bear's claws made contact with his blade instead of his face. The reverberating sensation of the hilt in his hand gave a moment of relief before claws bled through his blade like fire through frost. He jumped back, and brandished his ruined sword like a knife. The bear struck. Andarios maneuvered his body as the bear's other paw smacked him across the clearing and his back crashed into a tree. The bark behind him was a welcome comfort to the aching throb of his arm. Before he could breathe, the iron bear appeared. There was no escape as a skull rammed into his stomach, choking him of air. Andarios coughed and spit bile before the glint of metallic fangs relieved him of his breastplate with a horrific scream of torn metal.

His ears rang before gnashing teeth seeped into his leather armor and pierced his oblique muscle with a sickening pop and tear. He roared, far louder than the bear ever could. He swung an arm up. The broken blade jammed and held itself deep between shoulder and neck. Muscles strained as he wrenched the weapon free. He repeated the attack. Up. Down. Up. Down. Up. Down. The bear did not fall, but rose to its full height, claws high. Andarios' skin tore like cloth as he was dashed to the ground. His head slammed into the root of another tree. The broken sword protruded from the beast's neck like a tribute to its strength. The balmy chuffing of the bear's breath reached Andarios' face. Jet black eyes looked into his, no longer filled with fear but suffused with victory. Pain melted away from Andarios like snow. The warm hue of the trees haloed the milky features of his doom, like the sun greeted a sky it must share with the moon. He thought of his parents, and forced his breath to say their names out loud. Besides the thudding in his ears and the cry from above, the world was a perfect and beautiful haze. A tremendous weight slammed into him, and the earth pulled him in where there was nothing but darkness.

Bitter Breeze

Cinnamon, nutmeg, and clove clung to Kezerah's fingertips as she wiped her hands down her velvet dress. She hadn't had time to change between making the cider batches, and now rushed against the sun towards the Autumn Hall. Three glass jugs— still hot from boiling and steeping—balanced between her hands. Her foot caught on a stone, set into the pathway, and the weight of the middle jug left her precarious grasp. She watched with a slow rolling dread as it fell towards the ground.

Brown hands, long and nimble, snatched the falling jug right before shattering. "Whoa there," her father said, smiling as he helped her stand straight once more. "What are these?"

"I made cider," she said, "for Ambrose and Rorrik."

Elowren lifted his brows so high his dots of freckles followed. "How very hospitable of you."

"Yes," Kezerah slowed her pace to match his. She loved her father but despite his long gait, he traveled at the progression of a contemplative tortoise, "I've been a very gracious host."

"So I've heard," her father said dryly.

They entered the hall, and warmth escaped past her through the still open doors as Elize approached. "There you both are!"

Kezerah paused at Elize's tone, it sounded as if she were genuinely happy to see them. "Kezerah, could you please close the door? The cold air is getting in."

'Please?' Kezerah prodded the door closed with her foot, eyeing her mother. Elize's smile didn't falter, lips lost in the stretch of the grin. "I was afraid you'd miss the evening meal, it's getting late." This she said to Elowren.

"Never my dear. I was just assisting Kezerah with her Elastian hospitality."

Elize followed Elowren's gesture towards the cider, eyes widening at the soft amber liquid and swirls of spice. "An Autumnal miracle. Well done, Kezerah."

The praise washed over Kezerah like a hot bath in a chilled room, the shock of warmth both jarring and soothing. Kezerah shuffled her feet, unfamiliar with the sensation. "It's nothing really... Just a gift." She didn't dare mention she'd churned the gift out of spite rather than goodwill. Why ruin the moment?

Elowren nudged her with a lanky arm, then pointed. "Perhaps not nothing, but a beginning?"

She followed his line of sight. The tall corridor was bathed in rich orange from the setting sun. The large oak trees drank in the warmth from the window panes high above, and below her corner of the banquet table was much changed. Ambrose and Ikaika sat near each other, only one chair apart. The twins spoke to them, an animated conversation flowing between all four. Ikaika chuckled and a swell of hope rose in Kezerah. This was a start. Ikaika just needed a bit of time, and he too would come around. That's what Ikaika did.

"Well," she said with swagger, "I *am* the Soul Heir. Uniting kingdoms is sort of my specialty."

"That it is," Elowren said, then squeezed her shoulder. "But it's probably best you join them, to make sure it remains peaceful."

Kezerah nodded and started toward her seat, then stopped. She looked from Ikaika, to her empty spot, then Ambrose who occupied Andarios' chair. The next seat over; empty.

"Where's Dar?"

"He is on a scouting mission," Elize said, already moving towards her own seat. "I'm sure he's running late, per usual."

Kezerah didn't move. It *was* usual for Dar to be late for meals. But he was only ever late because *she* was. Kezerah couldn't help the small seed of unease that rooted in her stomach.

"But...he's stationed at the Solstice Gate. He should already be here."

"No," Elize said. "He switched in order to escort Prince Rorrik around the Winter Wood and Northern border. He'll most likely eat in the barracks with the rest of the soldiers." Kezerah once more redrew her and Andarios' argument. Not only had he spent the morning with Rorrik and gone riding with him but, '*He skipped the evening meal to spend time with him...*'

Elowren looked down at her, reassuring. "I know you like to think of the Winter Wood as adventurous, but Andarios is more than capable. I have every confidence in him."

Kezerah felt awkward standing there in the fire-lit hall. She watched the servants bring rolled honey ham and shucked corn in. The sudden chatter and clatter of food being served filled the space. "I couldn't agree more," said Elize. "We entrust him with you. Don't you also think he's capable?" Kezerah nodded. Of course he was capable, and yet, her sight swept past the guests—who clung tightly to their silverware, resisting the urge to eat without their monarchs seated—to the closed doors. What was wrong with her?

Elowren tried again. "If Lord Andarios and Prince Rorrik have not made an appearance by the end of the evening meal, we'll send a search party." Elowren chuckled. "And a proper chastisement for worrying you."

A plate was set at Elize's empty seat; her mother watched her with a tapping foot. Her tone edged out of affection and into a sweet warning. "Sit down, Kezerah. I'm sure your shadow will be along shortly." Kezerah's distress persisted, and she looked back at Dar's empty chair. "Kezerah, sit. Everyone is waiting to eat. It's rude."

Kezerah caught Ikaika's eye, the annoyance from earlier gone from his face. He simply looked happy to see her. He smiled, and the corner of her lips followed his. Maybe Ikaika knew when Andarios would return, or at least more about the situation. She took the third cider from her father and, with a mumbled apology, went to Ikaika.

He pulled back her chair. His smoky curls had been partially tied back, exaggerating his jawline. The obsidian of his eyes were depthless. They crinkled as he smiled down at her, and then his gaze dipped below her face. "Here, let me help you with the cider."

Kezerah followed his eyes to the cider she still held to her chest. "Ah, right."

He thumped the jugs down in front of Ambrose, ruining a joke he told the twins.

"Kind regards," Ikaika said, "from the Princess of Elastor."

Ambrose smiled, winking at Kezerah. "I'll enjoy every sip."

Kezerah rolled her eyes, and tried to ignore how clammy her palms had gotten. She wiped her hands down her dress again. They smoothed over a squishy bump in her pocket. She removed it.

"What's that?" Ikaika asked, inspecting the squashed yellow-brown lump in her hands.

"It's an egg tart," said Kezerah. "I meant to give it to Dar, but he isn't here..."

Ikaika's smile faltered. "You okay?"

Kezerah's mouth was dry, and suddenly swallowing felt inconvenient. "Mmhm."

"Thank you all for your gracious patience," Elize announced. "You may now all *sit down*, and begin the feast." *Sit down. Sit down. Sit down.* Kezerah opened her mouth to let in a few quick, short breaths.

"Kez?" Ikaika pulled her chair back a little farther, and offered it to her.

Kezerah's stomach turned. She felt torn, a puppet with two separate and bickering puppeteers. She should sit down. She couldn't. She just kept holding the egg tart, as if it were precious. If Dar had left this morning, he would have missed midday meal...but that would have been hours ago. Several hours ago. Even when taking their time, it didn't take a day to circle the forest border.

"What?" Ikaika asked. "What's..." He paused, and she guessed he must have listened to the pinwheel of her circulating thoughts, because then he turned to Ambrose. "What are you and your stupid brother up to?"

Ambrose pulled his shoulders back. "I've got two stupid brothers, so you'll have to be more specific."

"Dar," Ikaika said with impatience.

"Which manages to be neither of them."

"Earlier you said Dar was with Rorrik. Where are they?"

Ambrose raised his hands, looking between Ikaika and Kezerah as he reassessed. "I don't know. I just saw them riding out." He turned to Kezerah and spoke more earnestly. "I don't know where they are, I swear it."

Kezerah's unease unfurled and bloomed into dread. She dropped the egg tart. She made sure her voice carried. "I ask to be excused!" The hall deadened to silence.

"Your request is declined," said her mother. "We have yet to eat and your food—"

"I ask that a search party be sent out to look for Andarios and Rorrik."

"Kezerah," Elowren said, "as promised we will—"

"He's missing!" Kezerah couldn't stand the calm cadence of their voices, not when it contradicted every nerve in her body. A din of murmurs swept across the table. "We need to send a search—"

"Enough!" Elize said over top of her. "You will sit down!"

"I won't!"

"We can have a conversation about this without shouting." Elowren lifted his hands in a call for peace.

Kezerah's breaths came out in rapid succession, the room watched her with open concern and veiled amusement. Nobody moved. Nobody helped.

The chair to her left scraped back. "I'll go," said Ambrose.

"That's not necessary," Elize said. "Kezerah is just—"

Ikaika stood up on her right. "I will also go."

"Soul Heir Kezerah is looking out for the safety of my brother no doubt," Ambrose said, with a look at Kezerah. She looked away, knowing he had very well heard her singular focus for her friend. "I am inclined to trust her judgment. So, unless I am a prisoner here, I shall ride out immediately."

Her mother sat stiff in her chair. "But of course, you and Prince Ikaika may both go." Ambrose and Ikaika bowed, for once in unison. Kezerah followed after them, eyes on nothing but the door to outside. To Dar. Her steps were sure and flat on the stone floor.

"Kezerah, we ask that you—" her father's words were cut off by her mother's demand.

"Sit down, Kezerah. You have not been excused."

What started as a march, sped up until she sprinted towards the Autumn Hall doors.

"Kezerah!" Her mother called from behind her a final time.

Kezerah paused, hand heavy on the long hooked door handle.

"I'm going to find Dar." Her mother's stare prickled at her spine, her muscles nearly halted in place by sheer rage. She knew if she looked back she'd see the warning there, that if she took another advance forward she'd be made to regret it.

But Kezerah possessed no stronger conviction in the world than to take her next step. She jerked the doors open and dashed out, letting the cold air in.

IT WASN'T until Kezerah rode Soot that she realized she was not just accompanied by Ambrose and Ikaika, but the entirety of Rook's royal guard. Rook himself did not seem pleased, and caught up to her on horseback.

"You've upset your mother so greatly that she's collapsed in the dining hall."

Kezerah made an unkind noise. "Sounds a bit dramatic to me."

Rook glared. "So does leading the entire royal guard out on a search and rescue for two incredibly capable soldiers in the middle of a dinner party."

"I agree," Kezerah said. "I don't know why you came."

"Then you misunderstand your position," Rook snapped.

"And you mistake your place." Ambrose's voice came up beside her. He looked both majestic, and keenly uncomfortable atop an elk. His posture was straight but his hands gripped the reins far too tight. "Or have you forgotten you're speaking to the Soul Heir, who is leading a search for what is now a missing prince under your care."

Rook ground his teeth together, but did not respond. Apparently, if he had lost his place, he'd found it again. No thanks to her. The last of her anger with Ambrose extinguished in a puff of smoke. Kezerah gave a curt nod in his direction just as Ikaika rode up beside them.

"I'm going to ride ahead," Ikaika said. "If I can get away from this mess of minds I might be able to pick out Dar's voice."

Ambrose and Rook stayed beside her and she watched Ikaika gallop off. Kezerah hated that she was stuck on Soot, the fat little pony trudging along at the breakneck speed of a slug.

"What is our next course of action?" Ambrose asked and looked at her. Kezerah returned the stare with startled panic. She had intended on riding out, and shouting her best friend's name at the top of her lungs. Not leading an army. Ambrose continued to watch her.

Rook raised a bristled brow expectantly. She wished he would lose his place again, because she had no idea what the protocol for rescuing someone was. She didn't even know if rescue was the word. She just knew, since leaving the Autumn Hall, her stomach had unknotted itself and she could breathe again.

The words escaped her like a whispered secret. A dull one, that everyone already knew. "I don't...I don't know."

Silence and hoof beats rung in her ears, and she loosened her reins to fiddle with Soot's dusty black mane. She wished she could disappear. She wished she was lost, and Andarios was in charge. He always found her.

"Split into three groups of five," Ambrose boomed out, like a boulder falling from a great height. "One follows the West Wall, the other goes along the coastline. Once you reach the tree line move inland and toward Mount Estora. The Princess, Queensguard Rook, and myself will lead the Northern group and we'll rally at the Aloran border wall."

Nobody hesitated. Even Rook fell into line, grouping soldiers into fives. Each party headed in their designated direction.

"Thank you," Kezerah managed, as they moved forward. Their pace was quick but less frantic. After a long silence she dared a glance at Ambrose, and found he watched her with a tilted head. More in speculation than admiration.

Hooves loud and fast came towards them, and their attention shot over to Ikaika riding their way. His voice sounded unmeasured, frazzled. "This way. I found Rorrik."

Rorrik.

"Where is he?" Ambrose was urgent. "What happened?"

'Look at me.' Kezerah thought to Ikaika. *'Look at me.'*

Ikaika did not, he still addressed Ambrose. "In the fields outside the forest...He's covered in blood."

"And you left him there?" Ambrose accused.

"Andarios?" It was a question and a plea. Kezerah watched Ikaika wince as she asked.

"Rorrik is alone."

Kezerah threw her legs off the pokey little pony and ran. She had made it yards before her legs shook, and Ikaika rode up beside her, offering a hand. She grasped it, and was lifted onto his elk with ease. Ikaika did not hesitate to wrap an arm around her waist, and then their mount spurred into action, leaving all else behind them.

Rorrik grew larger, a stark crimson to complement the yellowed grass and newly dead wild flowers, with rows of red forest behind him. Ikaika slowed them down but, to Kezerah's relief, didn't stop entirely.

"Where is he?" demanded Kezerah.

"Oh, I'm fine, thank you." Rorrik said, waving a hand down his blood stained appearance. "You should see the bear."

"The Bear?" At first, Kezerah thought he was referring to Andarios' growing nickname.

Rorrik nodded. "It got Andarios pretty badly along the chest, he—"

Kezerah whipped the elk's reins in the direction Rorrik had pointed. She hoped the pounding she heard was Ambrose catching up, and not her heart about to burst free from her chest. She looked towards a large white boulder she didn't recognize. When they got closer, she grew more confused.

"Summerlands..." Ikaika's breath was hot by her ear. "An iron bear."

They trotted forward more cautiously, and Kezerah's whole body trembled. The size of it stunted the tree. Its matted fur was speckled pink in some parts, and soaked red in others. Black bottomless eyes stared out at nothing and a purpled tongue drooled out from gleaming silver fangs and blackened gums. The claws, too, were silver, a true and shining metallic that didn't fit against the warm brown earth.

"What is it doing all the way down here?" Ikaika said in wonder, but Kezerah didn't care.

She clambered off the elk. Ikaika's hands slipped trying to catch her and she fell to the forest floor. She got to her knees before the scream built up in her lungs set itself free.

"Dar!" She repeated her call. No matter how she rubbed at her eyes, hot tears ruined her vision. Her throat grew raw and scraped as she cried out again, "ANDARIOS!" Their elk danced in place, alarmed by the violent tenor of the noise.

A groan to their left.

Bramble bit into her knees, calves and palms as she scrambled to get to him. If it was him. She had seen Andarios covered in mud, sweat, and even sometimes food, but never blood, and never this much blood. His eyebrows pinched together but his eyes didn't open. She shook him and felt Ikaika's hand snake around her.

"Whoa, whoa, Kez. Careful, he's got some nasty cuts."

'Cuts' didn't begin to describe the gaping wounds that slashed and extended from Andarios' shoulder to mid torso. A patch work of ripped cloth and dried leaves covered where it could. Kezerah heard a whimper and realized it was her.

"He's alive," Ikaika soothed. "He's just unconscious. I can hear him...dreaming." The way Ikaika said dreaming made Kezerah think a far less pleasant sort of sleep ailed him and she grabbed Andarios' hand.

"I can hear the rest of the party coming," Ikaika paused. "He's going to be alright, Kez. We've just got to get him back to the castle."

Kezerah nodded, but did not let go of Andarios' hand.

BLOOD-SOAKED AND MOANING, they had carried Andarios in, Rorrik not far behind. Dyllian, as well as other nosy courtiers, crowded the already packed infirmary. Their 'deep concern' threatened to drown out the head apothecary's demand for tools. The room reeked of a carnal aroma. The queen, too, occupied a bed, the king at her side. Ikaika turned away just in time to miss her vomiting into a bucket. Maybe there had been more truth than drama about her collapsing in the banquet hall.

"I don't need extra guards!" Kezerah said, still holding Andarios' hand as they situated him on a plush bed with white linens. A waste, as they were dyed crimson. "And I don't need a shorter curfew!"

"You're lucky that bear was dead by the time you got there!" Elize said, haggard and slumped over her bed across from Andarios. "Your choices put not just yourself, but your kingdom in danger."

"As if there's a scenario in which you ever approved of my actions!" Kezerah argued. "If it were up to you, I'd be in a coma, only capable of breathing."

Elowren's face looked like an old tree: stoic, unchanging, and incredibly tired of being a tree. "That's not true, Kezerah. But I do find further supervision and consequences to be necessary, given that you left the castle without proper protection, against orders."

"I was with Rook," Kezerah said, "and thank Thrice I left, or we would have all been eating pumpkin rolls while Dar bled out!"

"I bandaged him up," Rorrik interjected, salve applied to his shallow cut.

"With leaves!" snapped Kezerah.

An apothecary tending to Andarios bit off thread and strung it through a needle. Ikaika found he had nowhere to look as Elize wrenched the bucket back to her face. The needle went in and Andarios let out a howl of pain through a grimace.

"Here, bite this." The apothecary placed a strap of leather between Dar's teeth.

Elowren kneeled to brush loose strands from Elize's tightly bound hair. He looked back up after she'd finished heaving, and Andarios softened into heavy breathing. "I do not regret your actions, but the way in which you conducted them. Yes, you had Rook. Forcing him to leave your mother undefended as she—" Elowren looked over at his paramour, his eyes worried. "—Was once more overtaken by illness."

Ikaika looked towards Kezerah, but she seemed unbothered by the admission and tsk'd. "What? Did she want Rook to hold the bucket for her? She's the one always harping about her independence."

Elowren's voice became a warning. "Another disparaging remark towards your mother, and you'll go straight to your rooms and remain there."

It was impossible to tell which grip grew tighter as Ikaika assessed Andarios and Kezerah's hands.

Kezerah's eyes watered from anger. "If you think I'm leaving this room, then I hope you brought a sword, because you'll have to cut my hand off at the wrist."

"If you had that same passion for protecting your Kingdom," Elize said, pulling a kerchief out of nowhere to dab at her mouth, "maybe you'd put yourself in less danger."

"I wasn't in danger!" Kezerah shouted. "Dar was!"

"And where do you think that danger came from?" Elize hissed. "You think an iron bear—only seen in the winters of the Bastian glaciers—trotted merrily into our fortified woods?"

Silence joined the crowded room.

"It was planted there. Either because it is the place you most frequent, or because someone knew the Prince of Xenkesh would be there—under our care," Elize said with finality.

Elowren nodded. "Either way, until we conduct an investigation, the woods are not safe. You are not safe."

Ikaika shifted his feet. He couldn't help his rise in discomfort, because he had to agree. Kezerah had been foolhardy, without a plan, and he had encouraged the danger. He looked away, knowing Kezerah might seek him out for assistance.

"The bear has been sent to the butchers in the kitchens." Ambrose entered the infirmary alongside a chilled draft. Ikaika suspected he'd waited for his perfect moment of entrance. "It had minor lacerations along its neck. Possibly from a rope."

Elowren's face was solemn, his head dipped low. "It's true then. The bear was brought here."

"Are any of us safe then?" piped up Dyllian, with a look Ikaika's way. "Given that it was an Aloran bear..."

Ambrose's eyes traveled to Ikaika. "I can't say for sure. Luckily, we have an Aloran among us as an expert."

Ikaika's first thought was to grab the nearest herb jar and smash it against Ambrose's head. Unfortunately, throwing a jar at his brother would only prove Ambrose's case.

Kezerah swung to face Ikaika. Her maddened gaze seemed to look, not at him, but through him. Cold settled over his bones and he met her with a measured stare, his jaw tight. If she thought him capable of any involvement in this—but she turned her attention back to Andarios as he groaned and pushed his hair back.

"Let's not jump to conclusions," Elowren spoke to the room. "This night has been long and grows longer. Let's save these discussions for the morning when all is well."

"I'm not leaving." Kezerah didn't look away as she dabbed at sweat on Andarios' brow.

"Rook, please assure that guards remain with my daughter at all times," Elowren said. Kezerah opened her mouth to protest. "But, she may otherwise remain at Andarios' side as he recovers in the infirmary."

Kezerah closed her mouth again. The sharp nod of an agreement reached.

Awake

AN APOTHECARY DREW THE CURTAINS AGAINST THE twilight air of the herb-potent infirmary. The blood had been cleared away, the queen sent to her chambers, and spectators shooed off. After a restless night's sleep and a day of tedious study, it did not surprise Ikaika to see Kezerah right where he'd left her. Two guards stood in the corner, both surveying Ikaika as he entered. Their eyes flitted over him, hesitating on the rapier strapped to his waist. He gave a nod, and watched them pause before returning the gesture. *'Great, now they think Rorrik a hero and me an assassin.'* He picked up his pace and smiled at Andarios who, now awake, caught sight of him and smiled back.

"Sorry, I wanted to come sooner, but I ran into Biloba and they asked for our assignments."

Kezerah rolled her eyes. "At a time like this?"

He shrugged into a chair. "They spent a decade on Bethync, Kez, they're a bit removed. It was easier just to get it over with." He'd done hers too, but didn't want to appear hungry for praise.

"Well, you didn't miss anything," Andarios said, "apart from Kez snoring in her chair."

"I didn't snore!"

"You drooled too."

"How are you feeling?" Ikaika asked, before their bickering got out of hand. "Your stitches look...clean."

Andarios let out a raw laugh, more like a cough, and flinched. "Yeah, they feel like string keeping my insides from falling out."

Ikaika made a face. "What are you taking for the pain?"

"Yarrow for the fever, but I've got a concussion so I refused the poppy."

Given that Andarios' mother had been a renowned herbalist, Ikaika trusted he knew whether or not to drink a milk tea known for either deep sleep or death. "Do you remember what happened?"

Andarios gave a lopsided grin, but his eyes cautiously glanced at Kezerah, who frowned deeply. She must have gotten the longer version while Ikaika was away. "It's a bit fuzzy, but I think I got my ass kicked by a bear."

Ikaika snorted. "And lived to brag about it."

Andarios' expression grew serious. "Thanks to Rorrik." He shook his head. "I told him to stay up in that tree but, when the bear had me pinned, he jumped down—straight onto the bear—and killed it from behind."

Ikaika disliked the amount of reverence in Andarios' voice, but was incredibly relieved his friend was still alive to praise his enemy. He packed on a smile. "Well, I'm glad you're okay. Kez would have been insufferable without you."

This extracted a grin from Kezerah. "I thought you already found me insufferable."

He gave her a cursory glance; bags under her eyes and unkempt hair couldn't diminish her beauty. Ikaika wanted to ask Kezerah privately about last night, her look of distrust burned into his mind.

Andarios cleared his throat, reminding Ikaika to respond.

"Right. Yes," he said, fumbling with his words. "You're a terror." This earned a look of withering pity from Andarios. Ikaika attempted to recover himself. "Which reminds me. I believe it's been awhile since—" The guards reminded him they had an audience. He looked at the floor. "Since we looked at the cherry blossom tree in our courtyard. I thought maybe we could go—" He met her eyes again. Courage abandoned him like snow in spring. "...go tree-gazing, or whatever."

He expected her to say something clever, but instead she just looked at Andarios. "Oh, I was going to try and stay here tonight."

Ikaika's stomach dipped, and his ears grew feverishly warm. "Ah, okay. Not a problem. We have all the time in the world."

"Kez," Andarios said, "I'm not dying. Get some rest." He slid a private smile Ikaika's way. "Or, 'tree-gaze, or whatever.'"

Kezerah nibbled at her bottom lip with half glances to Andarios. "Maybe we could just stay here?"

Ikaika was being thrown scraps. He took them greedily. "Yeah, that's great."

A guard poorly disguised a scoff.

"Shut it, Fenn," Andarios warned, then winced with a hand to his chest. Kezerah knocked a dish of water over in a dash for a vial at his bedside. She applied a salve and swatted away Andarios' protests.

Ikaika looked over at the guard, Fennel, whom he'd sparred with dozens of times. "What's funny?"

Fennel squared his shoulders. "Nothing. Just doing my job, watching over the Soul Heir is all."

"Ah, okay." Ikaika's body felt tight, but he couldn't seem to release the tension. "Just wanted to be sure, since nothing funny has happened in the last twenty-four hours."

Something in Fennel's face hardened. "I'm taking it less lightly than some, of that I guarantee you."

"You think I'm taking this lightly?"

"Kai, he didn't say that," said Kezerah. "We're all just—"

"With all due respect, Soul Heir Kezerah, I *am* saying that," said Fennel. "You won't catch me trying to get cozy time in after my friend's been mauled by a bear."

"I'm fine, drop it," Andarios pleaded from his cot. "He just knows Kez needs a break and—"

"Where were you by the way?" Fennel asked. "Before the bear attack."

Ikaika couldn't believe he'd had the gall to ask. With one off-handed comment, Ambrose had poisoned people against him. "I was out looking for him, with the rest of you."

"No, he'd already been attacked. Prince Rorrik said they came across the bear midday."

'Prince Rorrik said.' Ikaika moved in close. His eyes level with Fennel's. "Go on, say it. Say it so I can do the math for you, you—"

A hand gripped his arm and drew him back. He let Kezerah pull him away. "Enough," she said. Ikaika wanted—needed—to break something. For the second night in a row, he realized just how much glass the infirmary had. "I know you had nothing to do with it," she finished. "I know you'd never hurt Dar." It wasn't enough. He needed her to say he'd never unleash a bear on the Solstice Court.

"But he's—"

"Princess Kezerah?" Nimah's voice rang out, distant behind the closed door. Kezerah muttered something to herself. "Ah, there you are." Nimah came in and caught her breath. "Your mother asked me to fetch you for the celebration."

Ikaika caught a glimmer of distrust pass through Kezerah's thoughts. "Why is everyone so keen on me leaving? I'm not leaving."

Ikaika felt himself tangled in the accusation, and rushed to her aid. "What's there to celebrate?"

Nimah looked at him as if the answer was obvious. Ikaika waited. She spoke carefully. "To celebrate the slaying of the bear, and the safe return of your brother, Prince Rorrik."

"Ah," Ikaika said, "of course." He didn't dare glance at Fennel, who was noticeably silent.

"Well, I'm not going," Kezerah said, returning to Andarios' side.

Nimah put fists on hips. "You'll have to eat."

"I'll just have some of Dar's food."

"You'll what?" sputtered Andarios.

"Princess," Nimah said, "your mother insists—"

"I can just bring food back," Ikaika said. "I don't mind."

Kezerah perked up. "Are you sure?"

'Absolutely not,' Ikaika thought. He wanted no part of a celebration for his brother. But after the conversation with Fennel, he'd decided it might be better to at least make an appearance. "Yeah, of course, it'll be great. We can 'feast among the'–erm..." he surveyed the cluttered shelves and tables, surgical instruments hung on hooks. "Scalpels." *'Not ideal.'* Ikaika internally groaned, until Kezerah's bemused smile warmed him and he smiled back.

"Well, it's quite cold," Nimah fretted. "Better to not be running to-and-fro."

Ikaika shrugged, eyes only for Kezerah. "Alorans can handle some bite to their breeze."

. . .

Mɪsᴛ ᴅᴀᴍᴘᴇɴᴇᴅ ᴛʜᴇ ᴇᴠᴇɴɪɴɢ. Ikaika shook out his curls as he entered the well-lit stone corridor. A soft pattering echoed on the glass dome as he followed string music through the Autumn Hall.

Without much interest or curiosity in these mature social gatherings, Ikaika found validation in how underwhelming they seemed to be. While similar to the feasts in conversational topics, more deals, highly political in nature, could also be heard throughout the drawing room. The Ralvens outwardly spoke to the Larkens about expanding crops, but Lord Ralven inwardly invested in foreign trade. The lord's mind alluded to plans to show his displeasure for a new irrigation by paying many off to deny they had Sway to begin with. It appeared the Ralvens also received payments to drum up trouble in the streets of Heartsglove.

The Lords of Heartsglove—frequent visitors of the Solstice Court—gave a passionate speech to the Regent Lord of Luka about intervening with the bandits that burned and hoarded crops in Luka. However, both nobles had already paid off the bandits in the capital and taken their cut of the sales, so they already knew the amount of Prevention flower stock to be sold at a higher minimum. Sickness roiled in Ikaika, all the false words jumbling with the truth in their minds.

In an attempt to push the thoughts out, he tried to focus on people's faces. Ambrose, of course, thrived in the middle of the room, flocked by admirers and false, high laughter. Next to him stood Xenkesh's Sword Master, Azalea, the most threatening woman Ikaika had ever seen. Her eyes bore the dreadful cold of wind in winter, hair sheared as if done in a temper and the remaining bits tied in a fitful knot: a mockery of an Aloran hairstyle. Both menacing and slight next to Ambrose, it made Ikaika unsure of her size. What did Eriko make of this hawk of a woman? His pulse jolted as her eyes clicked onto his like an arrow latched onto a target, and Ikaika averted his attention.

Rorrik, too, was easy enough to spot. He sported his same white and gold scaled armor, now outdone by a brilliant white fur shawl. A large goblet squatted between his fingertips as he told the story of his encounter with the bear.

"I told Andarios to run, to save himself. I had a plan after all, but a battle is a battle to The Bear, so he stayed to fight—brave man—he kept the beast busy while I enacted my strategy. We fought side by side until he fell, and I struck the creature from behind. Just in time it would seem."

"And not a scratch on you?"

"An iron bear might be quick," Rorrik said, with a swig of wine, "but let word travel to Alora and its Iron Queen: I'm quicker."

Ikaika walked over to the carafes of ciders, ales, and wines and poured a juniper ale. He took the first glass down in one go, the liquid leaving scorch marks along his throat. The next he tried to sip slower, as to not appear out of sorts. While his brothers had yet to notice him, others whispered as Ikaika passed by. Courtesy kept many from bringing the war up outright, but both sides under one roof appeared to have emboldened people's opinions.

"At some point the whole thing just becomes selfish," Liege Lumi of Aveltra said, speaking with Dyllian and his father.

"It depends on where you reside," Dyllian said. "While I understand it affects trade for port cities, the revolutionaries have made sure Elastor still functions as *Elastor*."

"Revolutionaries! Bah," Lumi sneered. "They're nothing but pirate apologists. They bypass trade for profit, and yell in the streets."

Dyllian puffed out his chest. "Have you bothered to listen to what they're shouting about? Fair labor prices, fair divides in *coin*— our actual functioning currency."

"I think those further from the crops would say the shares have been poorly divided. We all reside in Elastor, we all play our part," said Lumi.

"There are plenty of benefits to trickle down to less affluent cities," Lord Ralven quipped. "You may say we all reside in Elastor, but far more than that, we all reside in Thrice, and not all of Thrice *pays* its part."

Lumi looked at the pair in distaste. "I don't partake in conversations of prejudice."

"That may be," Dyllian said, "but, while you huddle in your cove, Alorans benefit off of hard earned coins. I only argue we benefit in return—"

"—Lord and Lordling of Ralven, are you insinuating that you see benefit to this war?"

Dyllian looked at the judgmental eyes upon him and sought assistance. "I simply stated that not all have to lose from the continuation of the war. Not that I benefitted."

Yara of Sorrel came to his aid, her rose-gold glass matching her hair. "Take Crown Prince Ikaika for instance. He's the last born in the Aloran line, but because of the war, he'll be a king."

The room quieted as thoughts grew louder, stunned at Lady Sorrel's callousness. Ikaika took a long sip of his drink, the fire burning down his throat far less excruciating than their stares.

Ambrose broke the tension after finishing his own glass. "Yes well, I can't be ruler of *all* the Thrice Kingdoms, can I? Someone had to pick up the slack."

Irritation pricked at Ikaika as guests chortled, the tension easing. He heard them all internally waiting for his reaction, his outburst. Some minds shifted to the bear. They could keep waiting. He wouldn't give these people anything to blather about in the coming weeks. He grabbed another glass, retreating to a corner to wait out the crowd around the food platters. He wished Andarios or Kezerah could have come. Though, at this moment he would have been thrilled if Willow or Whistle walked in.

Talk moved towards the Nighttide festival and upcoming plans for Yuletide. Queen Elize flitted around the room, attending all conversations seemingly at once. He glanced up periodically, as if to look engaged, and jumped. Ambrose leaned against the pillar beside him.

"Yara is an idiot," Ambrose said, low, while he allowed his wine to breathe.

"Are you on a first name basis with many idiots?" Ikaika asked, in no mood for his courtly games.

"Most certainly. She frequents the Trusol court, so she is one of many idiots I'm well acquainted with."

Ikaika realized he was being given the golden opportunity to speak, unfiltered, with Ambrose. "Perhaps there's a common trend you're missing between you and those you acquaint yourself with."

Ambrose stopped swirling his wine, eyes assessing him. "Perhaps if you better acquainted yourself with your role as heir, you'd understand the burden and responsibility of acquainting yourself with idiots."

Ambrose's condescension tightened Ikaika's grip on the fragile stem of his glass. "Of course you'd manage to turn friendship standards into a weakness."

"You think these people are my friends?" Ambrose's smile was feral. "Kings don't have friends, Ikaika. Kings have allies, or they have enemies."

"King Elowren has plenty of friends. Maybe it's just your standard of king that's lacking."

Ambrose straightened. "Elowren thinking he has friends is what got him into this mess in the first place. You think my—our—*Illija* would hesitate to destroy him if he joined my father? Or even got the impression he might? You think Kezerah is playing peacekeeper with both of us to be polite to her father's *friends*?" Ambrose's words harshened. "Wake up. The Solstice Court is beautiful, but it's a dream and Elastor has decided to remain asleep rather than face the people dying right outside its walls."

Ikaika didn't respond, he wanted to argue on behalf of his mother, but Ambrose's accusation of her had not been completely false. His moment to speak passed. Ambrose pushed himself off the pillar and left, taking the final word with him.

Ikaika stormed forward and grabbed a platter of meat and cheese off a table before he disappeared through the open terrace, and into the rain.

CURLS PLASTERED his neck and shoulders as he trudged back up to the infirmary. Comebacks and unused conversation pieces came to mind as he made his way back. Ambrose's cynical perspective had holes. Ikaika would be a king, he would have friends, and Ambrose could sit on his blistering throne, surrounded by the echoes of his own words.

Had Ambrose not bid to be Kezerah's friend? He'd have a hard time managing that once he—

Kezerah lay, slumped in a chair by Andarios' bed. Her head positioned on their friend's arm and shoulder like a pillow. A singular candle illuminated their corner of the room in an orange glow. Soft snores assured Ikaika they both slept deeply. Ikaika imagined waking Kezerah, and couldn't bring himself to it. He backed away once more, leaving the plate of wet brie and soggy sausage on a counter near Fennel.

Back in his room he pitched his clothes into a heap on the ground and donned a nightshirt. Ikaika feared he'd dream drift, but instead he remained in his own dreams: a long drawn-out duel with Ambrose, in which he was defeated again and again no matter how hard he tried.

Bonding

Kezerah woke to the sensation of missing her right arm. More alarming still, she'd dreamed her father had indeed decided to take a sword to it. She opened her eyes and exhaled in relief, moving it back and forth to wake it up. The numbness from resting it through the night, pinned to Andarios' side, had taken its toll. The moonlight laced the room with shadows and she tried to light a candle, which remained a stubborn, hardened puddle at the end of its wick.

Andarios grumbled as she paced the floor, quiet so she didn't wake him, and tried to shake away her restless thoughts. She'd almost lost him. Her mind tried to conceptualize life without Andarios and came up short. She was brought back to her screams in the meadow. Her inability to help him. She'd always accepted her failures before, but this would have been unforgivable. She rotated her arm again, aware her guards watched her in stoic silence. The room felt small. She wanted space. She looked at Andarios. She couldn't leave. The corners of the room began to knit together, shrinking as her fears grew larger.

She popped a lump of blue cheese into her mouth and continued to pace. Would someone have tried to hurt Andarios? Who had to gain?

"It's not even dawn," Andarios yawned. "Ugh, not even close. The night thrushes are still singing."

"How can you sleep knowing someone tried to kill you?"

Andarios laughed in the dark. "Nobody tried to kill me—Well, the bear did—I mean nobody planned to have me murdered by a bear."

"How can you be sure?"

"Because I'm not important enough."

"You're important to me." Kezerah frowned and ceased her pacing. The idea of someone trying to physically harm her was ludicrous, but if they'd wanted to send her a message...

The platter whooshed past her, Andarios using his Sway to pick around at the meats. "Ugh, Kez, this cheese is moldy."

Kezerah looked over at the guards, her breath short. "Andarios—your Sway!" she tried to recover her composure. "I mean, wow! Congratulations! You've—"

Andarios and the two guards chuckled. "Sorry," Andarios said, "with everything going on, I forgot to tell you, the jig is up. Everyone found out when I laid Rorrik out in the mud."

Kezerah didn't find this at all funny. "If my mother finds out—"

"She already knows." Andarios waved a hand, flippant. "She actually wasn't horrible about it."

Something ticked into place. Kezerah narrowed her eyes, cold crept over her body. "In what way?"

"She's letting me keep my rooms, and—Oh! She stood up for me when Rook assigned scout missions." Andarios gave a teasing side-eye towards Fennel. "Since I did get the best bracket score."

Her bones reached glacial temperatures.

"I don't feel well," she told the guards. "Can I please be escorted to speak to my father?"

"You're already in the infirmary," Andarios said. "It's probably just the cheese."

"It's not the cheese."

"We've been instructed to escort you only to and from your rooms," said Fennel.

"Until given further notice," said the guard who wasn't Fennel.

"I'd like to speak with my father," she stated again. There was a long silence. Kezerah closed her eyes, thinking back to Ambrose telling Rook—Rook of all people—what to do. She squared her shoulders and stopped the room's slow decline. "This is your further notice. I will be taken to my father, now. " Each word fell out of her steady and calm, weighed down by the gravity of her need. She turned to Andarios. "One of you—Fennel—will stay here with Andarios." She pointed to the other guard, sorry she didn't know his name. "You, with me." She marched past them, towards the door. Both guards grumbled to each other but bowed and followed orders as she descended the stairs, and stepped into fresh air. Kezerah made sure not to give her lead any slack.

She cursed under her breath as she neared her father's study. Light glowed from the crack under the door, but judging by the garbled voices inside, her mother had come up with the same idea. Kezerah stopped, and slid closer to the door.

"Princess—" the guard protested.

"Shh!" Kezerah hissed. "It's rude to interrupt a meeting."

She scooted closer, surprised not by the words spoken, but by who spoke them.

"I see no benefit in keeping her cooped up in her room—the castle, yes," said her mother, "but we have guests, not to mention a diplomatic duty to create better ties with Xenkesh."

"Not at the risk of her life," came her father's voice. "We have little to no information on what occurred in the Winter Woods. Until we know more, our duty is to our daughter."

"We'll keep guards on her, Elowren. She'll have a Queensguard by the spring."

"I don't think—"

"She's already isolated. I have leads on the bear from my Eyes. Let me follow them and make your decision in the morning."

Silence. Kezerah suspected an agreement of expressions rather than words had been reached.

The tap of her mother's dainty heels hit hard and fast on the floor. Kezerah backed up—and into her guard, who didn't budge. They glared at one another as Elize opened and closed the door.

Elize's earlier conversation seeped into her voice. "What are you doing here?"

Kezerah forced a smile. "I came to see you." This had not been the plan, but, since her first plan had already unraveled, she shifted it into something new.

Elize examined her, then her lips gave a tug at the edges: A *hint* of a hint of a smile. "You need something." She slowly yanked at her father's closed door. Confirmation that it was shut.

Kezerah shrugged. She had more options in confronting her

mother if she remained vague. Elize cast a casual hand to dismiss Kezerah's guard. "We'll speak in my rooms. Rook will see her back." The guard left without a word, and Kezerah followed her mother through the Winter Hall to her private chambers.

The last time she had willingly spent time in her mother's rooms, she'd been five. She had also been very small, and very, very lonely. Kezerah made sure she didn't falter in the door frame. Her eyes slid across the familiar room. Elize gracefully sat in her high-backed chair. Where she had always sat, so many years ago.

Kezerah recalled the hours spent on her mother's makeup, each line either perfect or erased. She'd sat dutifully on the low, padded seat beside her. Elize dabbed at her lips, then scrubbed the paint off with force. Kezerah sympathized with the paint. Hundreds of dresses had been tried on, then cast aside in frustration. Any thoughts of fleeing dashed away; Kezerah had nowhere to go. Elize finally turned as if just remembering her.

"Do you want to play the compromise game with Momma? Help me get ready?"

Kezerah remembered the eagerness she'd felt, the hunger for affection. She nodded. This game was simple. There were always two choices, and Kezerah would choose the one she thought her mother wanted.

Elize held up dresses. "Do we like this dress? Or this one?" Kezerah deliberated, then nodded at her favorite. If she was right, Elize would smile and put the dress on. If she was wrong...

"This dress doesn't compliment my figure. Did you not notice the color with my eyes? Remember, this is a dress for me, not you. Don't be selfish and try again. Which one is best for me?" Kezerah picked again. She wanted it to be right and true with everything she had. Then held her breath as she watched her mother try it on. Elize would look in the mirror, fresh-faced and no longer upset. "You did perfect Kezerah, this is just the right dress." Kezerah beamed, her breaths at first large, then calm and relieved. She'd made her mother happy.

"Can we play 'Run' now?" Kezerah asked, sliding off her cushion.

"Next time." Elize already walked towards the door. "We have your father's welcome home feast to attend. But," she said at Kezerah's frown, "you can sit next to me, and we'll play the silent game." She tapped Kezerah on the nose with a bright red nail. "I bet you win again."

It had been the last game Kezerah had won against her mother. That evening her father had come through the door with more than open arms; he had come with someone in his arms. Andarios. And Kezerah no longer needed to play her mother's games.

Andarios, Andarios, Andarios.

"So," Elize said, jarring Kezerah out of her thoughts. "What is it that you need from me?"

Kezerah kept her tone falsely doting. "Can't I simply want time with my mother?"

"Fourteen years says otherwise," Elize said, like a sweet berry with a tart aftertaste. "Cut to it, Kezerah, you know we're always better when we want the same thing."

Kezerah caressed the footboard of her mother's bed and traced a finger over the carving of a lamb. She'd never hesitated in an argument with her mother where Andarios was involved, but if her mother had tried to kill him? Kezerah treaded carefully.

"I wanted information on the bear." She brought her eyes up, gazing into Elize's impassive ones. "You told father you had leads. I want them."

Elize sighed and turned with disinterest. A basin of water sat at her vanity and she smoothed a cloth across her brow. "Of course, you've suddenly decided to be involved when your personal interests are threatened."

"Do you have leads or not?" Kezerah coaxed. "Are you stalling? Does the great Spymaster, self-made and confident, have no clue?"

"Honestly, Kezerah—"

"Or is it because the lead would be a circle?" Kezerah dented her nails into the footboard. "A snake eating itself." Elize looked taken aback. A feat. "Why don't you just tell me what you want? I'll give it to you. Do you want me to grovel? I'll grovel. Do you want me to sit and stare during a council meeting? I'll be there. Just leave my friends out of it."

"Just to be clear," Elize said, slowly, "you think I consorted with pirates, commandeered an Aloran Iron bear—one of this world's deadliest creatures—and set it loose in our home, on the off chance your leech of a friend might stumble upon it?"

Kezerah pushed the discomfort out of her voice. "Not by chance, you planned it."

"Ah," Elize resumed, squeezing the cloth into the basin, and wiping at the curve of her jawline. "Right, of course. Because I also knew where the bear would be at all times. Did I have the animal followed, or did I personally drag it around to be stationed where he might be?"

Kezerah disliked how absurd it sounded when played out. "Well, there was a rope."

Elize tossed her cloth into the water basin with a splash and burble and massaged her hands across her face. "All while planning a dinner party. My, you *do* have a high opinion of me." She turned to face Kezerah again. "It was somebody's pet, Kezerah."

Kezerah faltered, her hand falling to her side. "It...a what?"

"A domestically tamed animal kept for companionship. You must be familiar. An Aloran merchant was found in the Bastians, claiming, on a fishing trip, his 'pet' had gone missing. His attacked yours. That's the lead. The end of the line."

Kezerah shook her head. "I saw it. It was huge, and the way it attacked Dar, it didn't act like someone's pet..."

"Well, that's why it's illegal to have them as pets," said her mother, voice irritated and impatient. "And why it is that we need stronger border regulations. But you missed *that* meeting yesterday."

"I was a bit preoccupied."

"Yes, you do a fine job of 'sitting and staring', regardless of the location. What a fine queen you'll be."

Kezerah backed away as if struck. The hollowed-out pain in her chest intensified. Elize's brash blue eyes bore into Kezerah's with a knowing stare. She stopped her hand from wiping away tears. It only brought them to her mother's attention.

Then, Kezerah watched as Elize softened, her gaze more akin to the Lull. "You have been trying more lately though, haven't you?"

Her mother filled the gap of silence by walking over to her. A thumb brushed away the dampness at Kezerah's cheek. "Prince

Ambrose seemed so pleased after his trip down to the beaches." She tucked a curl behind Kezerah's ear. "It just makes me wonder what more you are capable of, for your kingdom."

Kezerah looked away, no response at the ready. Fingertips tilted up Kezerah's chin, and she looked directly into her mother's conviction. "Which is why I asked your father to lift your guard supervision. I want to see what you'll accomplish. I want to see your power."

"I don't have power." The words slipped out of Kezerah before she could stop them.

Elize dropped her chin and turned back towards her chair. She snapped her fingers. The door opened and Rook loomed in its frame. "See my daughter to the bottom of the stairs, then let her find her own way back."

Kezerah eyed Rook with dismay. "Why are you letting me go?" Surely her mother knew she'd never pass up an opportunity to roam free.

Elize didn't turn. "Because sometimes your father and I disagree, and sometimes, my daughter, it is you and I that see eye to eye."

Rook led Kezerah out and down the stairs, and released her into the cool Autumn night.

The grass made a small, shushing sound under her feet as she roamed towards the maze. It seemed the safest place to wander while avoiding explanation. Once hedges towered around Kezerah, she removed the hood of her cloak and shook out her hair. The silver moon waned into nothing above her, making the stars all the more bright.

She contemplated the hole she'd dug up to smuggle herself into Heartsglove. She chewed her bottom lip and thought back to the artist. His fear and her guilt. She might be without power, but people's false ideas of her could be dangerous. With a light shake of her head she banished the memory; a night in would be just fine. She needed to get back to Andarios soon anyway. A sigh wisped out of her as she lay down on the cold ground, delighted that the chill was waking her.

"That can't be comfortable."

She recognized the voice and didn't open her eyes to respond, instead letting a smile play on her lips. "Quite the contrary. I was just thinking how comfortable it is."

"Are you trying to convince me you're not cold?" Ambrose mused. He held his typical posture: arms crossed and shoulder leaning into a hedge. He seemed forever lopsided, and the thought made her grin. "I seem to be amusing you without even trying," he said, eyeing her curiously.

"And I thank you for it."

"May I join you? I admit, you make laying on frozen grass, mid-moon, look quite appealing."

She thought for a moment. Ambrose was fun to flirt with. It seemed to come as easy to him as breathing and she enjoyed the witty banter. However, she didn't fully trust her own wits when factoring in his close proximity.

She had paused too long.

"Perhaps not then."

"No..." She knew this was partially to challenge herself, and partially not wanting him to leave. "Join me."

He gave a large smile, straightened himself, and made it to her in one easy stride. Despite his broad frame, he gracefully flopped to the ground and looked up with a shiver. "Yes," he said, unable to veil his quivering body as he adjusted to the cold ground. "I can see why this is so—appealing."

She laughed, and he seemed to ease a bit. He brought his bare arms up to rest behind his head, hands interlocked.

"Here." She unfastened her cloak. "To disguise your discomfort." She draped her cloak over him, laughing at how it covered no more than his torso. The fleece pants he wore clashed with his black silken tunic, making the image all the more absurd.

His teeth chattered as he grinned at her, somehow the earnest attempt appeared charming. "It's—imposssibl-le t-to f-feel dis-ss-comf-fort-t, l-laying n-next-t-to y-you-ou."

She laughed again and laid back, the icy tendrils of grass tickling her neck. "I'm surprised you're braving the chill, to be honest. Do you wander my mazes often?"

He cleared his throat as he steadied his voice. "This is only my second time. I didn't realize they were your mazes—it was your mother who suggested it. She thought the walk might be nice when she saw me shivering yesterday."

Kezerah snorted. "Just like my mother to see someone shivering and send them into the cold."

"Despite the cold, I'm definitely not complaining." He shivered again and they laughed, looking up at the stars and souls that shone across the sky.

She leaned on her side, facing him. "Show me your magick," she demanded, suddenly eager. "Make yourself warmer."

He rasped a laugh but composed himself to speak. "It doesn't work like that, unfortunately. Bonding only allows you to cast illusions, or control objects. We can't actually affect other living beings; just make it look like we are."

"Like changing my eyes. Or sending a letter."

He nodded, allowing a flame to appear in his hand. He moved his other hand through it. "Here, try."

If anyone else had told her to stick her hand in an open flame, she wondered if she would have attempted it. With Ambrose, she immediately cast her hand in.

It was like sweeping fingers through the air. Despite how real it flickered with feigned affliction to her touch, it was not fire.

"Why does it work on objects but not people?" she pondered aloud, eyes still on the flame.

"When you Bond, you are binding yourself to an object permanently. Non-living organisms have a different...presence than living ones, although both have souls. They are reasoned with more easily. Humans, animals, living things—they have too much free will. It would be—" Ambrose shuddered at the thought, "—cruel. It's called Will Bonding, and it's taboo to even think of it really. Bonding yourself allows you to speak the object's language, but they don't mind being controlled." He paused a moment before amending. "And if they do, they'll tell you."

"Objects have language?"

Ambrose nodded. "All things do. My magick allows me to understand it. Things don't speak like we do; they feel, they desire, they exist without intent. When I look at that rock—" He dipped his head toward a rogue stone that lay between them, "—I can feel it before I command it. It wants to be—well, it wants to be a rock." He chuckled. "But it doesn't mind anything else I ask of it, as long as it gets to continue being a rock."

"What happens if you want it to become a sword?"

Ambrose grimaced. "How about a smaller rock?"

Kezerah shook her head, grinning. "No, I'll take a sword, thank you."

Ambrose looked at the rock, brow furrowed in concentration, keeping his breathing steady.

The rock shifted in shape, transforming into a sleek piece of steel with a silver hilt.

Kezerah picked it up, inspecting the weight. It was rough in her hand despite its smoothed edges, it felt uneven and heavy.

He smiled, amused by her confusion.

She watched as it flickered and, like a flame, went out, a small rock nestled in her hands.

Her eyes widened in surprise, and he continued. "All things have willpower. The Bond I've created is strong. I picked something with meaning to me, but no matter how strong a Bond is, if something does not align with what I have planned for it, it can fight it. A rock —this rock—does not want to be a sword, but it's much easier to talk a rock into being a smaller rock."

"Even though your Bond is strong?" Kezerah countered, remembering his boast.

Ambrose scoffed. "The closer the object's...substance is to my Bond, the better the translation. I'm honored it didn't deny me."

"Does your Bond object ever deny you?"

"Rarely, but..." Ambrose's thumb brushed his bottom lip in contemplation. "My Bond and I are aligned. Our desires are attuned. Our paths would have to be quite diverged for it to refuse me outright. That's why compromise is important."

Kezerah looked at the rock as he spoke but felt his eyes on her. She met his stare. She wished she hadn't. With just the forged fire illuminating his features, he looked unearthly, as if he, too, was just an illusion. His eyes burned emerald in the glow of the flames. His lips were full, absently smiling as if it were their natural shape. She felt drawn in, a moth to his light.

Mouth dry, mind hazy, she tried to break his spell. "What are you Bound to?"

He drew nearer. The hand holding his flame lowered. He appeared to not comprehend, tilting his head to the side as if trying to understand her words.

Then, the glint returned, and his smile a grin. "Not even for you, Princess. Once Bonded, the bond is permanent for the Bond Wielder's lifetime. The more people who know what my magick is linked to, the more vulnerable I am."

"Just the Bond Wielder's life, not the bond?"

Ambrose scrunched his brows, parsing her question. "Objects don't die as we do, but a bound object's soul will follow its Bond to the Summerlands. From there it's scholarly hearsay; the souls reset with the option of finding each other again in the next life."

"On the off chance someone foolishly bound themselves to a rock," she teased.

"Nobody in their right mind would—ah, I see." He stopped at her smile.

"Well," Kezerah laughed, "I've now narrowed it down to not being a rock."

Ambrose scoffed, eyes bright. "That you have. My soul is indeed not tethered to a rock."

"But, perhaps," Kezerah tapped the little pebble, "since you were able to change this temporarily, it's within the mineral family?"

Ambrose's amusement did not falter, nor did he react. He simply waited for her to give up. She felt a wall between them, and she desperately wanted to tear it down. A new thought occurred to her.

"What happens if someone were to take your Bond?"

Ambrose shuddered. "Ugh. It's awful. It's like being without water in the desert." He caught her look of confusion and amended. "Sickening, maddening. You don't realize how much magick you've got until it's ripped away, or weakened beyond use."

"Sounds like you've suffered the experience."

Ambrose shrugged. "I forgot mine in my room—early on—just after Bonding with it. I had to turn back halfway to Zelos, I was so sick. I've heard stories of weakened Bonds. Apparently, it's something similar...but the feeling is constant."

It sounded horrible. His discomfort clear, she tried a new method. She looked over his body, trying to make the movement seem playful, and relieved much of him stayed hidden beneath her cloak. His legs were crossed over one another, the picture of comfort despite the cold. Gold bands adorned his arms and emphasized not just his russet skin but corded muscle. He cocked an eyebrow, eyes searching and filled with humor.

Kezerah made her voice a comfortable drawl. "Since you're able to make a flame, that means your Bond must be on you. If it needs to be close at hand."

His smile widened, the flame extinguishing as he gestured down his large form. "By all means, search away."

She laughed, the spell finally broken as she sat up. He followed her and seemed relieved to be at least partially off the ground.

Ambrose interrupted the comfortable silence this time. "So, what brings a princess out of her bed, in the middle of the night, to stargaze while she freezes to death?"

"You're speaking as if I'm not here again," she teased.

He sighed, playing along. "What brings you, *Kezerah*, out here to freeze to death?"

She savored her name in the air as he said it. Then she thought of her mother and opened her mouth to divulge their horrendous conversation. His stare was steady, patient. He'd asked a question and resigned himself to wait for his wish to be granted. She closed her mouth and scuffed a boot.

He hugged his legs to him, to better hold in heat. "What is it?"

She tried to speak and found an ill accustomed shyness barred her path. "How did you find your power—Your magick, I mean."

"Is that what you mean?"

Kezerah fiddled with an ornate buckle on her boot. "Well, obviously you were born into being the crown heir."

"As you were born into being the Soul Heir," he agreed. "Yet, I think we both know it's the role we stumble into, not the power."

She snapped and unsnapped the buckle, not looking at him.

After a moment he spoke, his words measured. "I was angry at my mother." Their eyes met, knowing they graced the edges of dangerous territory. "She had burned a village to the ground, and I'd been just spans away. Right on the outskirts of camp. My father had taken me along because it'd been the role I was 'born into'. I'd known about the war, of course, I'd heard the stories. But when I entered a perfectly peaceful village, I couldn't imagine it." Ambrose closed his eyes, and Kezerah felt him drift into the memory. "Everyone was so friendly. They'd lavished me with gifts, let me sample all of the foods at their market, and invited me to dance at their festival. All because one day, I'd sit on a throne on the other side of the sands from them. It was the festival that disguised the first fires. She'd known when the dancing would take place. She knew our customs, our culture. I was still getting ready for the evening when I heard the first screams."

He swallowed, the atrocity clearer on his face than any details he could have given. Kezerah deliberated what she could possibly say. Not as a peacekeeper, but as a friend. He relieved her of the chance.

"I realized then that I'd been praised for a power I didn't have. The power to protect my people against those who wished them harm." He turned a fearsome gaze on her. "I wanted nothing more in this world than to possess that power. To take back what she'd taken from me.

"My mother left little in the way of heirlooms behind. That, or her first fire destroyed all but a few. I'd hoarded them, treasured them, and when I returned home, I let them go. I released myself. I took back the power she'd taken from me. That night I chose my Bond. The next day, I took my position as War Strategist. Because power is not found, or given; it's chosen."

Kezerah half believed she'd gain her Hold on Sway from the energy his words exuded alone. The way his need to protect drove his actions resonated with her to the core. But if she hadn't held Sway in the forest then it seemed that bit of power dwelled beyond her reach. His energy remained magnetic. As if his talk of strength had drawn her close, her legs leaned into his, their bodies turned towards each other's vitality.

"I'm sorry," she said finally, "for what happened to your village."

His hands dropped their hold of his legs to brush the smidge of grass between them. "Thank you." He gazed at her but Kezerah could tell he was far away. She wanted to bring him back. She inclined forward, her own hand in the grass shifted with her, just a nudge.

"You know, I—agh!" Kezerah clasped her stomach, the dull ache piquing into a sharp pain. Ambrose startled, suddenly panicked, and close by.

"What's wrong?" He looked around as if expecting to see enemies in the bushes.

A roiling bubble threatened to escape Kezerah. She put up a hand to stall him, her shy melancholy replaced by overt humiliation. "This can't be happening." She hadn't meant to say it out loud, but it couldn't get worse: she burped. "It's the cheese."

Ambrose's face remained stunned for several heartbeats. "The..." Then he barked a laugh, deep and full. "You have indigestion? Summerlands, Kezerah, I thought you'd been poisoned."

Kezerah gritted her teeth. "Yes, well, don't worry, you won't end up on a list of suspects. I think I just need to lie down."

Ambrose snorted and stood, extending a hand. "I'd be quickly waived as a suspect."

Their hands met and she was lifted without effort. Once standing, she didn't even reach his shoulder. "And why is that?"

"It interrupts my chance to participate in your late night activities."

She swatted his arm, and he feigned a flinch.

"Such as stargazing, obviously," he laughed. She held her stomach again, and he steadied her. "Shall I walk you back to your room?"

"Just the infirmary."

His smile dimmed. "Is it really that bad?"

"It's not that. I need to get back to Andarios, and I..." She trailed off, unsure how to explain the terror feasting on her heart. A peace had been made between them, but it had created a vulnerability in her she couldn't shake. As it turned out, he didn't need an explanation.

"I felt the same when we found Rorrik outside the woods," he admitted. Somehow, when he said it, it sounded brave, practical.

"How did you get past it?"

"I didn't," he said, as they began to walk. "I'm terrified of losing anyone I care about. But I also accept it's not always in my control. I fight what I can, but allowing fear to control me isn't an option. It only serves to let time with my loved ones slip away." The sprawl of the meadow appeared before them. The dual hymn of the night thrushes finishing their song penetrated the silence.

Kezerah looked from the infirmary tower to the Spring Quarters.

"What's your fear behind the fear?" he asked, the question felt intimate, like a secret.

"Losing him," she answered, her eyes on the tower.

"No, that's the fear. What's behind it?"

Kezerah didn't know. She looked up at him, and a strand of his hair fell forward into his face as he returned her stare. He lifted her fingers, a gentle gesture made illicit by the hush of night.

"Whatever it is, don't let it rule you. If the fear comes, fight it, but don't let it rule." His next words were a challenge. "Now, where shall I escort you?"

He walked her to her room.

My dear one

My dear one, I'm sorry to receive the news that your migraines have intensified. This is unsettling. Unfortunately, Amarus' forces have made some headway along our coast. As that leaves a clear line to Mellock, you can see why my leaving right now is impossible. Be strong, my son. The time for the Temples of Estora is nearing, but without adequate protection or the ability to get you there myself—due to my banishment while your brothers reside there—my hands are tied.

Please continue to focus on your breathing and distance your mind from the exterior world. This intense manifestation is a veiled gift. You must possess immense power to have it pain you so. Give Elowren my best, and if you are willing, describe your brothers to me in your next reply. I long to know how they have grown, it pains me they are so close. Although it is a blessing and relief that you can be at each other's sides.

All my love,
Your mother

Sword Masters

IKAIKA CONTEMPLATED WADDING THE LETTER UP AND tossing it into the fire, crackling brilliantly in his room's hearth. The violet-blue light of dawn did little to warm the space. If anything, it brought a cold, ominous chill, which suited his mood just fine. He folded the paper twice over, and placed it in the inner pocket of his tunic. He'd known the likelihood of leaving for the temples soon was low, but he hadn't expected to have no promise of going at all. The light made the throbbing behind his eyes worse. Each hue of the flame dappled and meshed with his surroundings. His stomach swam.

He took long, deep breaths, concentrating solely on the air as it left his body, feeling his chest expand and contract, his shoulders rising and falling. He tried to imagine his feet grounded to the stone like the roots of the large trees in the meadow. The pain remained but the aura around his vision receded, allowing him to calm his nausea with the next few breaths.

People began to wake up, their minds focused on breakfast. Then, inner voices rose as they found each other.

The distance between him and the other quarters had always felt so vast. He gritted his teeth, and fought back as his Melding expanded out like a blanket of sky. Gossip, reactions, ponderings all mixed together with half truths. It was going to be difficult to look Lady Sorrel in the eye after the—hopefully fantastical—obscene image that entered his mind while she spoke to Ambrose from across the table.

Ikaika grimaced. *'Right, distancing my mind from the exterior world.'* He tried to find himself. His hand reached out and palmed the dagger at his hip. The one given to him by Eriko. He remembered the moment, after the assassin had stopped breathing. Eriko had tried to assure Ikaika the assassin was dead, and showed him the dagger, meant for him, in the assassin. But Ikaika had already known. He'd died with him, trapped in his mind until it went dark. All of the man's vile thoughts snuffed out with a twist of a blade. He'd felt the Aloran steel go through; his ribcage opening to spill insides outside. Ikaika had suddenly feared for a woman he didn't know, a child he'd never seen, a family in a hot desert, a life in Xenkesh. Then, nothing. Ikaika had become nothing. Until Eriko shook him awake and gave him air. His mother had been swift in her return home, and swifter still in leaving it, as she mounted them onto her wolf.

"WHY DO WE HAVE TO GO?" Ikaika had clutched her waist as rocks and woods blurred on either side of them. The wolf's powerful claws bounded through the still-thawing earth.

"Because they might come back, and I can't stay to protect you."

"Who will come back?" he asked. "The man died." *I died.*

Illija's voice was hollowed out by cool wind as they crested a snow-capped mountain. "More will be sent, my love. I'm sorry, I can't take the chance."

"But who would send them?" Ikaika couldn't help himself. "Who would want to kill me?"

Illija had been silent a long time, steering the Iron Wolf to follow a river of opals. Then she spoke. "Amarus. The assassin was Xenkeshi, and the dagger you now possess is one I know."

But it hadn't just been Amarus who'd sent the assassin. His mother's hands hadn't clamped over his ears fast enough to protect the truth, as Queen Elize announced it casually upon their arrival.

"It seems he won't inherit anything, based on how poorly you are able to protect him from his brothers..."

His brothers. The reason his mother fought so hard—why she couldn't be there to protect him herself. His brothers: That did not want to be saved. That didn't want to know Ikaika. That wanted him dead and out of their way. He tried to want the same for them, but he couldn't do it. It disgusted him.

He'd always wanted to be a protector, like Eriko, for his sole purpose to be saving lives. But, despite his love of swordplay, he didn't know if he could take a life in order to save one. How did one rule if they couldn't protect their people? He didn't even know his people. Would they look at him as a pretender? A prince raised in Elastor trying to claim an Aloran throne? He was supposed to be home. He was supposed to be learning about his birthright.

But his mother had never pushed him like Kezerah's parents did. Her parents were protective to be sure, but they had always left room for her involvement.

He bit his lip, and paced, allowing himself to think his fears through. Illija never bothered with him because she'd always intended for her firstborn son's return. She had expected, *wanted*, Ambrose to take the throne. Did Ambrose desire that as well? He seemed to mostly just eat, drink, dance and flirt—That last one irked him. Ambrose seemed to desire everything, consuming them like food with his gaze: Kezerah included. The thoughts Ikaika glimpsed were often lewd, Ambrose's first assumption being that Ikaika had already bedded her.

He shut his eyes tight and massaged them out of habit, knowing this pain had nothing to do with his migraine. He stayed in his room until the fire died out, letting his anger cool alongside the embers.

Erratic knocks woke Kezerah. She leapt out of bed, almost tripping over a vase. Something must have happened to Andarios. Dresses littered the floor, and an overturned desk remained an obstacle when another knock—much more impatient—rapped at her door. Kezerah, determined to stay in her room, had decided late in the night to reorganize the space. She'd dragged several pieces of furniture to one corner, but found the larger fixtures too heavy to lift. Now the items barricaded the exit and she fought to dig herself out as her door began an orchestral drum beat. She wrenched it open.

"Dar!" Kezerah collapsed into his burly frame and outstretched arms.

"Hey—ouch—watch the stitches," Andarios said, hugging her twice as hard.

"Are you alright? What happened?"

Andarios' brows shot up. "Uh, I was recently attacked by a bear?"

"No, I meant—" What had she meant to say? That she'd feared his pillow would suffocate him? She tried again, soothed by his embrace. "Are you out for good?"

"I still have some healing to do. Rook put me on leave for a moon, and told me to stay in bed, but otherwise—" he shrugged with a yawn, "—just some salve and sleep should do it."

Kezerah stepped back, reluctantly. "Are you tired now? Should you sleep?"

"Hungry, more like."

She rushed past him. "I'll get you breakfast."

"You don't have to—"

But she'd already begun to back onto the stairs. "Need I remind you of the last time you refused to have breakfast with me?"

Andarios scoffed and raised his hands. "Fair shot. You can just wait on me hand and foot from now on, then."

The two stowed away in Andarios' room; Andarios on his bed and Kezerah situated atop a pile of pillows on the floor beside him. They ate off of overstuffed plates and spoke about anything and everything unimportant, until a thump rattled Andarios' door. The two waited, the door remained unassuming, regal in its confidence to be nothing more than a door.

"Was that...knocking?" Kezerah asked, playing the sound back.

"I think it requires more than one knock to be considered knocking."

"Not everyone practices percussion on people's doors, Dar."

A thwack once more announced their answer, somehow shorter than the first. They looked at one another again. "You get it." Andarios sprawled across his bed. "I'm injured." Prepared for that exact phrase to be uttered for moons to come, she wiped crumbs from her mouth and resigned herself to see who it was.

"It can't be Kai." She reached the knob. "He's—" she addressed Rorrik's shoulder and side profile, his posture somehow both disinterested and impatient, "training with Eriko."

Rorrik gave a sharp step back at the sound of her voice. "Oh, you."

Kezerah couldn't help but smile at the disinterest in his eyes as he gazed past her. With this fresh outlook on her social status, she widened the door's opening.

"Oh, Rorrik," Kezerah said, casting her voice back into the room. "Just who we were expecting." Andarios rustled behind her, adjusting to sit up.

Rorrik retreated farther from the threshold as if spikes protruded from it. "I stopped by the infirmary and noticed Andarios wasn't there. I didn't know if he'd eaten." A small knapsack disappeared behind him. "Looks like he did."

"There's more," Andarios said from his bed with a shrug, "if you want to join us."

Kezerah tamed her features to hide a frown she hadn't seen coming. Rorrik sidestepped with a lack of grace.

"Tch. With daily rankings about to start? I don't think so. A bear won't stop me from keeping up on my training." Kezerah released her scowl.

"Leave it, Kez."

Before she could decide whether she intended to leave it, Rorrik made it to the stairs. "Anyway, have fun with..." Whatever he mumbled in cowardice couldn't be heard as he disappeared down the archway.

Andarios curved a brow as Kezerah shut the door and turned to him. "Why do I feel like I'm suddenly in trouble?"

She dropped her arms, which had been crossed. "What, no, of course not."

"Then why do you look..." Andarios waved a hand over her posture and she worked to loosen it. He chuckled. "Like I'm in trouble."

Kezerah sighed, retaking her position on the pillows in front of him. "You're not in trouble. I just...do you..." She bit her lip, it seemed absurd. "Are you interested in him?" In the time it took to get the words out she tried to understand why she asked them. Then, she thought back to the egg tarts. Her mother had mentioned Andarios choosing to spend the day with Rorrik. After he'd denied time with her. Is this how it would be? Time bartered—*importance* bartered—between her and a fussy prince? He would laugh. Kezerah wanted him to.

Andarios did not laugh. Andarios did not smile. Andarios stared intently at a wall.

"Dar?"

Kezerah observed her friend as he rolled his shoulders and winced to hold a bandage. She couldn't believe how many rapid blinks she'd gotten in before he answered.

"I don't know, probably not."

The blinks increased. "Probably?" She sat close to him yet worlds seemed to separate their thoughts. She grasped out with words, fearing she'd been too closed off in her petty covetousness. "Because if so, that's great—I mean he's kind of a clump of bitter grapes—but if you want to—"

"I don't want to do anything with him," Andarios said in a rush. "I just...don't hate being around him as much as before."

Kezerah tried to work through this. "Well, I mean... Do you think he's attractive?"

Andarios turned crimson. "What does that have to do with anything? Stop blinking like that."

"I can't help it." Kezerah shifted so she sat on her knees and tried not to blink. "I just happen to think it has a lot to do with things."

He chewed on his inner cheek. "Well, I don't know if I do."

"That's okay." She moved to the bed. "But, maybe you want to find out?"

Andarios scooched passed her, and laid down. "Maybe, but...not with him. I don't know." He put an arm across his eyes. "He's not exactly a safe or viable option is he?"

Kezerah didn't answer, it veered too close to a line of thought she herself actively avoided.

"On account of being bitter grapes," he tacked on in her silence. They both gave the shaken laughter of an awkward conversation defeated by humor. Then, Andarios yawned. Kezerah felt a pang to stay, but willed her feet to stand.

"I'll let you get some rest."

He nodded. Kezerah had the urge to remove the arm still

covering his face, for their eyes to meet and for her to see that her best friend was still there. His breaths softened, then grew to small snores. *'Of course he is,'* she chastised herself. Both their attentions had been divided lately. Though *her* attention hadn't led to a bear attack almost separating them permanently.

She shook her body out and careened a heel to pivot towards the door. It had been a good morning. She'd just continue it with a bit of her own divided attention. The thought made her smile.

Heart lighter and opportunities for the day endless, she hurried to her room to fix her hair in the mirror. A grouchy Fennel waited outside for her when she finally emerged.

"You're supposed to have a guard with you."

"And here you are," Kezerah greeted. "Let's go."

She pranced down to the west training yards, feather light steps to match her mood. She'd watch a few training bouts, she decided. And, if it so happened that she caught someone to chat with between skirmishes, all the better. Any of her friends would do, just whomever happened to be there, she told herself.

"Oh, Kezerah, where have you been! Dyllian ate with us all through breakfast and wouldn't stop talking about the irrigation system," Willow complained as Kezerah and Ambrose sat across from her and Whistle for midday meal. "I know exactly how each family in Ralven feels about the delay it'll have on their crops going in."

Kezerah grabbed a roll dented with oats, sickles of apples, and then drizzled caramel and honey onto her plate. "Ugh, I'm sorry. He keeps trying to talk to me about it too."

Ambrose reached for a roll and their shoulders brushed. She wondered if it had been deliberate. It felt deliberate. If she elbowed him in an attempt to get another roll, would he know she'd done it on purpose?

"Kezi?" Whistle echoed Willow's earlier question.

"Oh, we were in the practice yards." Kezerah awkwardly grabbed butter while dodging the rolls.

"Ooh, did you see Eriko?" asked Willow. "I think he might be the best fighter in all of Thrice!"

"It wasn't until Prince Rorrik dueled him that people noticed," Whistle said, most likely to be contrary to her sister.

"All of Thrice?" Ambrose protested. "Lady Willow, I believe that's how false rumors are started."

"Or information is spread," Ikaika said, making an appearance to Kezerah's right.

Ikaika smelled freshly bathed and Kezerah wished she didn't smell like the barracks. She kept her arms at her sides, to better hide whatever odor she may be attacking him with.

"Sorry I'm late," Ikaika added to her. "I was in the northern yards, and lost track of time. Had I known you were in the western yards, I would have made an exception." Ikaika paused Ambrose's way. "Though the view is less appealing."

Ambrose only smiled at Ikaika, and Kezerah recognized the taunt and tried to balance it.

"It was on a whim," she said. "Dar kept talking about sparring practice."

Ikaika looked unconvinced, but relented. "Eriko's great, isn't he?" he asked Kezerah, and Kezerah alone. "I think the attention has gone a bit to his head. I've never seen him practice this much."

"Well, whatever it is," Kezerah said, "it seems to be working. He was unstoppable today."

This wiped the grin from Ambrose's expression. Now both looked mildly surly. *'Balance restored.'* She couldn't help but think this was becoming easier. Now friends to both of them, they'd grow on one another like wisteria vines in the sun.

Ikaika picked at his roll. "Well, maybe tomorrow you could visit the northern yards. I'd give you a sparring lesson. If you wanted."

Inflated by the ease of her success, Kezerah shrugged. "Perhaps I will."

Ikaika blinked in surprise, his shoulders straightened. "Excellent, I know just what techniques we'll start with."

Ambrose dipped his apple slice into her caramel. "Interesting that you think Ikaika capable of teaching such techniques. I hardly see him use any weapons."

'Perhaps weeds, in need of pruning, was the better metaphor,' Kezerah thought, as Ikaika watched the apple travel from Kezerah's

plate to Ambrose's mouth. "Better to wield one blade sparingly, than wield two and be just as useless," he said, gesturing down to the twin swords at Ambrose's sides. "I can't decide, is one your Bond, or are you waiting for an attack mid-luncheon?"

"On the topic of useless," Ambrose spoke as if conversing about the weather, "what exactly are you training for Ikaika? Do you intend on joining your mother's army? Or was the plan to simply continue hiding in the Solstice Court?"

"Ambrose," Kezerah warned. "Not here."

Ikaika glared, but Kezerah felt a chill as it slid towards her. "Not anywhere, I'm sure. Since it's a completely taboo subject."

He said it as if keeping score. She shrank back, wondering how many tallies he'd struck against her without her knowing. "That's not what I meant." It came out too quiet.

Ikaika, thankfully, returned his ire to Ambrose. "You must realize by asking if I intend to hide here, you're implying that the Solstice Court too is in hiding. Correct?" His eyes glittered with something unkind. "But of course you do. You stated it yourself last night, 'Elastor lives in a dream, and Elowren foolishly believes himself with friends.'"

Kezerah snapped her attention back to Ambrose. She searched for his shock, his affrontement at the lie. But Ikaika didn't lie, and Ambrose didn't look offended.

Ikaika slanted a mocking smile onto his face. "A lovely sentiment from their supposed allies."

"An ineloquent summary that only an Aloran is capable of, which skips the crux of the issue." Ambrose's tone turned from sour to true cold. "Whatever allows you to sleep at night, while Alora invades homes, and devastates families—"

"Families, *ha*. What a perfect descriptor, considering you now have children joining your war."

'Children?' Kezerah tried to follow, question upon question rose and fell from her lips.

"*My* war?" Ambrose's volume boomed, too loud. Heads swiveled towards the commotion. The twins shuffled down the table, muttering about getting more honey. "This is not my war," Ambrose continued, lower. "*I* am not the one setting *your* world on fire."

"No," Ikaika said, "you just help your father do it."

"Stop—" Kezerah demanded.

"If your mother is so righteous in her justice, then why does she never attack him, Ikaika?" Ambrose cocked his head to the side. "Why is it always the outskirts and never the capital?"

"Because she wants to draw your disgusting pig of a father out of hiding!" Ikaika hissed. "Because *you* are in the capital—

"I don't think—"

"No, Kez, he doesn't get to spew his twisted dogma and get away with it."

The truth crashed down around Kezerah. There was nothing she could say, no input she could have to cause a ceasefire. *Useless, powerless. No control.* Even if she'd heard them both out and formulated an opinion, they didn't want to hear it. No one wanted to hear her. They just wanted their sides heard.

Ambrose hadn't even noticed her try. "I was in Ravysh too, and she left nothing but burned bodies and—"

Her chest lifted and sank. She deepened her frown to stop her mouth from trembling, then forced it into a line. She couldn't take sides, but one action remained available to her.

Kezerah stood, the force of her anger crashing the seat back. "I think I've made myself clear. If I'm in a room where I'm unable to speak, I will choose a new room to be in."

Ikaika lowered his head. She didn't possess the resolve to look at Ambrose.

Silence stretched over two breaths. Kezerah stalked past her overturned chair, and retreated from the Autumn Hall. Her anger felt all consuming. How could they do that to her? Make her sit and listen to atrocities she wasn't allowed to weigh in on. Children, families, innocent people. People who had just as little control over the situation as her, torn by violence. She stopped and pressed hands to her face to try and block out the thoughts.

Footsteps padded behind her, and she spun on a heel. "Don't you dare follow—Dyllian," she seethed. "If you mention that stupid meeting I missed, I'll throw you into the Lull myself!"

Dyllian, mouth agape, looked very much as if he tried to reroute the trajectory of his conversation. "I'd never dream of it, Princess. I simply happened to be leaving as you did."

Kezerah huffed and started walking again.

"Quite the ruckus though," he continued. She waited to see if he'd give her the excuse to release her building temper upon him. "I remember when this place used to be peaceful. But, I suppose that would have been two princes ago."

She weathered his petty banter and forced her legs forward. She could be proud of that at least: both in upholding her duty as heir by not killing Dyllian and removing herself from the fray. Victory had never felt so much like defeat.

IKAIKA FOUGHT the urge to follow Kezerah. He knew better than to approach when her mood stormed like this. Moreover, the knowledge that he'd sunk to Ambrose's level sucked the anger right out of him. The rest of the hall tried to fill the awkward silence with chatter. Nobody talked about the outburst; everyone thought about it.

"Excellent," Ambrose muttered under his breath, his eyes accusatory and pointed at Ikaika.

Ikaika opened his mouth to retort. Ambrose had definitely started this. He clamped his mouth shut. He wouldn't continue to feed his brother's brutish behavior.

Ambrose pushed himself away from the table.

Ikaika watched Ambrose stalk out without another word or look in his direction. Rorrik, further down the table, left his plate and trotted after his elder brother like a scrawny wolf cub.

'Good,' Ikaika thought. Yet, he'd also lost his appetite. He tossed his napkin aside. Kezerah's rage wouldn't last forever and he'd make amends while his brother cast his chances away in the training yards.

In his rooms, he replenished his apologies. The vesper murmur of herbal mist from above dulled the intrusive push of thoughts. He in-took the calming aromas, lavender breaths becoming deeper until his lungs got their fill. He gave a long, final exhale and the voices dampened to whispers; Kezerah's thoughts pervading long past the others. She often didn't think in solid words but a swirl of images with emotions attached: a medley of disappointment and confusion next door that he worked to dispel with each drag of air.

The light in their courtyard deepened to vibrant magentas as the pink canopy of petals teased sunset. Ikaika decided he'd waited long enough. He lept from terrace to terrace, then knocked on the glass of her door.

His migraine dissipated; only silence followed. He shifted foot to foot until finally she unlocked the bolt, retreating back to bed afterward. Her body leaned against the headboard while she hugged herself close.

He sat across from her and mirrored her stance: knees locked to chest, hugged by arms. His chin dipped to his knees to meet her eyes. "Kez, I'm sorry. I let my temper get the best of me—let *him* get the best of me, and it got out of hand."

Kezerah's bottom lip slightly pouted. A puffiness circled her eyes; she had been crying. His shoulders sank lower. The idea that he'd played a part in her tears made him want to escape under blankets and never return. Instead, he scooted closer, forcing his head up. Their knees pressed together.

"I know it's hard to hold your opinions in. I know you're trying to be fair. I'm truly sorry for putting you in that situation," he said again, relieved to see her nod in acceptance.

"It's not just my opinion," Kezerah said quietly. "It's knowing I can't do anything about it. Not only may I not say anything, I can't *do* anything. And those people—" She stopped herself from saying more, from acknowledging which people she felt sympathy towards.

Ikaika wanted to scream.

If she knew what those people—Ambrose's father, Xenkesh, had done—she would feel differently. Sometimes he wished he didn't know.

Illija held back when speaking of her treatment in Xenkesh. However, over the years, the truth had presented itself quite clearly: in servants, soldiers, Eriko, and Illija's closest friend Castiel. Through whispered words and fragmented thoughts, Ikaika understood the picture. His mother had never loved Amarus. Their handfasting had been political and, in Illija's own words, illegitimate. One could not simply pair their soul to another. It required intent from both parties and Illija had loved Ozule, the younger prince of Xenkesh—Ikaika's father.

Amarus had known, and hadn't cared. He'd pushed for the handfasting regardless. She hadn't loved him when she conceived Ambrose, nor Rorrik, and she had not loved him when she attempted to flee with Ozule and conceived Ikaika. When Illija finally did escape with Ozule's help, only one of them had survived. Or two, if Ikaika counted himself. He had been born a mere moon later.

Alora fought to right an injustice, while Xenkesh pleaded innocence and martyrdom. Amarus might have fooled Elowren from an ocean away, but those in power could not be ignorant of what his mother had endured. Arrogant, self-assured Ambrose seemed particularly unfamiliar with ignorance. '*Whatever small poisons he put into Kezerah's head are working,*' Ikaika thought as she sympathized with the people of Xenkesh.

He placed a hand to rest on her knee. "Listen. I won't engage with him anymore, I'll—"

"No," Kezerah blurted, eyes widening. "We can't fix this if you don't speak to each other! Nothing will get solved, it'll just get worse."

"I can't fix things with him," Ikaika said. "It's not even just Ambrose that needs to be fixed. I—" He struggled on how to convince her the efforts she made were futile, without pressuring her to his side. "When the war is over, and Amarus is dead, Ambrose, Rorrik and I, we won't need to talk. My mother has this vision of how it will be but—" Ikaika shrugged his shoulders. This at least was a simple truth. "It's too late. Amarus won in that regard; her elder sons will never love her. Ambrose will rule Xenkesh, my mother in Alora, and Rorrik and I will be their heirs. Apart from trade relations, which can be done through Elastor, we won't need to talk."

Kezerah frowned, and Ikaika wondered where he'd lost her in the scenario. He played it back until she responded with slow deliberation.

"You know Alora will win? You think... Ambrose won't avenge his father?"

Ikaika tried to understand her tone, either a challenge or curiosity. "I believe, based on numbers alone, Ambrose doesn't stand a chance if he tries—and he knows it." Ikaika worded his next sentence as best he could. "Xenkesh can't last more than a few more years, by sheer...lack of soldiers alone. I didn't speak in hyperbole when I said there's talk of sending children."

Kezerah seemed to internalize this, and Ikaika waited.

When she continued not to speak, he pushed on. "But when the war is over, things will change, or can change," he said, testing the boundaries of the conversation. "Perhaps the treaty might even be rewritten. You might not have to be so... neutral?"

He rested his hand on hers, and hated that it felt forbidden.

She looked at him, soaking in the deeper meaning of his words. Her freckles saturated with the deepening color of her cheeks. He said nothing else, letting his suggestion linger, instead of overstating it, or making a fool of himself.

"Ikaika—I..."

He watched her: the small dilation of her eyes, the unsteadiness of her breath, and the parting of lips. Ikaika wondered what her reaction would be if he leaned in. If he closed the distance between their soft breaths. He ruminated on the thought; Kezerah liked daring, she liked danger. Perhaps she'd kiss him back, arch forward, opposed to him reaching. Her thoughts crept at the edges of his mind, opaque like fog. If he opened up to her, unfurled just beyond the fog...What if she recoiled, drew back. She'd fled to her room in an effort to not be pressured and here he loomed, ever closer. He wasn't Ambrose, and wouldn't try to be.

His next breath came and went, he drew back and rushed on, alleviating the pressure from her swirling thoughts. "A concept to be further explored, much later." He nudged her knee with his own. "No need for a mind-whirlpool," he teased as he quirked his mouth to the side, in the smile he knew she favored.

She smiled sheepishly—in apology, regret, relief? He couldn't know—and the tension ebbed away like an inevitable tide.

"I was going to visit Dar, see if he wanted to stretch his legs a bit," he said. "Did you want to come?"

She bit her lip. Ikaika tried to focus. She continued for a fraction of a breath longer. "That's alright, you go. Nurse will have a fit if she sees my room." She gestured around her, and Ikaika noted that a dresser blocked half the door. Perhaps a half truth, mixed with an excuse.

"Alright, I'll see you tomorrow then." He tried to make sure it didn't sound like a question.

"Of course!" Her grin made him grin, easing his anxiety some. "See you for Nighttide Eve."

"Yeah, see you then." *'Not a problem,'* Ikaika told himself. While loud proclamations didn't suit him, he possessed a quality he knew his brother didn't. He could be patient.

The gloam of dusk matched Ambrose's mood: muted, dim, and cold. Wooden swords batted against each other, but the fights in the western yards held no interest. He just stood, arms crossed, in the hopes he appeared too brooding to approach. He tried to muster the umph to speak to Kezerah, but his boots remained rooted in the mud.

Tomorrow would be a day of preparation for Nighttide. Elastor's day of silence, and a day of communication in a language he was mediocre in at best. A sprig of vermillion twirled down in front of him. He picked up the samara seedlet, and looked up at the barrage of red maple leaves it fell from.

Was he meant to stay through the season? He cursed his father for poor instructions. Then revoked it. He knew the answer. No, his kingdom could not afford for him to remain here. They couldn't afford his failure either.

A guttural grunt caught his attention and he watched, dull-eyed, as Eriko once again flung someone to the ground. He couldn't do this anymore. He pivoted to leave and stopped as Azalea stepped into the ring.

His Sword Master was on night duty, her schedule flipped with Eriko's in order to guard Ambrose and Rorrik's rooms. She'd apparently heard enough to stir her curiosity however, and strode into the yard right before her shift began. A silver-white bun was tied in a knot atop her head, highlighting the hair she kept shorn close to her scalp underneath: an Aloran fashion that only Azalea could get away with in Xenkesh, unscathed.

Ambrose eyed the dirt as she walked past him. Her pale, calloused knuckles cracked as she webbed them together, before grabbing a dull practice blade. The wind-whipped sound of her sword so familiar that Ambrose straightened expectantly: instincts at the ready.

She gestured towards Eriko without a word.

The crowd doubled within the first two blows.

Eriko lunged forward before sweeping for her right shoulder. Azalea ducked low, touching the ground as she whipped her calf to connect with his own. Eriko caught his fall, a knee pressed into the earth. Finished with her spin, Azalea sprung up and struck. He blocked from his downed position then stood.

Ambrose gripped the fencing, his shame replaced with anticipation. He couldn't decide if he wanted Eriko to fall fast for the glory of Xenkesh, or for the fight to be dragged out, for Ambrose's own dignity.

Grim-faced, Eriko reassessed his opponent's skill. Using his size as an advantage, he pushed her back, and worked to get behind her.

Azalea would have none of it. She cascaded her sword in a down swing. The hit loosened his grasp before she used the fence to ricochet forward. She crashed down upon him in a front kick and their blades clashed. Eriko lost his offensive hold, solely focused on keeping his hilt in hand.

Ambrose looked past the match, and spotted Ikaika with the Lord of Luka across the yard. Ikaika's posture matched his own: hands fastened to the rail and jaw set in determination. Ambrose pushed away from the fence. He needn't look so eager. Arms crossed, he smiled broadly instead.

Then, Azalea slid between Eriko's wide spread legs and shot up behind him like a viper. A sudden swing aimed for his neck and the winning blow.

Ambrose glanced at his youngest brother again, wanting to see his reaction. Ikaika smirked, his cocky grin snide as he nudged his friend and said something.

Eriko's sword moved faster than Ambrose would have expected. Instead of turning his whole body to block, he arched his blade over his shoulder, blocking Azalea at the last moment in what Ambrose had to admit was an impressive maneuver.

He twisted to face her again.

They circled.

Azalea's smile suggested violence.

Ambrose remembered the day that smile had been fixed on him, when he'd won not one, but both of his swords. He clutched his left blade at the memory, knowing she must have gone easy on him.

He noticed Ikaika watching just as closely, eyes calculating Azalea's moves. *'Let him try,'* Ambrose thought. Azalea didn't have moves, not in the traditional sense. Her battle strategy came from being unpredictable, completely in the moment. She was honed to deflect and fend off Mind Melders. Eriko, a non-Melder, didn't stand a chance.

Azalea pounced. Mid-strike, Eriko tightened his defense again. To prevent her sliding below him once more, his stance remained less firm. She gained traction, pressing her sword into his as he held her off. A head taller, Eriko used his upper body as leverage. Azalea bent back; her body angled like a stem about to snap.

Moments before the fall, she snaked a leg around Eriko's still feeble stance.

Eriko tumbled forward and Azalea twisted her body to fall to the side. In control of her fall, she rolled and sprang up. Then re-gripped her hilt in her left hand, her dominant hand. Eriko defended from the ground, but Azalea forced his sword down and away. Arcing her own to firmly rest against the side of his throat that pulsed with reddened veins.

The air thinned as everyone gasped. The yard went quiet. Ambrose found his hands bone white on the fencing again, unable to loosen his hold until the fight was finalized.

Eriko yielded.

Ambrose released his breath and his grasp.

The two masters stared at one another, neither breaking their form. Then, Azalea cut through the tension.

Her sword left his neck. *"Fesa Aveltra,"* she said in Aloran, hand outstretched.

Eriko scoffed and let her lift him. "Safe travels to you as well, Xenkeshi."

Azalea stepped away, her back not to him until she reached the fence posts. Fighters got back in line, demanding a turn, but Azalea denied them with a shake of her head. Her smile became more genuine as she hopped the fence. She stalked toward Ambrose, and her voice held the harsh, low tenor she used in lessons.

"Did you watch how I did that Your Hot-headedness?"

Ambrose scuffed a boot, arms still crossed as he admired the mud. "Yes, Azalea. Agile as always."

A sword tapped and lifted his chin. "I wasn't talking about the fight, Ambrose." While her glare was glacier blue, he heard the levity in her tone. "I was referring to once I'd finished."

Ambrose nodded, the sword bobbing at his throat. He knew he was being coached in grace, and when Azalea spoke, Ambrose listened.

"Good," she said, curt. "Now get back to practice. Don't make me fight another Aloran this trip." The sword lowered, and Azalea winked. "And, happy birthday."

Ambrose's returned smile faded as Azalea walked away. It should have been a perfect birthday present: Xenkesh declared the victor to a crowd consisting of his Aloran enemies and fair-weather allies. The sorrow still clung to him. It made his ribcage heavy and feasted on his heart. Azalea thought he'd failed in diplomacy. She overestimated him. He didn't want a win for his kingdom alone. He wanted something—some*one*—for himself. A selfish and weak desire his kingdom didn't have time for.

It was an act of survival that kept him in these training yards, where he'd been so elated and surprised to find Kezerah midday. He'd wanted to run after her tonight, to apologize, to grovel, as he was sure his brother did now. *Apologize* for defending his people. No, this place, this girl would not be his ruin. If she could hear and know what was said in that dining hall and do nothing, then she was nothing to him. Distance would help keep it that way.

The Eve

THE QUIET OF COURT WOKE IKAIKA EARLY ON NIGHTTIDE Eve. He got dressed in purple satin—as per tradition—nodded to the few nobles in the Autumn Quarters, and enjoyed a muffin while he walked the halls, eavesdropping on bits of thoughts as he went. He so often tried to reign in his mind that he felt entitled to the freedom just this one time of year. Many slept; their dreams just a wide array of people, places, and emotions. The sensation was akin to being back home, watching the lunar rainbows dance with colors across the Aloran sky. He walked through the spiral halls of the Spring Quarter, with no true direction but appreciating the endless stretch of dreams.

Kezerah's dreams tossed and turned. Flashes of boats docked and the black-robed monks of Bethync glided from the Solstice Bay towards the Solstice gates. This year, Kezerah had been meant to come into her magick to conduct the Elastian ritual herself. Tonight's ceremony would begin as the first stars alighted in the sky. Her fretful dreams erupted into nightmares as she tried to lift an enormous amethyst obelisk with her bare hands. A dizzying, falling sensation lurched through Ikaika as Kezerah fell through the sky and he had no choice but to press on, leaving the Spring Quarters behind.

Guilt loomed behind him as he walked. He wished his day of peace didn't have to be a culmination of everything Kezerah avoided.

For Elastians, today recognized Kezerah's first incarnation, Ellas' foundation of Elastor and his legacy of power. A man born without sound, the silence not only honored his memory, but allowed space for souls from the Summerlands. Souls who wished to join together at the thinned veil between their worlds. Ikaika found such belief's fascinating and liked learning the history, but avoided a heavy participation in either Elastor's culture or non-verbal language of Sway. It felt disloyal to celebrate Elastian holidays with an inability to celebrate his own. Nomadic stories spoken about the fire, in the old Aloran language, couldn't be so easily found at the Solstice Court. He was a guest, here to observe, but this was not his home.

Elowren's thoughts appeared as the king rounded the corner of the Winter Quarters. Ikaika smiled and bowed low to him as they passed. The king made quick comparisons between Ikaika and his mother. Ikaika's heart squeezed at the sight of his mother's face. King Elowren walked into the War Room (or Strategy Chamber as Elowren preferred them). He eyed the Thrice Kingdom's map with confusion but then his thoughts faded away, and Ikaika let them.

At last, he drifted outside: his finish line. The sounds of early morning greeted him. He plopped down at his favorite tree and opened his book to the final few chapters.

NIMAH WRUNG her hands as she walked up the stairs to the Queen's chambers. She'd splashed cold water on her face not once, but twice in preparation to ask for the night off, and still a weariness clung to the circles under her eyes. Moons ago, she'd gotten permission from Hanan to spend Nighttide with her youngest son, Asher. However, due to the uptick in the princess' protection, she now needed special permission from either the King or Queen. If only King Elowren hadn't been in a meeting, *'All I have to do is assure her the princess is behaving.'*

'Yes,' she thought, mentally mustering the determination she needed. *'Everything is fine. There are plenty of guards and servants to attend her.'* She reached the door and prepared to knock when the shock of voices could be heard through the large wooden door: the sound gave her pause.

"You came to intimidate me? Inform him he needs to have patience," Queen Elize's voice rang with authority. "He lives near an ocean. Tell him to boil the water and make do."

A deep voice responded, too low to be heard.

Nimah pressed her ear against the door. What was so important that the Queen would break her silence on such a sacred day?

"I'll be staying in town in case you change your reply," the voice continued.

"Be discreet. I won't clean up your next mess."

"I don't take orders from you, or any monarch," rasped the voice. "I did the job I was paid for."

"You were paid by those whom I pay. If you want to continue to be paid, you'll check in with me or His Majesty. Are we clear?" Nimah caught and held her breath during a static moment of silence. "Now go, before I send your hand in message instead of you."

Nimah panicked and scurried from the door, before realizing she had nowhere to hide. She rushed back and knocked on the door right as it opened. A thin man with shrewd eyes stared down at her. His shaggy hair looked unkempt; several rings decorated his scarred knuckles as he held the door open for Nimah to enter. She did not. She ushered a frantic flurry of Sway to explain to him, but he stopped her.

"Don't know what you're saying and don't care." His breath oozed. Nimah stepped back, he held his position.

"I—" It felt unusual to speak after withholding her voice so long. She looked past the man to her queen, her dark purple gown large and opulent. Elize gave Nimah an icy stare, waiting for her to regain her composure. Nimah gulped and tried again, but nothing came out.

Elize glared at the terrifying man in the doorway. "Don't you need to deliver that message to my dearest King? I'm sure he'll want the news."

The man moved past Nimah without uttering a word, not breaking eye contact with her until he was through the door and down the hall.

Catching her breath, Nimah bowed but remained in the doorway.

Elize already seemed impatient. "Why are you at my chambers without a summons?"

Nimah spoke low as to not completely dishonor the dead. "I only came to say that Kezerah sleeps, and—and that the day has gone well... and—"

"And?"

Nimah's nerves withered. "And, truly, the princess has been much better behaved of late." Her hands tightened on her apron, she needed to ask. "So, I was going to beg your permission, if I may, to… to—" She gulped. "It's just Asher—my son—he's in the kitchens, which has already prepped—"

"You'd like the night off."

Nimah closed her eyes with a nod. "Yes, my Queen."

Elize assessed her head to toe with a rhythmic tap of her nails. "How long were you at my door?"

The tapping continued in sets of three. "Only to knock, my Queen."

One, two, three, one, two, three, one— "The man you saw, he's a fisherman and brought salmon for tonight's feast." Nimah nodded frantically, fear gripped her lungs too tight to let her speak. "You did not see him, you will not speak of him, you will not recognize him if you see him again."

"Of course, yes, of course," Nimah choked out when Elize waited for her to agree.

"This request is an act of negligence. You may have the night off with your son, but only with the understanding that you have assured me my daughter is in no danger. If Kezerah comes to harm, it's you that will pay the price."

Nimah hesitated. Never in all her years had she trusted a ward more to misbehave.

"Are you wavering because Kezerah is *not* safe without supervision?"

"No, no," Nimah said. "I believe Kezerah has become more cautious of late. I think one too many surprises has calmed her appetite for adventure, for a time."

Queen Elize smiled. "Yes, let's hope that's the case, for both Kezerah's sake, and yours. Enjoy your night with Asher."

The way Queen Elize said Nimah's son's name rose goosebumps along her flesh.

"Yes, my Queen. I understand—very well, my Queen." And Nimah did understand. The moment she was excused she raced back to her rooms to check on her son and place a kiss on his cheek.

THE AUTUMN HALL'S stained glass, in sunset hues, cast down a kaleidoscope of shadows onto the purple satin courtiers below. Kezerah sashayed in, dressed in a dark purple tunic with elongated slits up the sides and matching pants: traditional, yet comfortable. It felt like liquid on the skin, easily slept in and challenging to wrinkle. Eyes alighted on her and she quickly spotted Ikaika sitting next to Andarios.

'*Ikaika.*' It was as if she had called out his name, he turned and smiled at her as she joined them. Sunflowers, antlers, animal skulls, and smoky quartz adorned the table along with pitchers of cider, roasted hen, and Xenkeshi caffeinated beans dipped in honey to keep you awake if you so pleased.

'*Did you nap today?*' Andarios asked, addressing both Ikaika and Kezerah. Ikaika cocked his head to the side at the Sway, not following the quick gestures. Kezerah closed her palms and rested her head on the side, pretending to sleep. While it was not a true Sway gesture, it got the point across a bit easier.

Ikaika shook his head in answer, understanding.

She popped a honey-dipped bean in her mouth to further illustrate she didn't plan on sleeping a wink more this evening. The crunch was bitter and acidic, the honey lending a sweet after taste.

The three of them continued their jumbled conversation of Sway and outlandish hand movements, later attempting a game of charades, which grew more absurd the more they played.

During Andarios' turn, Kezerah's attention trailed and she spotted Ambrose sauntering in. His plum-black satins made his movements all the more fluid. The purples also set the green off in his eyes. She forced her attention back on the game. Andarios pretended to be a horse. She muffled a laugh, but then heard Ambrose's deep, rich laugh stifled as well. Who had made him laugh?

He stood in his easy way, speaking with Whistle. It appeared slow going, as he answered with limited Sway vocabulary. Every other word punctuated by a nervous flourish of his hand. Kezerah's smile creeped along the corners of her mouth; his uncharacteristic uncertainty was endearing. Their eyes met, and Kezerah dragged her gaze away to meet Ikaika's knowing stare. She began the Sway for an apology but halted partway. She didn't know if she stopped herself because he wouldn't understand the gesture, or because perhaps she wasn't sorry.

Ikaika repeated the napping gesture she'd given him earlier. The gesture was clear, his expression was not. She got up to follow him, but gave a cursory glance to the head of the table. Conversation preoccupied her father, but her mother paused her Sway with Lady Sorrel to give her a warning look with a pointed glance at the setting sun.

Kezerah resigned herself with a huff of defeat; tonight's fun ended before the sun had even fully melted behind the high walls. She pushed off from her seat to prepare for her ceremony.

QUARTZ AND ONYX jewelry adorned her wrists and throat while servants switched out differing diadems. She liked the high collared black lace that decorated her skin with patterns. The long sleeves of her dress covered all but her fingertips, inlaid with rings. The black shift underneath was her only top coverage before the dress plunged into a smokey gray and black gossamer that billowed around her as she walked. Impatient hands pawed at her as she fidgeted in place.

'*Calm your breathing, Princess, or it won't fit right,*' Swayed a servant who tightened a thread at her hip. Several rows of bracelets, brandished atop the fabric and up her forearms, slid down as Kezerah paused mid-smoothing of her unrumpled dress.

'*They came to watch me fail, not to see if my dress fits,*' Kezerah quipped with ringed fingers. The servant didn't look up to see her answer. Left to a room silent in all but her thoughts she tried to calm her own nerves.

'*Why are you nervous?*' She challenged herself. '*You've failed this ceremony since you were ten.*' She'd participated since she could walk, but that had been the year she'd learned of Basha—a Soul Heir known for his tenacity in all things. He had developed Sway during the Eve Ceremony at her same age and been hailed a prodigy. In stark contrast, ten was the year Kezerah found out she most certainly wasn't one.

But she'd woken up from her nap today with a disorienting

conviction. She was tired of failing. She wanted to try. The admittance stole something she didn't know she possessed in such matters: pride. Kezerah's chest heaved, stopped short by a cinching at her back. Arms turned her gently towards her door, then her steps followed the slow procession. The door opened to her father, the black of his robes exaggerating the silver of his braids and the jewel-toned brown of his skin. He tilted his head at her expression and Kezerah gulped and raised her head higher. Elowren smiled and she knew he understood her. She would move the obelisk herself tonight.

It was rare to see monks leave the island unless they had finished up their time on Bethync, or their time on earth entirely. The Isle of Bethync served as passage between Thrice and the Summerlands. There, seconds dragged to minutes, minutes to hours, hours to days, and days to years, offering them extended lives of study and worship. Time was borrowed, however, not given, and what the monks took, they gave back upon leaving its shores. It showed in their many withered faces as they watched Kezerah descend the stairs and step out of the Spring Quarters.

Quills at the ready, and fathomless eyes upon her, the monks recorded history as she walked: The first Soul Heir to embody the Nighttide ritual without the ability to Hold Sway past her nineteenth birthday. Kezerah gave a lofty lift of her chin. Let them write down that she didn't care.

Those who did Hold Sway raised heavy pillars of amethyst quartz, up high in the air, before—in time with the stomp of feet from a gathering crowd—the pillars crashed to the ground, hard enough to shake the earth. The ground rippled with aftershocks and Kezerah knew if she were to be perched atop the western wall, she'd see the people of Heartsglove doing the same.

Then, all the nobility in attendance began a new Sway. Hands plucked at invisible strings in a tightened fist; a soul leaving the body, before one hand slammed back down onto the closed palm: The Sway for the Soul Heir. The Sway for Kezerah no matter what life cycle she was in or what form she took. It was her cue to enter the ritual in front of the Solstice Gates.

'*Soul Heir, Soul Heir, Soul Heir.*' The movements continued, and

Kezerah's shoulders stiffened. She knew her regal posture looked unnatural, thrust upon her instead of held up by her. The walk slowed, her parents on either side, until she reached the obelisk of quartz. The stone rose once more, and the sun's last grasp on the day dipped behind the hills. Kezerah kneeled on the ground. She reached out. The motion felt awkward, like being too aware of your steps and stumbling. She clenched her teeth.

'*Focus*' she commanded herself.

She was meant to stop the amethyst from rising again. She tried to picture herself powerful, commanding not just herself but the world around her. Her eyes surveyed her audience. The reverence people held for her never matched what she saw in their eyes once meeting her. They continued the steady Sway of her name. '*My title,*' she thought, '*I don't even have a name in my own language.*' Her soul inspired hymns yet she felt unknowable, fathomless by design. She saw the guards that Held Sway, Andarios among them, begin to lift the stone again. She slammed fists into the earth. The stomping ceased. The amethyst slab rose against her bidding. A horrific silence blasted through the clearing. A blur moved out of formation as Andarios gestured for the obelisk to drop, others followed in suit. It thundered to a halt and the amethyst became a jutting pillar of the Solstice Gate once more. Her farce ended, the bell tolled.

Nighttide

THE SUN SUNK BELOW THE HORIZON. FROM THEIR balcony, Ambrose felt the weight of silence alleviated. Whoops and cheers sounded alongside the gong of bells in the courtyard below. Music erupted, packing the air with life. Ambrose fastened the brocade-lined buttons of his new black tunic, the fabric's pattern lost between the shadows of the ensemble. He liked the meaning behind the wardrobe change, but liked color and vibrance more. While the day had been spent in respect of the dead, the evening would be about celebrating among them. The bells continued as the bedroom door opened and closed.

"Finally," Rorrik said. "You should have seen the glares I got in the yards earlier, as if sparring was considered speaking."

Ambrose had to agree, the lack of sound had been agonizing. He hadn't realized just how useless he was without words. But now, as he dressed for the celebration and dances below, he found words hard to come by. Fine, since Rorrik had more than enough to spare.

"Do we have to dance? I haven't formally danced in ages."

"Yes," Ambrose straightened his too-high-necked collar. "As royal ambassadors for Xenkesh we need to show respect for Elastian customs."

"They're not respecting our customs," Rorrik said, surly, "or we wouldn't have to dance."

This warped sense of culture bothered Ambrose. Celebrations in Xenkesh more often than not led to dancing. Xenkeshi dances were beyond the body. They danced because their souls did, because the music called to them, or their beings bubbled over with joy. However, King Amarus had stopped hosting such celebrations after the fall of Ravysh. While dancing in the cities could be found in abundance, the continued heavy losses were the nobility's burden to bear. To follow their failures with a dance or formal celebration would be distasteful.

"We're not in Xenkesh, and they're not Xenkeshi dances," Ambrose said simply. "Elastor is not at war."

Rorrik shared his signature sneer. "Many thanks to your princess."

Fully dressed, Ambrose reached for the door. "Let's go. You can sulk at the party."

"Wait." Rorrik lingered behind. "There's something I've been meaning to tell you."

"I don't like the sound of that."

"It's not bad! I just think you should know..." Rorrik shuffled his feet and Ambrose suspected it must be very bad. "While you were in Heartsglove, I made contact with an insider. A double eye, working out of the Solstice Court."

Ambrose dropped his hand. "What?"

"It's fine!" Rorrik put his hands up. "He's a Xenkeshi sympathizer—"

"Rorrik you don't have even a beginner's knowledge of working with spies."

"Well, I do now," Rorrik said. "I met with them in Heartsglove. There's an entire coalition down in the lower city."

"You went into the city?"

"As did *you*. But I didn't have a semi-combustible Princess with me. Anyway, they've been smuggling trade on the Lull to and from Xenkesh—"

"So, he's a pirate," Ambrose said, with disgust.

Rorrik scoffed. "Hardly, he just works with them. He's a spy. But he also doesn't like how passive Elastian government is. He's been working to upend it."

"So, he's a radical."

"Will you just listen? There's more. When I went with him to the meeting, they had a Xenkeshi with them. He said he sometimes worked with Father but to keep quiet about it."

Ambrose faltered then checked the walls, a finger to his lips. The walls—alongside disgruntled woes about the ground shaking—

relented and answered him. Nobody listened. "What did he look like?"

"Erm—grimy? But that's what you've got to do to blend in—"

Ambrose didn't have time for a lesson in amateur sleuthing. "Descriptors? Details? Jewelry?"

Rorrik frowned. "He had lots of rings and layers on. He's Xenkeshi."

"Any that stood out?"

"A ring shaped like a snake, I guess? Wait—do you know him? If Father sent—"

"No," Ambrose lied, "I don't know him. Sorry, go on with your story."

Rorrik searched Ambrose's eyes. Ambrose protected his brother with everything he had and raised a brow; impatient, interested. Rorrik gave in.

"Alright. Well, we went into Heartsglove, to an old hovel outside the Bliss—erm, Ruby district, it's called here. They wouldn't tell me the exact plans, but they were plotting a way to disrupt some sort of Aloran-Elastian agreement that'd been made. Then the Xenkeshi showed up. He told the insider he had something but that the payment could only be done through trade."

Ambrose rubbed at the sides of his eyes. He needed to sit with this, but he also needed to eliminate any lingering interest Rorrik might have in Thrice's crude underbelly.

"He wanted to buy from an Aloran smuggler, but..." Rorrik fiddled with his empty sword scabbard, his eyes cast down, "the rebels didn't have anything grand enough for the trade."

"You traded your sword?" Ambrose tried not to think of what he'd have to do to make sure a royal Xenkeshi blade wasn't implicated in a back-alley rebellion in Elastor. "So your 'insider' is not only a radical spy-pirate, but he's also destitute. Brilliant."

"He's against Aloran trade." Rorrik shrugged, nose upturned. "He has principles, I don't. So, I paid."

"You don't even know what you paid for."

"Well—" Rorrik sputtered, "—what kind of spy would expose their secret plans?"

"What kind of prince joins another kingdom's impoverished, radicalized pirate union!"

"Conducting business with a *Xenkeshi* spy!" Rorrik crossed his arms. "Come on, Ambrose, don't pretend that doesn't mean something."

Ambrose couldn't deny it. The spy Rorrik spoke of had become a necessary evil. After they'd lost their last Spymaster, Xenkesh had made a formal, *temporary*, agreement with a pirate captain named Syle. The pirate held influence over people of... much lower character. It was a makeshift bargain born from war.

Ambrose had been privy to Syle's whereabouts since their first night in the city. It made sense to have a connection outside of Elastor's own network to pass highly sensitive information onto his father. Yet, he'd already done that and watched Syle depart with his message, the spy's business concluded.

"You only saw the Xenkeshi one time, right? In Heartsglove?"

"Well...twice more, then yeah. I haven't seen him since."

"Oh?" Ambrose fought to not shake him.

"We were supposed to meet him on the coast, but something went wrong so we met him in the city after you and I argued and you stormed off. That's why I didn't tell you," Rorrik reasoned. "You've been so...in your head since we got here and if Father *did* send the spy..."

Rorrik hadn't wanted Ambrose to botch the mission. While this irked him, Ambrose had a crucial piece of information to take in. Rorrik's timeline meant the pirate-turned-spy had returned to the city, either of his own volition or on his father's orders. But his father would've told him, wouldn't he? Meaning Syle now acted alone.

The idea of that urchin skulking so near the Solstice Court and Kezerah sent a shiver up his spine. Ambrose calmed himself. It sounded as if Syle had—thus far—remained in the city.

He needed to collect his thoughts. An impossible task with Rorrik underfoot. "For now, let's get to the celebration. We'll be missed if we lag much longer."

"You're not mad?"

Livid. "Nope, just keep me informed from now on."

He forced himself not to skip steps on his way down the stairs. "And for now, let's stay out of Elastor's affairs."

THE MEADOW HAD BEEN TRANSFORMED into the night sky. People danced in preset twirls: live decoration added to the splendor surrounding them. On further inspection, Ambrose noticed tiny bugs auraed with light drifting around the maze adorned with shimmering gems. Lanterns in differing shapes, colors and baubles ran in criss-cross constellations. Carved squash filled with firelight haunted the grass and beaded crystals hung low on trapeze strings to join the stars with twinkling dots.

Ambrose readied himself to find Kezerah, then stopped. His priorities had shifted, he reminded himself. He would spend the evening bolstering Xenkesh's image and then depart for home.

"Like what you see?" Whistle came up beside him, her dress obscured by a thick, fur-lined cloak. It fastened at the collar and below her chest, accentuating the area.

He reached out a hand. "Of course. The day might have left me tongue-tied, but I can see what's right in front of me."

She took his hand. "Would you join me for my first dance?"

Rorrik grumbled behind them.

"Don't do anything stupid," Ambrose told his brother. Whistle beamed and he led her into the crowd of dancers.

CASTIEL BREATHED in and nearly drowned. Rain and wind ripped at his tied back hair. The ship groaned and his sails bloated with the Brash. Lightning hissed across the sky gifting him less than a naut ahead. Nights on these tumultuous waves were a deadly thing, but the worse their visibility, the more invisible they were to their enemy.

Illija made her entrance above deck alongside a crack and roar of thunder. The ship continued to tip and rock, the gales forcing them to shout side by side.

"I can feel their minds," Her braid fought its confines. The salt of the sea extracted the gloss from her skin. She rubbed chapped lips together and winced. "No words yet, but echoes..."

"What's wrong?" he asked.

Her brows pinched together. "It's hard to pinpoint. Their minds are... rested. Awake. There's a vibrance in the waking mind unlike a sleeping one. It's what makes dream drifting easier."

"There's bound to be shifts. Not all can sleep at once." He caught her arm as the ship pitched against a wave and she stumbled towards the banister.

"His ship will be at the back, closest to us," Illija said, replaying their plan. "How close do we need to be for me to board it?"

"Close enough to see it, for a start."

"Castiel."

Castiel didn't like this plan. It overutilized Illija and underutilized him. His fleet would take on the fight around them. But with Illija aboard an enemy ship, it left them vulnerable and hindered their ability to attack that ship. It did *not* hinder the enemy ship from attacking them. If Illija were captured, injured, or worse they wouldn't know in time to engage a rescue.

"It could be a trap."

"He has nothing more to trap me with. All of my sons are safe in the Solstice Court, you stand by my side, and we now hold his water supply along the Xenkeshi Strand. He has nothing, and he knows it. Give me the distance, Cas."

Castiel's huff was lost to the storm. "The scorpion can shoot about one naut of cable across. But to get an accurate enough shot to skim you over, without you being blown away first?" Castiel noted the tempest winds swirling around them and calculated further. "Perhaps...half a naut?"

"Half?"

"A fourth, if you're rational."

"That brings us too close!"

"It also gives them less time to notice a giant spear jammed into their mast, and you sliding down a rope cable to kill them," said Castiel.

"We'll be in range of their arrows."

"Which is why we should do a wide assault first. If he goes down aboard—"

"I won't spend the rest of my life *hoping* he died at sea," Illija said. "I'll do it myself."

"Irrational it is then. Half a naut is the best I can do. We have four ships docked and ready in Tierytide with five at our back. That should be enough to hold them off until you've returned, then we'll destroy what's left."

"No." Illija stared into the undying storm. "Once he's dead, they'll be offered a surrender and retreat."

"Lija, I don't know if—"

She pointed a finger straight ahead. "There."

Castiel followed her indication. Coal-black profiles haunted gray-black waves. Six dark sails and their ships flashed and evanesced into the night.

KEZERAH REMOVED her slippers to feel the cool dew of the grass beneath her feet. Shadows swept across the grounds as lords, ladies, and lieges danced. The satins switched out for traditional black fabrics to join the ancestors in their night of honor. She spotted Willow dancing with Liege Lumi: a beautiful pair in their obsidian gowns.

Dance partners appeared scarce, most people already dancing. Rorrik stood near the edge of the grass-covered stage but his posture looked too rigid to be any fun.

She followed his gaze and did a triple take as Ambrose and Whistle pranced past. '*When did that happen?*' She couldn't help but watch. Whistle was the best dancer among their friends, and the two together looked, admittedly, mesmerizing. They spun like whirlpools along the shore: fluid and forever twirling. Ambrose dipped Whistle low and Kezerah turned away.

"Am I still permitted to be your first dance?" her father asked, coming up beside her. "Or have you gotten too old for that tradition?"

She smiled, grateful. "Never."

Elowren took her hand and they swept into the middle, vassals naturally parting for their King and heir. "Did you enjoy your day?" he asked, switching hands so they could pull into the next step.

"It was uneventful, but I did sleep through some of it."

Her father's eyebrows rose in surprise. "Both characteristics I do not often associate with your days."

She shrugged. "It's worth it to stay up all night."

He laughed, spinning her. "I envy you your boring afternoon. I just managed to leave the Strategy Chambers."

Kezerah grew more attentive. "Anything interesting?"

Elowren *hmm*'d. "I'm not sure. I feel 'unusual' may be a more apt description." He looked over at Ambrose, who took creative privileges with the dance steps, lifting Whistle up and sliding her close to his frame.

Kezerah blushed, and Elowren chuckled. "He reminds me so much of Amarus when we were young."

She clung to the distraction, turning them away from the mirthful duo. "How so?"

Elowren, forever thoughtful with his words, spoke carefully. "Amarus was always very...magnetic. Lively in comparison to the rest of us. He enjoyed life."

Kezerah caught the past tense. "And now?"

Elowren shook his head. "Not in the way he once did. War changed him." His frown slid lower, and she tried to cheer him.

"Well, maybe when the war is over he can relax again."

She'd clearly failed. Her father only looked further away, despite answering, "Perhaps."

Kezerah thought back to Ikaika's declarative statements about the war. As she looked up at her father's face, lined with worry, she thought maybe the statements hadn't been unfounded.

The music shifted into something slower, and Elowren grinned in a way she knew she'd inherited from him. "I think my time is up. You seem to have another dance partner."

Kezerah turned and Ikaika smiled shyly as they approached. "Where have you been?" she demanded, eagerly intertwining their hands as she was passed from her father to him. Elowren smoothed her hair to kiss the top of her head before moving to the side.

"I took a late nap. I only woke up about half an hour or so ago," Ikaika said, apologetic.

She examined him, a black brocade outfit with a subtle design she could only see as it caught the lights. It matched his eyes perfectly, and she realized Ikaika looked striking in everything. She tried to picture him in her least favorite color, a salmon pink. Ikaika led the glide across the grass with ease and snickered.

"What's so funny?"

"Nobody would look good in that color."

She paused in confusion then took her hand away to hit him playfully. "Stop that!"

He laughed again. "I wish I could." Then his tone grew more tentative. "Although, I don't mind hearing you think I'm striking."

Her ears burned with embarrassment but he seemed different, too vulnerable to tease. A harp cascaded, signifying a spin, and her stomach mimicked the instrument's strum. She sifted through her thoughts then realized he could probably hear them and decided on the truth. "Well, you are..." she pushed the words out. "Striking, that is."

Ikaika didn't speak and she decidedly couldn't look up at him. She tried to regain herself, she was the bold one here. She forced her gaze to his and got lost in the starless night sky of his eyes right as he finally spoke, voice soft, "As are you."

Her heart thrummed louder than the harp. He had never spoken to her like this. She wondered if it was her dress. She suddenly felt more elegant than before. He smiled down at her, not the crooked smile, but a new one that pulled up on both sides.

The music faded and she thought of demanding they start back up again. She would have given a royal decree if that's what it took, but her mother's voice rose above the crowd, and she allowed the moment to fall away.

"I hope you all are having a pleasant evening, and have gotten a good day's rest to join us for the coming night." Elize spoke in her jovial tone she used on everyone but Kezerah. "While there are more dances to be had, I ask that you all join us in the banquet hall for our Nighttide Feast. May we enjoy this evening together, with the veil at its thinnest, so we might share it with our loved ones past."

Many clapped, and while the music started up again, it was not meant for dancing, but proceeding. The throng of nobles waded into the Autumn Quarter.

Kezerah wrapped an arm around Ikaika's outstretched one. They followed, bodies warm against the crisp night air. She went to sit down in her regular seat but found Dyllian already seated there.

"Dyllian, move."

He looked up at her, then pointed at an obsidian glass plaque with his name etched on it. "Sorry, Princess, it's designated dining tonight." He didn't sound sorry in the slightest. Not having a choice of seats ruffled her, and they started down the line, glancing at each placard.

They found Ikaika's first, seated between Rorrik's and Whistle's. Ikaika's face was motionless. "This will be interesting." He begrudgingly let his arm fall from hers. She left him to hunt down her own name.

She'd made a half circle of the table before holding back a groan. Her placard was firmly placed to the left of the double head, next to her mother. Luckily, Elize wasn't yet seated, so she didn't hear Kezerah's sound of disgust.

"Come now," Ambrose emerged at her shoulder, "I'm not that bad."

She looked at the seat to her left. "No, you're a lovely consolation prize. I'll have to thank my mother for her generosity."

His hearty guffaw startled Lady Sorrel who looked across at Kezerah with disdain, as if Kezerah had been the one with the booming laugh.

They sat and Ambrose angled his chair towards hers, leaning in with an elbow on the table. "You know, sitting next to the King and Queen is considered an honor."

"I think that depends on who the King and Queen are."

"Funny, I've always found your father quite charming."

Kezerah's retort came to her lips before she could pull it back. "I'm surprised you're not disappointed by the arrangement, seeing how Whistle is halfway down the table."

His grin grew unhinged with glee. She had the urge to slap him. "Is this...jealousy, I'm hearing?"

"Hardly."

"Well," he said, voice pitched low so only she could hear him, "that's a shame, as I'm quite pleased you're not seated next to my brother tonight."

"Funny, I always found Rorrik quite charming."

"Words uttered by no one."

"Oh? Is it only you who's sought after at the Trusol Court then?" She hoped her voice didn't betray the real question there.

Ambrose searched her face, and she did her best Ikaika impression: unreadable. She wouldn't be accused of jealousy twice in one evening. "I'm not usually the one who needs to do the seeking, if that's what you're asking."

"Must be nice."

Ambrose glanced across the table and back. "It depends on who's hunting."

Kezerah thought back to Heartsglove: how Kofi had looked at him, and later Ambrose's smile as the courtesan wrapped a silk scarf around his neck. He hadn't been complaining then. "Would that statement hold up on a second trip to the city? I can recall more than one hunt you seemed to enjoy."

Ambrose frowned. "For the time being, we should steer clear of Heartsglove."

"Why?" asked Kezerah, "Worried you'll be lured in?"

"I'm worried because it's dangerous." Ambrose's chair shifted, ever so slightly away from her. "You should keep to court."

Kezerah cocked her head to one side and wondered what she'd done wrong. "I was only teasing, Ambrose, I—"

"Prince Ambrose, nice to see you at this end of the table!" Her father's voice broke them apart.

Ambrose matched her father's cordial tone. "It's my honor, Your Majesty, truly. I thank you."

Elowren chuckled. "I take none of the credit. My dear queen is the mastermind behind the evening." He gestured to Elize as she sat, her dark eyes delighted by Elowren's words.

Ambrose raised a glass. "A gracious honor indeed."

"I only hope not to have missed something in preparation." Elize fretted, with false modesty.

"Well, now that you mention it," Kezerah said, pretending to ponder the thought, "the seating does feel a bit off."

"Don't be rude," said Elize, not looking her way.

Elowren, always the pacifist, attempted humor. "I'm not so bad, am I?"

"Someone already told that joke, Father."

Ambrose chuckled beside her. Kezerah tried not to feel relieved by it.

Elize looked past her, to Ambrose. "How are you enjoying your time at the Solstice Court?"

"Immensely," Ambrose said, politely. "I've been undone by the hospitality given to myself and my brother."

"I've seen Rorrik quite frequently in the training yards and barracks."

He nodded. "Rorrik is a born soldier to be sure."

"And how have you best spent your time?"

"While I, too, enjoy swordplay—" he cleared his throat, "—I've been more captivated by conversations this trip."

"Ah, well, then I hope my daughter can be a pleasant speaking companion for the evening."

Kezerah shot her mother a look, but it wasn't returned, her blue gaze fixed on Ambrose.

Ambrose's polite expression crept into a soft smile, his eyes drawn and lingering on Kezerah. "I could not conjure a better one from my imagination."

Her mother seemed pleased, if not a bit surprised, just as the food arrived.

A SLOW CACOPHONY built up around the table. Conversation flowed everywhere, the exception being Ikaika and his dinner companions. Whistle spoke often, seemingly attempting to coax something meaningful out of Rorrik, who sat stiffly next to him. Ikaika spotted Andarios seated toward the end of the feast hall, near some of the lower nobility that lived outside the capitals. Ikaika tried to share his chagrin with Kezerah, but she was too busy laughing with Ambrose and her father to meet his gaze.

The pain in his skull had felt manageable when dancing, but as more guests woke and joined the table, the pulse of pain grew substantially. Both lords of Heartsglove sat across from him and he attempted conversation.

"Heartsglove looks to be in full celebration tonight."

The paramours looked at one another, a private conference shared in a look. "Quite."

Ikaika didn't understand the chilled response. The aura of words and images were too blended together to decipher. He could see how many who didn't journey to the Temples went mad. The nausea in his throat promised the worst was yet to come. "In Alora, we celebrate the eel constellation this time of year ..." Ikaika's words wavered as intrusive thoughts struck him.

'Perhaps the bear was an accident...An Aloran sailor all the same...' Both Lords fiddled with their utensils rather than meet his eye.

Ikaika didn't bother finishing his sentence. He instead picked at his peppercorn mash and tried to shut out the noise. Maybe, if he imagined the clamor of voices smashing into the barriers of his mind as the crashing of waves? He tried it. It didn't work.

Neither master of Heartsglove ventured to save the fragmented conversation. Whistle, however, seemed to have worn Rorrik's poor mood down. He elaborately explained how he'd won his sword from his sword master. It was hard for Ikaika to believe considering how formidable Azalea had been against Eriko, who wouldn't shut up about her.

"Oh, no, it's a ceremonial blade. It's not on me. We choose a weapon for combat afterwards...My brother won two swords but my father said I even beat his time."

"You must be the best then!" Whistle flattered.

Rorrik preened then looked at Ikaika for the first time. "Well, there's not many here who could beat me, that's for sure."

Ikaika sensed the challenge. Admittedly, it was the wrong brother, but the pain creasing his temple didn't care. The urge to release his pent up frustration overtook him.

"Are you taking challengers?"

Rorrik smiled, cruel and eager. "You're implying it would be a challenge."

"You haven't managed to beat Eriko even once."

Rorrik glared, dissatisfied with the facts being announced in front of Whistle. "Eriko is a sword master, and twenty years my senior, *little* brother." Ikaika scoffed at the petty, ten moon differentiation between them. "He was also torn apart by Azalea, *my* sword master, whom I beat just last summer."

"In ceremonial melodrama."

"Did you just call our Sword Trials melodramatic? How do you win your weaponry, Aloran?" he lazed an arm on his chair's backrest. "Do you cheat and read the opponent's mind, taking what isn't yours when their back is turned?"

"Taking that which isn't yours is a Xenkeshi trait."

Rorrik's eyes flared, it made him look serpentine. "You're right. Alorans prefer to run."

"I guarantee, I won't." Ikaika's voice was steel. "Just try to recognize when the battle is lost."

"When." Rorrik didn't ask, only demanded a time and place.

'*Now,*' said the agony of Ikaika's pounding skull. Yet, laying Rorrik flat on the dinner table would probably go over poorly, and he intended to fight fair.

"After the feast, the Northern yard."

"The Eastern yard is closer. Need time to practice your breathing?"

Ikaika parodied Rorrik's grin. "I just want you to have a nice view of the Aloran Mountains as you fall."

AMBROSE ADMIRED the glass domed ceiling and smattering of stars. The moon's absence stole away any sense of time. It annoyed him that he didn't want the night to end. He and Kezerah had tempoed so naturally into conversation. Words flowed between them like the current of a river mill; each churn in topic building up to the next. He wondered if she felt the same.

Bites of delicious food caused a comfortable silence. Her mother chimed in just as Kezerah scooped a corn and pea medley into her mouth. "Have you asked Prince Ambrose to dance after the feast? I imagine he gets swept up quite quickly."

Kezerah, noticeably irritated, turned to Ambrose and, mouth full, asked flatly, "Wonta donce?" A piece of corn fell from her full lips.

With much difficulty, Ambrose subdued his face and bowed his head. "Most gracious of you, Princess, it would be my privilege." Kezerah mocked a curtsey while sitting down and Elize sighed, turning to Elowren for better conversation.

Ambrose imagined Kezerah dancing. She didn't possess a rigid bone in her body. She'd be playful, free. To dance with her would feel like dancing at home again.

Elowren rose to excuse the table and both Ikaika and Rorrik snapped out of their chairs as if struck by lightning then left the hall together.

Ambrose's nerves spiked. *'Fantastic.'* He deliberated on what to do. He and Kezerah stood and trailed behind the party of courtiers who'd begun to return to the meadow. Azalea loomed some paces back and Ambrose dropped his arm from Kezerah's.

"A moment," he said, "and I'll be back for that dance." He stalked over to Azalea, in the hopes that she could keep his asinine brothers from spoiling everything.

KEZERAH RESENTED the pang in her chest as Ambrose and his guard walked in Whistle's direction. *'Elowren foolishly believes himself with friends.'* She fought a building unease, one she'd tried to ignore on more than one occasion with Ambrose.

A tapping persisted at her shoulder.

Kezerah thought for a fleeting moment she'd turn to see Ikaika, but her smile dimmed as Dyllian outstretched a hand.

"Will you honor me with a dance?" She took his hand with a roll of her eyes. At least she'd be dancing when Ambrose came back. "Do you know this one, Princess?" he asked, the steps so simple it could only be an insult.

"Yes, it goes like this, right?" Kezerah stumbled and stamped onto his foot.

"Are you not wearing shoes?" He sounded appalled.

"No, I have a fungal infection that grew too severe," she said prettily. "I hope you don't mind."

Dyllian ignored her, "Actually, while I have you—"

"You don't have me. It's a dance, Dyllian, not an open forum." She counted the progression, anticipating when they could switch partners.

"Right, well, the irrigation is set to go in after First Thaw, so time *is* of the essence, you know."

Not even the recovery of her pride was worth this. She began to back away, but found her hand still caught in his. His grip tightened. She stared at him. Gaunt shadows drooped his features and a dull sheen glazed his golden eyes.

"Dyllian, let go."

"Kezerah, for once in your life," he hissed low, "listen." Her skin crawled and she applied more force to drag herself out of his grasp.

"While you make a handsome pair—" The tempest in Ambrose's glare undercut his jovial tone as he assessed their frayed stance. "—I'm afraid I was promised this dance."

Dyllian had the audacity to cross his arms. "We're in the middle of a song."

"Sorry, Dyllian," Kezerah cut in, "but decorum requires I honor my promises. We can continue this... in the next *council meeting*."

Dyllian looked to the dais, as if he planned to bring the pressing issue of dancing up to the queen herself. Then tossed his hands down, easily defeated. "Enjoy yourself, Princess. It's what you do best." He stormed off towards the hedges. *'Let him get lost.'* Kezerah thought before she shook the incident off and turned her attention to Ambrose. Her chin lifted. She still had more of her dignity left to defend.

A CANNON BURST and shattered the inseam of a far off Xenkeshi ship. Well underway, the battle shredded into worn red sails that battered against the wind. They'd finally arrived at Amarus' craft, recognizable by its weathered gold embellishments and ornate oak hindquarters.

A zeal spawned in Castiel that he hadn't felt in a long time. Their ship had closed in and he'd watched as a small force led by Illija, clad in blue and black and blood, dashed across the enemy vessel. Her palpable hunger drove the sharp dance of her sword, clearing a path only she could see. The ship rocked and tipped at the ocean's torment.

Castiel had seen her cut down the crew at a gruesome speed. She only ever stopped to read an opponent's thoughts or send them nightmares in their last glimpse of life. Souls tore from bodies like shooting stars: a cascade of radiant lights clustering together to shower across the sky. They flew east, and Castiel didn't bother a prayer.

A high octave flutter broke through the clamorous deluge. Castiel froze, then turned sharply to his cannon-handler. "Hold fire!"

His top-lark, high above, played their piccolo once more. Dull booms echoed from the sky but Castiel caught the second warble of notes. The top-lark had just announced ships approaching...from behind.

Castiel spit and cursed low. They were now the ones being flanked.

"MAGICK IS ALLOWED." Rorrik stalked ahead of Ikaika into the training yard. He was going to enjoy this. Andarios and Azalea stood at the mouth of the corral, backdropped by broad, cold mountains. It irked Rorrik that Ambrose had sent Azalea to oversee him after he'd already asked Andarios, but he supposed someone should keep him in check. Each sword in the barracks had looked too feeble for what he wanted to do to Ikaika. *Little brother,*' he thought, weighing the hollowed-out mace he'd chosen. He'd used the words in mockery, but Ambrose had referred to Ikaika as such on more than one occasion. Brother was a term earned. It was a bond deeper than blood, and he'd bathe in the Brash before he gave that title to this weak, sullen, imperious boy pretending he had any right to a throne.

Andarios crossed his arms. "Maybe magick should be left out of this one."

"No, done." Ikaika made small blocking maneuvers with a thimble of a sword. "His terms, his way."

"Kai." Andarios sounded impatient.

Rorrik smiled. He'd first viewed Andarios as an oaf, but that had changed in the forest. Andarios was one to have on your side and any chink in Ikaika's armor was worth noting.

"*Dar* is right," Rorrik said. Ikaika narrowed his eyes impossibly thin. "A brawl match then, no magick, first blood."

"That's not what I meant," said Andarios. "Clean as in fair, sparring rules. No blood."

"I can take him." Ikaika's arrogance followed him into a ready position.

"Yeah, that's not what I'm worried about either," Andarios looked over to Azalea. "Are you going to stop this at all?"

She returned his exasperation with an impassive expression. "Magick, first blood, no foul play." Her eyes landed on Rorrik and he scoffed. "Let's get this over with."

"Why are you here?" Kezerah asked mid-spin.

Ambrose finished the twirl and thought through his answer. Kezerah carried herself with more vulnerable curiosity than anyone he'd ever met. If he lied, he had a feeling she'd sense it. She tilted her head, gaze open and aware.

"I don't know." Honest *enough*.

"Alright then. Why do you *think* you're here?" Apparently 'enough' wasn't enough for Kezerah.

Ambrose prepared half truths in his head and watched her eyes sharpen.

She didn't trust him.

Something about that made his stomach turn. Why? What did he have to lose?

Her.

Fine then. He'd already decided to leave. Better he lost on his own terms.

"I think I was meant to seduce you, bring you to sympathize with my side, and..." Ambrose thought back to Syle lurking somewhere in the city, "I think I have more allies than I realized to help me do it." Their gazes bore into one another's. Ambrose feared her lips would bruise from how she forced them together.

The silence lasted too long. She turned her face away, bestowing him with her side profile. Her eyes glistened like early morning dew. Ambrose's heart dropped, his hands shook slightly.

"Oh," she murmured, "that's all."

He changed his mind. He suddenly wanted to remove the truth from her memory as quick as he'd given it to her.

The string instruments dipped into a slower melody with drawn-out notes. They moved in a sedated spin only an Elastian dance was capable of. Her hurt and disappointment surpassed the rage he'd expected to have thrown at him. He'd endured her anger, and now wished for it. Instead, she slipped away from him, like fine sand through his fingertips. An abrupt and sharp panic gripped him. He tried desperately to fill the space with words.

"You have so many expressions," he blurted, interrupting her brooding. "I know exactly how you're feeling, it makes it...easy—refreshing to talk to you. I'm not constantly guessing what to do next." He recognized the agitated frown on her face, far better than pain.

"Does every conversation need a battle plan?" She challenged him with a stare worthy of combat.

"I am my father's battle strategist." He gulped. "But since we've met, I've realized any plan is futile. You just scatter the board for the next round." She furrowed her brow, more perplexed than angry.

"That is...not quite a compliment."

"You don't seem won over by compliments." He wrapped a hand around her waist, following form and pulling her close. The sheer lace of her gown sent his thoughts in a thousand different directions. *'Right, dancing, speaking.'* The steps called for them to break apart, he did so quickly and pulled her back in close. "You've only ever given my truths the time of day."

"Ah," she appeared to muster up her best airy tone. "So, it really is that easy then. What a disappointing game that must have been."

"On the contrary," his breaths were feather light as the words escaped him, "I've never enjoyed losing a game so much in my life."

Time ceased as Kezerah's eyes searched his. He couldn't hear the music anymore, just the vibrant beat of his heart pounding in his ears. She began to say something, but then looked at the musicians. Ambrose realized the song had stopped. His moment at its end, he opened his hands to release her.

"In the city, you told me they dance differently in Xenkesh." She tightened her hold. "Teach me." The instruments started up again.

"WHERE IS HE?" Illija stood body to body, face to face with a woman. An insignia marked her as the captain of Amarus' royal battalion. Injured from Illija's earlier attack, the captain had tried and failed to ambush her. Now, she stood disarmed; locked between the master cabin door and Illija's sword pressed to tilt up her chin.

Illija had swept the entirety of the above deck. There had been plenty of storage barrels, weaponry and, of course, a full crew aboard. All the Xenkeshi soldiers dressed in the armor of Amarus' personal battalion with various levels of Bond magick. Could Amarus truly sit below in his cabin while his entire crew was massacred? Of course he could. "Your king is a craven and a leech. Don't die for him." The captain's teeth gritted and lips parted, but still she said nothing. Illija lowered her sword to the captain's throat and stepped back, applying pressure. "Where?"

Fire arrows shot through the sky, curving above them before falling to stick in the deck. What was that, a signal? A misfire? Nobody should be attacking this ship with both monarchs aboard. Before Illija had time to process, the captain began to laugh. Illija frowned, taking in the captain's wave of thoughts. *The barrels.* Illija followed the thought with her eyes while the madwoman crowed in manic delight.

Then, the captain reached out and, open-palmed, grabbed the sword by the edge and pulled. The blade seeped in. The woman choked a laugh with her final breath. Illija let the body drop to the floor. She stared a moment before eyeing the many wooden casks dotting the ship.

A whiff of gore, seasoned by sea salt, surrounded her. She withheld a dry heave as she stalked over to the nearest barrel. She hefted the lid. A new smell, as familiar as home, wafted up to greet her. Inside, fine, bright flaxen dust filled the drum to the rim. The odor was akin to a match snuffed out, or rotten eggs. Sulfur dust. Barrels and barrels of—

Illija whipped around to her ship. Six additional Xenkeshi galleons splintered around her vessel like jaws in a cave.

Illija's panic harmonized with the roar of waves. *"Castiel!"*

Her ship burst into a pyre with black tendrils of smoke higher than Estora.

Illija didn't think. Her boots pounded across the deck. Her legs screamed at the velocity of her sprint. Another flame-engulfed arrow whizzed past her. It did not miss. The bolt hit a nearby barrel with a thunk. Heat and light singed and blazed at her back and Illija dove into the Brash.

RORRIK EXPECTED to dislodge Ikaika's wiry blade immediately. The mace swung, Ikaika pivoted. The spiked cudgel continued its forward momentum. Ikaika jabbed out. Too fast. Rorrik needed to slow him down. His chestplate thrummed, hungry for battle, for impact. Rorrik aligned himself with his Bond. The metals of his mail relied on strength and vitality. The blade across from him hissed with an acute clarity. *'No, it would not weigh itself down in this way. It refused strength in turn for artistry. It wanted to carve blood from Rorrik's flesh like a sculptor to clay.'*

Ikaika smirked. Rorrik shivered and returned to his mace. The hollowed-out core solidified. This time when he swung, the mace connected with Ikaika's bloodthirsty sword then continued on to jam into its master's stomach.

The padding stopped the spikes from penetrating skin, but Ikaika gasped for air. Rorrik used the falter to kick his boot out towards Ikaika's sword hand. His foot slammed into thin air and he stumbled forward as Ikaika dodged and rolled. A whoosh and lash of pain flared along his right arm. Rorrik cursed and flung out, but Ikaika had gotten behind him. He spun as more welts built up on his neck, back, and legs. A point jabbed in the soft bits between his arm and side. Everywhere he turned Ikaika wasn't there. Every pivot resulted in a bite of pain.

"You coward! Fight me!"

"What, you think it's the wind hitting you? You're slower than your mace."

Rorrik flung away his mace and struck out. The club stuck in the ground and Rorrik slammed into Ikaika.

The two tumbled and, to Rorrik's satisfaction, Ikaika's blade fell aside. Ikaika pitched forward and connected. Rorrik's body hit the fencing with a ricochet that shook his jaw. Stupid move. Rorrik lunged. As expected, he had more brawn than Ikaika and pinned him long enough to draw a fist back. The moment he connected with Ikaika's jaw his chest eased. A spasm shot through his knuckles and up to his shoulder. He shook and flexed his fingers for another hit.

"Hey! That's first blood!" Andarios shouted.

Rorrik glared down into fathomless eyes and a torn lip. Not enough.

"*Rorrik,*" Azalea warned and started forward.

He reached for his mace an arm's length away. Ikaika spit, and Rorrik sputtered as hot spittle spattered across his vision. Then his hearing faltered as Ikaika's own fist crashed into the side of his face. Before Rorrik could fully register the pain, Ikaika's head arched back, and his body bridged and twisted. Rorrik lurched to the side. Ikaika's leg snaked around and reversed their positions. It happened too fast. Rorrik still clung to the mace but couldn't move it as Ikaika drew up behind him, locking his arms high above his head. Pressure squeezed at his neck and shoulder and he was pulled onto his knees. Against his will, Rorrik's grip slackened. *No. No. No.* But Rorrik couldn't move. He was clamped in place.

"Kai! It's done!" Andarios' voice was underwater, but he seemed closer now. Rorrik's head swam. "He's disarmed, defenseless."

"So was I."

Rorrik's arm twisted at an unnatural angle. Bile climbed his throat as his shoulder made a sickening pop. Like lightning before thunder, a flash of pain erupted before the ringing in his ears began. Rorrik might have cried out, he didn't know. His vision missed parts, a portrait with burns puckering across the canvas. Then the pitch of black between stars engulfed him.

KEZERAH'S MIND tried to keep pace with her heart as they swept across the meadow. Ambrose had rushed his confession out and she tried to make it stick. He'd arrived with ill intent. Ikaika had been right. But had she been wrong? Could Ambrose not both need an ally but want a friend, or a...? She blushed, forcing her gaze up. She'd requested a dance but now conflict troubled Ambrose's handsome face. She'd wanted the boy who spoke about weaving with his family, who'd laid with her in the grass while admitting their fears. But perhaps she'd misread him once again.

No, she knew he was there. She'd seen him before.

Kezerah guided them through the crowd to the place he'd last been vulnerable with her. They slowed once in the maze. Wordlessly, she reached to smooth out the lines in his features. Her fingertips brushed across the creases above his brow. They did her bidding and his face softened. Ambrose cleared his throat, as if coaxed from far away.

"Xenkeshi dances," he said, low, before he spun her around and pulled her to him, "have no rules." Kezerah's arms crossed as he drew her in closer, every curve of her pressed against him. His hands held her with confidence and he explored down from her shoulders to arms, in order to reach her hands again. He moved his body to the beat of his own imagined tempo. Her back to him, she followed, hands hugged at her waist as she moved to the music. His energy heightened and she inhaled as his fingertips grazed her hips. He reversed her to their original position and slowed his movements into the Elastian dance.

He smiled now and they drifted farther into the maze. The lanterns dimmed with distance. Only the fireflies illuminated Ambrose as he dipped her low again.

The breadth between them closed once more and Kezerah knew her pulse betrayed her every time his hands brushed her. She also knew what she wanted in this moment, and that if she didn't stop their dance soon, it would lead somewhere she wasn't meant to go. Somewhere selfish. Her mother always accused her of selfishness.

Ambrose brought his lips beside her ear. "Where's your mind?"

"I—" Perhaps she was selfish. Perhaps she wanted to be. "Here."

"Good." His smile shone with the word. "I want you here."

Ambrose stretched an arm out, still holding her tight, he whipped her towards a hedge before pulling her back, curling her into his arms before she faced him again.

"Show off."

He scoffed. "I've never denied that."

She was coiled against him, wanting him to continue speaking in her ear.

"What is it that wins you over?" she asked. "If honesty is all it takes for me, what about you?" He didn't answer. The glint in his eyes seemed to dare her to seek it out herself. "If I call you handsome, you would simply agree." They followed the curved path towards the pocket of grass at the maze's center.

"Well, I don't think I'm the *most* regrettable person to dance with," he agreed, with a smile.

Before the final turn she stepped forward, not disentangling from his embrace but leaning into it—into him—she put a hand to his chest. The threads of his fine Xenkeshi silk tunic sighed as she drew her hand down it. Ambrose's chest caught and held as she surveyed him. She looked up, pleased to see her own curiosity mirrored there, along with a hungry, metallic heat in his gaze.

"Ah, it could be touch, then." She purred, allowing him to tighten his hold around her further. "An arrogant man *would* wield a weapon he himself is weak to." Lower, lower still she brushed her fingertips as she spoke. Each word held his attention.

"I've been called arrogant," Ambrose confessed, his voice quiet and unconfident. The hand stopped at his ribcage.

Her other hand admired the angle of his jawline before rounding the curve of the golden bands that adorned his arm. They threatened to singe her with their heat, the metal hot despite the autumn air. She could feel each tense of muscle as his body reacted. Ambrose now appeared unwilling to speak, not wanting to interrupt her exploration of him.

"Hard to believe," she said, "with all your well-crafted words that a simple touch would be your undoing..."

"I assure you," he breathed, "you're undoing plenty."

They were too close now. Their dance at a standstill and voices low. She traced her hands back to his shoulders. "Really?"

"Are you unaware of the effect you have in that dress?"

"No," she said, mischief taking root. "Please elaborate."

He appeared less amused, an intensity to him as he said all at once, "You look otherworldly, like a sprite of Bethync come to embrace me in death."

She nudged him, playful. "Or to drag you back from the Summerlands to do it all over again?"

"That's the problem. I think I would let you drag me just about anywhere."

"Then I suppose you're lucky I'm not a temptress," she teased, heart fluttering at his confessions.

He looked down at her. A spark of green caught each time a firefly dawdled by. "Aren't you?"

"You tell me." She glided away from him in a slow spin. Then looked back, pleased with the awe on his face as he drank her in. She'd awed herself as well, shocked by her ability to be so forward. It felt like releasing her hair from tight braids, or the upward swing of climbing a tree.

Ambrose didn't hesitate to draw her back to him. This time, when he dipped her low, he removed his hand to caress down her laced front. She arched up in reaction and gasped before he spun her again, dizzier from his touch than from being twirled across the grass. She laughed in exhalation as they circled, foreheads touching each time they drew back together. If this was how the Xenkeshi danced, she was ruined for all future dances.

Her feet lost purchase in the grass. She tilted back, falling. Ambrose caught and followed her as they pressed into a nearby hedge. Leaves bunched against her back, twisting into her hair. His body was close, pressed into hers so that she was molded between his shape and the foliage behind her.

He straightened himself but didn't pull away. Instead, he kept one arm wrapped around her waist. With his other hand, he brushed a curl from her cheek. The heat from their dance increased every small sensation. Color rushed up from her toes to her ears, covering her body in a blush. His eyes bore into hers and she thought if she stared long enough she might forget her own name.

He reminded her, his voice just a rasp, "Kezerah." Why, when he said it, did it sound like a whole new name?

"Yes?" she heard her voice whisper.

His hand was like fire as it rose from her hip to smooth up along her dress before tracing along her collarbone, her neck. Then finally, carefully, he brought his fingertips to rest under her chin. She looked up at him through her lashes, but he tilted her to face him, their noses touched, lips just breaths apart. Her face cradled in his hands. She tried to break his spell by closing her eyes, but his stare still remained vivid in her mind, his warmth grew nearer. She felt herself lean in to meet him, and her breath caught just before his lips brushed her own.

"Rorrik is in the infirmary," Ikaika interjected from behind Ambrose. The chill in Ikaika's voice turned Kezerah's body to ice.

They broke apart. Ambrose's face looked pained as Kezerah recoiled, then he registered Ikaika's words.

"What? What happened?"

Unable to look Ikaika in the eye, Kezerah instead looked down at his boots. He wore practice armor covered in mud.

"He lost a duel," Ikaika said. His voice sounded like a stranger's, remote and foreign to her.

Ambrose spoke, tight-mouthed. "You two really couldn't keep it together for one night?"

Ikaika matched heat with cold. "Amusing, I was about to say the same thing to you."

Ambrose crossed his arms. "If kissing lands you in an infirmary, I'd say you're doing it wrong."

"That would depend completely on whom you're kissing, don't you think? Considering her favoring either of us starts a war."

Kezerah flinched, coming back to herself. A war. Death, families torn apart, homes ruined.

"I'm no Mind Melder," Ambrose hissed, "but I'd say that plan mirrors your own."

Ikaika laughed darkly. "My plan? I didn't have a plan. I wasn't raised to take advantage of those I care about."

"Don't," Ambrose commanded. "Don't speak on topics you know nothing about."

"Because you know so much? Ambrose, you were three years old. Whatever lies your father fed you—"

"My father does not lie to me. What did your mother tell you when she left? That she'd be right back? Where is she Ikaika? It's been a few years."

"She's seeking vengeance against the monster that locked her in a tower!"

"Monster?" Ambrose scoffed. "My father didn't slaughter an entire village in the night, filled with innocent people!"

"You're such an idiot. *She went there for you*! Because she knew you were there. If you hadn't been there, she wouldn't have been."

"Liar!" Ambrose lunged.

Before Kezerah could move they were upon each other, Ambrose's large frame dragging Ikaika to the ground as Ikaika's arm snaked around the back of Ambrose's neck.

They rolled, and she found her voice. "Stop! Ambrose, Ikaika! Stop it!"

This time they did not stop.

Ikaika's padding gave him an advantage to equal Ambrose's size. She ran forward, wishing whole heartedly she held Sway to rip them apart. Then suddenly, they were. Both boys slammed into opposing hedges. Ikaika looked like he planned to get up and go at Ambrose again.

Kezerah looked down at her palms. Had she done it? She looked up to see her father. Both of Elowren's outstretched hands restrained them with a Hold on Sway, preventing them from getting up.

"This ends here," Elowren's voice boomed in absolution. "This ends now," Ambrose and Ikaika stopped struggling, Elowren looked at the two of them, then locked his eyes on hers, anger and disappointment evident on his face. "Is that understood?"

Everyone nodded.

"Good, you're all needed in the Strategy Chamber."

He released them.

Ambrose asked before standing, "Rorrik—"

"Is being treated in the infirmary. He requires a splint," Elowren finished, with a glare in Ikaika's direction. "But he will heal. Come, the news is urgent."

Treaty

The walk from the maze to the War Chamber felt incredibly long. A complex mixture of vexation and elation swirled through Ambrose. His head spun. He tried to focus, mind muddled from almost kissing Kezerah, then ending up on the ground with Ikaika. The two trailed behind. He made sure not to look back at them. He imagined them whispering to one another; Kezerah assuring Ikaika it had all been a mistake. That he'd been a mistake.

Elowren led them with notably brisk steps. Back straight, gaze forward. Ambrose hoped he hadn't just ruined ties with the king. He should have held his temper. Damn Ikaika for getting under his skin, and damn himself for allowing him to. He damned Kezerah too, for good measure, but knew that was unfair. It was his own fault.

He'd shared a side of himself that felt like stepping into fog. No up, no down: each step a chance at free fall. Their dance had exposed more and more of him with each step. The truth had seemed to thrill her, and terrify him. And yet, he could not get her expression, upon Ikaika's entrance, out of his head. He'd watched her pull away, leaving him captured in the dream. He understood clearly now. Kezerah's feelings for Ambrose derived from somewhere fanciful and ethereal, while her feelings for Ikaika firmly rooted themselves in reality. In the drawing rooms, Ambrose had urged Ikaika to wake up, yet he'd been the one caught in the clouds.

Ambrose rolled his shoulders. His black rage boiled at Ikaika's other accusations: that his father would be cruel enough to lock his mother away, or his mother fragile enough to let him—like some princess in a tower.

Ambrose remembered her leaving, soundless in the night. That had been the easy part. It had been her return that raided his nightmares. Ambrose had cried for his mother, and his mother had come. The sight of her had terrified him, so much anger, so much blood. She'd stomped toward him, purposeful and ferocious. Her footfalls made heavier by her stomach, full with Ikaika.

Then Azalea's arms wrapped around him, not with words of reassurance for Ambrose, but a promise of violence against her Queen. Illija had faded back into the pitch of the doorway: A wraith vanishing into mist and smoke.

Until her armies returned. Again and again and again to burn down his home and attack his people. *'If you hadn't been there, she wouldn't have come.'*

Ambrose tried to pry his mind away from the image of the small child crying out for her mother, her tiny hand desperately grasping his as he helped her look, knowing her mother was no longer there. His throat caught as the smell engulfed him, choking him. He tried to swallow but couldn't.

A hand squeezed his bicep: Elowren. Ambrose tried to catch the breath that escaped him in a gasp. Elowren held his stare with patience, hand still steady on his arm.

Ambrose breathed in again, this time it came out smoother. He nodded, and looked away. Elowren released him.

They entered the War Chambers.

Ambrose distracted himself by looking around at the immense room. Maps, notes, and a large table carved into the shape of the Thrice Kingdoms stood before them. Miniature towers in the three crown's colors: amber, amethyst, and Aloran's glacial blue, marked the positions of the war. He examined them, seeing if anything had changed since his last council meeting. The portion of the Strand that snaked through Xenkesh had more Aloran figures on it, a small barricade piece on its divide. This troubled him. He pointed to the piece.

"Why is this barrier here?" he asked Elowren, as Kezerah and Ikaika followed through the door.

Elowren answered with practiced neutrality. "It is a dam. Alora currently controls the water supply emitted by the Xenkeshi Strand."

Ambrose went numb, ears ringing. The Strand encompassed nearly all of Xenkesh's water supply.

"When did this happen?" he demanded. He knew his tone was too rude to address a king but he didn't care and Elowren remained patient.

"Alora laid siege the moment you docked in Aveltra."

Truly ill now, the anger in Ambrose's veins kept him upright. "Why was I not told of this? Are you not our ally?"

But of course he knew the answer just as Elowren calmly stated it. "We are, as we are Alora's. We do not interfere in either affair. If your father had chosen to inform you, I would not have prevented him."

"Then why are we here now?" Ambrose demanded, thinking of his people going without water for weeks, the Lull's salty waves a reminder of their thirst. Ikaika also examined the map in a careful circle. Ambrose noted his brother didn't shy away from him, despite their brawl. He also noticed Ikaika's split lip. He envied Rorrik and fought the impulse to reassert himself as a threat. Ikaika's padding could only protect him from so many blows.

Elowren seemed to sense this, and moved between them as he spoke. "Because we have reached a turning point in the war, and because your father is no longer able to contact you as he pleases."

Ambrose went very still. "Where is my father?"

Elowren steepled his fingers, voice grave. "A messenger delivered word this evening of your father's capture by Aloran forces. I have written to confirm with Queen Illija, but the message will take time to return. However, this letter just arrived via a Xenkeshi spy which confirms enough."

Elowren took a scroll from his breast pocket and Ambrose snatched it from him. Reading over the words twice to be sure.

Elowren,

 If this letter finds you, I've made contact with one of my spies from inside the Aloran armies, based along the Xenkesh Strand. My army was defeated in an ambush as we attempted to reclaim our water supply and every soldier, but myself, was killed in the battle. I understand your position and do not seek your aid as anything other than a messenger. Ambrose is King Regent until I am either returned through trade or executed. Please tell my sons I love them, and for Ambrose to not forget what I told him upon our last meeting.

Thank you, old friend.

-Amarus Xenkesh, King of Xenkesh.

Ambrose's hands shook as he read the words over and over again, 'executed' seeming to become more and more bold as he scanned the page. The news of the dam now seemed so manageable compared to this.

"What happens now?" Kezerah asked her father. She sounded far away, like an echo.

Elowren answered Kezerah but spoke to the room. "It appears we are at a crossroads. As King Regent, Ambrose will need to decide how he wishes to proceed. Our treaty, our alliance, is still in place if all so wish it, but it does not yet bear your seal. If you wish to remain in the treaty—" Elowren gestured with his hands, a parchment cascading through the air to the open table. He addressed Ambrose directly now. "Then you will need to sign the agreement of the terms decided by myself, Illija, and your father before you. It is also possible for you to cease battle with Alora—as I'm sure they will do—ending the war."

There it was. An end to the war, at the expense of his father's life, and the countless others who had so long sacrificed for their kingdom.

Elowren hesitated.

"Or?" Ambrose prompted him.

"Or, you could choose not to sign. I would permit you to return to Xenkesh, and the procedure from there would be of your own volition—As would mine." Elowren's tone made the threat he posed as an opponent clear.

Ikaika spoke. "What cause does my mother have to leave Amarus alive?"

Ambrose's temper flared, relieved for the release at a target. "Is his capture not good enough for you? You need his head before the night is through?"

Ikaika seemed more controlled in temper than earlier, or more removed overall. "I simply mean, knowing my mother and the hatred she has for your father, that it's out of character for her to leave him alive."

"You speak of her brutality as if describing her favorite color," Ambrose said in disgust.

Elowren raised his hands and Ambrose silenced himself, being thrown across the grass still a vivid memory.

"It is unlike Illija...to take prisoners." Elowren chose his words carefully. "However, they apprehended Amarus at the Strand in Xenkesh. Your mother is in—"

"Thistle," Ikaika finished, "or well on her way to Tiertyde, as is Amarus himself. I received word from my mother that his navy had made headway."

"A miscalculation I myself made," said Elowren. "It appears he sent his personal forces on without him, choosing to try and take back the Strand with an alternative infantry."

Ambrose ruminated on his brother's accidental slip. Amarus had never planned to take to the seas himself. The attack had always been meant as a naval battle that disrupted Aloran-Elastor sea-faring trade and an eventual ground assault. Ikaika believed Amarus would attack Tiertyde himself. Which meant his father must have found the spy nestled in their court. The excitement of the revelation fell away. He had no way of asking his father to whom he'd dispersed the information.

His father had left him with many unanswerable questions. Why had Amarus sent his personal infantry for a direct attack on Tiertyde? Ambrose had warned him of Illija's ability to come up from behind. Why risk his best soldiers? This wasn't a move his father would usually make, but coerced by a halted water supply? He must have grown incredibly desperate. Why hadn't he summoned Ambrose back to court? Ambrose could have helped...Could he still? He looked over the letter again, picking it for information not on the page.

'And for Ambrose to not forget what I told him upon our last meeting.'

This Ambrose knew, and remembered well. He had played it back several times since coming here, trying to gain direction.

Upon adjourning the council meeting, Amarus had requested

Ambrose stay behind. The Aloran army had made camp along the Strand, headed east towards what Ambrose now realized must have been the beginnings of damming their water supply at its divide.

AMARUS HAD SPOKEN LOW, the words solely for Ambrose's ears. "I know the consequences of war affect you greatly, my son."

Ambrose answered automatically. "I understand their necessity to protect us."

His father nodded. "But you disagree with my choice of bringing in more soldiers."

It was not a question, and Ambrose responded honestly. "I don't know if lowering the age of recruitment will benefit us. Children of that age can hardly lift a sword, let alone Bond." As he said it he pictured Rorrik at that age and the idea made him sick.

His father looked solemn but did not contradict him. "My hands are tied. Illija invades with more and more force each day. If I do not act, she will soon overwhelm us." He paused, then said thoughtfully, "But you brought up fair points in this meeting, Ambrose, and I do not disagree with your assessment. If we had more allies, or could even reason with the Alorans to seek peace..." Amarus combed through his thick beard with fingers in contemplation. "Perhaps it's time we seek you Haven in Elastor. Ikaika has been there for some time now. Maybe the time with Elowren has softened his heart, or perhaps the young princess can be reasoned with."

Ambrose had seen the ability to stall the age amendment made in the meeting. "If that's what you wish, I'll go."

Amarus nodded. "Then it is agreed. You and your brother both —yes both of you, don't look at me like that—You both will go to Elastor, and seek an alternative to this war. But Ambrose, while peace is the ideal, I ask you, as a King, do not choose what is right. Choose what is right for your Kingdom."

HIS FATHER HAD EXPECTED Ambrose to make the best choice for Xenkesh, for his people. Had he not done that by seeking out favor with Kezerah? Was there more he could do now?

He looked at Ikaika, whose expression simmered with loathing just below the surface. Ikaika had no attachment to Amarus or his brothers, and nothing to lose from their defeat. He couldn't be reasoned with. Ambrose knew Kezerah cared, and that he presently cared too much, but that needed more time, and time was not something his father could afford.

He looked down at the page again, the possibility of his father's execution excruciating. *'until I am either returned through trade or executed.'*

'Returned through trade.' He looked back up at Ikaika, seeing him not as a younger brother, a romantic adversary, or Aloran scum, but as *the* Aloran scum—the only heir to Alora. His mother's precious son. *'Do what is right for your Kingdom.'*

He folded the paper away into his pocket. "May I have the evening to converse with Rorrik on the news of tonight?" He looked away from the treaty, knowing that if he signed it now, his options would be limited. He dared not finish his thought, knowing Ikaika could very well be privy to them.

He held the weight of Elowren's gaze until Elowren turned away. "I will have your decision by morning."

Ambrose began to bow, then caught himself. As a king, he no longer had anyone to bow to.

He moved to leave, and Kezerah looked as if she might say something, but stopped herself. Ambrose imagined it had taken a lot of effort and thought bitterly that the effort had possibly been made on Ikaika's behalf. He made a quick exit, shutting the door, just a little too hard, behind him.

THE DOOR SLAMMING INVITED a new layer of silence. Ikaika stared at the map but his vision blurred and ears rang. For once, he felt pain without a migraine. He was aware Kezerah stood next to him, but she kept her eyes averted. It was as if his mind had slowed, choosing only to play the moment of Kezerah and Ambrose together in the maze.

Why couldn't he have just left Rorrik wailing in the practice yards? His fury had been satiated the moment he'd dislocated

Rorrik's shoulder, with nothing but guilt left behind. Rorrik's crumpled form had possessed Ikaika to think he should make amends. The empty feeling in his chest had compelled him to get Ambrose in order to do so.

For the thousandth time, Kezerah leaned into Ambrose's embrace, gazing at him as if he were the moon and stars. A fresh wave of nausea rolled through Ikaika, and he suddenly needed to be as far away from her as possible.

"With leave, Your Majesty," he forced out indifferently, "I'd like to return to my rooms."

"Yes of course," Elowren said. Ikaika caught Kezerah's movement from the corner of his eye. "Kezerah, I would like you to remain behind for a word."

Elowren's tone quickened Ikaika's pace to the door. While unaware of how close Kezerah had come to breaking the treaty, Ikaika guessed the king worried for its health. Elowren needn't fear, however. Ikaika never intended to report Kezerah's choices to his mother. Unlike King Amarus, Ikaika had been raised to release those disinterested. He thought of the Xenkeshi king, captured and awaiting his fate. He wished he felt satisfaction from the news. Yet, when he turned inward, only the hollowed out pain surfaced. He knew at that moment, he'd never had what it took to be a king. All he could think, when he'd looked at a map—colored with his kingdom's victory—and back at Kezerah, was that none of it seemed to matter anymore. He left the King of Elastor to confer with his heir.

"I'M GOING to make this abundantly clear, so that there are no questions or missteps in the future," Elowren said. Kezerah stared at the door Ikaika had walked out of, his steps as silent and empty as a shadow. Her heart twisted and she kept her eyes low, as her father continued stonily. "Our villages remain safe, our crops growing, our people fed, because we are not at war. A war that precariously resides on either side of our borders, and relies on our complete impartiality with either ally."

"Yes, Father."

"I allow you much because I understand the burden placed upon you. Do not force my hand in regaining some of that control."

"Yes, Father."

"You may dance, speak, and treat them equally. You may not show favor, bias, or prejudice one way or the other. From here on out, if you dance with one, you dance with the other next, or you dance with neither one. Do I make myself clear?" He enunciated the last question.

"Yes, Father."

His tone softened. "I know you and Ikaika are close friends. I know the way he looks at you makes things more difficult."

Kezerah wanted to plead for him to stop. She lowered her head. If only he knew how horrid she'd been. How close she had come to ruining everything. What would he think of her then? He would be disgusted by her treatment of Ikaika, by her. Tears pricked at her eyes and she rubbed at them. She had shown him enough of her weaknesses for one night.

"But perhaps some time apart is necessary."

"How much time?" The words caught in her throat. Even now it felt like too much time had passed. The moment lingered and Kezerah snapped her head up to survey him. Her father, renowned for reassurance, had nothing to say. He allowed the silence to speak for him.

"Father, please, no." She knew how pathetic she sounded, knew she proved his point. She begged regardless. "I'll do what I'm told. I'll behave. I promise I will. Please."

He looked at her, immense sadness and pity in his eyes. For a heartbeat, she hated him for it.

"Once the treaty has resumed, I'll move Ikaika to the Winter Quarters. He can join the night regiment and get some training in—his migraines are lessened when most are asleep. It will be pleasant for him. You will be seated with us at meals. Andarios may join you, if he wishes."

This was it. The cumulation of her failures. She'd always been better in theory, and now she paid the price for her efforts. Efforts that had never amounted to enough.

He seemed to be waiting for her answer. She managed to breathe out, "Yes, Father," one last time before he excused her to her rooms. Straight to her rooms.

THE BITTER BREEZE blew in from the north. Ambrose cursed Alora under his breath as he bundled his black silks more tightly around him. The Winter Quarters appeared to be the most worn of the castle wings: drafty halls, carpets run through by frequent comings and goings, and an absence of sun that graced all other castle wings. Ambrose wondered why Elowren chose them as his quarters, and not one of the grander chambers.

'Because he puts others before himself,' he thought while he stalked towards the infirmary. *'Because he's good.'* Ambrose wanted to be good. He knew his father was good.

Ambrose recalled his father long ago speaking of Elowren kindly, but in the same breath calling him a fool. Was Elowren a fool? Ambrose didn't know anymore. The king didn't carry himself like one. Perhaps that was a luxury that came with years of peace.

Ambrose pressed his lips together, and winced at their dryness, chapped from the cold. Thrice, he hoped they hadn't felt like that when he'd begun to kiss Kezerah. An almost kiss. A stolen moment. Ikaika's jealousy and possessiveness all over his face. Ikaika could go on believing there had been no plan in place for himself, that he had been raised better, but Ambrose knew a side of their mother that Ikaika did not.

Illija's battle strategies were methodical, drawn out: the long game. Ikaika might not have been aware of why he had been placed here, but Ambrose knew better. Ambrose just didn't know why *he* had been placed here. His father's erratic choices in his absence left him all the more displaced. He'd thought he'd known why he was in Elastor. He'd believed that he understood.

"Just a bit longer, and we'll release Prince Rorrik back to his rooms," said a wan-faced healer, standing in the small infirmary door. Ambrose thanked the healer and turned on a heel. The music beckoned high spirits to frolic in the grass. Ambrose tramped around the party's back, giving it a wide berth. Nobody would catch him dancing anytime soon.

Once in his room, he fell onto his bed with a huff. The parchment crinkled in his pocket and he straightened it out to look it over again. Whatever Amarus' original plan, it must have failed. Now his father requested his son's help, and Ambrose was hesitating.

Why? What did Ikaika matter next to all that this letter stood for? *'He's my brother.'* Ambrose fought the sentiment. Sentimentality bore little weight in the decisions of a king. *'Do what is right for your Kingdom.'* His father was right for his kingdom. He needed his father, he needed to be callous. He closed his eyes. Ikaika was petulant, arrogant, easily influenced by his mother and boring. His decent qualities hidden in some delusion only Kezerah could see. Ambrose rolled his eyes. Perhaps he could do what his father asked of him.

"Alright, before you say anything—It was a draw."

Ambrose shoved the paper into his pocket, then sat up to look Rorrik over. Gauze wrapped his arm, suspended from a sling, a plum-black bruise stamped on his jawline. Ikaika, too, quite clearly harbored pent up frustration. And had taken it out on Rorrik.

"It's worse than it looks—Dar can tell you."

Ambrose shook his head. Their circumstances felt as battered and bruised as his brother. He had no desire to tell Rorrik their situation. He didn't have a choice. They needed to act fast. He pulled the letter back out, handing the crumpled contents to Rorrik. "Father's been captured."

Rorrik's eyes scanned the letter over. His free arm shook as he held the paper up to one of the lanterns. "We need to take Ikaika captive, now," he said after reading.

Ambrose loathed the spike of envy he felt for Rorrik's immediate conclusion. He stayed seated, hands planted firmly on his legs. "Let's talk this out. If we do that, I don't know if Elowren will let us rejoin the treaty."

"Forget the treaty! We have to get our father back!" Rorrik's words echoed Ambrose's heart. He just wished he could shut off his mind, and the sharp twist in his gut.

"I know," Ambrose said. "I just want to make sure we're making the right decision. Acting in haste could ruin everything."

"Acting without haste could kill our father," Rorrik said. "Ikaika will be in bed. We have an ally in the city. There's a loud party outside, and the streets of Heartsglove are full. We need to act."

Rorrik's rash, foolhardy, and fiery temperament often worked against him. His moves ranged from predictable to repetitive, the most bold attack always played. But Rorrik was also right. For this plan to work, it would have to happen tonight. *Now.*

Ambrose thought through how it needed to be done. He needed to get into his brother's rooms unseen. What would he do if Ikaika was in Kezerah's room? Or if she'd chosen to visit him? Kezerah would fight him. He would have to disarm her. Ambrose dropped his head between his arms, and tangled hands in his hair.

He couldn't do this.

"Ikaika has Haven here—" Ambrose's voice sounded dull to his own ears. Perhaps he wasn't actually speaking. "—An attack on him would be an attack on Elowren. We gain our father, but lose too much in exchange." Silence buzzed between them. One heartbeat. Two. Three.

"Say it," Rorrik hissed.

"Say what?" Ambrose asked, confused, guilty.

"We lose too much in the exchange *for our father's life.*" Rorrik's whisper pitched as he made his accusations. "But what do you gain from it? A crown, peace, a lovely princess, perchance?"

Ambrose stood. "You're tossing peace in the middle as if it's a copper among silvers." Rorrik's words shook him, as did the fear they might hold even an ounce of truth. He didn't know what held him back. Not usurping his father but... "I'm not making these decisions lightly, but I am making them as a king. As father asked of me."

Rorrik rattled the paper, like a threat. "I read the same letter you did. Father's intentions, *the King's* intentions, are clear. We are meant to bring Ikaika to Xenkesh and make a bargain for his life."

"And if she does not accept the exchange?" Ambrose let 'she' linger, not wanting to unhinge Rorrik, or himself further. "She is ruthless, Ror. She *left* us, she *left* Ikaika." He heard his voice break and he hated himself for it. "What do we do then? Tuck him back in his bed, and tell Elowren, 'Sorry, we thought that kidnapping scheme would pan out better. Here's your ward,' and hope he lets us back into the treaty?"

Rorrik stared back at Ambrose in either pity or disgust, or both. "Ambrose, if Illija kills our father, we kill Ikaika. That's how hostages work."

Ambrose thought he might throw up. He made his voice low, trying to reason with him, with himself. "If we kill Ikaika, kill our *brother*, we will never have peace. We lose this war."

Rorrik, for once, matched his cool tone. "What makes you think that Illija will give us peace? Was it not you that she barged in on, covered in the blood of our people? Only fleeing when the fight was lost? Is it not odd that she always avoids crossing the Xenkeshi border herself, but burns down a village that you're in?"

Rorrik's words hit their mark, Ambrose faltered at how close they echoed Ikaika from earlier. '*She went there for you.*'

"If the burning of Ravysh is truly upon my shoulders," he said, "then I will request Illija's terms for peace. If it's my death she requests, then you will be king." Ambrose became more and more certain as the words came out. He would relent himself if it meant sparing his people's lives. That, he could live with or die for. He would not become a monster for peace. "The war will end with you."

Rorrik shook his head, eyes awash with bitter tears. "Ambrose..."

Ambrose needed to placate him, until the treaty was signed, until he could sign his father's life away. "We can speak more in the morn—"

The reverberation of bells and shouts startled them into silence. Ambrose pushed himself in front of Rorrik as he opened the door. Rorrik followed.

Servants dashed through the halls, opening and closing doors, and yelling to one another.

"What's going on?" Rorrik asked, watching the chaos in the pre-dawn night. Guests came from their rooms, and lanterns were relit, ensconcing the dimly lit corridor. Was Elastor under attack? But no. The servants did not scramble or flee, they checked guest rooms like an activity much practiced.

"Check the walls!"

"The stairwell is clear!"

"They're searching for something," Ambrose said.

"Hey!" Rorrik yelled. They jumped to either side of their door as guards pushed past. The guards ignored him, as closets opened and beds were checked.

Ambrose spotted Lady Sorrel in the hall. Her head craned out one of the corridor's high arched windows, hands drawn up to her high collar and light orange hair spun into a braid for the evening.

Ambrose approached her. "What's happened?"

The noble woman smoothed out her long satin nightgown, not in modesty, but appraisal. This was usual of Yara, but now her movements appeared more like a nervous tick rather than true flirtation.

"I'm not entirely certain of the details, but it appears both Princess Kezerah and Prince Ikaika... are missing."

"Missing?" Ambrose knew he'd misheard.

Yara Sorrel nodded, thin lips grim. "A guard found the princess' bed empty, then checked Prince Ikaika's. I heard the servants gossiping as they came up the stairs. Apparently there was a note and everything. They're gone..."

The ground became too light and Ambrose too heavy. He ignored the dropping sensation in his stomach and tried not to jump to conclusions.

Rorrik did it for him. "Well, there goes the treaty."

Capture

Fresh from the meeting with her father, Kezerah erupted into a world drained of color. She flung herself onto her bed, then soaked her mattress in tears. Her heart, which had felt like an empty well in the Strategy Chambers, now overflowed and overwhelmed her.

'Be calm, neutral, impartial—'

It had always felt so simplistic to her, so within her abilities. She'd been informed relentlessly since she could walk: Don't pit kingdoms against each other. Easy. Unless you were an idiot.

She attempted to scour the emotions from her face with the back of her hand. The deluge persisted. Hot tears and a runny nose refused to cease. Instead she thrust her face into her pillow, and released a muffled scream.

'I am an idiot,' she thought, allowing herself to drown low in her thoughts. *'I'm ridiculous.'* Because if it had not been Ambrose—quick, witty, and passionate—it could have been Ikaika. Ikaika, who had been her late night confidant, and endless source of both comfort and glee; who tolerated her fully and made her feel beautiful.

She hadn't noticed her feelings for Ikaika the same way she never noticed breathing. It happened effortlessly and naturally. Unfortunately, she wasn't permitted to breathe. Nor dance, nor do any of the things she desired to do, nor kiss whom she desired.

'That would depend completely on whom you are kissing... Considering her favoring either of us starts a war.' Ikaika's words. Cold, remote, removed. She had failed him.

She had tried her best and, as expected, fell short. Perhaps she'd avoided trying her entire life because, in her heart of hearts, she'd known this would be the outcome. Yet, she'd never been able to conjure the horror of seeing Ikaika's disgust and disappointment in her. The shocking memory of him emerging from the shadows mingled with her feelings of elation just moments before in a dizzying contrast. He hated her. He must. He couldn't. She couldn't imagine a world in which Ikaika looked at her the way he had. The idea of him never being accessible through their balconies again churned her stomach. She'd fix this. She at least owed him an apology for the pain she had caused him. She'd start there.

It was well into the evening now, but the night was still wrought with the sounds of celebration. Right now, her parents would be distracted by party guests and paperwork. By morning, her forbiddance to speak with Ikaika would begin.

Time had passed. Would he see her? She wiped her eyes and remembered Nurse wasn't there to attend her. With effort, she removed her dress. A layer of gossamer tore and she didn't bother with the bracelets. She laced up her boots, changed into the first plain dress she found, and opened her balcony doors.

Ikaika's rooms were dark, but they often were. She lifted the latch, fearing it would be locked but relieved when it rose. Her eyes adjusted to the darkness. No lantern lit for late night reading. A pile of clothes tossed in the corner. His bed lay empty. She spun around the space.

No Ikaika.

Had her father already moved his rooms? No, many of his belongings remained: books in place and bed made. She walked over to it, the scent clean and familiar, then she spotted the parchment on his pillow.

IKAIKA'S HEAD could not break away from Kezerah's thoughts, her mind in a never-ending loop. He thought witnessing her moment in the maze with Ambrose had been horrible. Kezerah's perspective of the moment collapsed him onto his bed. Mercilessly it continued, and Ikaika pressed his face into his pillow as if that could stifle it.

'Arms wrapped around her. Her name. His name. Warmth at her lips. Ikaika's own face, unfeeling as he interrupted them.' Unfeeling? How could she read him so wrong? It had felt like his blood had been replaced with glacier water, pain tore through his mind and soul as the two of them embraced.

It began again, this time with echoes from the guards' thoughts in the corridors, and the nobility in the meadow. His mind unraveled.

He could sense Kezerah's emotions heightened as she thought through them: Sadness, confusion, and fear roiled out of order as her mind spun. What did she fear? Did she think he would seriously hold the treaty against her? Was she sad because her father would undoubtedly put an end to her and Ambrose's flagrant flirtations?

He found himself analyzing her every laugh at Ambrose's lewd humor and bile rose up in his throat. He couldn't think like this, not with everyone else's thoughts claiming purchase in his mind.

He got up, grabbing a piece of parchment from his desk and dotting his quill with ink. With each word he became more and more sure, as if the promise of relief staved his mind from feasting on thoughts. He regained enough control to get his words out.

Your Majesty, King Elowren.

I must thank you for graciously welcoming me into your home. It has been both my honor and pleasure to receive Haven as your ward. I have learned much, and know there is still much more I could learn. Unfortunately, I am unable to do so. I have left for the Temples of Estora. I fear if I do not make the journey now it will be too late. I write this to you not only in thanks, but as proof that there has been no foul play. I have been fairly treated, well past what anyone deserves. I leave of my own free will, and will journey back to Alora after I have completed my training in one year's time. For now, this is goodbye, but I look forward to seeing you as an ally in our many years ahead.

Sincerely,

Ikaika, Crown Prince of Alora

He donned his cloak and quietly moved outside his balcony doors, then grabbed the ledge of the tower, and climbed.

KEZERAH LET the letter drop from her hands: a goodbye not even addressed to her. It slid back onto the pillow as if never picked up. Ikaika was not just gone, he wasn't coming back. Her breaths came out in short rasps. It wouldn't be a night regimen, or sleeping quarters that kept them apart. Ikaika was leaving—Ikaika had *left* the Solstice Court—left her. He'd stolen away in the night to be away from her. He was probably halfway to Heartsglove by now.

Heartsglove.

Ambrose had acted strangely about Heartsglove. He'd said it was dangerous. Did he know more, could he help? Kezerah banished the thought as she had it. Had she learned nothing? Ikaika would never listen if she brought Ambrose with her. She paced near the balcony. She wouldn't endanger Andarios, but if Ikaika was in danger, whether he forgave her or not, she couldn't leave him. She'd find and warn him before he got too far. The girl who begged in the Autumn hall for help was of no use here. She had ignored her first instincts and relied on aid to save Andarios and had nearly run out of time. She could use her shortcut to the city through the maze. If she hurried, she could cut Ikaika off by at least the Lunar Channel. She nodded, a plan in place.

Without looking down, Kezerah grasped at the notches in the wall outside Ikaika's door and climbed. It took all she had not to run as she moved through the halls, staying in the shadows as people wandered past. Each bend along the way, she expected to catch up, but Ikaika was nowhere in sight. She fastened her cloak tightly as she stalked past party-goers. Her shoulder's only relaxed as she reached the maze.

Focused on her task, Kezerah loosened the stones she had meant to wriggle through on her first journey into Heartsglove. She flattened onto her stomach and inched her way through the small hole. The hard earth tore several seams in her dress and cloak, metal bracelets getting caught on loose rocks. She didn't stop to remove them. Everything but forward momentum felt like it leaked away too much time.

She landed in a small stream. The water soaked her boots, as it rushed past her into various paths to reach its destination. She followed the water's irrigation until she saw the passage she'd been looking for: a thick grate barring her way from the crops outside the walls. Kezerah pulled, and it groaned as it gave way despite its heft. One leg, and then the other, Kezerah slid down the stone drain, and kicked the next grating with ferocity. Each slam of her boots into the corroded iron crumpled the bars, loosening it until, finally, it clattered down to the base of the castle. Bits of stone fell to the ground along with the bent grate. She followed it, and landed on the wet soil as it trickled into the crops stretching out before her.

Kezerah felt a moment of triumph but refocused. Find Ikaika. Warn him away from the city, and then explain tonight. What she would explain, she didn't know, but once she found him she knew it would come to her.

She looked at the surrounding crops, expecting to see nothing but feeling disappointed all the same. She ran down the trail, not stopping to catch her breath until she reached the bridge arching over the Lunar Channel; the ice opals inside rendered invisible by the new moon.

Heartsglove's nighttime festivities glittered as if only just getting started. Strings of lantern light criss-crossed from building to building. Caravans opened wood paneled doors to display makeshift puppet shows. A Bethync monk stood on a platform, retelling Ellas' story while drums beat to the Sway of earthquakes. Swaths of black fabrics danced in celebration. Heartsglove made a swarm of ants upon fallen fruit look less packed together. Panic seized her as she realized she would have to spot Ikaika in a crowd of thousands.

Sellers bellowed their prices, and chords strummed in all directions. The memory of Ikaika squeezing her hand as they wove through the streets openly mocked her. She recognized the fish seller. She pulled her cloak all the tighter about her hair and cast her eyes down, waiting for him to stop shouting. He turned to her.

"Ah, come to buy some sweet fish? It's an Aloran delicacy!"

She shook her head and kept her eyes trained down. "I'm hoping you've seen an Aloran boy—or young man. He's about this high, tan, dark curls, dark eyes and wearing all black."

He'd turned his attention elsewhere as she described Ikaika, and rolled his eyes when she finished. "Young lady, it's the Nighttide Festival. 'Wearing black' is not a useful descriptor." He scrutinized her muddy dress: a dark emerald velvet noticeable in the light. She cursed. She did not need more to make her stand out. "Unless one was describing yourself," the merchant added with disapproval. "Didn't your mother teach you to respect the dead?"

Bells sounded repetitively in the distance, and she wondered at the time, not having the moon for reference. She rushed on, not bothering a goodbye. Other vendors all had similar responses. Though one woman kindly asked, "Where did you last see him? Maybe he went somewhere familiar you both might find?"

At first Kezerah found the advice useless, but then an idea formed. She thanked the woman and retraced her steps, in search of the curry tavern they'd eaten in. If the same server was there, they would recognize Ikaika, and possibly point her in the direction he might go in order to get to the Temples.

Deeper in the city, the road became impossible to walk, let alone run. Traffic stood still as bodies smashed together. At this rate it would be impossible to catch up. She made a turn off the main market street. The further she journeyed in, the further off the sounds of the market became. Soon, little to no people passed by in the alleyways. Relief fell upon Kezerah, nothing but her feet and the soft sound of taverns with closed doors could be heard. She picked up her pace to offset lost time. Well into darker side streets, she kept an eye out for the green beetle she remembered being stamped on the sign above the entrance.

She wished she had Ambrose as a guide—the memory of his steady confidence through the streets at once reassuring—then she cursed herself for the thought.

Kezerah stopped to rub at her toes through her boots, tightening the clasps to better secure her aching feet. She knew she took too long. The streets zig-zagged beyond the complexity of someone used to familiar castle grounds all her life. She sped up, choosing a turn at random. Then another.

As she turned again, the alley came to an abrupt end. She kicked the wall and let out a growl of frustration. This was useless, she was—

"You appear lost." An unfamiliar voice said from behind her.

She turned, a narrow man with a shaggy beard walked toward her. A cross alley separated them, but as she looked, another, wider man appeared on the left of it. "No sign of him this way—oh." The shaggy man held up a hand in silence. The wider man followed the first's line of sight and fell into step.

Whatever their business in this alley, Kezerah wanted no part of it. Her eyes darted from one to the other, then she steadied her breathing, and spoke with as much confidence as she could muster. "No, I just don't have a strong appreciation for walls—" She gave her friendliest flash of teeth. "Thank you, I'll be on my way now."

The first man kept walking towards her, two more followed behind him. He smiled. "Listen, if you're lost, we can help you get where you need to go. Unless... you're also looking for someone? Maybe we can help." The slimy texture of his voice ruined his words, and the fact that another man now moved in from the street to her right.

She counted their growing numbers. Five. '*Sure,*' she told herself, '*I can take on five men with the fighting lessons I quit when I was ten.*' She internally cursed herself for losing interest in useful skills so easily. "No, that's alright," she kept her tone light. "I'm being expected at the Green Beetle—by several burly men with war hammers, so I'd best be on my way."

She made as if to move, to test their reactions. It wasn't good.

A few chuckled, but held their positions, each barred her option for escape.

"I've never heard of the Green Beetle before," the slimy man said, conversationally.

"Oh really? They have the best curry in Heartsglove." She heard the flicker of fear in her own voice and tried to swallow it. "You should try it." She moved to the right, where just the one man stood, thinking she could likely slip past him.

"Maybe I will," the man said, toying with her as he raised hands glittering with rings. "I have heard of the Solstice Court though," he grinned yellow teeth. "They've been waking the dead with their bells clanging. Half of the Elastian royal guards are in the market now searching for their missing prince and princess."

The lackeys looked to their assumed leader, and back at her. Kezerah knew that wide-eyed recognition when she saw it. She needed a new tactic.

"Ah, sounds like they'd pay quite a lot for a princess' return. Unharmed." This seemed reasonable. They'd stumbled across the Soul Heir, what left was there to do but catch and release her for a reward? The man stalked close enough now she could smell him, ale and several days sweat potent in the air.

"We're already being paid." He snapped his gold clad fingers.

Kezerah tried to flee the moment the Bond magick activated. Her bracelets locked into place around her wrists while her boots came together by their metal clasps. Momentum worked against her and Kezerah tripped and slammed against the side wall. One of the man's calloused hands caught her bound wrists. Kezerah withheld a yelp and tried to steady her breathing.

"By whom?" she asked, eyeing his rings. "Xenkesh?"

The man spoke, and she turned away from his breath, "Not today."

"You won't receive a higher reward from either neighboring kingdom," she asserted. "We are allies to both. Your effort is wasted."

A laugh passed around the circle.

"Yes, your 'peace' is something we're all well aware of." He moved his other hand down to her neck. She shuddered, trying to break free of her bindings with minimal results. "But I've found that desperation for power and control always leads to the best pay."

A man in the back shifted from foot to foot. "But, uh, what about the prince? Don't we need him to—"

"This changes our plans. I'll get word to mine, you to yours. Tell the little lordling we have the Soul Heir. Let him decide if he still wants to divide our resources."

'The prince.' Ikaika. Kezerah struggled harder. Whatever these people wanted, the fact that they looked for Ikaika meant he was in danger. Her bracelets welded tighter together and dug into her wrists and arms.

The shaggy man leered down at her, then his hand returned to hold her jaw, his rough thumb rubbing her cheek. "You know, you're actually quite the looker up close." He smoothed the thumb to brush against her bottom lip.

Kezerah lashed forward, biting down with as much force as she could manage. She spit out the foul taste of mold and tried to break free with his concentration shifted.

The bracelets slackened momentarily as he jerked back. Then the back of his hand connected with the left side of her face and she crashed to the ground, smacking hard on the stone street. She cried out and pain jarred her head and vision. She'd never been struck before, the shock and humiliation of it almost worse than the ache in her cheek and temple. Her mouth was too wet; she spit to breathe, seeing blood splatter out as she did.

Murmurs and objections passed through her captors. "Oi, you can't—I mean... she's the Soul Heir," one said.

A force connected with her stomach, leaving her gasping for air. Several of her captors took fretful steps back alongside hushed shouts of panic. The Bond Wielder sounded impatient.

"I don't pledge myself to any of your earthly propaganda." Hands scraped and grabbed at her shoulders and waist as she was lifted. The briny smell of the sea made her wretch. The pain in her stomach doubled when she was roughly flung over the leader's shoulder. Kezerah cried out as the lack of control in her limbs mingled with the pain. "Now, tell your leader to meet us in the Ruby hideout before I see just what your savior of storms can do."

The lackeys scrambled. Her captor began running too. Kezerah's head lifted and fell, a disorienting pang shot through her right temple from where she'd hit the ground. *'Scream,'* she thought. *'Scream.'* But she was dizzy, and what she managed came out stifled and weak.

Cobblestones blurred beneath her. Echoes of footsteps and a ruckus of voices caused her further confusion. Alleyway after alleyway rushed by, the warm glow of Nighttide festivities right out of reach. Cloth flaps brushed past her in a torrent of red and silk as they entered a house. More voices joined and stairs creaked beneath them. Each step shortened her breaths and a tumultuous fear began to build up in Kezerah. The man's hold on her slackened. She fell back. The lurch of her stomach only stopped when she dropped to the ground. Her body hit a splintered wood floor and a new wave of agony surged through her side.

Her bracelets unclasped and reclasped behind her. A door opened and closed, excitement and arguments muffled on the other side. Kezerah took in her new surroundings. She must be close to the main road. The light that filtered through the singular window—coated in ages of dust and grime—looked like the smolder of lanterns. She squinted through the gloom. Broken cider bottles and old wine crates littered a corner of the otherwise incomplete and abandoned room.

The door opened once more. The slimy man entered. She recalled his touch and recoiled, her legs scrunched up while her arms remained bound behind her.

Then, a second figure walked in.

"Dyllian."

Kezerah didn't understand. His familiar features in this strange place immediately relieved her. She forced away her first thought, that he'd come here to save her. He looked too at ease around the debris and scum. She settled into the truth of it and glared. "It's a shame my opinion of you is so low, or I might have been surprised."

His pale face returned her disdain from under his cloak like an irritated moon. The hood dropped back in a belated reveal. "Admit it," he said. "You're a bit surprised."

"Not in the slightest," Kezerah lied. "I saw Ruby district scarves as we came in. Desperation suits you."

"I don't—this is a hideout," he snapped. "The location is meant to keep meetings discreet." Fear fled her as she surveyed him, his stature more similar to a rat than a person. This was Dyllian, easily riled and forever pompous with bluster.

Kezerah cocked a brow. "I know how brothels work, you don't have to spell it out for me." She leaned forward, wishing he were in spitting distance. "Don't tell me you're still waiting for that dance."

Dyllian burned such a deep red Kezerah wondered if he would continue straight into purple. Vanquished by innuendo. Unfortunately he was not.

"You know, when Syle found the Soul Heir skulking in the lower city, I didn't bat an eye." Dyllian surveyed her with a shake of his head. "Others don't see you. They're all in wonder of you. Don't get me wrong, my parents also fed me stories of Ellas, Ioni, Basha and all of your ilk. The first time I visited the Solstice Court I couldn't wait to see my stories come to life. Everyone crowded in to see this supposed living myth, and I pushed my way to the front. Do you know what I saw?"

Kezerah adjusted her weight and braced herself to better withstand Dyllian's confirmation of all her fears. "A really bored twelve year old?"

"I saw nothing. I saw a girl playing dress-up; pantomiming old traditions and being doted upon for what she couldn't do. You're not a symbol of hope, you're a halt in progress. You are as unchanged as the first time I met you." Dyllian paced and threw a hand her way. "And you know what? You ending up here tonight proves it all the more. You're a puppet in need of puppeteers, a figurehead meant to be led into a decision rather than make it yourself. You were supposed to be more than some girl sneaking off in the night!"

Kezerah expected the truth to hurt, but the blow struck without momentum. A subdued hit compared to what she told herself. She already knew what she stood for and how she matched up beside it. "I wouldn't have ended up here if you hadn't brought me here. I was —" Her mind returned to her, "Where is Ikaika?"

Dyllian crossed his arms. "We don't know. We haven't found him yet. I didn't necessarily order your abduction," he said with a pointed glare at the Bond Weilder, Syle, "—but there's undeniable merit to the leverage that feeds into my plans."

"Don't forget that it benefits more than just your cause," hissed Syle. "We're not done here." Kezerah flinched at the sound of his voice. But they'd just given her important information. Ikaika was safe. The aching in her ribs lessened as her body untangled itself in relief. Now, she needed to find out more.

"Why do you want Ikaika? He's not your monarch or your kingdom's heir apparent, demanding terms from him won't lead to anything."

Dyllian looked at her, head tilted to the side in disbelief, a frown creased his brow. "How is it you never ask the right questions? Not even by chance. Don't you want to know what *you're* doing here? What merit *you* might *finally* pose?"

Kezerah frowned back. "Isn't it coins? For—I don't know..." She thought of what leverage she could have. You couldn't kill the Soul Heir without throwing the world out of balance. Even harming her could be dangerous. She could be kidnapped—clearly—but then what? Anything Dyllian gained monetarily would be lost the moment she returned; a punishment she'd already begun cooking up. "No, I'm out," she said, with a shrug. "It seems like an idiotic choice to me."

"You must know why you've been brought here," Dyllian urged. "You can't be so wrapped up in your messy infatuations that you have *no* idea."

"Well, I haven't exactly been kidnapped multiple times, Dyllian." Kezerah said, irked by his impatience. He waited a beat longer, as if she'd decipher his cryptic wording. "Do you want me to pretend like I know?" Kezerah offered. "Nod along and such?"

"Wow. You really don't have a solitary clue. That's absurd. But, I suppose it would require you to care about anything your subjects care about."

"If you tell me, I bet I'll have at least one clue of what you're talking about."

Dyllian stamped his foot. "The Irrigation plans, Kezerah! The plans I've been trying to explain to you since you signed them!"

Kezerah couldn't help but gape. "You...you kidnapped me... because you don't like the plumbing?"

Dyllian grabbed the hair at his scalp as if trying to remove it. "You insolent, careless—It's not just plumbing. The Ralven province has supplied the majority of Elastor's crops since the founding of our kingdom. My ancestors chose our land—strategically—because it crosses paths with the flow of two rivers. Now, you want to divide our labor, our Sway Holding farmers, to deviate crops to other provinces—Luka, the Edge—and force our hand to assist the competition in crop growth."

"Those are all Elastian Provinces," Kezerah argued. "All benefiting from bringing more food to Elastor." Kezerah pondered a moment more, eyeing the door. "You have a small army outside.

Do *they* care if your province is just as profitable as other provinces?"

"They care for the funding it brings. And they care for the cause those funds help support. Not that you'd know anything about that."

Kezerah recalled when she and Ambrose had left the fray of a rising crowd. She lifted her chin. "They want fair trade for their profits." Pleased by the taken aback expression on Dyllian's face, she expanded, quoting what she'd heard the protestors chant in Heartsglove, "Fair wages for fair work."

"And why do you think they aren't getting fair pay for their work?" Dyllian challenged.

Kezerah wrung out her dried up wealth of knowledge. "I don't know that they aren't. None of the lieges have come forward saying the wage fares are too low."

"Because they aren't. The *trades* are. Because Elastor allows for bargains instead of pay. I won't be delusional enough to assume you've looked at a map of Thrice, but do you know what borders Luka?"

Kezerah ignored the jibe. "The northern half of Luka bleeds into Alora."

"Alora," confirmed Dyllian, "the very non-Elastian territories that disturb our trade and benefit from King Elowren's lax border lines. Alora, who doesn't trade in coin but wares and cloth and labor. Which benefits exactly no one in Elastor."

Kezerah dug deep in the recesses of her mind to remember that chapter in her text and hoped it wasn't one Ikaika had done on her behalf. "We need trade with Alora just as much as we need trade with Xenkesh. Aloran trade differs, but it's always of fair value."

"We need coin to function within our own economy," said Dyllian. "Ralven loses every year to a forced trade with border nomads because we can't refuse Aloran 'payment'. Then you dedicated an entire water system to benefit them and further the growth from surrounding provinces?" He shook his head. "At first, I thought you'd made the plans out of spite. Some childish retribution for that incident at Yule. My father encouraged me to try and charm you, to regain your favor."

"Well, you've definitely charmed me, Dyllian. Never have I wanted to assist you more." Yet, something in Kezerah hesitated. She did want to assist people feeling underpaid for their work. She recalled her temperament when buying bananas. She would not make rash decisions on this trade. But she would talk to her father. "Why didn't you or your family bring this up in council meetings? The irrigation, yes—" she rolled her eyes, "—but why not the pay upset?"

Dyllian straightened his cloak, indignantly. "There is a hierarchy within our nobility you couldn't begin to understand."

"Your father is a lord of a province. He's meant to bring up lower lieges' concerns. The *people's* concerns."

"Of course we have our rank and stations. But between the elite, there are rules. Order. A way things run. My family always has and always will be at the top of that order. We've earned it. We earned our lands fairly during Ellas' founding, and have supplied Elastor with the majority ever since. I've been tasked with leading this rebellion because our family respects traditions while accepting change. It's a large operation and I assure you, everyone is playing their part. But too many opinions in one place turns to shuffling cards without a clear or dedicated plan for where or how they fall. She—I have a plan. The lack of funding gets in the way of that."

"But why would that plan need Ikaika?" Kezerah tried to catch her words up to her spinning thoughts. The Ralvens needed coins to fund a rebellion they refused to advocate for. They wanted to personally gain, which the irrigation system got in the way of. Which helped them fund the rebellion. The rebellion that they didn't want to end in compromise. Why? When the only outcome that could lead to was— "War?" Kezerah tried to understand. "You want war with Ikai—with Alora? Just so you don't lose money and status from other provinces getting a cut?"

"Believe me, Princess. I'm not the only one with the scales tipped in favor of war."

"Do the people following you know that?" Kezerah gestured bound hands at the door. "Do they know there are other ways? Ways you haven't tried, like speaking on their behalf for trade reform?"

Dyllian turned hastily to Syle, who braced a hand on the doorknob and waited a heartbeat, before shaking his head in some sort of confirmation. Dyllian returned his attention to Kezerah again. "Keep your voice down! People know as much as they need to know to execute the plan."

"And who decided it was up to you to execute this plan? Your father?" Kezerah asked. "Since obviously you didn't want your *monarchy* involved."

Dyllian smiled. "You would like to know wouldn't you? But unfortunately I'm pressed on time and can't teach an entire lesson on the obvious tonight. No, tonight you're going to have no choice but to honor my request for your irrigation system."

"Fine. You want me to, what?" Kezerah asked. "Talk to my father? Plead your case?"

"My father and I already tried speaking to the king," Dyllian said, his face puckered. "You know what he told us?"

Kezerah rolled her eyes with a huff of breath, "I'm guessing something akin to 'no'. Get on with it, Dyllian."

"He told us it was up to you. That the project was completely and utterly in your hands. He refused to touch it without your say so."

Kezerah in-took breath, achingly touched by the gesture.

Dyllian didn't seem to find tenderness in the sentiment. "He used our lands as a trial experiment for your rule. My family has had to rely on smugglers and pirates to make our trade quotas and still turn our usual profit."

A word snagged in Kezerah's ears. It tugged at her and she followed it as Dyllian continued to lament. She looked at Syle guarding the door. Dyllian's disdain for his bordering neighbors. Her mind picked at thought threads.

"And once Lumi took over Port Aveltra—"

"Pirates," Kezerah interrupted.

Dyllian stopped. "Have you been listening to—"

"You..." Kezerah fit another piece into place. It was easier to think once his mouth shut. She glared at Syle. "You're working with pirates. You gain from cutting border ties with Alora," Kezerah looked up sharply. "You need Luka to remain weak." Dyllian didn't feign innocence, his chin ticked up a notch. "The bear was your doing."

Dyllian dared shrug, arms still interlocked. "I tried getting your attention. When that didn't work, I called in a favor." He gestured to the slimy Xenkeshi. "I admit, I hadn't originally planned for Prince Rorrik to take part, but can you imagine?" He shook his head, marveling at the concept. "We wouldn't have had a choice but to join the war. And with Alora to blame, the option of which side we joined would have been made for us." His frown creased as he came back to himself. "A shame it didn't play out."

Rage swelled in Kezerah and she burst forward in her bindings. "I'll have your titles stripped." Her legs fumbled and she crashed to the side, held up by the wall. "I'll see you and your entire family exiled!"

"You're really not in a position of power here, Princess," Dyllian said, gesturing to her off kilter position on the ground.

"What's your 'improved' plan then?" demanded Kezerah. "Go back to the Solstice Court with my signature?" Kezerah mocked Dyllian's voice in a high-pitched wheeze, "Soul Heir? Haven't seen her. Oh, but looky here: her signature on these plans just dropped from the clouds!"

"Of course I have a bargain for you," Dyllian shot back. "Truly," he muttered, more to himself than her, "imagining you during a diplomatic crisis makes my skin crawl."

"You sicked a bear on my best friend!" Kezerah said. "Your chance for bargains has ended."

"Princess," Dyllian seemed to be trying to regain his calm, he spoke through his teeth. "You're tied up on the floor of a smugglers' den. You voluntarily left the Solstice Court." He tilted his head to the side. "I know you hide your shame well, but even you must know just how catastrophic it would be if people found out you put *yourself* in this situation."

"I don't care. You tried to kill Andarios," she spat. "Your punishment will be far greater than anything my father can conjure."

Dyllian looked unbothered. "You know, it's funny you mention your father. He entered the maze rather late, don't you think?" Kezerah's heart faltered. Dyllian smiled. "From my view—after you jilted our dance—it looked as if he missed the most pivotal part of the evening. I'd say that's worth bringing up when I'm given my trial." She imagined Dyllian lingering in her maze, a voyeur to her cataclysmic evening. She swallowed, and fought back against embarrassment. "Unless, you decide perhaps that a trial would no longer be necessary?"

Kezerah smoldered like a flame without enough kindling. Dyllian looked smug as her face betrayed her. "Change the plans, and nobody knows what a failure you are. Change it, and you go home, I go home, and we live our separate lives." He paused dramatically, as if allowing her the time to contemplate.

She glared at him. "Go on, Dyllian. No half measures, finish your threat. If you have the spine."

"Must you always be so brutish?"

She waited.

"Fine." He mustered courage somewhere within his bony exterior and moved in close to return the stare. Kezerah wondered how much blood there would be if she bit him and how bad it would taste. "If you don't change the irrigation plans, all of Thrice will know just how much danger they're in by letting you run free. How you fled the safety of the capital to look for your supposedly neutral ally, endangering us all, right after kissing the other one. King Elowren will have no choice but to lock you away and rule to prevent a war. Or join with Xenkesh to withstand Queen Illija's wrath at being betrayed."

A myriad of fears tore through Kezerah all at once. Her father would do anything to keep her safe. In turn, he expected Kezerah to do anything to keep Elastor safe. She had failed. Her father wouldn't. Despite her trying, her chest rose and fell with panic. Dyllian had won.

He pulled back. "We both have something to lose, and something to gain here. That's how a bargain works."

"What happened to not having time for lessons on the obvious?" she seethed.

"Quite right." Dyllian straightened and rummaged in the pocket of his cloak. He produced and unrolled a document. Her document. Her plans. "I've already made the changes," he said. "All I need is your signature." He used his foot to slide over an overturned wine crate and placed the plans before her. A grid map of Elastor, dusted with prints, hard work and her handwriting scrawled across her vision. Her firm signature penned at the bottom.

Kezerah looked up from the plans to give him a vacant stare. Then rolled her shoulders, the metal of her adhered bracelets digging in. "Did you want me to sign with my teeth?"

Dyllian sneered and nodded to Syle. "Keep her legs bound."

A click and tinkling sounded as her bracelets loosened and fell down her arms. Kezerah massaged her wrists up to her elbows.

Dyllian handed her a quill and shuffled back in haste like a crustacean.

Kezerah spun the calamus between her fingertips, the feather twirling above. If she signed it, Dyllian would have to set her free. He had no other recourse. Suspicion would fall on all of Elastor if she weren't found. She couldn't be easily hidden, nor contained. This left keeping his mouth shut to his benefit. It would be as he said. A ruse would be created, and she'd be returned.

Kezerah tapped the point on the paper; so like that day in her father's study, her unsure hand steadied by his words. *Someone's best is not a request for perfection.* These changes reflected someone else's desires, her work no longer legible on the page. *Then, this Kingdom has been given all it can ask of you.* She looked at the assured slash of her name, the proof of her efforts indenting the parchment. If she didn't sign away her best, she'd be confined to her rooms, or worse. The 'worse' outcome terrified her, unknowable in its severity. Ambrose echoed like a warning, *If the fear comes, fight it, but don't let it rule.* Her best always seemed to come up short, was it worth fighting for?

She set the quill down on its side. "No," she said. "I won't sign them."

Up until this point Dyllian had stood waiting, his stare intent and eager. He tensed, his feet seemed to move without him as he stumbled forward. "You have to. If you think I'm bluffing, think again. I have nothing to lose if I return empty-handed."

"But only you have to gain from these changes. I can't sign off for the good of one at the detriment of many." There was no telling how far Dyllian would take his blackmail. She would own up to her mistakes and face her father and Illija for judgment. She would fall at the queen's feet, postpone her ascension to the throne. Perhaps she'd suffered being puppeteered by her parents, but they had proven to have her kingdom's best interests at heart. Dyllian had not.

"What about my detriment? The detriment to the Ralven family."

Kezerah shook her head. "We can work something out with the disbursement of wealth. If the Ralven lands are truly in dire straits we'll look into it. I don't have my father's ledgers but—"

"Don't pretend you're going to do something after years of nothing!" Dyllian snapped. "After ignoring me every chance you had!"

Kezerah rolled her eyes through closed lids, exuding a calm she didn't feel. "I shouldn't have ignored you, Dyllian, I realize that now." She swallowed back bile. "I apologize."

"Now that you've been gagged, tied up and blackmailed!"

Her facade of calm fissured. "Maybe if you weren't so–so–" She gestured up and down his frame. "*You*, I would have listened!"

"And if you weren't *you*, we wouldn't be here." His voice sounded feverish, he looked ill with anger. Then, a stony glaze cut across Dyllian's expression. His mouth firmed into a line. "Right. But you are you. And we're here." He sounded so reasonable Kezerah sagged her shoulders in relief. "If you won't bargain with me, maybe King Elowren will bargain with Xenkesh for your return."

"I—what?"

"Syle, get in touch with—"

A crash and the clang of metal shuddered the door. Dyllian and Kezerah both looked to the Xenkeshi—Syle—for answers. He touched the doorknob only for the door to fling back and slam directly into his face. Kezerah felt her boots unclasp as Syle hit the floor.

Andarios, clad in plum-purple stained armor and white hair streaked back with sweat, burst into existence.

"Dar!" Kezerah worked at her buckles to remove them alongside her many bracelets.

Andarios looked around wildly and Kezerah watched his face

shift from distress to a tired relief. Yells called out from the stairwell and Andarios backed up towards her as he faced the door, sword drawn.

"Are you alright?" Andarios' sword aimed forward, his voice like an urgent stranger. Kezerah noticed and tried to un-notice the red smear that ran up the metallic gray of his blade.

"I'm fine, just sore ribs."

It was the wrong thing to say. Andarios jerked his head back to examine her. She forced herself up to prove how well she fared and was rewarded by a sharp, intense pain that caused her to double over.

"What did you do?"

Kezerah raised her head to see Andarios spoke to Dyllian, who had removed himself from the situation, now placed in a corner. Dyllian didn't answer. Footsteps thundered up ailing stairs, before the remaining assailants from the alley swarmed at the door.

"How did you get past without fighting all of them?" Kezerah asked in awe.

"I burst in and raced straight up here, I didn't really stop to say hello." Andarios thrusted to block a sword that swung towards him. "Can you move?"

"I think so."

"Good." Andarios blocked and backed into her. "Shadow me."

Kezerah understood. She took a weighted breath before she straightened and pressed her back to his. Her focus drew to his movements, an old game turned into a challenge. Steel screamed against steel and Kezerah leaned back while Andarios pushed forward, then sidestepped to block a blow from his left. Pivot, shift, thrust. A thud. A hand dropped into her line of sight. Kezerah closed her eyes. They moved across the room, Andarios leading the fight to give them the wall advantage. Light leaked through her eyelids.

Kezerah's stocking stepped into a puddle of something warm and thick. *'Don't look, don't look, don't look,'* she told herself.

Andarios jerked to the side. Kezerah followed. Her eyes snapped open as he let out a low hiss and cursed. A fresh red gash ran along his right side. Kezerah turned out of sequence, unable to help reaching toward it.

"Formation, Kez!"

It was too late, Andarios pulled right, while Kezerah remained behind. The ruin of the room revealed itself to be worse than her imagination. Bodies, no longer assembled, made a mess of the floor. It looked like a painting composed by a violent hand. Andarios, the artist, fought the final two.

"That one's Bonded!" Kezerah cried out, her fear taking on new heights as she watched Andarios fight Syle. It looked nothing like the skirmishes in the training yards. Kezerah didn't know how to gauge his success. She took a step back, giving him the breadth he needed.

Andarios pinched two fingers together and twisted and Syle doubled over in pain. The Bond Wielder turned his attention to Andarios' sword from his downed position. Andarios' hilt glowed a dull orange. He growled through a grimace and held on tighter as his sword burned his hand. Andarios repeated the Sway for pain and Syle's body bent at odd angles. He screamed and writhed in pain. Oiled features contorted; ring-drenched fingers curled into fists as he convulsed.

The second man ran forward and Andarios kicked him back. Then, Andarios pivoted the muddy sole of his black boot and stamped down on Syle's convulsing torso, holding him in place. Kezerah watched a sword—twice as thick as her forearm—jam into the shuttering man's heart. He gasped. The sudden silence interrupted by the gush of blood that spilled from him as the blade withdrew. Several smashed rings twitched on the stone floor. A trickle of light—no larger than a firefly—extracted itself from one of the rings, a matching sliver of luminescence drifted from the man's chest. The two lights danced about each other before tangling into one, and darted high above and through the open door. From there she knew it would travel east, past the Isle of Bethync, to the Summerlands. Syle's body went limp, eyes unseeing but mouth still snarled in pain as his soul and Bond left him.

The second bandit regained his posture and lunged once more. Andarios heaved his sword, but she saw the fatigue there. She needed to help him.

Kezerah forced all her thoughts and intentions on Andarios. If she were ever to Hold Sway, this would be the time. She breathed low and deep, raising her hands to create a gesture.

She was jerked back by the wrist.

Dyllian. She'd forgotten him, crouched in the corner. He dragged her to him, pulling her close. Kezerah felt the icy, cool threat of metal pinprick below her collarbone.

"Stop," he commanded. "Drop your weapon, or mine pierces her heart."

Andarios released his hold on the bandit, who slumped to the ground, and faced them.

"Dar, don't listen," said Kezerah. "He's bluffing. He wouldn't dare."

The sharp sting of his knife made Kezerah gasp as Dyllian drew blood.

"What do I have to lose? What fate awaits me after you arrest me and I'm brought back to court?" Dyllian growled. "See if I don't take you all down with me!"

Andarios' eyes darted from Dyllian, to Kezerah, to the dagger, and back to Kezerah. The man behind him began to rise.

"Andarios, don't you dare!"

Kezerah watched his eyes make the choice, his hand slackened its hold on his sword. Before she could think, she used the only weapon she knew she had. Herself. Her own hand tightened over Dyllian's grasp on the hilt and she pressed the blade in.

"What are you doing?" Dyllian shouted. She felt him fight back, his feigned courage dissolving into panic as she did his job for him.

"Kezerah, no!"

The knife dug deeper. Kezerah felt it tear through several layers of flesh, each one offering resistance before it yielded to the next.

The heat of it was excruciating.

Then, the whole of her began to tear away. It started in her abdomen. As if trillions of roots and sinew pulled taut and snapped free from her. Her body convulsed, and she fought to keep her fist tight around Dyllian's. She thought she shook, violent tremors sending her stance off balance, but Andarios stumbled too. The man behind him fled, scrambling on all fours out the door. Cries could be heard through the window. Shouts and panic and screams and howls of wind replaced the festivities.

"Let me go! Let me go!" Dyllian begged.

She couldn't. Kezerah's soul felt eager as it ascended. It rattled up her ribcage, hungry for light. A sudden and electrifying burst fractured the dark of the room, accompanied by a deafening, crackling resonance. Kezerah felt like the storm came out of her—through her. She was a cyclone unleashed from a bottle, a star jutting forth through the sky, a ruination of clouds and power.

She wondered why she had ever remained in such a fragile shell when the earth itself trembled in response to her celestial fury. Glass shattered and warmth encircled her to the sound of a scream at her ear. She reveled in the comfort of being engulfed by flames.

But then, a shift. Her clouds began to recede, her waves calmed, and the thudding no longer came from thunder, but her heart, with warm hands placed atop it.

Kezerah's eyes fluttered open, and the swelling in her chest returned to a pain entirely human. She coughed out a sob, then screamed the scream she had meant earlier, her body curling in on itself as sounds returned to her. As she returned to her body.

"Kez! *Kez!*" Andarios' voice was almost unrecognizable in its anguish and urgency. "It's alright, it's me! It's okay now. It's okay!" His large hand soothed her hair, then propped her head up. Kezerah became aware of the ground.

Andarios' ash white hair looked matted with specks of red in stark contrast. His chest heaved and his eyes smoldered gold in the dim light. Her tears blurred his face. She hadn't even known she'd been crying. Kezerah tried to speak and whimpered. It both shamed and relieved her. She felt more like herself. More human. More senses returned, the air was thick with an odd stench. Something putrid and burned.

He hushed her in soothing. "It's okay, I promise. We're going to get you home."

Kezerah lolled her head to the side. "Where's Dyllian?"

Andarios' hands were quick and soft, turning her away. "Kez— Kezerah, look this way, eyes on just me, okay? I'm going to lift you up now."

He spoke to her slowly, movements all the slower. His hands drew her to him, placed carefully under her back and legs, cradling her like a child. She didn't care, she clung to him as he lifted her.

"Don't look down."

"Is Dyllian—"

"Shh," he pressed his cold cheek to her too hot forehead. "Don't worry about that right now. Let's get you home...Just promise me you won't look down."

Kezerah closed her eyes in a silent oath.

She did not open her eyes again until they exited the hovel. The city was a shambles. Soldiers thrust buckets onto fires while people tended to each other, surrounded by overturned carts, and houses unnaturally slanted. Animals roamed free of their stalls and the earth smelled like the thick fresh damp of rain.

"What...what happened?"

"A...storm."

"A storm? On the mainland? From the sky?"

Andarios fought the answer, "No, from you."

"Did I Hold Sway?"

His brows pinched together. A wrinkle of emotion etched into every line of what had once been a youthful face. He shook his head so faintly she almost didn't catch it. He wet parched lips by rubbing them together then formed the words, "No, not Sway. I don't know what you—what that was, but it wasn't Sway."

In the pause she took to try and understand, Andarios hailed a guard. Kezerah turned her face away in order to not be recognized, her hood up to obscure her hair. Andarios' hands jostled beneath her, a sign he used Sway to converse with the guard rather than let her hear him. Kezerah nuzzled deeper into his shirt as the tramp of boots went to investigate whatever horrors they'd left behind. That she'd left behind. Kezerah's mind looped back in on itself every time she tried to recall the scene after she'd evoked her soul's wrath. The fatigue of effort finally won out, and she focused once more on her surroundings.

They neared the lights of the upper street market and Kezerah's original purpose jolted through her.

"Ikaika! We have to find him."

"They're looking," Andarios sounded eerily calm. "but a witness from a curry tavern said he left the city hours ago."

Kezerah wondered if she would have ever caught up to Ikaika.

The noise of the city intruded on her brooding. The unbearable image of a blood-spattered Andarios carrying her through the streets as she lay weak and limp in his arms prompted her.

"Do we have to go through the market? Maybe I can walk."

"You're not walking," he assured her, but he banked left and kept a block away from the crowds. "Besides, think of how heroic I'll look carrying you."

Andarios *did* look heroic. Upon reaching the Lunar Channel, they were met by over twenty soldiers on horseback. Kezerah recognized Andarios' grey mare, saddled in her gift of yellow garnets. He spoke to a captain and explained he believed her ribs to be bruised rather than broken. He also mentioned she might have a concussion and denied his horse, instead offering to carry her back himself. They relented easily. The soldiers dispersed to carry the message back that Kezerah had been returned safely.

"Everyone knows?" she asked, miserable.

"Erm, not the details but... that you were missing was definitely pieced together. Hey," he said a bit more urgently, "stay awake. We need to take you to the infirmary before you go to sleep."

"Mmm," she hummed, her eyes closing.

"We were briefed on the letter from Ikaika," he said tentatively. "I knew his migraines were getting bad but..."

Now awakened by an entirely different ache, she fought to admit the truth to him. "It was my fault," she said, the confession making her feel both better and worse. "He saw Ambrose and I...and we were, well—we almost kissed and he—he left."

Andarios' brows rose high into his shaggy white hair. "You *kissed* Ambrose?"

"Shh! Not so loud."

"Yeah, fair shot, considering it could send our Kingdom to war— Oh Kez, I'm sorry. Don't cry." She did anyway, and he changed tactics. "I mean, yeah, the all-encompassing war bit would be your fault, but Ikaika leaving isn't."

"It is. We were dancing and I, he—"

"Yeah, yeah, he fancies you. We all know that. But you fancying someone else doesn't make him leaving your fault. That's his choice."

"He knew I had feelings for him too... or at least, I think he did."

"He also knows that too leads to an all-encompassing war," Andarios countered. "Not to mention, speaking from experience, you're a perfectly fine friend even without a constant need to kiss you."

She snuggled into his arms, squeezing him in a hug, prepared for the throbbing in her ribs. "You are, without a doubt, the best friend anyone could ever ask for."

He laughed, carefully walking her up to the Solstice Gates. "I know."

Assumptions

The bell clanged again in mockery of Ambrose's naiveté. He had traded his father's life for a fool's treaty. The future monarchs meant to uphold it had run away together in the night. All guests had been ordered to remain in their rooms. Rorrik had ignored this order after seeing Lord Andarios pass by, but Ambrose remained. The buttery light emitted from their lanterns provided a false sense of calm—ruined by the bells—as he stared out at Heartsglove's twinkling lights from his balcony.

Over an hour had passed and the Solstice Court continued to toll. *'Long. Gone.'* each gong seemed to say.

He and Rorrik had packed to leave after first light, deciding to rest before making the lengthy journey: first to Port Aveltra and then home. Ambrose would need to meet with the Quintet Counsel before going forward with any decisions, but a plan had begun to form that he wanted Rorrik's opinion on. Once Rorrik began speaking to him again. Rorrik had requested special permission to help the search party, but Ambrose suspected he'd only gone to avoid him and help one soldier in particular.

Ambrose had no such vestige of interest in someone who chose to be lost. He had sat there last night and chosen Elastor, Ikaika, their treaty—*her*—over all that he held dear. She hadn't even cared or bothered to look back. He tensed his jaw against the sting that rose up his sinuses and pushed at his eyes, unable to look away from the balcony and city below. Like a fool.

The sun rose over fields and homes.

A troop of soldiers gathered at the bridge, stopping people from coming and going. A lone figure moved towards them.

He narrowed his eyes, trying to better see, but darkness still clung to dawn.

The army dispersed out in different directions, and the figure continued on through the gates.

The bells ceased.

Ambrose watched the figure subtly shape itself into a large man carrying something.

Ambrose rushed out the door.

He hurried down the stairwell passage, his mind singularly focused on the figure. The man had been carrying not something, but someone: the fiery red hair identifying her immediately.

AMBROSE WATCHED Andarios bring in a badly bruised and bleeding Kezerah, and thought he would implode from guilt. The bitterness drained from his limbs and he forced himself not to crumble. The cost of his pride and dignity felt too high. She looked so small cradled in the lord's arms. Then, healers gathered her up and whisked her away to the infirmary before he could process that she had ever truly been there.

He approached Andarios, unused to the height disadvantage. Until this moment, Ambrose realized he'd yet to speak directly to Kezerah's best friend. "What happened?"

Andarios looked tired, sweat and bits of blood soaked his clothes. Arms free, he stretched them, catching his breath. From a distance this boy had always looked friendly, but as Andarios sized up Ambrose, he appeared guarded.

"She was attacked in the city."

"Attacked? How? Why?" Ambrose tried to puzzle through the last few hours, trying to see how these events had played out. It made no sense. "Where is Ikaika?" His stomach writhed in distress, and he tried to ignore it.

Andarios looked at him, surprise cracking his armor. "On the way to Estora. Where have you been?"

'*Sulking in my bedchambers...*' he thought. "I've been preparing to depart for Xenkesh. I have responsibilities that I must attend to."

"Oh yeah, Kez mentioned you're a king now," Andarios said with a scoff.

"You're definitely not supposed to know that, nor say it aloud in public."

Andarios lifted his hands in mock surrender, looking over at the Spring Quarters. "Was there anymore to this interrogation? I want a bath."

"No, I'm most certainly not finished," Ambrose said. "Who attacked her?"

Andarios frowned, it looked unpracticed, citrine clad eyes assessed him head to toe. "For now, and unofficially, bandits," he said finally, "but the leader I killed was Xenkeshi. He was Bound to this." Andarios held up a ring: A metallic snake coiled into a band, eating a now-cracked piece of amber. "I watched it break open as I killed him." Ambrose stared at Syle's ring. "Rorrik tipped me off on her possible location. Lucky for all of us, Rook told me to stay behind." He patted the bandages still healing from his brawl with a bear.

Ambrose decided Andarios of Luka was not a force he intended on reckoning with. "My brother has a chaotic moral compass." A guilty one most likely. But Ambrose didn't know how The Bear would take to knowing—what Ambrose suspected—was Rorrik's involvement in his attack.

"He also knew where the hideout would be," Andarios said. "The hideout with a Bonded Xenkeshi."

"I will have my people look into it." Ambrose reached out for the ring. He couldn't bring himself to regret Syle's death, but he needed the mercenary pirate not to be traced back to his family. The soldier continued to stare at him, and Ambrose caught up. "My family had nothing to do with the attack on Kezerah. But unfortunately, neither amber nor snakes are exactly rare in Xenkesh. It'll take time." He kept his hand out-stretched, authoritative.

After another hesitation, Andarios dropped the ring in his palm.

"I'll investigate any connections, I swear it," Ambrose vowed.

Andarios nodded, and the tension in his shoulders relaxed. "I'm going to take that bath now," he said. "Have a safe journey back." He walked off towards the Spring Quarter with not so much as a bow of his head.

. . .

AMBROSE KNEW three conversations needed to happen before he departed, the first two with Elowren. He approached the king's steward, who made him wait in the hall before being led again to the War Chambers. The king had repeatedly used the term 'Strategy Chambers', but Ambrose knew this to be a futile effort. One couldn't avoid war in a room exposing it. The Solstice Court practiced neutrality, but neutrality was a concept. It couldn't exist outside of ideals. This autumn had proven that. Eventually, Elastor would have to admit the true practice was in complacency. They would have to choose. Ambrose aimed to give his kingdom its best chance for when that time came.

Elowren stood with his back to him, hands clasped behind him and shoulders slouched forward.

"Come in." The king sounded tired; last night's events bled into the morning. He glanced over briefly as Ambrose approached. Whatever he saw in Ambrose's face smoothed the tension on his brow and he returned his attention back to the table.

Ambrose's final steps felt unusually heavy. He looked down at the array of light blue pieces that infected his kingdom. His heart also felt the weight of the conversation. He would do what he could to have those pieces removed, to have his kingdom whole. His father had been a good king. What would Ambrose need to be to obtain peace? He looked to Elowren.

"You know it's odd," Elowren said, not looking up. "Amarus has always been such an inventive and resourceful leader. To jump into a battle without his own trained battalion..." Elowren trailed off, shaking his head.

"My father is ambitious," Ambrose offered, he didn't know what else to say. His father had caught him by surprise as well.

"Ambitious, but not reckless." Elowren spoke more to himself, then shook his head and pulled his focus away to smile at Ambrose. "You wanted to speak with me."

Ambrose swallowed. "I want to sign your treaty—" He paused. This was the formality, but the next words came out more difficult.

"And I wanted you to know, I intend to make peace with Illija... if she allows it."

Elowren's eyes gentled. He looked hopeful but tinged with sadness. Both of them knew what must come before any such event. He reached out and squeezed Ambrose's shoulder. "I do not understand all of Illija's motivations. Your mother is a secretive person. However, I believe that is very much a possible future for you both."

Ambrose nodded, trying to rein in the king's optimism. "I must first speak to my counsel." *'And my brother,'* Ambrose thought, knowing Rorrik still intended to attack The Strand.

Elowren nodded, understanding the logistical proceedings necessary. He Swayed the treaty over and handed Ambrose a quill.

Ambrose looked down at the signatures scrawled across the page: Illija, Elowren, Elize, Amarus. His father's amendment signature was written in a thick red ink, his flamboyant flair evident even in a political document. Ambrose's heart squeezed in his chest.

He bent low, pressing the ink to the parchment.

When finished, he stood back. His penmanship had been graceful and sure. Without hesitation. *'This is the kind of king I must be: One who knows what he wants and assures it.'* He reached out his hand. Elowren returned the gesture and shook it, long-boned fingers firmly locked with his. Ambrose felt powerful, one decision made, one more to make. He lingered. His tongue stuck to the roof of his dry mouth, suddenly he stood boyish and awkward.

Elowren's voice grew curious, "Was there something more Ambrose?"

Ambrose didn't know how to start. He'd watched countless noble houses make these arrangements with one another. Xenkeshi royalty often went the route of quick and practical handfastings. His father had once solidified—then nullified—a pairing for Ambrose, right before his eyes. But his father could no longer do that for him. Ambrose didn't know the first thing about how this was done. *'Know what you want, assure it.'* He thought through his words carefully. "If there is peace between the Thrice Kingdoms, then there would be no need for...impartiality."

"Correct," Elowren agreed, though a question still hung in his voice.

Ambrose had hoped Elowren would understand his subtlety. He realized he still held the king's hand and stepped back. His face reddened. His nerves threatened to flee. He cleared his throat and forced confidence into his next breath. "If that becomes the case, may I ask for Kezerah's hand?"

Elowren's eyebrows rose in surprise. He had evidently not understood the subtlety. "They are not my hands to give, as they are attached to my daughter's wrists."

Ambrose stared at the king, unsure how to make it clearer.

Then Elowren's face broke into an amused grin, so like Kezerah's that Ambrose nearly rolled his eyes at him. The king continued, "Unlike the Alorans and Xenkeshi, Elastian's do not partake in political handfastings. You will have to ask her yourself—" his voice grew stern. "—*After* peace has been secured. Kezerah is finding her place of power right now, and until that place is understood, it would be unwise to put such a proposition before her."

Ambrose swallowed. This had not been the answer he'd hoped for. He had meant to return to his counsel with a well-developed plan and Kezerah's future alliance secured—for reassurance to draw back forces. Elowren's gaze assured that his answer didn't intend to budge. Ambrose had once believed Elowren malleable. He no longer thought this. It appeared Ambrose would need to go about his goals in a different order.

He nodded and bowed his head not just to a king, but a parent. "I shall not place the burden upon her."

DAWN HAD BROKEN, but the light that diffused between the leaves glowed soft, the day still new in its possibilities. It did not uplift Ambrose's spirits. He walked into this battle unarmed. This conversation with Kezerah had many possible outcomes—though the promise to Elowren complicated them—and now conversing with a king seemed far less intimidating than speaking with that king's daughter. Kezerah had only ever given Ambrose the benefit of the doubt. She'd trusted him until he'd broken it, then tried again. The moment Ambrose had believed himself scorned he'd assumed the worst of her. She must have noticed his absence from her search party... Ambrose braced himself and opened the door to the infirmary to find out.

The earthy smell of dried herbs clung to the air. Plants were suspended on hooks along a back wall filled with shelves of multi-colored tinctures and bottles. A healer ground down an aloe vera plant at a long work bench, their eyes assessing Ambrose before bowing and returning to their work. Then Ambrose took in Kezerah. As it turned out, he could easily keep his promise to Elowren and found himself utterly undeserving of any such request.

Kezerah lay propped up on a bed, snugly fitted into an alcove window draped in curtains. The daylight that streamed through the white gossamer brought her injuries into an even starker prominence. Purple bruised her cheek and under her eyes while bandages wrapped securely around her torso. He stopped, the memory of himself brooding in his room preventing even one more step. How dare he approach her, after believing she'd run off from her duties to be with his brother. Kezerah reached towards the curtains in an attempt to draw them back. Her hand then quickly jerked down to hold her side. The healer set down their pestel, but Kezerah raised a hand in protest. "I'm fine."

A new wave of shame crashed over Ambrose, and he took a step back.

Kezerah caught the movement and winced before looking down and away. Evidently, she held the same opinion he did. Even so, he owed her an apology.

He walked over, and kneeled before her, bowing his head. "Kezerah, I'm so terribly sorry."

She hesitated, then spoke. "What in all of the Thrice kingdoms are you apologizing for?"

"I should have been there. I should have searched for you."

He kept his head low. The silence lasted long enough that he glanced up. Her features twisted briefly in anguish before settling into a smooth mask. He looked back down.

She touched his chin, summoning him. "You have nothing to apologize for. I—I make for a terrible monarch."

It was his turn to be confused, then he realized he hadn't asked why she'd gone in the first place. Considering where his assumptions had gotten him last time, he would hear it for himself.

"What were you doing in the city?"

She lowered her eyes, but her voice was steady. "I went after Ikaika once I found out he had left." This revelation shot too close to his original assumption not to sting.

He nodded, grabbing a chair, and he sat down. "Regardless. I should have looked for you."

"We are obligated in no such way." Her voice sounded strange, serene.

"Maybe not, but I feel quite obligated." He couldn't keep the bitterness from his words, but he intended to be straightforward in this. There would be no confusion left behind.

"I should apologize for that as well," she held up a hand to stop his interruption, her gulp seemed to go down dry. "I'd be lying if I said I didn't enjoy your attention, even if I suspected the original intentions behind it." Kezerah paused, her words became almost too quiet to hear. "I felt power and wielded it." Her voice cracked. Whatever she spoke about, it stretched beyond their flirtation. She stared down at her hands like they were unwelcome entities.

When her stare returned, Ambrose met violet brimmed with a pain he knew all too well. He'd seen it after he'd lost his first battalion and forced his face up to a mirror. The same fear ensconced Kezerah now. He scooted towards her, wanting to comfort her, then halted when she recoiled and continued in a voice that shook.

"You were right, power is chosen. But that doesn't mean it's earned." She sighed and seemed to return to herself a little. "I pursued time with you at the risk and disservice of those I'm meant to protect. My kingdom, my father, my duty as future queen. I have power, I realize that now. But it is unearned. I will no longer wield it so lightly. I will no longer play with hearts so lightly."

Ambrose longed to tell her that he would free her of her burdens, that he would bring peace and she would pledge to nothing and no one she did not want to. But he heeded Elowren's request: until he had peace in hand, he would not promise it to her.

"I'm sorry," she said, interpreting his silence as wanting more from her.

He shook his head. "It is you who has nothing to apologize for," she started to protest but he continued. "It wasn't something I truly intended either—my fondness for you that is," he scoffed. "It's not your fault you beat me at my own game. As I said in the meadow, my intention was quite the opposite. You were to swoon over me."

She fought a wan smile, choosing to say nothing.

"No witty quip about my presumptuous assumptions being my own ruin?"

"I wouldn't want my quips to be taken as flattery."

Ambrose noted her calm tone with new clarity. "No, rejection I can manage. This I can't abide. You must be yourself with me."

Kezerah inclined her head to one side. She spoke slowly. "By choosing to accept my duties, I am directly choosing to not be myself. *Especially* around you."

He continued to shake his head, unwilling to continue conversing further with this blank mask. "If you choose to be impartial, and show me no favor, fine. Consider yourself released from assumption. I won't presume you are anything but your nature." He flashed her a smile. Her lips slowly curled to smile back, albeit shyly. A light crinkle appeared on the stem that sloped into her soft button nose and the freckles atop it. His heart danced in his chest. "If you smile back at me, I will assume it's because you want to smile." He took her hand, which looked so small in his. "If you take my hand in yours, I will assume it is because you wish yours to be held."

She looked down at their hands. "I've never seen someone so passionately despair about the refusal to flirt," Kezerah said, tentatively. His delight must have registered on his face, because she matched his grin.

"The damage to my ego would be irreparable. I do what I must to survive, and I can't survive in a world where you are not yourself." Then he released her hand with an effort to remain casual, and stood. She looked stricken by his abruptness. He'd meant to leave her wanting more but couldn't leave with that look on her face. "Resume your letters to me."

She gave more of a cough than a laugh. "Only the first was mine, my mother took up the task after that." Her eyebrow quirked into a wry look. "I don't bother with fruitless activities."

"All the more reason. Write to me." He cocked a grin and backed away. "I promise, this time it will be fruitful."

"Maybe."

Ambrose nodded. While he'd promised not to presume anything, the expression that flickered across her face gave him hope. He closed the door quietly and prepared to return home, in whatever form that took.

Choices

It had been less than a week of soups, healing, and being trapped in her own thoughts. Both Willow and Whistle had doted upon Kezerah in the infirmary, conversation never dithering beyond her getting well. However, the moment the apothecary gave her permission to leave, the orders for an audience with her parents arrived.

Kezerah had prepared for her mother's fury and father's disappointment. She had not prepared for Andarios to already be waiting in the hall outside the thick double doors as she approached.

"No," she whispered upon seeing him. Elize's threats in the foyer from weeks ago came back in vibrant color. *'Continue to defy me and you'll have no idea where he goes.'*

Andarios fidgeted from side to side and Kezerah's stomach twisted.

"It'll be fine," he tried to assure her.

Hanan opened the door and Kezerah flung herself forward. "What is Andarios doing here? He has nothing to do with this."

Hanan looked startled, hands raised. "I'm unaware as to the context of Lord Andarios' summons. I've only been sent to let you both inside."

They walked in. The doors closed behind them with an echo in the empty, stagnant throne room. Kezerah's eyes searched the chamber. The formality of the place did not reassure her. As one of the more modest spaces in the castle—a room not of finery but necessity —her mother always complained it was small and sparsely furnished. No loose weapons, no shields. The banners of Elastor swelled against a draft in the stone walls, situated behind two wooden thrones upon a dais. Kezerah's breath rose alongside her anxiety the longer they waited.

The doors on the far side of the room opened.

Her parents entered, flanked by their personal guards. They sat ceremoniously in their individual thrones, guards on either side and Hanan unobtrusively stationed in the corner. Kezerah examined her father's face for pity and found none. How could Andarios truly be punished for her actions, sent to Luka or worse? She would not allow her choices to inflict damage on any more people. Her nose flared as she waited to speak, words at the ready. She needn't wait long, King Elowren began the proceedings immediately.

"Kezerah, upon receiving direct orders from me to distance yourself from Prince Ikaika, as to restore balance and peace between our precarious alliances, it is my understanding you did the following..." Kezerah longed for the warmth in her father's voice, absent of late, as he cleared his throat. "You brazenly defied orders by leaving your rooms—where I'd sentenced you for the night—you entered Ikaika's bedchambers, broke curfew, fled into the city wearing sacrilegious garments that shamed both your station and your ancestors, all while endangering the crown." Elowren's hands curled at the armrests of his throne, eyes bright. "I also have cause to believe you inflicted harm on yourself, at the risk or purpose of hurting others. Am I correct?"

Had she meant to harm Dyllian? She couldn't remember. Only that she'd wanted Andarios to be safe, that Dyllian held a knife, and that something awful would happen if she drew close to death. Dyllian had begged her to let go but she couldn't. *She couldn't, she couldn't, she couldn't.* Her guilt weighed her down like a crown never could.

Her father repeated himself all the more firmly, enunciating each word. "Am I correct?"

She managed a nod but she fought for Andarios. "Andarios had nothing to do with my choices. He is the one who saved me from the rebels—"

"Bandits," Elize corrected. "Any official rebellion is still under investigation."

Kezerah dared a glance at Elize who wore a facade of indifference, dark blue eyes piercing in contrast. "Regardless. He saved me."

Her father cocked his head to one side. "Yes, and while it has nothing to do with your indiscretions, I thank you for reminding me to add, *'being apprehended for ransom,'* to the list. It is true, Andarios acted with great bravery, also being the one to raise the alarm to your absence in the first place."

Kezerah looked from her father to her mother and back to her father again. "Then—then why is he here? If he did nothing wrong then why is he being used for my punishment?"

Elize scoffed in irritation, and Kezerah sent an icy glare in her direction.

"Punishment?" Her father pondered her for a moment, the two trying to understand each other. "Andarios might be the only reason you are still alive. I owe him such a debt that I may never repay it. What I offer him is to put his skills to use, and promote him as your Queensguard."

Kezerah's legs grew weak with relief as she took in his words. "So, he is not to be punished?"

"That is a matter of perception," her mother cut in.

Kezerah ignored her and took Andarios' hand in a squeeze.

He squeezed back, then seemed to realize they expected him to speak and let go, bending into a kneel. "I thank you, Your High Majesty, and humbly accept the position offered."

"Excellent," Elowren said. "Although this is being done out of order," he said wryly, glancing at Kezerah. "Andarios, I grant you the position of Queensguard. Your duty is to guard Crown Princess Kezerah, Soul Heir of the Solstice Throne in the Kingdom of Elastor. This is a permanent appointment in which you are expected to guard her with your life. You are granted the authority of her safeguard in all matters and above any and all ranking positions. You may choose another trusted and ranked officer to alleviate you for training, meals, and rest periods in which Kezerah is unable to accompany you due to her own duties. All choices are made for her benefit, for the throne, and for Elastor. Do you accept this duty?"

"I do," Andarios said, head low.

"Then rise, Queensguard Andarios of Luka. Join her side, and may you never leave it."

Andarios straightened, formally moving to stand at Kezerah's right. Their hands reclasped and Kezerah's heart momentarily rose with pride. The clammy grasp of his hand told her he held back emotions as well. Andarios, forever at her side.

Elowren continued gravely, "While that was a bright interlude, there are still darker topics to cover." Either the room grew, or Kezerah shrank under his stare. "Kezerah, you have shown me you are not only ill-prepared for the responsibility of a throne, but lack the self-control and discipline to lead. You have broken my trust and flaunted the freedoms granted to you. You are hereby sentenced to your rooms, unable to leave apart from council meetings and training with Sword Master Eriko. He has graciously agreed to train you in a weapon of your choice, as he will be staying with us for the foreseeable future. I will never see Elastor so defenseless again."

Kezerah bowed her head. "Yes, Father."

"This time, I will have you look me in the eyes as you pledge your word."

She diminished further at his flat tone and hard features. Her father's returned trust would be hard won.

She looked him directly in his honeyed brown eyes and pledged, "I will do as I'm told. I will remain in my room. I will keep peace and balance among our people. I will honor our kingdom and its name. I will not fail you again."

With each word she worked to lock herself further and further away, out of sight as to not do more harm. As she finished he looked sad. She began to lower her head once more, then lifted it.

"I request to attend a formal council meeting to discuss the reb —bandit situation. Before you pass judgment, I'd like us to better understand the effect our agreements with Alora may have on our merchant class."

Elowren straightened his shoulders. "The trade situation with Alora is quite precarious at this time. I'm afraid I'm currently unable to contact either of our neighboring monarchs."

"The situation in Elastor is precarious as well," Kezerah said, "possibly more than we originally realized."

Her father conceded. "The individuals we managed to apprehend and those still being investigated will be given a fair trial." Kezerah winced, Dyllian would receive no trial. His objections and opinions died with him, died because of her. "We will use their testimonials to look into further compromise. Your meeting will be arranged."

"Thank you." Kezerah had no more in her. She'd taken the first steps; she didn't believe she could take one more.

Elowren nodded. "I ask Queensguard Andarios to escort you back to rest."

Kezerah turned to go when her mother spoke, "I have some points of my own I'd like to discuss."

'*Of course she does.*' Kezerah whirled sharply, wondering what her mother possibly had to add to her being practically imprisoned.

"Of course, my dear, I was unaware. I apologize," Elowren said, voice filled with concern at his possible slight.

"As we have discussed previously, I do not think locking our daughter away is to her benefit," Elize said, eyes on Elowren.

"And," Elowren said, patience eternal, "as discussed, it is not for punishment, but protection." He broke his gaze away from his paramour to speak directly to Kezerah. "I believe you can benefit from more direct routes to your duties in order to prevent...poor choices made from spontaneity. And due to recent spontaneities, it is pertinent we all remain united on this front, on the chance our neighbors choose to take advantage of this potential weakness."

Kezerah knew he danced around the truth with his words. She had made a spectacle of herself and in doing so, flaunted Elastor's greatest weakness.

"Kezerah has been punished for her actions, but her actions were damaging."

"Yes, Mother," Kezerah quipped, unable to take many more insults. "That is usually why punishments are administered." Elowren looked at her with disapproval and Kezerah bit her tongue, locking that away as well.

Elize continued, "Yes, there has been punishment, but not prevention. Your bout of hysteria in Heartsglove by now is widespread. Though not to its full significance, fortunately, your fixation on Ikaika has, I'm sure, reached Xenkesh. It should also be noted that the King Regent left hours after and no doubt felt your insult."

Kezerah's eyes narrowed. Her mother truly enjoyed applying salt to an open wound.

"King Regent Ambrose does have other purposes for returning to Xenkesh," Elowren assured her.

Elize turned to him in frustration. "King Regent Ambrose is far from the only voice being heard in Xenkesh. He is but one piece on an ever-changing board. If he has allowed the insult, it will not be overlooked by others."

"What do you suggest then, my dear?"

"What your dear friend Illija suggested so many years ago," Elize said. Kezerah scrunched her brow. The queen of Alora had suggested a punishment for Kezerah, years in advance of her ruining everything? "I believe Kezerah should participate in a treaty tour of sorts. I say we use this time not as simple protection, but production. We shouldn't just lick our wounds and hope our neighbors forget, but use it as a show of strength."

"A tour..." Kezerah knew she spoke too slowly. "—as in leaving court?"

"Leaving Elastor," her mother said, voice like silk. "You would visit Xenkesh and Alora both, just like you've always wanted."

"Elize, have you lost your mind? We can't—"

"Everyone believes we can't," Elize said, "because they believe us weak. Only reliable in our inaction. Right now, what happened in the city is seen as an accident. We need to show our people—all of Thrice—we have nothing to fear."

'What happened in the city.' Kezerah pictured the fires and shambled buildings, the screams—his screams. *I couldn't stop, I couldn't, I couldn't—*

"I can't." Kezerah shook all over. Andarios pulled her close.

"You can," Elize said. "You can see the world, breathe in new scents, taste fruits that never reach our shores."

Elowren's brows knit together. "I don't think—"

"Dyllian." The name stuck in Kezerah's throat. "Dyllian is dead because of me." Hot tears lined her lower lashes.

"Dyllian is dead because he was a traitor to his kingdom," said Elize.

Kezerah shook her head. "He should have had a trial... I didn't mean—"

Kezerah felt her knees buckle beneath her and she covered her tears with her palms. Then, hands firmly gripped her shoulders. Her father, off his throne, kneeled before her.

"We know you didn't mean to hurt anyone." He cradled her curls in his hands. "It is on all of us that you haven't been better prepared for what you must be." His voice carried as he spoke to her mother, still seated. "I believe we need more time to discuss this, privately. Kezerah is—"

"Kezerah is meant to be Queen, and has yet to pass judgment even once in her life."

"Elize, look at her. It's cruel to ask her for what she's not yet ready to do."

Her mother's voice trembled. "What is cruel, Elowren, is coddling her so she is found defenseless; allowing her every whim and illusion of freedom, so that she runs boldly into danger, and is taken unaware by what evils roam the world just out of sight."

Her father's hands tensed at her shoulders. Kezerah wanted to reassure him the fault was hers, not his. He'd done nothing but provide her with chances. Chances she had squandered at every turn.

Elize seemed to soften in his silence. "My dear," she soothed, "I understand your fear for our daughter. I fear for her as well. I fear for her vulnerabilities. My actions may seem rash, but they come from love. We've tried your way, look at where we are."

Kezerah looked to her father, wondering why he didn't answer. But he looked conflicted, unsure. She rose, and her father released his hold, stepping back to the dais. She stood on her own, fighting a battle against her greatest desire. "I'm not—it's not safe."

"I'll be there," Elize said simply, "and Andarios will protect you. You won't have to face your fears alone."

Andarios would be there, protecting her, by her side while she saw the world. Aloran lunar rainbows and Xenkeshi rain dances dangled within reach. She just needed to reach out and grasp—

"No." Andarios broke her dream-like haze and it hurt like a cut.

"On what authority were you given to speak?" Elize hissed in his direction.

"On the authority that upholds the laws of Elastor," Andarios said. "On the authority granted to me to 'safeguard in all matters and above any and *all* ranking positions.'"

"That's an *ancient* semantic by-law not meant to be invoked upon the royal family."

"And yet, as a law, it still applies."

"You'd use your first act as Queensguard to deny her freedom?" Elize challenged. "A chance to be an ambassador and voice for her kingdom?"

Andarios folded his arms. "I'd use it to deny you accompanying her."

Kezerah's ears rang as the room lost all range of sound, she and her parents stunned into silence. Granted nothing but a speechless audience, Andarios continued, "As you've pointed out, Kezerah has not been given challenges befitting someone meant to rule. One form of 'coddling' shouldn't be traded out for another. It's as dangerous as any other threat. Either *Kezerah* leads her tour, or she doesn't."

Elize found her voice. "How dare you—"

Andarios turned to face Kezerah. "*I* know you're capable, but *you'll* never know until you take action without someone telling you to."

'*Say yes,*' her heart begged, '*live, be free, see the world—*'

'*Selfish, selfish, selfish*' her mind warred.

The last time she'd followed her heart she'd hurt everyone around her. She was dangerous, she would unleash havoc on the world if left to her own devices. Andarios waited patiently, no judgment to guide her either way.

"I don't know."

"That's alright," her father finally spoke again. "Ambassadorship is not learned overnight. Your same restrictions will stay in place but if lessons in this area are among them..." Elowren breathed deep, as if uncomprehending of his own words. "We can add it to your list of duties."

"Well, if I may be permitted to speak in my own throne room," Elize said, "I strongly suggest we start in the capital of Trusol, since Xenkesh suffered the larger offense in Kezerah's transgressions." Her mother looked at her pointedly. "Just as well, since Prince Ikaika has obviously tired of her antics."

Kezerah clenched her teeth and pushed past the jibe.

Her father spoke slowly, eyes on his queen. "This can not be decided in haste. I'll need to send word to both Illija and Ambrose. We need time for preparation." He turned to Kezerah. "Depending on your choice, when you make it."

Elize clicked her nails against her armrest. "We'll allow her the night to think it over, and discuss it in the morning during our council meeting."

"If that's all," Andarios interrupted, his tone flat, "I'd like to escort Her Majesty back to her rooms."

"I think that's best," Elowren agreed.

Her friend fitted an arm about her waist and guided them away.

ANDARIOS FRETTED over Kezerah's muted walk to the Spring Quarters. However, upon their arrival, he became spoiled for choice on which battle to face first. Hanan directed servants to carry Kezerah's belongings out as they began to enter. Kezerah, still quiet from the emotional barrage of the throne room, watched as her only possessions were carried off.

"What is this?" Andarios demanded, fed up.

"It has been instructed that Princess Kezerah's chambers be moved to the Summer Quarters, where she will continue her time until further notice." Hanan said, dodging one of the beams that made up her bed's canopy.

Andarios checked Kezerah, in the hopes of seeing her mood even slightly improved by the news. Her eyes seemed to lock on each servant, her surveyal becoming more frantic. "Where is Nurse?"

Andarios withheld a curse under his breath. Hanan's face grooved into a long frown and Andarios gave a frenzied shake of his head from behind her.

Hanan considered Andarios only a moment before he answered,

"Nimah Olenia and her sons are no longer stationed at the Solstice Court."

Kezerah spoke as if the word had to be fostered and grown from a garden overtaken by weeds. "...Why?"

"Kez," Andarios drew her back a step. He wanted her away from here, away from this conversation. She held firm.

"Due to her negligence during Nighttide, Her High Majesty deemed her no longer qualified for the position."

"It wasn't her fault," said Kezerah, her voice small. Andarios sagged in relief, glad Hanan had stopped the story there. As of yesterday, many considered the entirety of the Olenia family missing. Word had wafted through the barracks like a foul whisper when Terryn Olenia had not appeared for his drills. Rook had immediately dismissed the claims and labeled Terryn a deserter. Andarios pulled Kezerah again, she moved easier. "It wasn't her fault..."

"I know," Hanan said, too tired to be sympathetic. Andarios steered her towards the stairs that connected Spring to Summer before the withered steward could say anything more.

They followed the trail of servants down the halls. The quarter always looked unusual in the autumn chill. The open courtyard's midsummer pole stood neglected; its multicolored ribbons tangling in the breeze. The tiled murals of suns trailed a path to the second floor where an abandoned cluster of tables overlooked the Lull Sea.

He guided her to a table at the railing, and they sat in silence, watching the slow slaps the ocean made against the castle's cliff.

"We'll wait here until your room is finished," he said. Kezerah only laid her head down on the table, cushioned by her arms.

Anger boiled up in Andarios all at once. Elize had turned yet another one of Kezerah's greatest desires into a punishment. His friend's move to the Summer Quarters now tainted by her being confined to them. Suspicion curled in him as he thought of Elize's other decree: the treaty tour. He palmed his sword in its sheath. If Kezerah decided to go, she had mere moons before being tossed into the world. He needed to be prepared. *Kezerah* needed to be prepared. He alone had been the one to treat her as durable. Everyone else treated her like blown glass: delicate and best left out of reach. Words his father had Swayed to his mother once, after Andarios had fallen down, bloomed in his mind.

'Shields cannot be made without hammers.'

Kezerah had just been hit with several hammers.

His mother's retort upon picking Andarios up and setting him back on his feet: *'And a good blacksmith knows with just how much pressure to hit, and when to let the metal breathe.'*

Andarios took in a shuddering breath, and looked out to the sea. He would do all he could to prepare Kezerah for the world, but he would also be there to lift her back up onto her feet.

WHEN HER CHAMBERS WERE READY, the two journeyed over to her new rooms. Andarios allowed Kezerah to enter first, taking a moment to speak with Rook. When he followed after her, he found much of the layout unchanged. Her wardrobe, bed, bath, and mirror held a similar position to her previous arrangement. The most notable change was her view; no longer a small, pink-hued courtyard, but a wide spread of turquoise blue.

"It's a pretty great view of the ocean," he said, trying to cheer her up.

She looked at him dully, and he decided to try again later. Kezerah flopped on her bed as he explored, never being allowed in her room in the daylight. (Well, never being allowed ever, but not having any daylight opportunities before now.)

He busied himself by looking through her accumulated trinkets at her vanity, several small stones he recognized as ones they had collected over the years. He then held up dresses ten sizes too small to his frame in another attempt to get her to laugh. She snorted at the sight of a salmon pink dress with feathers, but then she frowned and he quickly put it away.

He spotted a sliding door that at first glance had appeared to be a seam in the wall. He slid it open.

"Oh!" he said, surprised to find his things moved in a mirrored position to his previous bedroom. He entered briefly before coming back through. "Well, this will make sneaking into each other's rooms easier!"

She got up, intrigued and temporarily distracted. "The best part of sneaking in was the *sneaking.*"

He elbowed her, making sure to not get her still mending ribs. "I'm pretty sure *I* was the best part of the sneaking, thanks."

She pretended to consider for a moment. "I suppose you're right."

He could tell she was far from her usual self, but used levity to keep her standing. "Come on, you're always better at finding the nooks and crannies. I bet there's at least one spy hole in my room."

Curiosity got the best of her, and Andarios watched as she went straight to his wardrobe, attempting to drag it from the wall.

He walked over, easily pulling it back. She glared at his arm, as if personally affronted by his muscles. Something glimmered in her eyes. Good. A prideful Kezerah meant a focused Kezerah. He liked when she aimed to best herself.

He flexed a bicep so she'd glare up at him instead. "What's that Xenkeshi proverb? Don't envy, compete?" he asked, knowing Kezerah could always be egged on by a dare. "You want the world to move for you, put in the work."

"Those Xenkeshi are arrogant."

"Smart too," he snorted, "if you exclude Ror."

Kezerah smiled, freckles dancing.

Once both sets of chambers had been explored thoroughly, Kezerah retreated back into bed, seemingly fed up with being locked indoors. Andarios didn't press her further, knowing she probably needed the rest.

"I'm going to relieve Eriko at your door for a while."

"Why is Eriko at my door?"

"Well, when we first got to your room, I kinda assigned him," Andarios admitted. "He doesn't really have a place to go at the moment since—" he stopped himself from saying, 'since Ikaika left' and corrected, "—since you went to the infirmary."

She did not miss his amendment and brought her knees to her chest and laid on her side. "Oh."

. . .

ANDARIOS SHADED his eyes with a hand on an open, wrap-around terrace with a view of the sun as it journeyed to the Autumn Quarters. He hoped the guards stationed on the roof did their job. Before, his guard duties had always been in the Spring Quarters (closed off and heavily surveyed) or the Solstice Gate (a small road that funneled people in and out single file). The Summer Quarters bore danger on all sides.

The meadow sprawled to his left, with crowds of apple trees and passage to the beaches below. The sound of the sea at his back eclipsed more nuanced noises, and the Winter Quarters to his right connected in a jumbled way that left blind spots in his surveillance.

He watched the guards on each quarter's parapet move in a comforting to and fro, their shifts about to end as the sun ticked towards the hills. Andarios' legs grew antsy and he shifted his thoughts alongside his feet.

He tried to grow accustomed to the idea that he now outranked all but Rook, with command encompassing all but the royal family. His actions in the throne room had been drastic, a law only meant to be evoked in extreme circumstances: wars, famines, coups and attempted usurpings of the throne. But hearing Elize declare she'd accompany Kezerah had provoked something visceral in Andarios. Words to explain it skirted out of reach, but the certainty of his actions fastened around him like armor. He shook the thoughts away alongside a shake of his shoulders and distracted himself by musing at the image of refusing Hanan entry.

Footsteps fell upon the stairwell. Andarios spun, at the ready, but was disappointed when one of the only three people he couldn't readily refuse walked toward Kezerah's door: his least favorite at that.

Elize wore her crown differently than Elowren and Kezerah. For one, she *wore* it. Kezerah rarely kept hers on, and Elowren preferred his silver circlet, the color blending in with his hair. No, Elize never settled for less. Several quartz stones jutted from carved antlers, intertwined with silver bindings, woven into her peach hair by braids. It looked as if she had royalty literally growing out of her head. One would not easily believe she had been a Lower Lady of Sorrel before becoming first Spymaster, then Queen. She walked as if she expected him to move. He had no intention of doing so unless commanded. He stared stonily at her.

"I wish to speak with my daughter," Elize said. She always sounded shrill to Andarios, like she did a bad imitation of herself.

Her words were not a command, and he took advantage. "I shall inform her of your wishes," he said, sounding bolder than he felt.

Elize's lips pressed together in a thin line. He made his exit into the room quickly.

A dark red fluff, semi-submerged under the covers, served as the only sign of Kezerah's presence.

"Uh, Kez, your mother would like to speak with you."

Kezerah groaned, fluff sinking below the blankets. "Ugh. Tell her I'm dead."

Andarios held back a grin. "I already told her no once this lifetime. I'm fairly certain she'd kill me for a second."

She sighed. "Bring her in."

Andarios did not intend to 'bring' the Queen anywhere, but he opened the door and gestured in invitation.

Elize strutted in, giving the space a cursory glance of disapproval. "I will speak to my daughter, alone."

He bowed, closed the door, and pressed against it, listening to the conversation unfold with clarity.

"How are you enjoying your room?" Elize asked conversationally.

Kezerah didn't answer.

"All you have done for years is ask to leave the Spring Quarters. I thought you wanted this. Your ultimate badge of maturity."

There was a moment of silence, then Kezerah's tired voice, "If you're here to gloat, get it over with."

Her mother tsk'ed. "We needn't always be at odds. When you were little, we were inseparable. We could be that way again. I only want you to act like a queen—"

"Yes, I'm well aware. I plan on keeping the peace, I—"

"No, Kezerah, not like your father. Like a queen." Elize went on softer and Andarios strained to hear. "You need to tell your father you will go on the tour."

"I don't know if I'm going."

"Of course you are. You won't give up this chance to spite me."

"It's not that...I just..."

A moment passed. "Have I not compromised enough for you? Have I not given you everything you've ever asked for?"

Kezerah didn't answer.

"Did you ask for more freedom, and less eyes upon you?"

"Yes."

"Did you ask to be moved to the Summer Quarters?"

"...Yes."

"Have you not always wanted Andarios as your personal guard? To have your shadow forever at your side? Who do you think approved that? The decision must be unanimous."

"Of course, but—"

"Then tell me, what more can I give for you to lend a bit of your will to my cause."

"I don't want...I'm sorry." Kezerah sounded in a fog. Andarios thought about cracking open the door to see her expression but thought better of it. "You've given me everything I want."

"Everything *we* want. All I ask is that you admit to yourself that you want to go on the treaty tour."

Andarios waited for Kezerah to argue. "I want to go on the treaty tour." She sounded quiet, as distant as Bethync.

Elize responded with a coaxing authority. "You will go to Xenkesh and continue to foster ties with Ambrose, as you did here."

Andarios narrowed his eyes, hearing Kezerah repeat the words back word for word. Something didn't feel right. A lightheaded nausea rolled over him. He backed away from the door. Air would help. Fresh air. He could hear neither mother nor daughter. Kezerah murmured something too soft. Elize responded just as low.

Andarios knocked himself into the door with a thwack of his shoulder. It shook and the conversation ceased.

"Sorry," Andarios hollered out, "tripped!"

"We'll speak more on it later." Elize's voice drew nearer. "But I'm glad we better understand each other."

Andarios scrambled to the side just as the door creaked open.

Elize glanced back to the room, lips pinched in agitation, then firmly closed the door. She turned to Andarios. "The next time you trip, fall forward."

Both cast their eyes to the rail and bannister before them, and the implied drop below.

The moment lapsed and she continued with sharp authority. "Nobody may go in or out. Food may be placed at her door, and I will send for someone to draw a bath."

Andarios came as close as he could to a bow, but his loyalty to Kezerah made the action difficult.

Elize noticed the slight and assessed him, displeased with her findings. "You may be her Queensguard, but do not think I forget that you're still the Edge scum that weaseled its way into my castle walls."

Heat rose to Andarios' neck and cheeks. When he again said nothing, her lip dragged down in the corners. "Keep your grime off my daughter."

She turned and strode away. The breeze attempted to lend fluidity to her ridged gown, and failed. Then, finally, her crown of antlers disappeared down the open air stairwell.

Andarios could hardly let Eriko get in position before he crashed open Kezerah's door. She had not answered him when he called for her, and after opening the door he'd merely seen a lump in the covers. As he made his way over, the lump shook, and he knew she was crying. After soothing her with circular motions up and down her back, he decided on the tried and true method. "I'll be right back," he promised and jogged down the stairs to fetch a tray of tarts.

HOURS LATER, when it had grown dark, Kezerah followed Andarios onto their joint balcony to watch the moonrise. Kezerah nibbled on the last of the tangerine tarts Andarios had brought her. Below, the Lull kissed rocky cliffs in quiet whirs.

"I've said it before, and I'll say it again: the view is the best part," said Andarios. They watched the luminescent halo of the full moon rise above the stretch of tranquil waves. Lunar lilies yawned open behind them on the balcony's trellis as the buds drank in the moon's glow. The Summer Quarter beaches stretched further south, making the drop a lethal one. Kezerah's stomach dipped, and she leaned into the spinning sensation while she continued to gaze at the rocks jutting up as if ripped violently from the sea.

"Why do you do that?" Andarios asked, as she stepped away from the rail.

She took another step back. "Do what?"

"You always look down. I know you're afraid of heights."

"I am not. I climb things all the time."

Andarios rolled his eyes. "You most certainly are."

Kezerah loved Andarios, but having someone know you so well meant sometimes they knew things you did not. She thought about it.

"I like controlling it—me. Knowing I could fall, feeling my body plummet, and choosing not to stop it. It makes me feel like if I were to fall, I'd be master of the action." Master of her own life and choices. She possessed so little control over her body, sometimes she pondered whether it belonged to her at all. From the inside out, others dictated and decided the bounds of her dominion: Her opinions, how she expressed them, her clothes, her day, her life and ultimately how long she chose to live it. Even the apothecary hadn't hesitated to stir Preventions into her stew without telling her until afterwards, and there would be a day she'd be expected to stop taking her Preventions to send her soul on. To continue on her line and never-ending cycle unto herself. *'Unless I fell. Nobody controls that but me.'* Until her soul or whatever had erupted out of her released itself. That she knew from her taste of afterlife she'd experienced in Heartsglove. No decision, not even death, would solely be hers it seemed.

Kezerah shivered and moved within reach of Andarios who looked thoughtful. "I suppose that makes sense," he said.

"That, I think, is the first time you've said I have sense."

"You don't gravitate toward it often," he teased.

They lapsed back into silence, and Kezerah wished she had stones to toss, anything but continuing to be in her thoughts. She would request Andarios get some tomorrow. They could skip stones together.

"So…What did your mother say?" Apparently, Andarios' mind had been on a completely separate path.

Kezerah thought back, the sensation caused her mind to grow hazy. "I was so upset, I don't think I even really listened," she scoffed and knew it rang false.

Andarios kept his fixed position, gazing at the view, but he side-eyed her. "I heard we're going to Xenkesh."

Kezerah didn't want to talk about this right now. The itch of her mother still lingered on her skin, she rolled her shoulders and looked over the edge again. "Yes."

"And you're okay with that?"

The waves subtly creeped higher. She felt near them, and far from her body. The vertigo gave her the sensation of floating. "Of course. It's everything we've wanted." If she jumped, she knew she'd fall right into the sky. Something tugged at her. Her hand, a hand. Andarios' hand held hers.

"Hey," he pulled her close, away from the edge. Her mind stopped twirling up. "Something's wrong. What happened?"

What happened? *What happened?* A fragile twig in Kezerah's resolve snapped, and every pent-up emotion she'd dammed up spilled out.

"I killed someone, that's what happened," Kezerah said with ferocity. The catharsis pushed her next words out with force. "I killed him without even trying. My body destroyed another person, and I couldn't stop it."

Andarios waited, allowing her fury.

"And she just expects me to go? To leave? To be unleashed for something as mundane as border relations?" Kezerah shook her head. Her breathing became heavier as she seethed. "But it's not just her. It's everyone! Everyone expects something of me: that I be diplomatic, behaved, well-mannered, demure. That I be fair, *impartial.*" The last word felt repugnant on her tongue as it left her mouth. "Even Ambrose and Ikaika—Ambrose came here to court me, and Ikaika left because he thought he'd succeeded!"

Hot tears wet her eyes and she pressed her palms to them, willing them back in and failing. "I control nothing. Not even my own body." She had *erupted.* Her body had not been hers but someone—

something—else's. *'Not Sway,'* Andarios had said. Not the magick she longed for. Not the magick meant to connect her to Ellas, to her true self. She wanted to open her ribcage, hollow out the imposter bits and see what she was left with, if anything at all.

Andarios' sad eyes reflected hers. For the third time that day, he held her as she cried, petting her hair while she soaked through his cotton night shirt.

Finally, he guided her back to bed, curling the blankets around her like a cocoon. Her eyes dried, and she knew even if she wanted to continue, she had nothing left inside her. He moved to leave, and she broke out of her bundle of blankets to grab his hand, dragging him back. Their hands locked together. His tightened around hers like a natural instinct.

Andarios' hands did not give her the tingling sensation that Ambrose or Ikaika's did. While rough, each groove was familiar, shaping into hers as if completing a pattern. Kezerah looked up at him and felt him pull back. Kezerah's voice came out quieter than she intended, a vulnerable murmur.

"Stay with me."

Andarios looked down at her. He seemed to assess something in her features, always recognizing her before she recognized herself. His jaw clenched and unclenched; lips set in a line. Then, finally, more to himself than her, he gave a sharp nod. Returning to her side, he crawled in. His burly frame took up a great deal of the bed.

He nudged her with a low chuckle. "Don't be such a bed-hog. Scoot over."

She laughed, curling into the corner and enjoying the warmth as he wrapped his arms around her: a perfect combination of hard muscle and supple body fat for Kezerah to snuggle into. Her body secured into his shape.

Andarios was the exception to Kezerah's earlier sentiment. He never asked nor expected anything from her: her sole companion until Ikaika's entrance into her life, her very best friend. Nowhere did she feel more herself than fortified in his arms. It dawned on her that the only choice she'd ever made, fully, in this life was Andarios. They chose each other every day.

Her body shifted and she became acutely aware that his did too.

She tilted her head up and found that he seemed to be wrestling with his own thoughts, jaw tightened once more while hugging her close.

She brought a hand up as she normally did, tracing the line and easing the tension from his brow line to chin. Warmth flushed beneath his faded gold complexion. The tendrils of his fine white hair—messy from the time in the sea breeze—shaded his face. Suddenly their closeness became charged. The air grew heavier around them. Kezerah's curiosity piqued. New sensations between her and Andarios rivaled a peony found after First Frost.

As if also sensing the change, Andarios looked down, pondering her. She felt herself lean towards him, wondering why the thought had never entered her mind before? Had he ever shown interest? Had she? Was she supposed to now? Did she? His body went completely still, as if she approached stone with her lips and splayed fingertips.

"Kez."

Kezerah stopped. His voice did *not* carry the rasp or tenor of someone on the edge. She pulled back sensing...fear. She recoiled slightly in shame. "I'm sorry Dar, I have no idea why I—"

"No, don't." His voice sounded raw. "I was thinking something similar. It's just, I... I feel like I thought about it differently."

She tilted her head to the side. He loosed a long breath, looking at her bed's canopy for counsel. "I have never thought of you that way."

She felt a sting, and then cast it away. Just a moment ago she had admitted to herself she hadn't thought of him in that way either.

He went on in a rush. "Not that I haven't tried. I was actually confused that I didn't. I love you, adore you really." His voice shifted to earnest, the truth coming more easily as he went. "But, I would see the way Ikaika looked at you, and knew it was nothing like that."

Kezerah flinched at the mention of Ikaika. "That's okay. I can't be to everyone's liking."

Andarios shook his head. "It's not that either. I don't know if anyone is to my liking, not in that way anyway...I don't think—I don't know." He amended, "I feel love, but it's like the desire is detached. The way Whistle looked at me? I was petrified. And Rorrik is—well he's Rorrik."

She thought back to his admission in his bedroom, after Rorrik had left. "I'm sorry. You'd said you weren't interested and I—I wasn't thinking." She tried to wriggle further away, and Andarios brought his forehead to hers.

"I said I didn't care about attraction. And I don't, I probably don't care about...this either." he gestured vaguely at their pressed together bodies. "But *you*. I've never cared for someone so deeply. If there is anyone in the world that I were to try such an act with, it would be you."

"I know for certain it doesn't matter what we do," she said, and meant it. To lose Andarios was another beast entirely, and one she could not defeat. "I'll always be here, no matter what we choose."

"I meant what I said before. I don't need to kiss you to love you." He echoed her words back. "No matter what we choose."

Uncertainty buzzed through the silence. Then, Kezerah leaned in once more, making her choice and waiting for his.

For exactly three heartbeats, she lingered there, then Andarios' smirk rested lightly upon her lips, giving her his answer. Her lips pressed to his and it was like his laugh, sudden and meant just for her.

She allowed him time to pull away but instead his lips returned her advancement. Soft and curious, as if exploring his own limits and willingness. Andarios' arms, still wrapped around her, slowly unwound, continuing his exploration of her. She returned each gesture, both following the other's lead. Soft murmurs encouraged higher, lower, softer, more.

Her breath caught as fingertips brushed against areas she had been unaware were sensitive and he paused, eyes golden in the moonlight, questioning her. They froze and assessed if they would continue. "I'm alright, if you are..." Kezerah admitted, settling into her stillness—an act with little practice—and waiting for Andarios.

ANDARIOS AIMED to control his breathing. His mouth had moved awkwardly, trying to discern the patterns her lips made on his. He didn't know what was meant to be instinctual. It all felt clumsy, like shadowing with his eyes closed and only their words instructing him on what to do next. Their guidance delayed by kissing. Then, struck by the sensation he might never kiss again, he paused. *Kez*, he was kissing *Kez*. She was kissing him, and they were kissing. She'd seemed to pick up the cadence more quickly. Her lips soft on his, then encouraging when she liked something. Andarios tried to learn the language and write back. The soft caress down his neck and spine, he liked. The time she tried to press on top of him and accidentally prodded his new scar: he could live without.

She followed his lead, freezing in place, not breathing until he either resumed or retreated. She understood him, and he knew if he never moved again, she would continue to hold her breath, she would not advance without him.

Andarios advanced.

She shifted the power to him, and he took the lead, knowing this was not an action taken lightly. He moved slow. Slower. Hands inched from neck to shoulders, trembling as he brought them in to feel her breasts, and flattened against her nightgown. They felt as they always did pressed to him in an embrace: soft, lovely, and simply a part of her. He smoothed down to the small contour in her waist— the easiest place to grasp her when lifting her in the air, twirling her about as she laughed in his arms. The tremble that passed over her as he explored the divots of her hips, however, was an entirely new sensation. A flutter rippled through him. Something about her reaction had affected him.

He brushed lower and checked her eyes as Kezerah's breath caught, lashes still lowered, her tongue slid in his mouth to deepen their kiss.

He guessed she enjoyed that.

Emboldened by this, his attention returned to her mouth. Their breath was sweet from the citrus tarts he had smuggled in. Andarios' hand shook as it swept between her legs. He halted again. She met his gaze, seeming to search him for as many answers as he had questions. Could he do this? His body told him yes, achingly so. A muted scream next to his mind asked if he wanted to. Did he want to try? He knew Kezerah did, beyond their bodies' mutual reactions. Her eyes held her answer, waiting for his, only as sure of her decision as he was.

He would know after this. There would be no more staring at her in question, wondering why he didn't want to devour her alive, consume her body and soul, like he watched others yearn to do. But he also thought he might know already. He might be able to disentangle himself from her, and she would nod, accepting him. Everything would go back to the way it was. He liked things as they were. Andarios *loved* things as they were—loved her. Could he love her more? The answer flew to his mind as easy as a song. *'Impossible.'*

He didn't just love her with his heart but the whole of his soul. No missing piece existed to make him more complete. If he made this decision it would be for his curiosity alone. To see what he liked and know what he didn't. To answer his own questions and fend off everyone else's. His eyes hadn't left hers.

"Okay."

"Okay," she whispered back.

He plunged back into the kiss.

Kezerah no longer waited on him. She worked on his belt as he slid her satin shift up her waist. His task easy, he returned to help her complete hers.

Without breeches, he felt odd. Off balanced. He calmed himself by touching a hand over her smooth skin, mesmerizing beneath his sword-weathered hands. Her small fingertips caressed and tickled as she ventured across his chest, unbuttoning him. He jolted as she tapped a deep purple bruise from his battle in Heartsglove. Two more buttons and she followed the textured scar that now ran from shoulder to torso and heat trailed behind her caress. Andarios removed his shirt, helping her hands that seemed to have no idea where to venture. The sudden warmth of the room helped his nerves as they both fumbled, now unclothed.

He pulled them briefly apart, and Kezerah finally caught her breath, seemingly satisfied with a lack of air for the sake of kissing.

He grinned at her, not surprised in the least that his friend would choose kissing over oxygen. She smiled back, and he used the small ceasefire to admire her. Kezerah naked was beautiful, her expression exuding delight in having no barriers placed upon her, no matter the size or silk.

He told her so, needing her to know just how magnificent she was. He could tell by the look in her eyes she believed him. He kissed her softly again. Kissing was fine, he supposed, but he thought it time to move forward.

His body adjusted atop hers in a way it had never been before. Countless years of sleeping in a tangled heap—arms and legs meshed together, hands clasped and bodies hot—and it had never been like this. He was slow, and achingly gentle. A butterfly's wings on the breeze would have given more force than Andarios, as they united. His breath caught, and she held hers.

THEIR BODIES JOINED. A sound Kezerah had never experienced before escaped Andarios' lips, right in the shell of her ear as he returned to her. It was as if he had given her a piece of himself, something she was meant to hold onto and keep safe. She held him, and it was like two stars spinning out of the sky, entangled and determined to hit the ground together. This time his withdrawal was final. She continued to hug him close, the lack of him feeling unnatural. Until he returned her embrace, squeezing her close to make up for their separation of souls.

"I'm here," he breathed, voice unsteady, as he fell back on the mattress, pulling her with him. "Right here."

The two held each other. They had become as physically close as any two beings could be, and the revelation on the other side had not surprised either of them. They had already been this two-souled creature. They had already chosen each other long before exploring their bodies' limits. Now they just knew that no matter what they did, who they were with, or where they were, they were always this. They were always best friends.

Kezerah sank into the thought, knowing as Andarios' eyes fluttered shut that he was right alongside her. Their breaths matched until his deepened, his barrel chest rising to press flush against her cheek. Air escaped her in a yawn, and she followed him into a deeper sleep.

KEZERAH AWOKE to the sun glinting through her windows, the curtains still drawn. By now, servants usually shuffled through her room, preparing her for the day, but there was nothing to prepare her for. She lay there in her nakedness, completely at peace as Andarios snored softly next to her, eyes covered by his disheveled hair. She felt light in such a way that if she had chosen to float up to the ceiling, she believed she could. Her body felt newly hers and she reveled in it.

Andarios groaned as the sunshine leaked, level with his face. He covered his eyes with an arm, and she laughed. "I was having a good dream," he muttered, fighting his wakefulness.

"About what?" she mused, happy to have him awake.

He turned his head to her, still trying to block the light. "The strawberry-filled pastries. You know the ones with the custard."

"Those aren't in season for moons!"

He rolled away from her dramatically. "Don't remind me." Then he paused and let out an abrupt laugh.

"What's so funny?" Kezerah asked.

"I forgot I was naked."

They both burst into a fit of laughter, the absurdity of the moment overtaking them. As their mirth subsided, they looked at each other. Unease forced her to swallow. What if they had altered their friendship in some way? She decided to tread across the unfamiliar the only way she knew how. "Well, erm—how was I?"

He snorted at her faux-casualness. "I think I should direct that question your way," he said, busying himself by searching the covers for his clothes. "I did the tricky part."

Their map became clearer, and her jaw dropped in mock horror. "You most certainly did not!"

Andarios threw her a wicked grin and rolled from bed. "I'm sure your next lover will appreciate the nuances of your technique." She tossed a pillow at him, grabbing another in case he continued to speak. He laughed, accepting the hit and raising his hands in peace. "Alright, I apologize, your skills are unparalleled, so much so that I'll never bother you, or anyone else, with the task—ever again."

"How diplomatic of you," she laid back, relieved to find Andarios to still be Andarios. "Well, I liked it," she admitted. "Though, I'd need to try it again to be sure."

Andarios eyed her warily, shaking his breeches up his legs.

"Not with you," she assured.

His smile eased and he pretended to wipe sweat from his brow. "Excellent," he said, all business now. "Because breakfast is waiting downstairs, and if you make me choose, you'll be sorry." He reached the door, then stalked back and kissed her lightly on the forehead. "But I'm glad I know. And that it was you."

Kezerah warmed at their newfound understanding. "Me too."

She did also, however, hold a deep sense of satisfaction that their friendship remained largely unchanged, and that Andarios had left with his shirt inside out.

Elize

THE   CARRIAGE   RATTLED,   WOODEN   WHEELS
uncooperative against the change from dirt to sand. The province of
Sorrel boasted an odd mixture of coastal salt breeze, slopes of grass—
yellowed by the heat—and a ceiling of smoke plumage from the
neighboring war. Elize hated it.

Her stomach could have been roiling for any number of reasons:
the thickness in the air, her sallow homelands, the jostling of her
body as the carriage's driver dismissed the need to avoid large rocks.
Elize knew it was none of these things however, and it made the
illness bubbling through her all the worse.

To think she had asked for this, gone out of her way for this.
Every time she left court, and the sickness overtook her, it felt like a
bout of madness. She wanted to turn back, to tell Elowren that Yara's
farce of an emergency was just that: a farce. She thirsted for a gulp of
air that tasted of sweet floral oils on her tongue; craved being in her
own bed, and near her petulant daughter once more. Instead, she laid
her head back on the cushion of her finely-padded caravan, and
imagined commanding its driver off a cliff every time they hit a stray
stone.

Oftentimes, a Bond Wielder recounted being apart from their
Bond like an emptiness inside them: a hollow incompleteness difficult to describe without a welling of tears, or a hand to the heart. In
Elize's experience, it was no such thing. She didn't feel empty, or
incomplete. She felt rotted out, like a dough-soft apple left out in the
heat: past the point of sweetness and into a velvet mold only worthy
of early Autumn bees. This is what it was to be Elize, away from her
Bond. To be away from Kezerah.

The carriage stopped, a door opened, and years of practice

allowed Elize to gracefully hide her disdain from her tormentor. The driver, in the lavender velvets of Elastor, bowed and gestured, making way for his queen. One dainty foot after another, Elize exited.

From the corner of her eye, Rook dismounted his large war horse. Then, all was right as he became the shadow that loomed at her side. An Honorguard was a traditional role. It dated back to a time before Elastor, when it was the duty of the monarch's paramour to control the kingdom's armies. Now, this duty fell to the guard themselves; a sacred right and devout life meant to be honored by serving only two purposes: kingdom and, in this regard, queen. The Edge scum, Andarios, sullied the title. Anger rose in Elize that rivaled her rotted core. She breathed harshly through teeth.

"Your High Majesty?" Rook, ever attentive.

"I'm fine. The air doesn't agree with me." Not a complete lie when breathing in the smoldering mixture of the sea and battle debris. She loathed that even under her rule, her home smelled this way. She pondered if Sorrel would always smell like this.

'No,' she told herself, *'not as long as I have a say.'*

And as they approached the Sorrel manor—modest to the point of shameful, with its worn stone and peeling roof—Elize had a lot to say.

Yara of Sorrel stood in the poorly lit doorway of Elize's old family home. Yara looked as weary as her manor house, her fretful fingers un-clasping and re-clasping themselves. The wisps of her rosy copper hair escaped a hasty up-do bun. Elize wondered how many hairstyles her cousin had gone through in order to quell her anxiety. The queen's mouth pinched together, assessing Yara's Xenkeshi silk gown that hung ill-fitted on her narrow frame. Whatever her anxiety, it was not Elize she aimed to impress.

"Welcome, Cousin." Yara gave a too-taut smile as the stone step beneath Elize shifted and groaned underfoot. "I know you wanted that repaired—It just seemed wasteful to put it in right before winter. We don't get snow, but the nights get cold." Yara rushed on at Elize's expression, snapping her fingers to summon servants to retrieve the queen's coat. "But of course you know that, I don't know why I'm blathering. I suppose I'm not used to company."

"I come every year," Elize said.

"Yes, but you don't—" Sure Yara had meant to say *'you don't count,'* but had thought better of it, Elize arched her brow. Yara nibbled at her lip, and tried again. A wise choice. "Your visits always put everyone at ease. The cotton farmers still asks after your health every moon, during taxes."

Elize flitted her eyes over Yara's dress once more, pointedly. "And when you buy your clothes, I'm sure."

Yara blanched, but Elize had no time to shame her cousin's wardrobe loyalty. She pinched at the fingertip of her gloves, fitted finely over slim-boned hands. "Is the cellar prepared?"

"Yes, of course."

"Has the wine shipment arrived?"

"Um, well, not yet. There has not been word, but I suspect it's just running late."

No wonder the Lady Sorrel looked distressed.

"I thought you had the order confirmed, Yara," Elize said, the glove whipped free of the hand. The next one tugged off with more force.

"I was given notice that it was to arrive tonight," Yara assured. "I'm sure there would have been contact if it was not able to dock on our private port."

"You suspect one moment, and are sure the next," Elize said. "I suppose I'll wait then, since you're so certain of its arrival."

"I'll make us tea. It shouldn't be much longer," Yara said, rushing ahead through the foyer and into the small sitting room.

Elize looked over the estate as she always did. Floral armchairs faded by time and wear, a rug left to unclosed curtains looked sun splotched and moth ridden. The air from outside seeped into the dust, creating debris. Too many candles clustered around the room, as if not to illuminate the space but warm it. The fireplace had its own cluster and Elize wrinkled her nose. A hearth was the center of every home. It didn't do well to show the cracks in ones' foundation. The corner of the room held an outline of what had once been a grand mirror and chest of drawers. An image of her mother brushing her hair, while seated at her vanity, grew vivid in Elize's mind.

Her mother had been inhumanly beautiful. Cream-smooth skin, hair a lush, thick bronze, and eyes of lake blue. Her father spent the majority of his day off in the fields to ensure the cotton harvested on time. It had not been an easy life. Elize herself had needed to help at the loom for Sorrel to produce enough to sustain itself. She remembered complaining to her mother when her fingers rubbed raw against the fabric after hours of labor.

"Not forever, my love," her mother would say, kissing her fingertips. "You're far too clever to stay here."

"What about you?" Elize had asked. "You cannot want to stay in this horrible place."

"Where I come from, a girl could do far worse than making pretty dresses."

"Pretty dresses for other people," Elize muttered. "How did you get away?"

The front door opened and shut. Heavy boots shuffled in the foyer. Her mother stood, eyeing herself in the mirror, brushing a finger sensually across her mouth. Her lips deepened a shade, glossening as she smiled down at Elize. "I was clever." Then she moved towards the door, greeting Elize's father with sweet nothings and a kiss.

It had not been until the Bane Harvest—the plague that had swept over Alora and Elastor—and her mother's death, that Elize had understood. Her father had been without magick, and she had believed her mother to be without magick as well. The laws of all Thrice Kingdoms required each magick user—whether it be Bond magick, Mind Melding, or a Hold on Sway—to register their manifestations.

When her mother's hand had gone limp in her hold, a shattering crack from downstairs had startled Elize. Her heart fissured. She'd understood the mirror, her mother's prized possession, brought from her home in Xenkesh, had broken. Her mother's hair dulled before her eyes. Her face became pocked and hard. Her lips thinned to match Elize's own mouth, and she knew what her mother had hidden from her, her father, and the world. Bond magick. Strong

Bond magick, if her mother's constant mirage was any indication. Which meant Elize either took after her father; magick-less or her mother; powerful. She assured herself of the answer and willed it to be.

Elize had planned, and she had waited. She bided her time to be sure that, whatever her Bond, it would be strong. Nothing had been good enough. Until she became pregnant. After years of tried and failed attempts, of yearning and wanting, what stronger bond was there? It had been taboo, and Elize understood why. Many would not be capable of handling the amount of power and control she had possessed upon her daughter's birth. Her first few years with Kezerah had been extraordinary. The human will bent and broke under her gaze. Each intake of breath had been laced with the ability to wield other's desires and manipulate the world around her like clay.

Then, Kezerah had grown up, apart from her, and Elize's magick dwindled. Half the time she couldn't tell if her Will-bond or her status commanded the room. It became a careful balance of meeting her daughter's desires, and keeping her close, under control. Kezerah proved to be a selfish creature. A sprinkled illusion of choice often sufficed, but never amounted to enough.

"King Elowren seemed more manageable," Yara said conversationally, taking a sip of her tea and tearing Elize's eyes away from the empty corner where the vanity once stood.

Elize sat. "Yes, much easier this past season." She had no intention of talking about the intricacies of puppeteering those closest to Kezerah. Traditionally, the more kindred a soul was to a Bond Weilder's Bond, the easier that soul outside the Bond could be controlled. Elowren should have been putty in her hands. Yet. Any more than silencing his protests or forcing a blind eye to her dealings proved a challenge. It hadn't always been so, nor would it be.

"You and the Princess must have been quite aligned." Yara winked, it was much closer to a delayed blink. "Should I order a dress for a handfasting ceremony soon?"

Elize cast her eyes around the room for listeners. It had been cleared of all but Rook. She shot her cousin a meaningful look. "Not just yet. First she needs to perform her duties in accordance with the peace treaty. Then she may begin courting for a paramour."

Yara snickered into her tea. "I envy her resolve when it comes to the Crown Prince of Xenkesh."

Elize didn't bother with a response and again looked towards the door.

"I forget how irritable you get when you're away from—erm, Court," Yara sighed.

A knock sounded at the door. Her cousin stood quickly, and hurried out of the room. When she reappeared, she smiled impishly.

"Cousin, the shipment of Xenkeshi wine has just arrived. If you would like to find a bottle to your liking in the cellar?" Finally, Elize set down her untouched tea and smoothed out her dress as she stood.

"Yes, please escort me."

Yara led her through the kitchen, the wood-slab surfaces still covered in that day's flour. Rook stationed himself outside a worn door as she entered. Elize signaled and the door closed, damp darkness enveloping her and banishing Yara from sight. Then, she waited.

Tendrils of multicolored fire snaked up and around fingertips, illuminating first a hand, and then a broad shouldered silhouette. The fire danced and painted a man's face in shadows. A trimmed beard, firm brows and heavily lined and lidded eyes blurred through the Miraged blaze. While he wore Elastian attire, his swagger as he moved toward her was anything but. Coconut oils slicked back a mane of hair and his tailored beard concealed age and accentuated his laugh lines. The flame's colors continued to oscillate as it glowed in his palm, changing his eyes.

"What? Not happy to see me?"

Amarus, King of Xenkesh, for a moment was all grins. Just a flash of teeth and a twinkle of eyes in the dark. Elize composed herself with a tilt of her chin. Her anger put her beyond petty antics. He leaned in. "Come on, Elize, do you really want an apology every time something doesn't go your way?"

Elize's anger did not falter. She leaned away. She wouldn't play his games tonight.

"You ruined everything!" She spat. "All my preparations, all my planning, and for what?"

Amarus' smile broadened. "Oh, are we cutting out foreplay

then? Getting straight to it?" he stepped closer. Her only options to either step back, or make her stance firm.

Elize didn't move. Instead, she smoothed out the thick material of her embroidered bodice, and tried to appear more concerned with her apparel than his proximity.

His smile remained in place, but his tone soured. "In order for our joint goals to be achieved, I need to not be dead," he said. "Unless *your* ambition is to rule without me?"

She caught the true avid green coloring of his irises as he searched every inch of her for a hint, a reaction. His mouth was still playful, but his eyes were marred with distrust. Elize rolled hers. "Don't be ridiculous. Of course I wish to rule by your side."

Amarus let loose a jovial laugh, a rich throaty baritone. It made the juxtaposition of his words more biting. "That's less believable when you tell my spy I should drink salt water, and then have him killed."

"I didn't kill him," Elize said, irritated. "I threatened him."

"Then why is he dead?"

"Because he worked alongside a radicalized group to kidnap my daughter," her whisper grew louder and faster in tempo, "and it's those dramatics and hasty conclusions that led to all of our ruined plans. It's *I* who should be suspicious of *you*, Amarus. How am I to know your intentions? When you change our plans—"

"Your plan, not mine!" Amarus swung his hand out in a demand for silence, "You took too long. I handed over my sons—at great personal risk, mind you—with the promise of your great powers at work, and all I'm given back is a lovesick fool and nothing to show for it!"

"Your sons," Elize stamped forward. "All I have done is sculpt pottery from the silt I was given! You said they would be ready, that they would easily fall in line! Your eldest took a moon just to ask Kezerah for a dance! Your youngest went rogue and joined my rebellion in purchasing an iron bear for some off-kilter scheme without my say-so!"

"Your same rebellion who 'kidnapped' your daughter? Sounds like a hoax to me."

"It's been dealt with."

"Admit it, you started something and couldn't stop it," Amarus said. "You're only as good as a regent to our people and they don't respect you."

"It was a single faction! My insurgent misfired and he paid dearly for it."

A dark chuckle, "From what I hear, that misfire caused quite the burn."

Elize's patience felt like glass blown to the point of shattering, "And what of your misfire, Amarus? I've had reports of several ships' debris, and yet, your captive is described with silver hair. Did you forget what your beloved looks like?"

"A matter also being dealt with." Amarus' voice dropped low. "More easily accomplished if, for once in your life, you have good news for me about Ikaika."

"My people are on his trail as we speak."

"So, once again, the answer is no."

"Fine. I've tried reasoning with you. If you are going to blame me for every one of your mistakes—" She turned towards the door and Amarus grasped her hard on the arm.

"Alright, alright." He jerked her back to face him. "It wasn't *all* your fault. Ambrose did not exhibit the forethought I had expected. His actions, or lack thereof, complicated your position."

"Why didn't you just tell him from the start!" Elize attempted to tug her arm from his grip and it tightened. "Every time I felt his soul it was ruptured with indecision." She stilled and he released her to brush a hand through an already groomed beard.

"Ambrose is not easily coaxed, as I'm sure you're aware. He is headstrong and independent, but he also bears a most unfortunate moral compass that sometimes spins away from me. If I'd given him direct orders..." Amarus rolled his shoulders, "I can't guarantee he would have followed them."

"It sounds like," Elize said, through her teeth, "you are telling me you have no control whatsoever of our situation. Yet I'm dealing with the brunt of this failure."

"I'm not raising pawns, Elize! I'm not Willbound to my own offspring! If you were better aligned with your daughter, you wouldn't need to poorly puppeteer my sons!"

"You were supposed to help me!"

Elize wanted to claw at her own face. She had spent years planning, testing and extending her knowledge of her magick. She had tinkered and experimented with human nature, found patterns in behaviors, and bonds between beings. She had done all she could to improve the Bond she and Kezerah shared, through painstaking compromise.

It had been tedious work, small manipulations through her precarious power, completely set to the tune of Kezerah's mood and emotions. It wasn't enough to feed into Kezerah's wants, she needed Kezerah's desires to match hers. Yet, Kezerah's scope so often fell short beyond herself. So much of what was important, she refused to see.

Old traditions and a lack of order plagued Thrice. It needed quelling, rules, and a united front. As it stood, too many opinions had created lands full of strife and disarray. Elize would bring the kingdoms together; she'd see an end to disorder, to war.

First, Xenkesh needed to be put in order. Easily accomplished with Ambrose next in line to both the kingdom and Kezerah's heart. If Kezerah aligned in this need, it all fell into place. A handfasting, a pairing of souls. With their souls paired together, Elize's Bond would partially tether with Ambrose and, by proxy, her Bond magick would extend to him. Amarus would become nothing but a footnote in her story.

Not even Illija would stand a chance against the combined strength of Elastor and Xenkesh. Alora would finally be swallowed whole. Its customs and currency done away with, a popular idea thanks to her long-stirring rebellion.

This just left Elastor itself: a kingdom crafted by rebellion and will. One that worshiped a soul rather than any one person. Elize didn't need a title. She had that. She needed the power and control only found behind a symbol. She needed what Kezerah wasted. With Kezerah and Elize aligned, not a soul in Thrice could resist her. A ruling figurehead with Elize at the helm.

"I've tried to help you." Amarus sounded so reasonable, so insistent. "It's not meant to be done."

Her eyes shifted from his. "It was working. Kezerah hasn't

obeyed me so easily since when she was a small child. I could feel my power rise by the day."

"I have no time nor patience for your novice control over your Willbond," Amarus said. "Admit it—when the time came, you got greedy."

"Greedy?" She hissed, as she looked him up and down. "All you had to do was sit and wait. If you wouldn't have thrown your tantrum, both of our goals would have been actualized." She could not believe his assumptions of her. She had shown her loyalty in offering Ikaika twice over now.

Amarus stalked away from her, only to turn back towards her with a flair of his hand. "I told you exactly how long I could hold Illija at bay. If Ambrose hadn't sent me word, I would have had even less. I would have been finished!"

Elize did not buckle under his intimidation. "Lower your voice," she commanded. The words ached the rot in her gut without her power to control him. "I did all I could to keep Ikaika and Kezerah apart and draw her interest towards Ambrose. It was your son who denied every invitation to my court due to his 'headstrong independence.' There wasn't anything more I could do."

"You could have handed Ikaika over ages ago. As soon as you had him in hand."

"And how would that have looked? How swiftly do you believe Illija would have taken my head? Or Elowren for that matter, if he suspected. You said you wanted Ikaika. I had every intention of giving him to you, *without* endangering my position or severing my growing Bond with Kezerah."

Amarus looked around the damp space, "So, where is he now?" Fire twirled in his theatrical search for Ikaika. "Where is your half of the bargain to use my sons?"

Elize let him play out his impatience, mastering her own. When Amarus appeared finished, Elize continued. "I told you. They're searching the countryside for him now. I did not expect Ikaika to act so irrationally. Outside forces got in my way—*you* got in my way."

"If you were as powerful as you pretend to be, I wouldn't have been able to."

This stung more than Elize could show. All of her magick and countless compromises were null, dependent on Kezerah's desires and whims.

Amarus spoke kindly: a hearth on a winter's night. "If you can't control your daughter—or *anyone* for that matter—what use are you to me?"

Elize's heart pulsed out of rhythm, his words from so long ago setting the tempo. *'less—less—less'.* He saw her as less than he was, less than Illija, useless. But no, not anymore. He would see.

"Am-Amarus. I'm sorry, I feared Elowren finding out. I have to be so careful. Everything must look natural."

Amarus' posture changed at her meeker tone, he swept closer. "Then take care of Elowren, for us. We don't need him," he assured, a hand slid down the curve of her hips.

She melted into him. "You know how important it is that my reputation remains intact. Elastor's throne cannot be usurped. If Kezerah suspects either of us, it will weaken the Bond and our chances of keeping her in line."

"And you don't think your daughter ready to rule? For you to pull her strings and swear fealty to us both?"

"She will be. I just need more time," Elize added pointedly.

Amarus sighed heavily. "Time is running out. I am losing this war. I cannot outlast these plans you have made. Illija needs to be stopped—now. Or I, and you, will lose everything."

"I've come up with a new—"

"No more of your schemes. They don't work. If they did, this war would have ended four years ago. We should just have it done with and arrange their handfasting. Ambrose is charming, they'll pair swiftly and we can start fresh."

Elize had to work to keep the tightness from her features. She could bear no more children, and knew what he implied of Kezerah's fate. She spoke carefully. "*Starting 'fresh'* implies at least nine moons of waiting, need I remind you. No soul, no Soul Heir...and the Bond only transfers in theory."

Amarus didn't answer.

The topic conceded, she continued on. "As I was saying. I *have* made arrangements. Kezerah will be in Trusol by the Fire Festivals. The news should arrive by the time you return to court."

"Oh?" Amarus looked taken aback. His brow furrowed in pensive confusion. "That is...ideal for me, but Elowren spoke of this long ago, and showed no sign of relenting."

"Yes, well. That was before Kezerah and I aligned."

"You've fully re-aligned with her?"

This removed a fraction of her satisfaction. "Not, fully. But close. I have but one more obstacle in my way." Elize sucked in air, thinking of Kezerah's shadow and how soul-shatteringly dreadful she'd felt on the precipice of his demise. "Which is why I will not be joining you this summer."

Amarus looked suspicious. "A personal sacrifice you need not endure."

A sacrifice indeed and a painful one at that. It would be excruciating, but necessary for her to execute all of her goals. Kezerah needed to be away, and it was imperative she became attached to Ambrose, who held a legitimate claim to both Xenkesh and Alora.

"As you said, you have gone to great personal risk. It is only right that I match you. Perhaps I am the schemer, but it is you that best delivers the results."

Amarus grinned as his nose dipped to hers, their faces now temple to temple. "Are you saying I'm a better match-maker? That my romantic prowess is greater than yours?"

Elize rolled her eyes, but she couldn't help that her cheeks grew pink, glad that the flames disguised the blush. "I'm saying, perhaps you'll have more luck—but she may not leave the Trusol court. I want her under heavy guard, lock and key." A pause, then Elize added, "And she must always take her Preventions."

Amarus' breath matched the sweet wines of his kingdom, his voice all the sweeter in her ear. "Of course. No damaged goods." His words trailed down her neck. "But I prefer my plans to have promises." Then to her collar bone, and up the left side of her throat. "I will not be denied an easy victory again. I want to rule with you. Don't make me kill you instead." This, she knew, was not a front. She recanted.

"If I don't succeed...we can do it your way. We can start over." She'd rather die than intentionally kill her Bond but that didn't matter, she promised it anyway. Better he believed himself indebted to her than running his own scheme to mussy hers.

Amarus' stare became momentarily bemused as he drew back in surprise. "Well, then—" he pulled at her hips, cinching the two of them together, "it seems we have regained our footing."

His expression signaled the end of his interest in the conversation. He brought her face close to his and gathered her to him. Elize knew she held nothing next to Illija's beauty, but it had taken a war for Amarus to realize he didn't want something untamed. She allowed him to cage her in the embrace. The kaleidoscope of fire around them disappeared as their mouths met, and both parties were left in the dark.

Thank you for reading The Solstice Court. Please consider a quick review and/or a star rating. Positive or negative, I am grateful for your feedback.

Amazon review page: Link

Goodreads review page: Link

Storygraph review page: Link

The King of Xenkesh

Oars lapped at the Lull. Ambrose gazed out from his ship to the jeweled horizon of his home. The early morning warmed his back as it rose behind him. Ambre Cove, his namesake, peeked out in a dash of crimson, beckoning him to Elastor's Port Aveltra and its honeyed-red stone shores, rather than forward to Tempestor Port. He wanted nothing more than to answer the call, to drift into the salt and sea foam, and immerse himself in a world not his own: any world that didn't have him sailing back to claim his father's throne.

Ambrose rubbed at the briny crust at the corner of his eyes, built up from lack of sleep. He had always slept well aboard ships, but this past fortnight he would have been lucky to shut his eyes long enough to enter fitful dreams. More often, he was wrenched back out of sleep before dreams came, like a fish jerked from waves.

"How much longer?" Rorrik asked from behind him. Ambrose turned to see who his little brother pestered, as he knew the question couldn't be directed at him. Rorrik hadn't spoken to Ambrose since they'd boarded.

The shores of the sacred island loomed like an ink blot on an otherwise blue topaz sea. Lord Fathym—*Captain* Fathym aboard the ship—raised a hand up until it hovered just below the sun, then ticked his hand down, one span at a time, to level with the horizon. "Two sun-spans, maybe three? By midday at the latest, Your High-ness," Fathym answered. "We're still benefiting a bit from the Bethync winds."

On cue, lightning rippled and thunder cracked behind them.

Rorrik startled and immediately checked to see who'd caught his flinch. His eyes met Ambrose's, then, just as quickly, he left, stomping below deck. Ambrose turned back with a huff of breath. He couldn't blame Rorrik. After all, Ambrose had sentenced their father to death.

When faced with the choice of capturing and ransoming their brother, Ikaika, in exchange for their father, Ambrose hadn't simply hesitated. He'd chosen. The choice had cost them their father's life. Any day now, Ambrose knew he'd receive the letter. He wondered if Illija would send the information personally or if he'd find out through King Elowren. Ambrose supposed, between the two, he'd rather be given the news from the king of Elastor than his mother. Elowren had been kind. The latter would probably send his father's head in lieu of writing.

Once in Xenkesh, he'd need to move quickly. Ambrose knew what Illija was capable of. He needed to speak with the Quintet council and be granted permission to first levy an attack against the barricade damming his water supply along the Strand. Then, once his people had access to water, he'd ascend the throne and prepare to fortify the city. Illija had always been too afraid to attack his father head on, preferring to attack outside of Trusol Palace, such as far-off Broxen. With his father dead, so too was the promise of safety within the walls of his capital.

The rays of sun on his back intensified. Gulls squawked and dipped toward the ever-growing shore. Houses crafted from sand and clay stratified the cliffs in a collection of colors and encircled Tempestor Port. Swirls of cumin and coriander mingled with the balmy sea air, and Ambrose inhaled his home with closed eyes. He wanted to smile. He wanted to cry. Never had Xenkesh's seaport filled him with so much dread and longing.

The ship docked. They offboarded to the sound of haggling, laughter, and a slew of percussion instruments playing to their own tune. Food stalls and caravan carts littered the midday streets alongside bargain bins. Everything out in the open air and soaking up the sun. Meats sizzled on charred sticks and ample pods of smoked cardamom were stirred into large pots for the boiled catch of the day.

Crowds of people bumped into their future king without a second glance.

Ambrose could not fault the slight, as none knew his face beyond vague rumors. Xenkeshi did not worship their monarchs like Elastians did. They relied on them. His people expected the Xenkesh line to keep them safe, as they had since before the dawn of Thrice. He wondered if that promise had ended alongside his father's rule; that Ambrose would be remembered by his failure to act.

Azalea moved in close, his Sword Master playing at bodyguard, not only to dissuade someone accidentally pickpocketing their prince, but from those in the palace who *could* recognize him. His stomach twisted at the thought, clearly in line with Azalea's own as she whispered, "If Lady Xakai isn't at the West Exit, we turn around and sail for the Solstice Court."

Yes, Xakai. Ambrose at least knew his long-time playmate, trusted confidant, and liege of their richest port town, would hear him out. He swallowed his mounting anxiety behind a wan smile. "What, miss their egg tarts already?" She granted him nothing but stoicism in return.

"We don't know the state of the council, and you *know* Jai has been frothing at the mouth. We can't afford to walk into a coup—" They had rounded a cluster of melon stalls, stacked high enough to topple, to reveal Xakai at the far end of the market.

Beside her, large lizard-like creatures stretched and jostled for space in a pocket of the market square. All four of the komodai cramped together gave the illusion of a viper pit, iridescent scales ranging from pearl to emerald to obsidian writhed together in a tangle. The overgrown thunder of reptilian beasts hissed at passersby. After a moon of elk and horses, their size loomed larger. Four thick legs ended in powerful clawed paws, setting them apart from their serpentine counterparts.

Ambrose smiled, a salt-laden breath caught in his lungs. "Drum!" The crown prince's saunter broke into a sprint, and moments later he pressed his face into Drum's elongated neck. The shadowy black of his scales caught the light like oil. "Summerlands, Drum," Ambrose crooned. "I've missed you."

Drum shook in a low rumbled response. A slitted slate eye

glinted dangerously as a forked tongue snaked out to catch the air. His muzzled maw prevented the full hiss and snap of his jaws. Satisfied Ambrose was not an imposter, the scale-armored drake shifted his massive head forward to rub Ambrose's side and shoulder, careful not to rub against the grain of his scales and permanently mar him.

Finally, Ambrose took in the rest of their newly formed party, Azalea already speaking with Xakai and several soldiers sporting Tempestor insignias. While Xakai's attendance boded well against a coup, he was uncertain what all they knew of his father's capture.

King Amarus had written to Ambrose directly, stating his elite mission to break the dam barring Trusol's water had failed. Because the king had led the attack himself, surely they knew him to be missing. Did they know of his fate? Why hadn't they stopped him? Ambrose banished the accusation as he made it. Nobody 'stopped' his father from doing anything. He was sure they tried, which was more than Ambrose could say for himself.

Next to him, Rorrik greeted his pearlescent komodai with a bit more reservation, but Ambrose caught the small smile on his brother's lips as he mounted. Ambrose did the same. It felt incredible: sturdy yet fluid, like holding command over the tides. A rush of exaltation buzzed through him, and he had to tamp it down with the memory of why they were here.

He swiveled Drum toward the rest of his entourage, joined at the West Gate. He took closer note of Xakai as she mounted a younger, still-green komodai. The lady of Tempestor had changed her hair since last he'd seen her. Black braids swirled into a semi-bun at her neck. Her dark brown skin glistened with the heat from waiting outside. She wore no armor; diplomatic raw silks wrapped around her shoulders and chest before giving way to skin and returning to a saturated red linen which flared out before bunching at her ankles.

"The Quintet awaits your presence," Xakai said.

Ambrose nodded. His rule might be precarious, but at least it hadn't fallen before the rise. He decided to test the waters. "I suppose I should thank you for not usurping me then." The dark pitch of his humor fizzled out under the blaring sun.

Xakai turned back, brown eyes lined with kohl. "It's good to have you back." Her face performed a studious calm unnatural to her.

Ambrose's heart sank. Xakai could never withhold a moment of snark said at the wrong time. The inner court must know the gravity of the matter, perhaps even more than he did. He wondered how the spy must have described his deceit, his lack of action. He decided to spend the ride in silence rather than try to keep a façade in place. Mirages were his father's specialty, but his father wasn't here, a fact for which Ambrose bore the blame.

Iron talons dug deep into the hot sand as they followed the southern coastline toward Trusol Palace. The Lull crept closer, and the komodai skittered across the rising tide like skipped rocks. The terrain gave way to cliffs, and red stone shifted under the weight of drake and rider as they scaled harsh drops into jagged stacks. Relief flooded Ambrose as the plateau opened to a large arena of dens that sloped into Trusol Palace's northern wall.

Once his jaws had been freed, Drum slid into his den with a hiss, powerful tail whipping behind him with no care for the handler who jumped out of his way. Ambrose turned to a small enclosure that led up and into the inner palace. He took a large breath, knowing it would need to last him as he began to deal out a string of orders.

"Summon the Quintet Council to the War Room," he told Xakai, who bowed and moved without question. "Azalea, get a tally of our numbers in the barracks and how many can be spared from Zelos and Broxen." Ambrose moved toward an iron-caged hoist with two armored guards on either side to levy it. He entered, a stormy Rorrik at his side, and nodded to one of the guards. She bowed, and the hoist-door swung closed like a curtain. The sound of wrung chains could be heard outside. Ambrose and Rorrik ascended into the air at an uneven tempo. The clicking of metals joined the silence of their turbulent climb.

"Ror—"

"No."

Ambrose ground his teeth together and fought for patience. "Rorrik, I'm sorry. I know you're angry with me, but—"

"I don't want to hear that you're sorry," Rorrik said. "I want to hear that you're *angry*."

"Of course, I'm angry! More than angry, I'm furious. All I want is to have Father back," Ambrose insisted, "but I can't only think of myself, or you, or even Father. I have to think of Xenkesh, *all* of it."

The hoist shuddered, signaling its stop. Rorrik faced Ambrose, his pearl-white armor smudged from their cliff-side ride. "Killing the heir to our enemies would have done nicely for Xenkesh."

Ambrose challenged his brother with a stare. Rorrik stared back with eyes identical to their father's, not a trace of Illija in sight. "You don't mean that. You don't think the solution to our problems is killing our brother."

"Don't you dare!" Rorrik spat as the iron door began to slide open. "Don't you dare imply he's family. Not when our father is under his craven mother's blade!" The doors revealed splashes of color; an audience of Xenkeshi courtiers kneeled to greet them. Several looked up at Rorrik's raised voice and eyed each other.

Ambrose cursed and pulled at the doors. They resisted, and he felt his Bond interpret for him, shutting them back in and enclosing their argument away from the crowd. He no longer had the luxury of patience. He moved in close, voice low to combat Rorrik's outrage. "We will show a united front," Ambrose commanded, "or I will make the hierarchy between us unquestionable."

He rapped Rorrik's shoulder, freshly out of a sling from his battle with Ikaika. "In the view of others, I am your king. Not your brother, not your friend. Xenkesh is crumbling all around them. I will not let my people believe it falls apart from within."

Rorrik looked ready to argue. Ambrose hunched low, emphasizing their heights. "I also have no intention of repeating myself." Rorrik's gaze broke away. "Rorrik."

Rorrik's body tensed, his neck rolling and cracking as his mouth worked to form the words. "Understood."

Ambrose didn't move.

Rorrik looked like a kernel about to pop. Then, when it was clear they went nowhere without his full and secured loyalty, he added, in a breath, "Your Sovereign Grace."

Ambrose pulled open the door, stepped into the crowded hall

and announced to all in earshot, "I will meet with my council now." The two Xenkeshi brothers walked past their kneeling subjects toward the opposing wall where wrought iron doors loomed tall, inlaid with scarlet tiles and trimmed with gold as sleek as honey. And as the soon-to-be king approached, the entrance opened to welcome him.

**See what happens next in The Solstice Heir.
Available wide:**
The Solstice Heir

Gratitude

I am humbled by how many kind souls brought this book to life. Thanks to each and every one of you, and here's a list of just a few:

To my partner, **Vincent**, for your tireless patience, your clean-ups, your amazing dinners, and keeping me hydrated while I wrote this book. Thank you for spending hours listening to me complain about formatting, photoshop, and the humbling activity that is marketing. Thank you for troubleshooting new programs, computer glitches, and cropping the image when I threatened to toss hours of work against the wall. Thank you for all the times you allowed me, guilt-free, to put this book above groceries, new work clothes, and personal hygiene. You are beyond any 'paramour' I could have conjured up, and I'm glad you're mine.

To **Yumi Yamamoto**, my editor, and the first person to read my book (when it still looked like a 300 page essay without paragraphs and a lot of commas). You have been a relentless champion of my writing journey. I am forever grateful and in awe of you. You've taught, inspired, and encouraged me from day one. Never have I felt so lucky to accidentally dm someone.

To **Mom**, for raising me with magick, allowing the use of the name Kezerah—I hope I did teenage you a bit of justice—and for running astrology charts for all my characters (so we could overanalyze them and their poor decisions for hours). You have inspired me and my creativity in so many ways. Thank you.

To **Dad**, yeah you get the dedication *and* the acknowledgments. Thank you for my work ethic, my diligence, and endurance. If you, my viking of a father, hadn't raised me to weather every storm, I would have quit on draft two (it was a doozy).

To **my grandma Laine and my grandfather Mike**, for

supporting Vince and I both in the most uncertain time of our life; for housing us when we were between homes and allowing me to toil away in your basement on this first draft.

Thank you to **my brother, Aristotle**. You are—hands down—the coolest person I know. You've done more than inspire some of my best one-liners and character quirks. You motivate me every day to be better, not just as your older sibling, or myself, but for the world. Thank you for having a lion's heart so I could be brave too.

To my Alpha Readers: **Lindsay, Han, Vincent, and Madeline** who approached my fourth draft with the utmost tenderness and care.

Thank you to my cartographer **Shyanne Garland**, who labored and crafted my world into a beautiful map.

Thank you to those who donated and supported me with words of encouragement and community. **Anjelica Apodaca, Xavier Dunn, Soleil de Zwart, Kat Reed, Theresa Hanno, Harry Gray, Jess Sheppard, Hide Miyake, my aunt Constance and Lindsay Lamp.** There are so many near and dear friends and family on this list. I appreciate you all so much.

Thank you to my Beta Readers: **Rachel Shepherd (my #1 fan), esme, Lisa, Joelle G., Mikai, Sarah, and Bára**. I was absolutely honored by your honest and thoughtful feedback. You made a process I was dreading into one of my favorite parts of the writing experience. I hope you can see your hard work reflected in this draft, because it made all the difference in the world.

To my proofreaders: **Vincent Kronberger, Lindsay Lamp, Han Jutting, and Madeline**, for reading this book multiple times in multiple forms.

And to **my best friend James.** You showed me what a best friend could be. I'll never settle for less. You are in every page of this book.

About the Author

Jade proudly hails from the north and claims Juneau, Alaska as her hometown. Though admittedly, Portland, OR brewed her the best cup of coffee during an all-nighter studying at PSU. Jade's degree and interests are social psychology and family studies, with a soft spot for child development.

When writing, she most likes to explore complex family dynamics and magic systems set in queer-normative worlds.

Now, nestled in Gifu, Japan, days are spent talking with students, writing books, and exploring the countryside with her partner and one real, one imaginary rabbit (Whimsy and Lancelot respectively). If she takes days to respond to your email, it's not because she dislikes you. It's just an Aquarius thing and it can't be helped.

Links to Jade-related places: https://jadejuniper.carrd.co

instagram.com/jadejuniiper

goodreads.com/JadeJuniper

youtube.com/@JadeJuniiper

Also by Jade Juniper

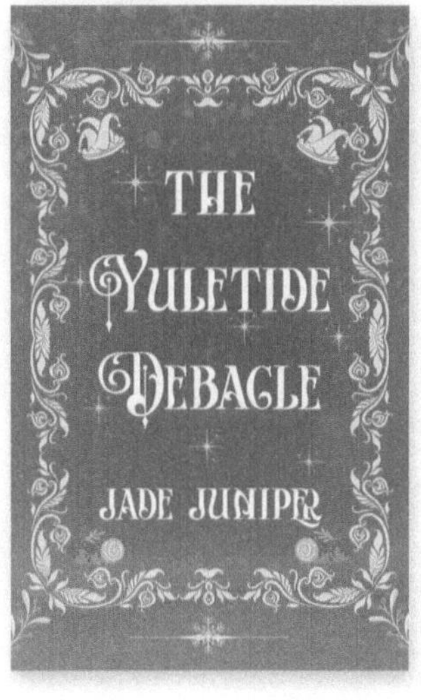

The Solstice Heir

The Yuletide Debacle

(Newsletter Exclusive)

Book 3

(Coming soon)